THE NIGHTINGALE NURSES

Helen is at a crossroads in her life as she battles with her domineering mother over both her love life and her future career.

Dora can't stop loving Nick, who is married to her best friend, Ruby. But a dark secret has the potential to destroy Ruby's marriage.

Millie is anxious about her fiancé being sent to Spain to cover the Civil War, and things only get worse when she encounters a fortune-teller who gives her a sinister warning.

With war looming in Europe, the women of the Nightingale have to face their own challenges, at work and in love.

THE NIGHTINGALE NURSES

THE NIGHTINGALE NURSES

by

Donna Douglas

Magna Large Print Books
Long Preston, North Yorkshire,
BD23 4ND, England.

British Library Cataloguing in Publication Data.

Douglas, Donna
    The Nightingale nurses.

    A catalogue record of this book is
    available from the British Library

    ISBN   978-0-7505-3938-8

First published in Great Britain in 2013 by Arrow Books

Published in Large Print 2014 by arrangement with
Random House Group Ltd.

Magna Large Print is an imprint of Library Magna Books Ltd.

Printed and bound in Great Britain by
T.J. (International) Ltd., Cornwall, PL28 8RW

Acknowledgements

The Nightingale Nurses would not exist without the help and support of a lot of people. First, I'd like to thank my agent Caroline Sheldon for encouraging me to take on the project in the first place, and my new editor Jenny Geras for taking me on and becoming a part of the Nightingale world. I'd also like to thank the whole Random House team, especially Katherine Murphy for keeping the production on track, Andrew Sauerwine and his great sales team for getting the book into the shops, and Amelia Harvell and Sarah Page for making sure people heard about it.

I'd also like to thank the Archives department of the Royal College of Nursing for their tireless help in tracking down facts, the Wellcome Library and the Bethnal Green Local History Archives. Not to mention all the brilliant nurses who have shared their stories (most of which are too shocking to include!) and the lovely readers who have taken the Nightingales to their hearts.

Last, but not least, I would like to thank my long-suffering husband Ken, who has put up with more hysteria than any man should ever have to suffer, not to mention coming home every evening to find me wearing the Pyjamas of Doom as deadline approached. And my daughter Harriet, who read each chapter as I wrote it, cheered and booed and cried in all the right places, and whose comments and enthusiasm kept me going. Sorry those sad bits made your make-up run on the bus...

To Ken, Harriet and Lewis

Chapter One

'Pay attention please, Nurses. The next six months will be the most important of your lives.'

The classroom instantly fell silent. Florence Parker the Sister Tutor stood on her dais and surveyed the rows of third-year students over her pebble glasses. She looked like a sweet old lady with her comfortably plump figure and white hair drawn back under her starched cap. But no student ever made that mistake twice.

'You have almost completed your three years of training. But you mustn't get carried away with your success,' she warned, her Scottish accent ringing around the walls, which were lined with diagrams of the human anatomy. 'There is still much ahead of you. In October you will take your State Examinations. Once you have passed those – if, indeed, you pass them–' she eyed them severely '–you will qualify and be able to call yourself State Registered Nurses.'

Sister Parker allowed a brief ripple of excitement to run through the young women assembled before her on wooden benches before going on. 'After that, you may choose to continue your training in another field, such as midwifery or district nursing. Or you may be invited by Matron to become a staff nurse here at the Nightingale. But I must remind you, this is a very great honour, and only the very best will be selected.' Her gaze

13

picked out Amy Hollins on the back row, twirling a strand of blonde hair around her finger as she gazed out of the window. 'Those who are not invited will, of course, be free to apply to other hospitals.'

Not that anyone would want that. The Florence Nightingale Teaching Hospital might be in a humble area of London's East End, but it had an excellent reputation. Every student wanted the chance to call herself a Nightingale Nurse.

'And then, of course, there is the Nightingale Medal itself, which is given to the most out-standing student in each year.' Sister Parker gave a nod towards the far wall of the classroom, filled with photographs of previous winners. 'That is something for you all to aspire to.'

She looked straight at Helen Tremayne as she said it. Helen sat in the front row of the class as usual, slightly apart from the other girls, tall and ramrod-straight, not a hair on her dark head out of place. If she didn't win the Nightingale Medal, Sister Parker would eat her cap.

'And now, girls, I have your ward allocations for the next three months.' She went to her desk and pulled out a sheaf of papers. 'As this is such an auspicious occasion, I thought I would hand them out rather than putting them up on the notice-board in the dining room.'

She started to move along the rows of benches, selecting papers and placing them down in front of each girl. As she did, she heard the whispered prayers from the other side of the classroom.

'Please God, don't send me to Female Chronics.

14

I don't think I could stand three months of Sister Hyde!'

'I hope I get Male Orthopaedics. I've heard it's an absolute riot.'

'As long as they don't send me down to the Fever ward,' someone else sighed.

'What about you, Hollins?' one of the girls asked.

'I want Theatre,' Amy Hollins declared firmly.

Then you'd better buck your ideas up, Florence Parker thought as she placed the paper down in front of her. Hollins stared back, her blue eyes insolent in her doll-like face. The blonde curls that peeped from under the edges of her cap tested the limits of the hospital's strict dress rules. Perhaps if she put as much energy into her studies as she did into her social life, she might have the makings of a good nurse. But the reports that came back from the wards made the Sister Tutor despair.

She made her way back to the front of the class and placed Helen Tremayne's paper down in front of her. She didn't make a grab for it like the other girls did but sat perfectly still, eyeing it warily as if it might bite her.

'Female Medical!' said Amy Hollins, screwing up her paper, her voice full of disgust. 'That's so unfair. Everyone knows old Everett is as mad as a bat.'

'If you're unhappy with your allocation, I'm sure Matron would be pleased to discuss the matter with you.' Sister Parker glared across the classroom at her. Amy blushed, her expression still mutinous.

The Sister Tutor turned back to Helen, who had finally steeled herself to turn over her paper.

'I hope you at least are satisfied with your allocation, Tremayne?' she said, peering at Helen over her spectacles.

'Yes. Thank you, Sister.'

'Your mother told me you were very keen to work in surgery. She mentioned you might like to be a Theatre nurse when you qualify?'

Helen looked up at her, and Florence Parker caught a flash of dismay in her large brown eyes before her gaze dropped again. This was news to her, Sister Parker could tell. Poor Tremayne, always under her mother's thumb.

'I'm not sure I'd be good enough, Sister.' Her voice barely rose above a husky whisper.

'Och, I'm sure you'll have no trouble. You are an excellent student, Nurse Tremayne. I daresay we'll be seeing your picture up on that wall of Nightingale Medal winners, before too long.'

'I daresay Mummy will see to that, too.' Sister Parker picked up Amy Hollins' spiteful whisper from the back row. 'It must be nice, having a mother on the Board of Trustees!'

Helen must have heard it too. She ducked her head, the tips of her ears burning bright red under her smooth dark hair.

Sister Parker remembered her last meeting with Constance Tremayne, when she had marched into the classroom and demanded that Helen be allocated to Theatre. After more than forty years as a nurse, Florence Parker did not scare easily. But Mrs Tremayne had made her feel like a terrified probationer again, being hauled in front

16

of Matron.

She glanced back at Helen, picking at her bitten nails. Whatever Hollins might think, Florence Parker couldn't imagine it was very nice to have Mrs Tremayne for a mother.

Helen heard the squeals of laughter drifting down the stairs when she returned to the nurses' home with her room mate Millie Benedict after their duty finished that night. It was past nine o'clock and most of the nurses were preparing for lights out at ten, unless they were lucky enough to have a late pass or brave enough to risk sneaking in through the windows.

'Listen to that,' Millie said, as they took off their cloaks in the gloomy, brown painted hall-way, taking care not to let their feet squeak too much on the faded lino. 'It sounds as if some-one's having a party.'

'Hollins,' Helen replied. 'I heard her planning it during supper.'

'I'm surprised Sister Sutton hasn't heard them, all that noise they're making.' Millie glanced towards the Home Sister's door. 'That's typical, isn't it? Hollins and her gang can get away with having a party, but if I so much as drop a hairpin on the floor Sutton's banging on the door, threat-ening to send me to Matron.'

Millie pulled an expression of disgust. She was every bit as blonde and pretty as Amy Hollins, but with none of Amy's hard edges.

'Perhaps she's asleep?' Helen said.

'Sister Sutton never sleeps. She prowls the corridor all night with that wretched little dog of

17

hers, waiting to catch us poor nurses in the act of enjoying ourselves.'

They climbed the stairs, taking care to miss the creaking step hallway up that always brought Sister Sutton out of her lair. The dark polished wood was uneven under their feet, worn down by the footsteps of generations of weary young girls just like them.

As they reached the second landing, they heard another muffled shriek coming from the other end of the long passageway. Millie turned to Helen. 'Will you be joining the party later, as they're your set?'

Helen shook her head. 'I have to study.'

'I'm sure it won't hurt to give revision a miss for one night?'

'Not with the State Finals six months away.'

'The others don't seem to care too much about that.'

'Perhaps they're more confident of passing than I am?'

Millie laughed. 'Hardly! Everyone knows you're one of the best students at the Nightingale. You should go, Tremayne. You know what they say about all work and no play...'

'I told you, I don't want to!'

Helen started up the steep, narrow flight of stairs that led to their attic room before Millie could argue any more. She didn't want to tell Millie that she hadn't been invited to join the party, or how humiliated she had felt, sitting at the other end of the dining table while the others made their plans. She knew she should be used to it after three years. But it still hurt, even though she tried not to show it.

When a set of students joined the Nightingale for training, they tended to stick together as a group. But right from the start, Helen had been set apart. The other girls were wary of her because she worked hard, and because her mother was on the Board of Trustees. They quickly decided Helen was too much of a swot and a teacher's pet to be included in their plans. Helen sometimes wished she could explain that she only worked hard to please her mother. But she wasn't sure anyone would listen.

As if she could read her thoughts, Millie said, 'Perhaps if you made more effort to join in, they might feel differently about you.'

'To be honest, I don't really care how they feel,' Helen replied. 'I'm here to work, not to make friends.' She parroted the stern instruction her mother had given her the one and only time Helen had tried to explain how lonely and left out she felt.

Millie stopped, halfway up the stairs. 'We're friends, aren't we?'

Helen turned to smile back at her. 'That's different.'

It was impossible not to love Millie – or Lady Amelia Benedict, to give her her full title. She was simply the sweetest girl Helen had ever met. She even looked sunny, with her bouncy blonde curls and wide smile. There were no airs and graces to her at all, even though she was the daughter of an earl and had been brought up in a castle in Kent.

Millie and their other room mate Dora Doyle were in the year below and had come into Helen's

19

lonely life like a breath of fresh air nearly two years earlier. They had refused to be put off by Helen's shy reserve. It was thanks to their friendship that she had learned not to mind so much when the other girls in her set were spiteful to her.

Her friends had also given her the confidence not to run away when she met the love of her life, Charlie Dawson. Between them and Charlie, Helen was the happiest she had ever been. Even though her mother's shadow still fell over everything she did.

'I should think so, too!' Millie beamed, then added, 'And you really mustn't mind about Amy Hollins. She's an awful cat. I can't say I'm looking forward to spending the next three months with her on Female Medical!'

Their room was at the top of the house, long and sparsely furnished with three beds tucked into the sloping eaves. A dormer window cast a square patch of silvery moonlight on to the polished wooden floor.

Millie shivered. 'Why does it always seem so cold up here, even in April?' She reached for the light switch, flicked it – then let out a cry of dismay.

There was a girl sprawled on the middle bed, fully dressed, her stout black shoes poking through the bars of the iron bedstead. Her left arm dangled off one side, still clutching the limp remains of a cap. A wild mop of red curls fanned out over the pillow, hiding her face.

At the sound of Millie's cry her head jerked up, revealing a freckled face bleary with sleep.

'What the – oh, it's only you.' Irritable green eyes peered out from under the ginger hair. 'I thought there was a fire.'

She sat up slowly, stretching her limbs. 'I must have nodded off. What time is it?'

'Nearly half-past nine.'

'Really?' Dora Doyle snatched up her watch from the bedside table and held it close to her face, squinting at it. 'Blimey, I've been asleep for two hours.'

'Had a hard day?' Helen said sympathetically, easing off her own shoes. Her feet throbbed in protest.

'You could say that.' Dora rubbed her eyes. 'Sister had us cleaning the ward from top to bottom all day. I've been up and down, cleaning windows and turning mattresses and damp dusting. I ache all over. I'm glad tomorrow's my day off. I'd probably be too stiff to get out of bed otherwise.'

'I know how you feel. They always seem to work us harder on our last day, don't they?' Millie rifled in her chest of drawers and pulled out a lighter and a packet of cigarettes. She took one, then offered the packet to Dora.

'I hope you're going to open a window?' Helen warned, unpinning her cap. 'You know Sister Sutton can smell smoke a mile off.'

'Yes, yes, don't fuss so, Tremayne. We're not going to get you in trouble.' Millie reached up and unlatched the window, pushing it open. Then she sat down and lit Dora's cigarette for her.

'So where are they sending you next?' she asked.

Dora took a long draw on her cigarette. 'Casualty,' she replied. 'How about you?'

'Female Medical. Although I'm not sure what Sister Everett will make of me.'

21

'She'll be fine,' Helen said. She pulled off her starched collar and examined the raw mark on her skin where the starched fabric had chafed. 'She can be slightly eccentric, but don't let that fool you. She's as sharp as a tack when it comes to the patients. Knows all their notes off by heart and expects her nurses to do the same.'

Millie chewed her lip worriedly. 'I wish I were going to Casualty with you, Doyle. I've heard it's so much fun down there.'

'If you don't mind severed limbs and people dropping dead at your feet!' Dora sent a stream of cigarette smoke up through the open window into the chilly night sky, then twisted round to look at Helen. 'Where are they sending you, Tremayne?'

'Theatre.'

'Oh, how exciting!' Millie joined in. 'I'd love to be a Theatre nurse.'

Dora cackled with laughter. 'You? In Theatre?'

Millie frowned. 'What's so amusing about that?'

'No one would ever send you to Theatre. You're far too accident-prone.' Trust Dora to spell it out, Helen thought as she pulled off her apron and stuffed it into her laundry bag. Typical Doyle, always blunt and to the point.

'No, I'm not.' Millie looked so injured, Helen couldn't help smiling. She glanced at Dora. She was fighting to keep her face straight too.

'Let's see…' Dora pretended to consider. 'Remember that time you cleaned everyone's false teeth in the same bowl and then couldn't remember which set was which? And what about the time you gave a patient a delousing treatment and accidentally bleached their hair?'

'And don't forget nearly drowning Sister Hyde with a soap enema,' Helen put in.

'All right, all right. You've made your point,' Millie sighed.

She looked so dejected, Helen's heart went out to her. 'You more than make up for it in other ways,' she said soothingly.

'Like what?'

'Well ... you're very kind, and compassionate. And you have a way of talking to people that makes them feel better. Everyone adores you.'

Millie had a way of winning people over. Even grumpy Sister Hyde on Female Chronics had been a little tearful when Nurse Benedict left her ward.

Another muffled squawk of laughter came up through the floorboards, followed by a crash.

Millie shook her head. 'They're asking for trouble down there.'

'What are they celebrating, anyway?' Dora asked.

'Bevan's got engaged.' Helen wriggled into her flannel nightgown. 'Her junior doctor popped the question two days ago.'

'At this rate there won't be any of us left after we qualify.' Millie looked down at her bare left hand. She wasn't allowed to wear the engagement ring her journalist boyfriend Sebastian had given her before he left for an assignment in Berlin. 'It's so silly, really. You'd think they'd let us carry on working after we get married, wouldn't you?'

'I don't know what Sister Sutton would say about having husbands in the nurses' home!' Helen smiled.

23

'You're not moving Seb in here,' Dora warned. 'It's bad enough with the three of us.'

'Can you imagine?' Millie laughed. 'No, I'm sure they could make some arrangements, though. It seems such a waste, to spend three years training and then have to leave.'

'I don't think Bevan is too worried about that.' Helen picked up her hairbrush. 'From what I could make out, she can't wait to say goodbye to the Nightingale and all its rules and regulations.'

'Well, I don't want to leave,' Millie said. 'I'd like to stay on after I get married, if they'll let me. But I don't suppose I'll get the chance. Once I'm married, that's it.'

'You could always put off the wedding?' Helen suggested.

Millie shook her head. 'I've already kept poor Seb waiting long enough. And I suspect my grandmother would have an absolute fit if I told her we were postponing the wedding. She's desperate for me to marry and produce a suitable heir to inherit the estate before anything happens to my father.'

She was so matter-of-fact about it, Helen could only marvel at her. Millie had a huge weight resting on her shoulders. The future of her family depended on her producing a son. She had been groomed by her grandmother for a suitable marriage almost from the moment she was born. Millie had made a brave bid for independence by training as a nurse. But they all knew her freedom would have to end one day.

'How about you?' she asked. 'When are you and Charlie planning to get married?'

24

Helen pulled a blanket around her shoulders to keep out the chilly April air that blew in through the open window. 'I'm not sure. I'd have to talk to my mother...'

'You're over twenty-one, surely you can do as you please?'

'Even so, my mother would expect to be consulted.'

'I don't see why she would object. Charlie is adorable, and anyone can see the two of you are head over heels in love.'

Helen glanced up into Millie's candid blue eyes. If only life was as simple, she thought.

'Can we stop talking about weddings for five minutes?' Dora interrupted them sharply.

Millie turned to her, startled. 'What's wrong with you?'

'Nothing. I'm just sick of hearing about people getting married.' Dora took off her shoes and climbed on to her bed, leaned out of the window and stubbed her cigarette on the ledge, then tossed the stub into the night air.

Before Millie could reply, Sister Sutton's voice rang out from the passageway below them.

'Lights out at ten o'clock, Nurses.'

Millie and Helen left Dora changing into her nightclothes and joined the line of girls shivering in the passageway outside the bathroom.

'You don't have to stand here with me, you know,' Millie reminded Helen, pulling her dressing gown more tightly around her. 'You're a senior. You could go to the front of the queue.'

As if to prove her point, Amy Hollins, Brenda Bevan and a few of the others from her set drifted down the passageway from Hollins' room and elbowed their way straight into the bathroom, laughing at the glaring faces of the junior students who had to move back to let them in.

'I might as well stay here.'

'Suit yourself. But you know they'll take all the hot water before we get there, don't you?'

'I'm sure there'll be some left for us.' Helen smiled.

Millie sent her a narrow look. 'You know, you're not nearly bullying enough,' she said. 'I bet you don't make pros do all the dirty jobs on the ward, either.'

'I don't like ordering other people around.'

'In that case, you'll never be a ward sister!' Millie nodded towards Amy Hollins. 'Perhaps you should take a few lessons from her?'

'I don't know about that!'

Millie paused for a moment, then changed the subject. 'Doyle was rather cross earlier, don't you think?' she commented. 'What do you suppose is the matter with her?'

'I don't know. Her friend is getting married tomorrow, and Doyle's a bridesmaid. Perhaps that has something to do with it.'

'So she is,' Millie remembered. 'But I still don't see why that should make her so irritable. If anything, she should be happy about it.'

'I suppose so. But you never really know what she's thinking, do you?'

Helen had been intimidated by Dora at first, the way those green eyes looked out so challengingly at the world, as if she would take on anyone who came near her. She had come to understand that was just Dora's way, that she was a typical East End girl, down to earth and fiercely proud. But she kept her feelings locked away under a tough exterior.

'Perhaps she's just upset because she has a ghastly dress?' Millie suggested.

'You could be right,' Helen agreed. Whatever was on Dora's mind, Helen doubted they would ever find out about it.

Chapter Two

Rain wept over the back streets of Bethnal Green on the day Dora Doyle's best friend Ruby Pike married Nick Riley.

'Talk about April showers!' Ruby grimaced, clearing a patch on the steamy kitchen window to look down over the back yard. Even though it was the middle of the afternoon it was as dark as twilight outside. 'It's coming down in stair rods.'

'Come over here and keep still. I'll never get this seam straight if you keep running off,' Dora mumbled through a mouth full of pins as she knelt at her friend's feet.

It was chaos in the Pikes' crowded kitchen. Ruby's father Len jostled at the sink with her brothers Dennis and Frank, all trying to shave in front of the tiny scrap of mirror. Her mum Lettie was cleaning shoes at the kitchen table, a pinnie fastened over her best dress.

Meanwhile, Dora was on her hands and knees,

doing a last-minute repair to the bride's hem.

It was the last place she wanted to be. But Ruby was her best friend, they'd grown up next door to each other in the narrow, cramped tenements of Griffin Street, and Dora had made a promise that she would be bridesmaid.

'I dunno why you're bothering. I'll look like a drowned rat by the time I get to the church anyway.' Ruby sighed. 'My Nick will probably run a mile when he sees me.'

'If he turns up!' Dennis suggested cheekily.

'He might do a runner,' Frank agreed. He and Dennis looked at each other, then both broke into song: '"There was I, waiting at the church" – ow!' they chorused, as their father fetched them both a slap round the ear.

'He'd better bleeding turn up or I'll have him, I don't care how big he is. He's had his fun, now he's got to pay for it!' Len Pike grumbled.

'You, go up against Nick Riley? I'd like to see you try!' his wife sneered. 'He'd make mincemeat of you!'

Len Pike huffed and blew out his cheeks, but they all knew Lettie was right. No one in their right mind would ever take on Nick Riley. Even by the tough standards of the East End, Nick had a reputation.

'He'd better bloody turn up, that's all I'm saying,' Len mumbled. 'He's got you into this mess, my girl, he'll have to get you out!'

'That's enough!' Lettie scolded him. 'You don't have to tell the whole world our business!'

'I've got news for you. The whole world already knows!' Len Pike scraped at his chin and flicked the bristly soap towards the plug hole. 'There's only one reason a girl gets married this quick, and that's because there's a baby on the way. What I want to know is, why you have to make such a show of it?' he said, picking up the tea-towel to mop his face. 'Why couldn't you just go off and do it quiet in a register office, like any decent girl would?'

'I don't do anything quiet, Dad. You should know that!'

Ruby winked at Dora. Everyone said Ruby Pike had more front than Southend, and she was proving it today. Even in her demure wedding dress, she looked like one of the film stars she followed so avidly in *Picturegoer*. The bias-cut silver morocaine clung lovingly to her generous curves. She'd styled her hair like Jean Harlow, the platinum-blonde waves curling softly around her pretty face.

No wonder Nick hadn't been able to resist her. There weren't many red-blooded men in Bethnal Green who could.

'Why shouldn't my Ruby have a white wedding if she wants one?' Lettie defended her. 'This is her big day and I won't have anyone spoiling it for her.' She smiled fondly at her daughter. 'Baby or not, she and Nick would have got wed sooner or later. You only have to look at him to see he's besotted with her.'

The needle caught the end of Dora's finger, making her yelp.

'Careful!' Ruby frowned down at her. 'I don't want you getting blood on my dress.'

'Sorry.' Dora sucked her finger. As she did, she glanced up and found herself meeting Lettie's hard dark stare. Even her wedding finery and the unfamiliar slash of red lipstick she wore didn't soften her thin, bitter face. There was a warning look in her eyes that made Dora uneasy.

The back door crashed downstairs, in the Rileys' part of the house.

'I expect that'll be my Nick, on his way to church,' Ruby said with a smile.

Dennis went to the window and looked out. 'I can see June Riley, wearing a daft titfer covered in feathers.'

'Let's have a look.' Lettie peered over her son's shoulder down into the yard. 'Look at the state of her. She can hardly walk in a straight line. Fancy being half cut this time of the morning, and for her own son's wedding,' she tutted.

'Where's Nick? Isn't he with her?' Dora heard the tremor in Ruby's voice.

'I expect he's already gone,' Lettie soothed.

'I didn't hear him leave.' Ruby's plump mouth pursed. 'I'm going downstairs to look for him.'

She started for the door, but Lettie stopped her. 'You can't! It's unlucky for him to see his bride before the wedding.'

Ruby hesitated, then turned to Dora. 'You go,' she said.

'Me? But I haven't finished sewing...'

'That doesn't matter. I want you to go downstairs and see if Nick's gone.'

'But–'

'Please, Dora. Be a mate? I don't want to get to church and find out he's left me standing at the altar!'

Dora saw her friend's nervous smile, stretched

almost to breaking point. 'All right,' she agreed, standing up and brushing down her dress. 'But I'm telling you now, you haven't got anything to worry about.'

Downstairs, all was in darkness. Dora knocked on the Rileys' kitchen door and held her breath, counting to ten.

One … two… She stared at the peeling paint-work.

Five … six… She took a step backwards, already retreating towards the stairs.

Nine … ten. No reply. She had turned to hurry away when the door flew open and Nick stood there.

Seeing him almost stopped Dora's heart in her chest.

No one could call Nick Riley handsome, with his flattened boxer's nose and brooding expression. But there was something compelling about the intense blue eyes that scowled out from under a mane of dark gypsy curls.

She looked away quickly, dragging her gaze from his unbuttoned shirt. 'Sorry,' she muttered. 'Ruby just sent me down. She wasn't sure if you'd already gone…'

'I was just leaving.'

'Right. I'll tell her…' Dora started to turn away, but Nick called her back.

'Wait. I need your help.'

She looked around, dry-mouthed with panic, looking for a way to escape. 'I'm needed up-stairs…'

'Please.' Nick's voice was husky. 'It's Danny,' he said.

The Rileys' kitchen was a cold, unwelcoming place, stinking of damp and rancid fat. The walls were furred with black patches of mould. The houses in Griffin Street weren't palaces, but most of the women Dora knew tried hard to keep them clean and tidy. Except for June Riley. She had always been more interested in her next drink or her latest man than in looking after her two sons.

Dora averted her eyes from the dirty dishes littering the table and went over to where Nick's younger brother Danny sat huddled in a corner of the room, his knees pulled up to his chin, face buried against them. He was half dressed in shiny suit trousers and a grubby vest, his feet bare.

'I was helping him to get dressed when he suddenly decided he wasn't going to come,' Nick said. 'Now I can't get him to budge. He won't even tell me what's wrong.' His gaze was fixed on his brother. 'He's always trusted you, Dora,' he said gruffly. 'I thought you could talk to him.'

She glanced at Nick's profile then at Danny, shivering in the corner. 'I'll try,' she said.

'Thanks.' Nick went over and crouched down beside his brother. 'Danny?' He put a hand on his shoulder, but Danny flinched away. Dora saw the look of pain flash across Nick's face. 'Dan, Dora's come to have a word with you. You like Dora, don't you?'

Danny didn't move. Nick straightened up and turned to Dora, his face beseeching.

'Look after him,' he whispered. 'And if anyone's hurt him, or said anything...'

'Just go and finish getting ready,' she said.

As the door closed behind him, Dora went over to where Danny was crouched and sat down beside him, carefully rearranging her pink dress around her so it didn't pick up too much dust from the floor.

'Now then, Danny ducks, what's all this about you not wanting to go to your brother's wedding?' she coaxed softly. 'We can't have that, can we? You're his best man. He's relying on you.'

Danny lifted his head slowly to look at her with red-rimmed, watery eyes. He was as pale as his brother was dark, with thin, gangling limbs that made him seem all disjointed angles.

'Th-they said I sh-shouldn't go.' He sniffed back his tears. 'Th-they s-said I – I'd l-let everyone down.'

'Who said that?' But even as she said it, Dora already knew the answer.

'F-Frank and D-Dennis.' Danny wiped his nose with his wrist. He was nearly eighteen years old, but still had the innocent, vulnerable mind of a child. Easy prey for cruel thugs like the Pike boys. 'They s-said Nick sh-shouldn't h-have me as his b-best man because everyone will l-laugh at m-me.'

'No one's going to laugh at you, sweetheart.' Dora smoothed his fair hair back off his face. Not while your brother's there, at any rate, she thought. Nick would string Frank and Dennis up if he knew they'd been tormenting Danny. 'You don't want to take any notice of that pair. They're just bullies, that's all.'

'I'm f-frightened of them,' Danny mumbled. 'And I'm f-frightened of R-Ruby too. She just laughs when they s-say things to me.'

'Does she now?'

Danny nodded. 'I h-heard her telling her m-mum she didn't know why Nick had p-picked me to b-be his best man.'

Dora fought to keep her temper. It was no less than she'd expected from Dennis and Frank, but she was disappointed in her friend.

Danny couldn't help being the way he was. He'd been left brain-damaged by a terrible accident when he was a child, although there were many in Griffin Street who suspected that it was his violent father Reg who'd caused the injury, shortly before he abandoned his family.

Most of the neighbours treated Danny with kindness and understanding, if only because they were afraid of his older brother. Dora hadn't expected Ruby to be so cruel. After all, she and Danny were going to be family.

'Well, I'll tell you why, shall I? Nick picked you because you're his brother and there's no one else in the whole wide world he'd want to stand beside him at his wedding. And I'll tell you something else, too. If you aren't there he's going to be very upset and disappointed. And you don't want that, do you?' Danny shook his head. 'So why don't I help you finish getting ready? We'll find you a nice shirt and tie to wear, and comb your hair and make you look like a proper gent. How about that?'

Dora stood up and put out her hand to help him to his feet. Danny hung back, still reluctant.

'Wh-what if I l-let him down?'

'You won't, love. And don't forget, I'll be there

with you. I can help you if you get stuck with anything.'

He regarded her with wary eyes. 'You pr-promise?'

''Course I do.' Dora offered her hand again. 'Now let's get a move on, or we'll all miss the wedding!'

She was helping him to put on his tie when Nick returned.

'Everything all right?' he asked, his eyes fixed on Danny.

'I think so.' Dora straightened the knot and turned Danny around to face his brother. 'What do you reckon? Will we do?'

The warmth in Nick's smile as he looked at his brother was like the sun coming out from behind a cloud.

'Very nice,' he said in a choked voice.

It was a moment before she realised he'd shifted his gaze to her, and another moment before she could react.

'Well, I'd best be getting back. Ruby will think I've deserted her!' She hurried for the door. Nick followed her.

'Did he say what was wrong?'

Dora glanced past his shoulder at Danny, admiring himself in the kitchen mirror. 'It was just nerves, that's all.'

'Are you sure that's it?' Nick's eyes narrowed. 'I meant what I said. If I thought anyone had been having a go at him–'

Dora thought about Ruby. 'He'll be all right,' she said. 'Weddings just bring out the worst in people, that's all.'

35

'Tell me something I don't know.' Nick looked grim.

Dora stepped into the hall, but his voice stopped her in her tracks. 'You look lovely.'

She felt herself blushing to the roots of her red hair. 'Pink isn't really my colour,' she batted away the compliment. 'But Ruby likes it, so–'

'What Ruby wants, Ruby gets,' Nick said.

Dora smiled wistfully. 'It seems that way, doesn't it?'

She stared at the staircase in front of her, that led back up to the Pikes' part of the house. She knew she should walk away, but her treacherous legs wouldn't carry her.

'I'm sorry,' Nick said.

'So am I.'

She managed the few steps to the foot of the stairs. 'I don't want to marry her,' Nick blurted out.

Dora turned to face him. She wanted to shout at him, to tell him he was being selfish, but he looked so wretched she couldn't bring herself to do it. Besides, she felt that if she let herself go even for a moment and allowed herself to show any emotion, she would be lost.

'You should have thought about that before you got her pregnant, shouldn't you?'

'Don't you think I know that? I made a mistake. If I could turn back the clock–'

'You can't,' Dora cut him off coldly. 'It's too late now.'

'It doesn't have to be.' He took a few steps towards her. 'If you just say the word, I'll walk away.'

She looked over her shoulder at him, knowing

36

the look of desolation in his eyes mirrored her own expression. For a moment, it almost seemed possible that they could do it, that they could snatch their happiness and run with it. All she had to do was say the word...

But then she remembered Ruby's face, radiant with optimism as she put on her wedding gown.

'You have to do the right thing by Ruby,' she said. 'We both do.'

His broad shoulders slumped. 'I know,' he sighed.

'You wouldn't do it anyway,' said Dora. 'I know you, Nick Riley. You would never walk away from her, not while she's carrying your child.'

His mouth twisted. 'I wish I could.'

'I don't. Because then you wouldn't be the man I fell in love with.'

The words were out before Dora could stop herself. Neither of them moved. She could feel the heat of his body close to hers and she knew she should step away but she couldn't, because she knew it would be the last time he was ever this close to her.

It had taken her too long to realise she was in love with Nick Riley. Growing up next door to her, he had always seemed so remote, a tough, troubled young man struggling to look after his sick brother and drunken mother. It was only when she started as a student at the Nightingale, where he worked as a porter, that they had got to know each other.

But by then he was courting Ruby. And by the time Dora and he realised how they felt about each other, his girlfriend was pregnant.

37

'I love you too,' Nick said, his voice gruff with emotion. 'I just wanted to say that one more time, before–'

'Before we have to forget each other,' she finished for him.

'I'm not sure I can forget you.'

'You must,' she insisted. 'For the sake of Ruby and your baby, from now on we have to be strangers.'

Ruby Pike, or Ruby Riley, as she was now called, downed her third port and lemon, determined to enjoy herself. All around her the Rose and Crown rang to the rafters with laughter, singing and merriment. Even her mum and dad weren't at each other's throats for once, as they stood arm in arm around the piano, singing 'If You Were the Only Girl in the World'.

This was her big day, but none of it seemed real. She hadn't ever believed it would come to this. Right up to the moment Nick slid the wedding band on her finger, she was sure something would happen to stop it. When the vicar asked if anyone knew of any reason why they shouldn't lawfully be joined, her heartbeat had crashed in her ears as she waited for someone to speak up.

But no one had. And now they were married, bound together for the rest of their lives.

Ruby's hand shook as she tipped back her head and sank the last of her drink. She wished Dora were there. Her friend had slipped away straight after the ceremony, saying she had to go back on duty. Ruby knew it was a lie, but she hadn't argued.

'Good thing too,' her mother had whispered, as they watched Dora leave, head down and coat collar pulled up against the rain. 'You want to watch that mate of yours, Ruby. I reckon she's sweet on your Nick.'

As if Ruby needed telling. She had been aware of the tension between them for months, even before they understood it themselves. 'I trust Dora,' she said. 'She'd never do the dirty on me. She's too good a friend for that.'

Not like me, a voice inside her head added. If she was honest, part of the reason she had wanted Nick was because she knew her mate liked him.

'And what about him?' Lettie had nodded towards Nick, who was straightening his brother's tie. 'Do you trust him?'

'We're married, ain't we?'

Her mother sent her a scathing look. 'You're a fool if you think a wedding ring makes a blind bit of difference to a man.'

Ruby watched Nick, fussing over his brother with so much affection, and felt a pang of jealousy. 'I'm going to make sure he never wants to look at another woman. You wait and see, he'll soon forget all about Dora Doyle.'

'Well, I reckon if anyone can do that, it's you.' Lettie smiled at her admiringly. 'He's lucky to have you, love.'

Ruby tried to remind herself of that as she gazed around the pub. All around her were the disappointed faces of young men she had turned down, local boys she'd toyed with and then rejected. Even now she was a married woman, they still watched her longingly. She was Ruby

Pike, she could have had any man she wanted in Bethnal Green. And she'd chosen Nick Riley. He should be on his knees giving thanks to God, she decided.

But deep inside her there was a knot of tension that just wouldn't go away.

'Rube?' She almost jumped when she realised Nick was standing over her. His smart wedding suit only seemed to emphasise the taut muscles of his body, as lean as a fighting dog's. 'I'm going outside for a breath of fresh air.'

'You will come back, won't you?' she blurted out.

His dark brows drew together in a frown. 'What kind of a question is that?'

'I dunno.' She felt suddenly foolish. 'Take no notice of me, I'm just being daft.'

She looked away, but his fingers tilted her chin and turned her face up to meet his. 'Ruby, look at me.' His eyes met hers, intense and direct. 'We're married, all right? I ain't going to let you down. I'm standing by you.'

'I – I know.' She bit her lip, feeling wretched. 'Kiss me,' she pleaded.

He looked around. 'What, here? In front of everyone?'

'Why not?' She rose, pushing her chair back with a clatter. The port and lemons made her unsteady on her feet and Nick's hands came out to catch her as she stumbled. 'You ashamed of your wife, or something?'

She wound her arms around his neck and moved in for a kiss. Nick tried to offer her a peck on the lips but Ruby buried her fingers in the

40

springy thickness of his curls, holding him fast as her tongue boldly probed his mouth. She felt the stiff resistance in his body for a second before he yielded to her, as he always did.

Their kiss brought a riot of catcalls and cheering from the crowd.

'Oi, you two! Save it for the wedding night!' someone shouted.

'They've already had that, from what I've heard,' someone else said, then shut up as Nick pulled away sharply and turned to scowl at them.

'It doesn't matter anyway.' Ruby laughed defiantly, holding up her left hand. 'We're married now. It's all legal and above board.'

'Better late than never!' another brave soul shouted from the back of the bar.

Ruby was still smiling bravely and laughing off everyone's jokes when Nick slipped outside a few minutes later. She waited until she saw the door close behind him, then turned to her brother Dennis.

'Get me another drink,' she said, thrusting the glass at him. 'And make it a double this time.'

'You want to go steady, you know.' Lettie appeared at her side. 'You don't want to get squiffy.'

Ruby stared at her mother. A network of fine purple veins stood out on her thin, flushed cheeks, and her hat was squashed into a strange, lopsided shape where someone had sat on it. 'You're a fine one to talk!'

'I'm not expecting, am I?' Lettie plonked herself down on the bench next to her. 'You're having a baby, remember?'

'How can I forget?' Ruby murmured, moodily

41

tracing a sticky beer ring on the table in front of her.

Lettie squinted at her. 'You're in a funny old mood, all of a sudden. What's the matter?'

'Nothing. It's just–' Ruby started to speak and then stopped herself.

'I know what this is about.' Lettie pulled off her hat and plonked it on the table. 'You're worried about what I said earlier, ain't you?' She pressed one thin, clawed hand against Ruby's shoulder. 'You don't want to take any notice of me, love. You're right, you and Nick are properly wed now. He's not going to look at anyone else, especially not an ugly mug like Dora Doyle. Not while he's got you.'

Dennis arrived and put Ruby's drink down in front of her, then held out his hand for the money. Ruby shot him a filthy look and he retreated sharply.

'Besides,' Lettie went on, slurring her words, 'you're expecting his baby. And that means a lot to Nick Riley, whatever he lets on. I know I've said some things about him in the past, but I'll say one thing for him: he's a grafter. You'll never have to worry about him providing for you and that kid–'

'There is no kid,' Ruby blurted out.

Lettie frowned in confusion. 'No what, love?'

'I'm not pregnant, Mum.' Ruby lifted her gaze to meet her mother's. 'There is no baby. There never was.'

Lettie's mouth opened and then closed again. 'But I don't understand...'

'I lied,' Ruby said simply.

'You mean, you–' Lettie's gaze dropped to

42

Ruby's belly, then back up to her face. 'But why?'

'So he wouldn't leave me.'

It was Nick's fault. He'd pushed her into it. Ruby knew he was going to finish it with her, cast her aside for Dora, and she also knew that she loved him so much that if he told her he didn't want her any more, it would be the end of her world.

And so she'd panicked and told him she was pregnant. And those words had changed everything.

The drunken flush drained out of her mother's face. She stared at Ruby, as if she couldn't make up her mind whether to laugh or cry.

'You silly cow!' she said finally. 'You mean, you've let all the neighbours gossip about us for nothing?'

Ruby's mouth twisted. Trust her mother to worry about something like that!

'You've got some neck, I'll give you that much.' Her mother shook her head slowly. 'So what are you going to do now?'

'I don't know.' Ruby shrugged. 'I hadn't thought about it.'

'Typical!' Lettie snapped. 'That's your trouble, you're always opening your trap before you've had a chance to think about what you're doing.'

'I'll tell him it was a false alarm, that I got my dates wrong.'

Her mother regarded her shrewdly. 'And how do you think he'll take that?'

'I'll find out, won't I?'

'You do realise he might leave you?'

Ruby shook her head. 'He won't. Anyway, he

43

couldn't divorce me. He wouldn't have the grounds, would he?' Men could only divorce their wives for adultery, not for lying.

Besides, people like them didn't get divorced. No matter how unhappy they were, they just put up with each other until death parted them. Her own mum and dad had been living under the same roof for more than twenty years, even though they hated the sight of each other.

'There are worse things in life than divorce, my girl. You don't want to be married to a man who regrets it.' Looking at her mother's face, so full of sadness, Ruby wondered if she was thinking about her own loveless match. 'It ain't no life, believe me.'

'Who says he'll regret it?' Now they were married, Ruby intended to make sure Nick didn't have a single moment of doubt. 'Anyway, I'll probably get pregnant soon enough,' she added.

'You'd best make sure you do, my girl, just in case he gets any ideas,' Lettie warned. 'And when are you going to tell him the truth?'

The door opened and Nick appeared. Ruby felt herself smiling as he threaded his way through the crowd towards her.

'Not tonight,' she said. This was the happiest day of her life, and nothing was going to spoil it.

Chapter Three

'You there. What do you think you're doing?'

Dora looked round at the sound of the sharp reprimand. A small dark woman in the grey uniform of a ward sister was heading purposefully towards her. It was barely seven o'clock on a Sunday morning, and Dora had just walked in through the doors of the Casualty department for her first day on duty. Surely she couldn't have done something wrong already?

She relaxed when the Sister barrelled past her towards an elderly man, huddled under his coat at the back of the room on the last of the rows of empty wooden benches.

'Were you asleep?' The nurse stood over him, hands planted on her hips.

'N-No, Nurse.' Dora saw the old man tremble, and felt for him. His white hair was straggly under his shapeless hat, and he looked as if he hadn't had a decent meal in days.

The Sister eyed him beadily. 'I've seen you in here before, haven't I?'

'No,' the old man said.

From somewhere beyond the waiting room came an unearthly howl. Dora jumped, but the nurse did not flinch. Her attention was still fixed on the old man.

'Yes, I have. Don't you try to get one over on me, my man. I've warned you about this before.

This is a hospital, not a public dormitory, I will not have members of the public wandering in to have a nap. Now be off with you.'

'But, Nurse–'

'I said, be off with you!' She lifted him bodily from the seat and propelled him towards the doors. For a small woman, she was surprisingly strong. 'If you want to sleep it off, try the local library,' she called, closing the doors firmly on him.

She turned, saw Dora and her eyes narrowed. Dora flinched, afraid she might be next to be ejected. 'Are you the new student?'

'Yes, Sister. I'm Doyle.'

'I'm Sister Percival, and I am in charge of this department.' She rapped out the words like bullets from a machine gun. She was a neat little woman, bristling with energy. Even when she was standing still she seemed to be moving, her fingers drumming, dark eyes darting. 'Well? Don't just stand there gawping at me. Get to the Operating Room and assist Dr McKay with his severed arm.'

Dora looked around her. The waiting room reminded her of a church, long and echoing, with tall windows down one wall and a set of double doors at one end. At the other was a high wooden desk like a pulpit, with a young staff nurse in a blue uniform seated behind it. In between were rows of benches like church pews, empty apart from a woman with a baby in her arms and a man clutching a blood-soaked handkerchief to his temple.

'Sorry, Sister, I don't know what I'm supposed to do–'

Another howl ripped through the air.

'Good heavens, don't you students ever think for yourselves?' Sister Percival pointed towards a door beyond the counter. 'Over there, girl, behind the booking-in desk. Now get along with you. We deal with emergencies here, and that means there's no time for dawdling.'

Dora went through the door and found herself in a short tiled corridor. Several doors led off it, all bearing the words 'Consulting Room' followed by various numbers. At the far end was a door marked 'Operating Room'. But Dora didn't need to be told that – the screech coming from the other side of the door told her all she needed to know.

Dora took a deep breath, pushed open the door and walked in.

She nearly ran straight out again when she saw what was waiting for her. A man lay on the operating table, roaring and cursing with pain, blood pumping from the yawning gash on his forearm. She caught sight of glistening muscle, sinews and bone, like the diagrams in a textbook brought to life in front of her eyes.

And so much blood. No textbook could have prepared her for that. It soaked through the towels, shocking scarlet blossoming on the stark white. Thick splashes dripped off the operating table, pooling at the feet of the doctor who stood beside his patient, applying a tourniquet.

He looked up at her over his spectacles. 'Ah, Nurse. Could you flush this wound for me, please?'

Dora rushed to fetch the saline solution, relieved to get away. The last thing she wanted to do was faint on her first day in Casualty.

The tourniquet stopped the worst of the bleeding, but warm, sticky blood still oozed over her hands as she tried to clean the wound. Dora averted her gaze as nausea rose up in her throat. She felt overpowered by the heat of the room and the sickly smell, like a butcher's shop on a hot summer's day.

The doctor took it all in his stride. 'I'm Dr McKay, by the way,' he introduced himself, as if they were guests meeting at a party. He was young, dark and slimly built, with a soft Scottish accent. 'And you are...?'

Dora regarded him warily over her shoulder. No doctor had ever asked for her name before. 'Doyle, Sir,' she whispered.

'Pleased to meet you, Nurse Doyle. And this is Mr Gannon.' He nodded towards the man on the bed.

'All right, Nurse?' he hissed through clenched teeth. 'You don't mind if I don't shake your hand, do you?'

'Ha! Very good, Mr Gannon.' Dr McKay chortled appreciatively. His eyes were a warm brown behind his spectacles. 'Mr Gannon has had rather a nasty accident at work, as you can see. But I'm sure we'll have him up and playing cricket again in no time.' He beamed.

Mr Gannon exhaled sharply, swearing under his breath. His face was white and slick with sweat.

Dora stared down at her hands, red and sticky with blood. They seemed to swim and blur in front of her eyes. The doctor's voice was coming from a long way off.

She quickly finished flushing the wound and stepped back. 'All done, Doctor.'

'Thank you, Nurse. Now, I'm just putting in a ligature in the main artery to control the bleeding points...' Dr McKay worked quickly and deftly. 'Have we met before, Nurse Doyle?' he asked.

She had been so busy watching him work, she didn't realise the question was directed at her at first.

'I don't think so, Sir. This is my first day.'

'That's odd. I'm sure I've seen you before...' He thought for a moment. 'I know! Jubilee Day. Your leg needed stitches.'

Dora stared at him in astonishment as it all came back to her. Last year, at the street party for the King's Jubilee, her sister Josie had gone missing and Dora had injured herself looking for her. 'How did you remember–'

He winked at her. 'I never forget a patient!' He turned back to the man lying on the bed. 'You see, Mr Gannon? Nurse Doyle survived my tender ministrations, so I daresay you will too. Now I'm going to give you a few more stitches to tidy you up. Do try to hold on, Nurse,' he added, out of the corner of his mouth. 'It really wouldn't do for you to faint in front of the patient, would it?'

'No, Doctor.'

'If anyone's going to pass out, it'll be me!' Mr Gannon said.

'As long as it's not me, we'll be all right,' Dr McKay quipped back.

Dora watched him laughing, bewildered. She had never seen a doctor joking with a patient before. But then, she had never heard a doctor say 'please' before, either.

Dr McKay pulled the last stitch tight, and snipped it off, then stood back to admire his handiwork. 'Beautiful,' he declared. 'Even if I do say so myself. What do you think, Nurse Doyle?'

'Very nice, Doctor.'

Dr McKay smiled and said, 'You've done a very good job yourself, Nurse. Well done.'

As Dora flushed with pleasure at the un-expected compliment, Dr McKay turned to his patient. 'We'll see about getting you admitted to a ward, Mr Gannon. We'll need to take care of you for a few days, make sure that wound is kept nice and clean until it heals properly. You can sort out the paperwork for me, can't you, Nurse?'

'Yes, Doctor.'

Dora went off, glad to escape from the dizzying heat of the consulting room. The sickly smell of blood still filled her nostrils.

She was making her way to the booking-in desk when Sister Percival stepped out from nowhere in front of her, blocking her path.

'Nurse! Where on earth do you think you're going?' she demanded.

'Dr McKay asked me to sort out a bed for his patient, Staff.'

'In that state?'

Dora looked down at herself. She had been in such a hurry to escape the operating room, she hadn't noticed her apron and dress were soaked through with blood.

Sister Percival's brows rose. 'Do you think it in-spires confidence and a sense of well-being, having you wander about looking like Sweeney Todd?'

50

'No, Sister. Sorry, Sister.'

Sister Percival sighed. 'Go and get changed. I will attend to the patient's paperwork. And be quick about it.' She nodded towards the rows of wooden benches, which had filled up since Dora had been gone. 'We have a busy day ahead of us, and I certainly don't need nurses slacking.'

Slacking! Dora wanted to shout at her retreating back. It wasn't even eight o'clock, and she had already been soaked with more blood than she liked to think about.

But Sister Percival was already off, addressing an old woman huddled in a corner. 'You there! I hope you're not thinking of sleeping here?'

Dora returned to the nurses' home to change, then headed back to Casualty. No sooner had she walked in through the double doors than the nurse behind the desk summoned her over.

'There you are,' she said. 'Percy was looking for you. One of the patients has vomited in Consulting Room Three, and she wants you to clean it up.'

'Oh, no!' Dora looked down at her clean apron and groaned.

The nurse smiled sympathetically. 'You'll get through a lot of clean uniforms in this department, I'm afraid.'

'Is it always like this?'

'Oh, it gets a lot worse than this, believe me. Sunday is usually a quiet day.' The nurse was a couple of years older than Dora, with a long, solemn face and heavy lidded grey-green eyes. The hair that peeped out from under her cap was the deep gold of honey. 'It's a bit busier at the moment because Dr Adler, the other emergency doctor, is

51

away at a conference in Switzerland, delivering some learned paper or other. He should be back in a week or two, I think.' Her voice was a slow drawl. 'As long as you keep on the right side of old Percy, you should be all right.'

'And how do I do that?'

'By doing everything twice as fast as she asks you to do it, and making sure you never let anyone sleep in here. Percy's got a real thing about it. They come in here a lot, poor old things, especially when it's raining. But Percy thinks they make the place look untidy.' She smiled at Dora. 'I'm Willard, by the way.'

She couldn't have been more different from Sister Percival if she'd tried. Where Percival fizzed with energy, Willard was languid and graceful. Dora couldn't imagine her doing anything at any speed, let alone twice as fast.

For the rest of the morning, Dora was kept busy. While Willard draped herself behind the counter, taking down the names of people as they arrived and managing them on a list in order of urgency, and Sister Percival prowled around the waiting room, making sure no patients died or, worse still, fell asleep while they were waiting, Dora and two first-years assisted Dr McKay in the consulting rooms. She cleaned wounds, changed dressings, applied hot flannels for shock, gave emetics and held hands. At other times she filled in paperwork, organised the transfer of patients up to the various wards, or got on her hands and knees and scrubbed up blood, vomit and all manner of other unpleasant things from the white-tiled walls and floor of the consulting room before the next patient arrived. It was astonishing how quickly she got used to the stench and the mess. She could hardly believe she'd turned so queasy at the sight of Mr Gannon's arm that morning.

And when Dora wasn't cleaning, or bandaging, or listening to the ward sisters carping about how they couldn't possibly accept another patient on their hideously overcrowded ward, she was fending off Nurse Willard's chatter.

The only thing Penny Willard did with any energy was to talk. Every time Dora skimmed past the booking-in desk, she would start again.

'I'm so glad to have someone my age to talk to at last,' she gushed, when Dora passed by on her way to collect another patient's notes. 'Percy's not a bad old stick, but she's ancient. And all she ever wants to talk about is her latest hiking holiday. Honestly, don't let her start telling you about the Peak District, because she'll never stop.' She rolled her eyes heavenwards. 'Do you have a boyfriend?'

Dora stared down at the notes she'd picked up. 'No,' she said quietly.

Penny sighed. 'Me neither. It's so hard, isn't it? My last boyfriend ditched me because we never saw each other. How can you court someone properly when you only get half a day off every week? And even then you don't know when it's going to be. I was for ever having to cancel arrangements, and in the end he just got fed up. He's going out with a shop girl now,' she said mournfully.

Dora had started to edge back towards the consulting rooms when the double doors opened and Nick Riley came in, pushing a wheelchair.

53

She stood, frozen, as he approached the counter.

'I've come to collect a patient for Holmes ward,' he said gruffly, his gaze fixed on the floor.

'Consulting Room One.'

Dora listened to the rattle of the wheelchair as it disappeared down the corridor. She felt as if she'd been punched in the stomach.

'I know what you're thinking.'

She glanced up in dismay. Penny Willard sent her a knowing look. 'He is rather attractive, isn't he? If you like that brooding sort, I mean. But I'm afraid he's taken,' she sighed. 'He got married yesterday.' She shook her head. 'It's sad, isn't it? The best ones get snapped up so quickly.'

Nick returned, pushing an elderly man in the wheelchair. He didn't glance Dora's way as he headed for the double doors.

'I know what you mean,' Dora said.

Helen and Charlie heard the guard's whistle as they were buying their tickets. They reached the platform just in time to see the Southend train disappearing in a cloud of blackened steam.

'Well, there goes our day out at the coast,' Charlie said, as it rumbled out of sight.

Helen stared after it. 'Oh, Charlie, I'm sorry. If Sister Sutton hadn't insisted on me going to church this morning...'

'Don't worry, love. It's not your fault.'

'But you were so looking forward to it!'

'I'm sure there's another train later. We can have a cuppa in the station buffet and wait. We've got all day together, after all.' He took her hand. 'Come on, I might even treat you to a currant bun, if you're good.'

Helen smiled reluctantly as he led her back down the platform towards the buffet. She had been looking forward to their day out too. For the first time in a month she had the whole day off. It was a good day for it; the relentless rain had finally given way to a crack of blue sky and spring sunshine, although darker clouds lingered in the distance.

Charlie had been keen to show her the seaside town where he'd spent so many happy childhood holidays.

'You mean to tell me you've never been to Southend?' He'd been genuinely shocked when Helen had asked him about it a few weeks earlier. 'Blimey, girl, you don't know what you're missing. There's all sorts there. The pier, Kursaal amusement park, the planetarium. You can even get a special lift that takes you up to the top of the cliff. Or we could just go cockling on the beach.' He laughed at her blank expression. 'Don't tell me you've never been cockling, either?'

'I don't even know what it is.' But she knew it didn't sound like something her mother would approve of.

They found a table in the window of the station buffet, and Charlie lined up at the counter to order their tea and cakes. Helen offered to help, but he was insistent.

'You spend enough time waiting on people,' he said, pulling out her chair for her. 'You deserve to be treated for a change.'

She watched him standing in line, leaning heavily on his stick. She worried about how he would manage with a tray of tea things, but knew better than to question him. Losing his leg in a factory accident had made Charlie fiercely independent and determined to prove he was just as capable as any able-bodied man.

He was certainly a man in her eyes. Helen felt quietly proud as she noticed the girl behind the counter smiling at him, so tall, fair-haired and handsome.

'Was she flirting with you?' Helen teased him when he returned to their table.

'Just a bit.' He grinned back. 'But she gave me an extra big slice of sponge cake, so I'm not complaining.' He slid the tray deftly on to the table with one hand. 'See? Not a drop spilt.'

'I didn't think for a moment there would be,' Helen replied primly.

'Of course you didn't!' Charlie pulled out his chair and sat down, shifting his leg stiffly into place. 'Well, this is nice, isn't it?' His mouth twisted. 'Tea and a stale slice of cake in a station buffet. Don't ever say I don't know how to treat a girl.'

'I don't mind.' Helen smiled, pouring the tea. 'We can pretend it's the Ritz.'

Charlie looked at her consideringly. 'You know, you're not like other girls, Helen Tremayne.'

'I know.' She grimaced.

'I meant it as a compliment.' He reached across the table and laid his hand on hers. 'I love you. Have I told you that recently?'

'Charlie!' Helen glanced around, heat rising in her face. 'People might be listening.'

'I don't care. I'd shout it from the rooftops if I

could get up a ladder!' He grinned.

Helen handed him his cup. 'You're incorrigible.'

'And you use too many long words.' He picked up his fork and started digging into his cake. 'Come on, then. How was your first day in surgery? Seen any gruesome operations yet?'

Helen shook her head. 'They wouldn't let me near anything like that,' she said. 'All I have to do is sterilise the instruments, make sure the surgeons have exactly what they need laid out for each operation, and then scrub down the theatre afterwards.'

'Sounds like a lot of hard work to me,' Charlie said through a mouth full of cake.

'It is,' Helen admitted. 'Everything has to be just right. And all the surgeons have their different preferences when it comes to the instruments they like to use, and there's hell to pay if you get it wrong. Like yesterday, when Mr Latimer was doing a laparotomy, and I put out the Dever's retractors...' She broke off, seeing Charlie's fork poised halfway to his mouth. 'Sorry, you don't want to listen to me going on and on about hospitals and operations, do you?'

'Who says? I wouldn't have asked if I didn't want to know, would I?' Charlie shook his head. 'Stop apologising. You don't go on and on, and even if you did, I love listening to you. Your work is a lot more interesting than my woodworking factory. Who wants to hear about boring old lathes?'

'I do,' Helen insisted loyally.

'Well, I don't want to talk about them.' Charlie put down his fork and sat back. 'So what are the people like? I suppose the Sister's just as fierce as

57

all the others?'

'Worse, if anything!' Helen shuddered. 'Theatre Sisters have a reputation for being a tough and unforgiving bunch, and Miss Feehan more than lives up to it. She turns me into a nervous wreck even when she's trying to explain something. I nearly fainted dead away yesterday when she was describing how to take instruments out of the steriliser. And as for the surgeons ... they're absolutely terrifying. They're treated like gods. The only time they notice us nurses is when we drop an instrument, or take too long passing them something, or breathe too loudly.'

Charlie laughed. 'They don't tell you off for breathing, surely?'

'Mr Latimer does. He has to have complete silence while he's operating, apparently. He once had a junior nurse thrown out for sneezing while he was trying to take out an appendix.'

'So there are no handsome young surgeons I need to worry about?' Charlie lifted a quizzical brow.

Helen pretended to think for a moment. 'Well ... there is one,' she admitted slowly. 'He's a registrar on Gynae. Tall, dark and a devil with the ladies, apparently. I haven't seen him operate on anyone yet, but the Theatre nurses all seem to find him very dashing.'

'Oh yes?' Charlie's smile faded.

'Unfortunately, he also happens to be my brother.'

He looked up at her sharply. 'You mean William...'

'Of course I mean William!' Helen burst out

58

laughing. 'All the nurses think he's the bee's knees, although I can't imagine why he sets everyone's hearts aflutter.'

Sometimes she didn't know which was worse: being Constance Tremayne's daughter or Dr Tremayne's sister. Either nurses were especially nice to her because they wanted to get close to him, or they shunned her because he had broken their heart. Life had calmed down in the past few months since William had fallen in love with a girl called Philippa, but his reputation lived on.

She saw Charlie's crestfallen expression and stopped laughing. 'Charlie? You surely can't imagine I'd notice another man, handsome or not?'

'I wouldn't blame you if you did.' He toyed with the crumbs on his plate. 'I'm not much of a prospect, am I? A crippled costermonger's son from Roman Road. You could do a lot better than me. I expect your mum thinks so, too.'

'I don't care what my mother thinks.'

His blue eyes glinted with amusement. 'Yes, you do.'

'All right, perhaps I do. But not where you're concerned. I was all ready to elope with you to Scotland, remember? When she threatened to send me away?'

Her mother tried to pack Helen off to another hospital when she'd first found out she was seeing Charlie in secret. She had come round once she'd realised how strong her feelings for him were. But that didn't mean she was happy about it, or that she'd given up trying to part them.

'I'm glad we didn't run away,' Charlie said.

'So am I.' It was he who had changed his mind,

insisting that he didn't want to ruin Helen's life. Not that her mother had given him any credit for that. As far as she was concerned, Charlie Dawson was dragging her daughter down into the gutter.

Helen looked at her watch. 'When did you say the next train was due?'

'Should be here in about ten minutes.' Charlie cleared a patch in the steamy window with his sleeve and peered out. 'It's gone very dark all of a sudden. I don't like the look of those clouds—'

No sooner had the words left his lips than a flash of lightning split the pewter-coloured sky, followed a second later by thunder rolling like an avalanche of giant rocks, shaking the window frames and bringing a deluge of rain.

Charlie looked rueful. 'I don't think we'll be going to Southend, do you?'

'I suppose not.' Helen shook her head. 'I'm sorry, Charlie.'

'What did I tell you about apologising for everything?'

'I'm so—' She saw his mock stern expression and stopped herself just in time. 'It's a habit,' she said.

'Then you need to break it. It's not your fault it's pouring down, is it? And I don't really fancy sitting on a beach getting drenched.'

Helen stared at the rain streaming down the glass, turning the outside world into a blur of dismal grey and washing away her chances of enjoying her day off. 'I suppose I should go back to the nurses' home and catch up on my studying,' she sighed.

'And miss spending your one day off with me?'

Charlie looked aghast. 'We won't have a whole day together for another month.'

'Well, we can't spend the day here.' Helen thought for a moment. 'I suppose we could go to the pictures, or take a bus ride up to the city?'

'I've got a better idea,' Charlie said. 'Why don't we go back to my house? We'll be back in time for my mum's Sunday roast, if we get a move on.'

'Won't she mind?' Helen asked. She knew her own mother would be aghast if a guest turned up out of the blue.

'You know my mum. The more the merrier, as far as she's concerned,' Charlie grinned. 'Anyway, she's got a real soft spot for you. She's always asking when I'm going to bring you round to ours. I think she wants to show you off to the neighbours!'

'Don't be silly!' Helen blushed.

'I mean it. She's always bragging about how her son's courting a nurse.' He stood up and offered Helen his free arm. 'Shall we go?'

Helen hesitated. 'Are you sure you don't mind about Southend?'

'We'll go another day. Now I've got a whole day with my best girl and my mum's roast beef to look forward to. What more could any bloke want?'

Chapter Four

Nick braced his muscles and hefted a chest of drawers on to the back of the horse-drawn wagon.

'Careful!' Ruby dived forward and snatched a box out of the way. 'You nearly smashed our new china.'

Nick watched her nursing the box to her bosom. They didn't have much new for their home, just a few wedding presents people had given them. There was a canteen of cutlery, a tablecloth, bed linen, and some cups, saucers and plates with a fancy flower pattern around the edge. Ruby had picked those and every night she took each piece out of its wrapping just so she could admire it. It made him smile to watch her running her fingers so lovingly around the delicate gold-painted rim of each cup.

'You do realise we're going to have to use that?' he'd said. 'Or are you planning to keep it locked up in a glass case?'

'As long as we're careful.' She held it up to the light. 'Look, it's so thin you can almost see through it. That's proper bone china, that is.'

'Dunno how I'm going to manage with it.' Nick looked down at his hands. They were made for knocking down opponents in the boxing ring, not for handling delicate china. 'Maybe we should keep it for when the new King comes round?'

'You can laugh,' Ruby said. 'But I want everything in our new flat to be perfect.'

He saw her expression turn sour as she stood beside her mother, watching the removals men start to load the wagon. Ruby hadn't been happy about accepting some of her mother's cast-off furniture, but as Nick had told her, beggars couldn't be choosers.

'I wish you didn't have to go,' his mother June said.

Nick turned to look at her as she stood in the doorway, arms folded across her skinny bosom, squinting at him through the smoke drifting up from her cigarette. He had never known his mother show any concern for him before. She only noticed he was there when she needed money.

Her next words destroyed any illusions he might have had. 'How am I supposed to pay the rent?' she demanded, her voice querulous.

Nick's mouth twitched. 'You had me going there for a second. I thought you might actually be bothered about me. But why change the habit of a lifetime, eh?'

'Why should I be bothered about you? You've been nothing but trouble to me since you were a kid.'

'Except when I'm paying the tallyman for you.' He lowered his voice. 'Don't worry, I'll make sure you keep a roof over your head. But you'll have to find some other mug to pay for your gin.'

'And who's going to look after our Danny?'

Nick shot a glance over at his brother, perched on top of the coal bunker. He liked to sit up there, out of everyone's way, and watch the world go by. But today his head drooped like a wilting

63

flower on his slender neck. Nick had to look away to stop the tears welling up in his eyes.

He hadn't been able to sleep for the past week, and not just because he and Ruby were sharing a lumpy single mattress in her parents' front parlour. He'd lain awake, staring at the ceiling until the pale dawn light crept under the curtains and he heard the sound of the milkman's horse clopping slowly up Griffin Street. Sometimes he thought he heard Danny sobbing in his sleep downstairs, and Nick's heart ached for him.

'You're his mother, you should look after him,' Lettie Pike said.

June turned on her. 'My son needs a lot of looking after. You don't know what it's like. A boy like that is a burden to a poor woman on her own.' She took out her handkerchief and dabbed at her eyes.

'He can come and live with us, if he's that much of a burden,' Nick said.

Ruby and her mother both whipped round to look at him. 'Nick!'

'Did you hear that, Danny? Your brother wants you to go and live with him.' June's face brightened instantly.

'C-Can I, Nick? Can I come and l-live with you?' Danny slithered down from the coal shed roof.

Once the idea had occurred to Nick, he wondered why he hadn't thought about it before. 'Well, I don't see why–'

'Sorry, Danny love, we ain't got no room,' Ruby cut in before Nick could finish his sentence.

'You've got a spare room, ain't you? Or he

64

could sleep on your settee,' June said. 'And he's as good as gold, really. He won't be no trouble.'

'I thought you just said he was a burden?' Lettie muttered.

Nick glanced at Ruby. Her face was rigid as stone, anger simmering in her eyes.

He turned back to his brother. 'I'm sorry. Dan. It might be best if you stayed here with Mum.'

'B-but I want to go with you! You s-said–'

'I'll come back and see you as often as I can, I promise.' Nick couldn't look into his brother's face. He knew if he did he would be lost.

'P-please, Nick! Don't l-leave me...' Danny threw his skinny arms around his brother's neck, clinging to him. Nick held himself rigid, not daring to hug him back.

'I've got to go, Dan.' He didn't like to show emotion, but his voice sounded thick and choked.

'Come on, Danny.' Ruby stepped in, gently but firmly disentangling his arms from around Nick's neck. 'It's not like we're moving to the other side of the world.'

'She's right, Dan. You can always come and see us.'

'C-Can I?' Danny wiped his face. 'Can I come and s-see you, Nick?'

'Any time, mate. You'll always be welcome.'

'Not if that missus of yours has anything to do with it,' he heard his mother mutter.

He was silent all the way to their new flat in the wagon, worrying about Danny. Seeing his brother in tears was like a knife in Nick's heart.

'I've been looking forward to moving into this flat for ages,' Ruby interrupted his thoughts. She swayed against him, rocked by the steady plodding of the horse. 'I hope you're not going to sulk all day and ruin it?'

'I just don't like seeing Danny upset.'

'He wouldn't have been upset if you hadn't told him he could come and live with us. You had no business putting that idea in his head.'

He stared at the backs of the removal men, sitting side by side on the long front seat. 'You're right,' he sighed.

'I don't know what you were thinking,' Ruby continued, her mouth pursed. 'Never mind upsetting Danny. What about upsetting me? I'm your wife now, Nick. You should be thinking about me before anyone else.'

Don't I know it? he thought.

As if she knew she'd gone too far, Ruby leaned against him, threading her arm through his. 'Please don't spoil this, Nick. Everything will be all right, you'll see. As soon as we've got settled in our lovely new flat, everything will be just perfect.'

Their new flat in Victory House was a palace compared to Griffin Street. No damp, no peeling paintwork, bedbugs or mice scampering out of the stove. The whole place smelled of fresh paint and polish, and the April sunshine poured in through the sparkling picture windows.

It made him laugh to see Ruby running from room to room, flicking light switches on and off, as excited as a child on Christmas morning.

'Oh, Nick, isn't it smashing?' she sighed. 'Look at that tap. Just think, you turn it on and hot water comes out. You don't have to boil a single

66

kettle. Who'd have thought you and me would ever be living in a place as grand as this?'

'It should be grand, the rent they're charging!' He was already doing the sums in his head, wondering how they would pay for it all. He'd be stretched to breaking point after paying his mum's rent too.

Ruby pulled a face. 'We'll manage.'

'Things are going to be tight now you've given up work.'

'Stop worrying!' She wound her arms around his neck, smiling up into his face. 'I told you, everything is going to be perfect.'

He kissed the top of her curly blonde head, breathing in her perfume, and tried to convince himself it was true. All right, it wasn't the life he had hoped for, and Ruby might not be the girl he'd hoped to marry. But it could have been a lot worse. He knew lots of men in Bethnal Green who would envy him, landing a cracker like Ruby. And it wasn't just her looks, either. Deep down, she was a nice kid with a good heart. She drove him mad at times, but she also made him laugh.

It wasn't as if she'd chosen to end up in this situation, any more than he had. Maybe, given the choice, she wouldn't have married him either. She was trying to make the best of the hand life had dealt her, and now he had to do the same.

He held her at arm's length, smiling down into her eyes. 'Come on, then. Let's have a proper look around this palace of yours.'

The flat consisted of a small hallway, which led to a sitting room, a narrow kitchen, bathroom, a bedroom, and a much smaller room, hardly bigger

67

than a cupboard, with a high strip of window.

'I suppose we could make this the nursery?' Nick said, peering inside. 'What do you reckon, shall we paint it pink or blue?' There was no reply. 'Ruby?'

He turned to look around, thinking she'd wandered off to inspect another room. But she was standing behind him.

'Rube?' She was so pale-faced and silent, he worried she might be ill. 'Are you all right?'

He saw her throat move as she swallowed. 'I've got something to tell you,' she said slowly.

'What is it?' He smiled. 'Don't tell me you're expecting twins?'

She didn't laugh. 'Nick–'

A sharp rap on the front door broke the tense silence, startling them both. A moment later the door opened and one of the removals men stuck his head around the door.

'D'you want us to start bringing this furniture in, guv?' he called.

'Just a minute.' Nick turned back to Ruby. 'What was it you wanted to say?'

'It'll keep for another time.' Her smile was back in place, as suddenly as it had disappeared. 'We'd best get unpacked or those blokes will start expecting overtime!'

Nick helped the men haul the furniture up the three flights of stone stairs. While he waited for them to huff and puff their way up the last flight after him, he paused on the narrow concrete walkway to admire the view.

The four squat red-brick blocks of flats formed a square, their walkways facing inward to overlook a small patch of green in the centre. Beyond the flats lay the rooftops of Bethnal Green, and beyond that the dock cranes that lined the Thames, reaching high into the sky. The air was filled with the acrid smells of the glue factory and belching chimney smoke. But below children played in the spring sunshine, chasing each other among the blossom-filled trees.

My kid will play down there one day. Nick couldn't keep a smile off his face as he thought about this.

It had been a shock when Ruby first told him she was expecting. But now he'd had time to get used to the idea, he realised he was looking forward to being a father.

And he was going to be the best father he could be. His son or daughter would want for nothing he could provide. He would see they were the best-dressed, the best-fed, the best-loved kid that ever grew up in the East End.

They would certainly have a better upbringing than he'd had, stuck with a drunk mother who had no time for her kids and a father who liked to teach his sons a lesson with the buckle end of his belt when he'd had a skin full.

Nick's hands balled into fists. It was a beating from Reg Riley that had left Danny the way he was, brain-damaged and helpless when he was just a child of twelve. Nick was still tormented by nightmares of seeing his brother smashed to a pulp and lying close to death in a pool of blood. He'd given his father a taste of his own medicine that night. Reg Riley had been so frightened of his sixteen-year-old son's rage that he'd packed his bags and disappeared.

But his old man had taught him a lesson, if only he'd known it. Nick would never lay a hand on his own kid, no matter what.

Chapter Five

The operating theatre was deep in the bowels of the hospital, a silent tomb of gleaming steel and glaring lights. The hissing, steaming autoclave and the heating pipes running along the thick stone walls made it almost too hot to bear, and Helen could feel perspiration trickling down inside her dress as she counted out the swabs for the next operation. She was glad they had lighter uniforms to put on for surgery, even though it meant changing in and out of her usual calico-lined uniform several times a day.

The next operation of the day was a perforated ulcer, and she carefully consulted the heavy ledger to check which instruments Mr Latimer preferred. As she laid them on the trolley, she remembered the mnemonic she had read in her textbook the previous night – knife, fork and spoon. Scalpel first, then forceps, then scissors. They looked so perfect and orderly, gleaming in neat rows on the trolley. Helen stood for a moment, gazing at her handiwork.

'Very nice, Nurse, I'm sure. Perhaps you should hang it in a gallery where we can all admire it?'

She swung around at the sound of Sister

Theatre's voice. Miss Feehan was in her early-thirties and a typical Irish beauty, with her glossy black hair, milky skin and brilliant emerald eyes. But behind that sweet face lurked the heart of a monster. And Miss Feehan's biting sarcasm seemed to cut even deeper when delivered in her lilting Irish accent.

'You do realise that if those sterilised instruments are exposed to the air for too long they'll be no use to anyone?' she snapped. 'Cover them with a cloth quickly, girl, or they'll all have to go back in the steriliser. And then you'll have to explain to Mr Latimer why his operations are being held up.'

'Yes, Sister. Sorry Sister.' Helen bobbed a quick apology and hurried off to find a sterilised cloth.

She was surprised to find her brother William scrubbing up at the metal sink. He was chatting amiably to Dr Little, one of the junior anaesthetists. He reminded Helen of a cherub in a Renaissance painting, with his round pink face and fair curls that almost reached the collar of his surgical gown.

They both turned to look at her when she walked in.

'Ah, here she is now,' William said. 'You'll have to watch yourself, old chap, my sister is a stickler for doing things properly. Helen, have you met my friend Alec? Alec Little, this is my sister Helen.'

'I've seen you in Theatre, but we haven't spoken.' Dr Little flushed a deeper shade of rose pink.

'What are you doing here?' Helen blurted out. Nurses were forbidden to speak to doctors unless

71

asked a direct question, but somehow her older brother didn't count. 'You're not with Mr Latimer.'

Junior doctors were arranged in groups, or firms, around one particular consultant or department. William was with Mr Cooper, the Chief Consultant in Gynae.

'So I am, but I have been selected to assist the great man today, as has Alec here. It's the most enormous honour for us, as you can imagine.' William's brown eyes glinted with amusement in his solemn face. 'Apparently we couldn't possibly call ourselves surgeons if we haven't witnessed the extraordinary talent of Mr Latimer. Isn't that right, Alec?'

'I thought you were here because Mr Cooper was busy with private patients all morning, and you had nothing else to do?' his friend replied in a deadpan voice.

Helen shook her head. 'You'd better not lark about during this operation,' she warned. 'I think you'll find Mr Latimer isn't as forgiving as Mr Cooper. He doesn't even like a sound while he's operating.'

'So we've heard,' William said. 'But I daresay you'll keep us on the straight and narrow, Sis!'

'I won't be allowed anywhere near you. I'll be next door, up to my elbows in steam and soapy water.'

No sooner had the unconscious patient been wheeled into Theatre than Mr Latimer made his perfectly timed appearance. He swept in to scrub up, flanked by a line of white-faced medical students. Helen was used to doctors being treated like gods, but Mr Latimer truly seemed to be one. His fearsome presence filled the room as he towered over his minions, all blazing amber eyes and a leonine mane of russet waves. His Theatre nurse fluttered around him like a handmaiden, helping him into his gown and fastening the ties while he stood in the centre of the room with arms outstretched. Helen almost expected the sound of a heavenly choir to fill the theatre.

She glanced across the room at William. She couldn't see his face behind his surgical mask, but the mischievous crinkling of his brown eyes told her he was thinking exactly the same as she was.

Once the operation was underway, Helen was banished to the sluice to wash and sterilise instruments from an earlier procedure.

Wielding the Cheatle's forceps, she reached into the steamy interior of the autoclave and pulled out a large metal tray. As she lifted it out, a cloud of scalding steam made her lose her grip on the forceps for a split second. She felt the tray start to slide and desperately tried to stop it. But it was too late. She could only watch helplessly as, in terrible slow motion, it slid from the forceps and crashed to the ground.

The sound was like the crash of a hundred cymbals, shattering the silence. A second later the door flew open and Miss Feehan appeared in the doorway, quivering with fury.

'What do you think you're doing?' she hissed.

'Sorry, Sister.' Helen couldn't meet her eye as she retrieved the tray.

'It's not me you should be apologising to, is it?' Miss Feehan's eyes blazed. 'Well, don't just stand there, girl. Put that tray back in the autoclave and resterilise it. And then you must apologise to Mr Latimer. He is most upset.'

'Yes, Sister.'

All faces turned to her when she stepped into the operating theatre. William regarded her with silent sympathy over his face mask.

Mr Latimer stared at her, forceps poised, but didn't speak.

Helen cleared her throat. 'Mr Latimer, I just wanted to say how sorry I am that I disturbed your operation.' Her voice was barely above a whisper, yet it still seemed to ring around the hushed theatre.

Mr Latimer said nothing. Helen squirmed as his amber gaze moved slowly down to her feet and back up to her face. Then, finally, he spoke.

'Go away,' he said.

She didn't need to be told twice. She backed out of the room, closing the door behind her, and fled back to the sluice.

I won't cry, she told herself over and over again, trying to blink back the tears of humiliation that prickled at the backs of her eyes. Hot soapy water scalded her arms as she plunged them in, but she was too mortified to care. Any minute she expected Miss Feehan to barge in and send her to Matron.

Luckily there were only two other procedures on Mr Latimer's list for that day. By four o'clock he had gone, and surgery had finished.

Helen was still at the sink, scrubbing blood from the joint of a pair of surgical scissors, when William and Alec came to find her.

'You mustn't take it to heart,' William said. 'It was an accident. They happen to everyone.'

'Not to me.' Helen held the scissors up to her eyes, examining them for imaginary specks. 'What kind of a nurse am I if I can't even sterilise an instrument properly?'

'Don't be so hard on yourself. You only dropped a tray. It's not as if a patient died, or anything.'

'Shall I let you into a little secret?' Alec said. Helen looked over her shoulder at him.

'What?'

'First you have to promise not to breathe a word. Not to anyone.' She and William looked at each other, then both nodded. 'Do you know why Latimer insists on total silence while he operates?'

'Why?'

'Because he's terrified of losing his concentration and making a mistake.' Alec glanced around him, as if to make sure no one was listening. 'Years ago, when he was first starting out, he left a swab inside a patient.'

'No!'

'That's what I heard. It didn't come to light until afterwards, when they were checking the swabs and realised one was missing.'

'What happened?'

'They had to open the patient up again to find it. There was a big fuss, of course, and Mr Latimer came within a whisker of being struck off. Ever since, he's been absolutely fanatical about no one uttering a sound while he's working.'

Helen looked at William. He seemed as surprised by the story as she was.

'Do you see what I'm saying to you?' Alec said.

75

'Everyone makes mistakes. Even someone as great as Mr Latimer.'

Helen smiled shakily. 'Thank you,' she said. 'That does make me feel better.'

'I'll tell you what would make you feel even better,' William said. 'Let Alec and me take you out for a drink this evening.'

Helen shook her head. 'I can't,' she said. 'I've got to study.'

William rolled his eyes. 'You work too hard.'

'And you don't work hard enough!'

'True. But don't tell Mother that, will you?'

'She wouldn't believe me anyway. You know you can do no wrong in her eyes.'

'This is true.' William sighed dramatically. 'Oh, well, if we can't persuade you to join us, we'll just have to go and celebrate by ourselves, won't we, Alec?'

'What are you celebrating?' Helen frowned.

'Surviving a session with Mr Latimer. I don't know about you, Dr Little, but I'm not in any hurry to repeat the experience.'

'Definitely not.' Alec shook his head.

'You're lucky,' Helen sighed. 'I have to face him again in three days' time. Even sooner if he's called to an emergency case.' She was already dreading it.

'You'll be all right, Sis.' William put his arm round her. 'And a word of advice,' he added. 'If you clean those scissors any more you'll wear them away!'

By six o'clock, she had finished sterilising, drying and polishing the instruments, and put them all away for the following day. She scrubbed the operating theatre until the white-tiled walls gleamed under the harsh glare of the overhead lights. Then she changed out of her uniform, wiped her shoes over with carbolic, switched off the lights and left.

Theatre was an eerily silent place to be when everyone had gone home. All the doors were locked, and the only way out was up the steep back staircase. Helen hurried along the passageway, her footsteps muffled by the thick stone walls. She was far too sensible to believe all the silly stories the other nurses told about the ghost of a former Theatre Sister who was supposed to haunt the place, but the darkness and the soft scuttle of the cockroaches coming out of their hiding places still made her heart race against her ribs.

She had almost reached the top of the back stairs when she heard the sound of breathing coming from above her. She paused, listening. Someone was standing in the shadows at the top of the stairs, waiting...

'Hello?' She called, trying to keep the tremor out of her voice. 'Is anyone there?'

She jumped as a heavy door banged shut above her. Whoever it was had gone.

Helen laughed shakily at her own foolishness. It was probably just a porter, or one of the cleaners. She had spent far too much time listening to Millie Benedict telling ghost stories after lights out, she decided.

But as she reached the top of the stairs, a curious scent caught her attention and made her stop again. She paused, sniffing the air. Was it her imagination or was that the scent of roses?

Chapter Six

'Go on, what happened then?'

Millie heard the voices as she opened the door to the sluice. Amy Hollins and another third-year, Sheila Walsh, were leaning against the sink, gossiping. They fell silent when Millie walked in.

'What do you want?' Amy demanded.

'Sister sent me to make an ice bag for the patient in bed ten.'

'Well, you'd better get on with it, hadn't you? And hurry up. We don't need Staff snooping around in here, wondering where you are.'

Millie felt two pairs of hostile eyes following her as she slid the block of ice into a sacking bag and started to chip away at it. They were silent for a moment, then Sheila said, 'Take no notice of her. Go on.'

'Well, he took me for dinner at the Savoy, and then we drank endless champagne cocktails in Harry's Bar...'

'You're so lucky,' Sheila sighed. 'My boyfriend can barely afford Lyons Corner House!'

'You're right, he does rather spoil me.' Amy simpered. 'He says nothing is too good for me.'

'So when are we going to meet this wonderful man of yours?'

'I'm not sure. He's a very private person.'

'So private you won't even tell us his name?' Sheila laughed. 'If you're not careful, we'll start

78

to think this Mr Perfect of yours doesn't even exist.'

'Of course he exists!' Amy's voice rose. 'I've got proof, too. He gave me this last night.'

Millie couldn't resist glancing over her shoulder. Amy had unfastened her collar and was delving down inside her dress. Millie caught a flash of gold before Amy turned on her, scowling.

'Haven't you finished that ice bag yet?' she snapped.

'Nearly.' Millie emptied the ice into a bowl and took it over to the sink to run it under tepid water to melt off any sharp edges. But her attention was still fixed on Amy and Sheila.

'It's beautiful,' Sheila sighed. 'But you're taking a risk, aren't you? You know you're not allowed to wear jewellery.'

'There's a lot of things I'm not allowed to do!'

Some whispering and giggling followed. Then Millie heard Sheila's shocked gasp.

'Oh, Hollins, you didn't!'

'Well, he'd gone to all the trouble of booking a suite. I couldn't disappoint him, could I?'

'What was it like?'

'It was blissful. The rooms looked over the river, and it had the biggest bathroom you could imagine–'

'I didn't mean the hotel room, silly!'

They shrieked with laughter. Millie turned back to her ice and let out a cry of dismay. She had paid so much attention to Amy Hollins' story, she hadn't noticed the ice melting under the tepid water.

Amy crossed the room and glanced over her

shoulder. 'Now look what you've done! You'll have to start all over again. Serves you right for eavesdropping on our conversation.'

'I wouldn't be eavesdropping if you weren't in here gossiping,' Millie muttered under her breath.

'Did you say something?' Hollins frowned.

Millie kept her head down. 'No.'

'It's a good thing too, or I'd report you straight to Matron.'

Millie went off to fetch more ice and left them giggling and gossiping together.

Coming out of the sluice, the first person she met was Staff Nurse Crockett. She was a squat woman in her forties, much older than any of the other staff nurses. Millie heard rumours that she'd stayed on Female Medical for so many years because she was devoted to Sister Everett.

If she was devoted then she had an odd way of showing it. The pair bickered constantly, and occasionally went for days without speaking. It made life very difficult for the students sometimes.

Today, thankfully, they were in perfect accord.

'We have a kidney abscess just come in. Bed Six, a Mrs Lovell,' she announced. 'Sister wants you and O'Hara to settle her in and give her a bath.'

The new patient sat on the edge of her bed, her coat pulled tightly around her in spite of the warm spring day outside. Katie O'Hara, another second-year student, was trying to coax her out of it.

'Come along, Mrs Lovell,' she was saying in her gentle Irish lilt. 'You'll feel better when you've had a nice warm bath.'

'I ain't staying,' Mrs Lovell growled. Her expression was truculent under her wild mane of

80

grey-streaked hair. 'I need to go, see. My family are off on the road and I've got to go with them.'

'I'm afraid you won't be going anywhere until the doctor has been to see you, Mrs Lovell,' Millie said.

'I don't hold with no doctors. And I don't hold with no hospitals, neither. I told 'em, I didn't ought to be here.'

'Yes, well, I'm sure the doctor will explain everything when he comes round.' Millie went to remove her coat, but Mrs Lovell lashed out at her like an angry, spitting cat.

'Don't you dare touch me!' she snapped, her black eyes gleaming. 'I told you, I ain't staying. I ain't slept under a roof in my fifty years, and I ain't going to start now!'

Millie turned to Katie. 'You hold her down, I'll get it off her.'

Katie shook her head. 'I'm not touching her,' she whispered. 'You know what she is, don't you? A gypsy.'

'What of it?'

'You have to be careful of gypsies. They have powers. They can put a curse on you, just like that.'

Millie laughed. But then she saw the terror in Katie's eyes and realised she was deadly serious.

'What superstitious nonsense!'

'She's right, my wench,' Mrs Lovell murmured. 'I can put a gypsy curse on someone, if I have a mind to do it.'

'You see?' Katie retreated a few steps towards the curtains. 'I'm not risking it, Benedict, and neither should you.'

'Oh, for heaven's sake!' Millie turned to Mrs Lovell. 'Look, I'm awfully sorry you haven't been able to go on the road with your family, but you're ill. You have an abscess on your kidney, and you need proper medical treatment.'

'I can treat myself,' Mrs Lovell insisted stubbornly, her arms folded across her chest. 'Romanies don't have any need for doctors and medicine.'

Millie suppressed a sigh. 'I daresay you're right, but we can make you better a lot quicker. And surely the sooner you recover, the sooner you can catch up with your family. You'd like that, wouldn't you?'

Mrs Lovell eyed her suspiciously. Millie saw Katie out of the corner of her eye, edging towards the curtain, but she stood her ground.

Finally, Mrs Lovell said, 'All right, then. Do what you have to do. But don't think I'm happy about it,' she added, shooting a malevolent look past Millie at Katie, who ducked away.

'Thank you. Right, let's start by making you more comfortable, shall we?'

She reached to take off the woman's coat, then let out a squeak of shock as Mrs Lovell's hand shot out, fixing around her wrist like a claw.

'Your young man's over the water, ain't he?'

Millie frowned back at her. 'How did you know that?'

Mrs Lovell grinned up at her, showing a few stumpy, misshapen teeth. 'You'd be surprised what I know, my wench.'

Ruby ran the tap in the sink and plunged her

hands into the warm soapy water. It was so much easier to do the washing when you didn't have to get up at the crack of dawn to heat up the water in the copper, or drag the dolly tub out into the freezing yard. She pitied her mum, getting up on a Monday morning, knowing she had a back-breaking day's work ahead of her.

But she missed it too. She and her mum would usually have a good laugh together while they worked, gossiping about all the neighbours and the goings-on in Griffin Street. It wasn't the same, rinsing out Nick's shirts on her own in the kitchen.

She'd thought she would enjoy the peace and quiet of having the place to herself, not having to put up with her noisy brothers or her mum and dad arguing. But sometimes she felt homesick for her family and for Griffin Street. Being stuck up on the third floor of Victory House with just a narrow concrete walkway outside her front door, she never saw her neighbours. She missed being surrounded by the world going about its business, people laughing, crying and arguing just a few feet from her back door.

She even missed Gold's Garments. That cow Esther Gold and her dad worked the girls hard, but there was still plenty of time for a laugh over the machines as they stitched and snipped.

She rinsed out the washing in cold water, then put it through the mangle and took it outside. Nick had rigged up a washing line for her, strung across the walkway. It was a brisk, breezy late April day and washing fluttered like bunting out-side the other flats.

'Someone's been busy, I see.'

Ruby looked around and saw a man dressed in a shabby pin-stripe suit and trilby hat.

'Always busy on wash day, ain't it?' he said. 'Although being a modern young lady, I suppose you've got one of them new washing machines to do it all for you? I've heard all you have to do is switch them on. And no washday hands!'

Ruby hid her hands in the folds of her skirt. 'Who are you?'

'I beg your pardon, Madam. I've forgotten my manners.' He raised his hat, revealing sparse greasy strands of hair stretched over his shining bald head. 'Bert Wallis, at your service.'

She had never been called Madam before. 'Am I meant to have heard of you?'

'Probably not,' he agreed. 'I represent Parker and Sons Credit Company. I expect you'll see me around here quite a lot.' His eyes scanned the flats. 'We have several customers in Victory House. Young couples like yourself, needing a bit of help to make ends meet.'

'Oh yeah?' Ruby flared up. 'Who says we need help to make ends meet?'

'Oh, don't take it the wrong way, Madam, I'm sure I didn't mean any offence,' he said hastily. 'It's just I know from experience how difficult it can be, when you're first starting out.' He glanced past her into the flat. 'Just married, are you?'

'Yes, as a matter of fact.'

'I thought so. Your husband's a lucky man, if I may say so.' He gave her an oily smile. 'And this is your first home together, eh? That's nice. But it's not easy, is it, when you first move into a place? I expect you're having to make do and mend with a

84

lot of old bits and pieces, aren't you?' He shook his head. 'That's a real shame. A beautiful place like this deserves to be done out nicely, doesn't it? Why should you start your married life with a load of old cast-offs when you could turn this place into a proper little palace?'

Ruby pursed her lips. She'd been saying the same thing to Nick the night before, but as usual he'd said they couldn't afford it.

'I can see you're the type of young lady who appreciates the finer things in life,' Bert Wallis said. 'You want everything nice, don't you? And that's where I come in.' He shifted closer, lowering his voice. 'You take out a loan with us to buy what you need now, and pay for it gradually, over the coming weeks and months.'

The truth dawned. 'A debt, you mean?' Ruby shook her head. 'My husband would never agree to that.'

'I told you, it's not what you'd call a debt. More like ... easy terms. There's no shame in it. Everyone's doing it, even the Hollywood stars.'

That caught her interest. 'What Hollywood stars?'

Bert Walls pulled a face. 'I can't remember their names off hand, but I'm sure I read about it in *Picturegoer*.'

Ruby paused for a moment, thinking. She'd seen a Pathé newsreel at the pictures of Claudette Colbert's home, and her bedroom was a dream. Ruby would love a glamorous new bedroom suite instead of that lumpy old mattress they'd borrowed from her mum...

She shook her head. 'My Nick still wouldn't

like it.'

'He needn't know.' Bert flicked his tongue over his lips. 'We could fill in the forms now and you could pay me back, just a couple of shillings a week out of the housekeeping. What could be easier than that?'

It sounded easy enough, she thought. They probably wouldn't even notice a few bob a week.

'Imagine showing off this place to your friends when you've done it out nice?' Bert's voice was so low, she could feel herself being drawn in, as if she was being hypnotised. 'You'd be the envy of everyone, wouldn't you? You could even get yourself one of those washing machines. Just think what a blessing that would be.'

Ruby stared down at her hands, red and roughened from the harsh green washing soap.

'Tell you what, it's getting a bit blowy out here,' Bert Wallis said, turning up his jacket collar. 'Why don't we go inside? Then we can have a nice cup of tea and I'll give you all the details...'

Chapter Seven

The first thing Dora saw when she arrived for her shift at seven o'clock was a man sleeping on the bench at the back of the waiting room.

Where had he come from? The porter had only unlocked the doors five minutes earlier. He must have been quick off the mark, she thought. Either that or he'd been crafty enough to get himself locked in overnight.

She looked around wildly, expecting to see Sister Percival bearing down on them, then remembered she wasn't due on duty for another hour. Penny Willard hadn't turned up yet, and Dr McKay was locked away in his consulting room. There was no one in the waiting room except her and the tramp.

Dora looked down at him snoring softly, stretched out on the bench, covered in a shabby black coat. He was a great bear of a man, with a shaggy head of dark curls. He'd taken off his shoes, and his big toes peeped out of holes in both socks.

'Excuse me?' She tapped his shoulder. He didn't stir.

She tried again. 'Excuse me ... Mister?' He stirred, grunted, rolled over and went back to sleep. He was young for a tramp, no more than in his mid-thirties by the look of him.

She shook him harder. 'Oi, you! You can't sleep here.'

The man opened one brown eye and looked up at her. 'Eh?'

'I said, you can't sleep here. This ain't a doss-house, y'know.'

'Oh ... right. Sorry, Nurse.' He sat up, rubbing his hand through his hair. 'What time is it?'

'Time you weren't here.' Dora picked up his shoes and handed them to him.

He stared at them in confusion and then back up at her. 'I'm sorry ... you want me to leave?'

'That's the general idea, yes. Unless you're ill and you want to see a doctor?' She peered at him. 'Are you ill?' she asked.

He looked dazed. 'Er ... no,' he admitted, looking sheepish. 'Just tired, that's all.'

'So you thought you could sleep it off in here?'

'Well, yes...'

'Park bench not good enough for you, I suppose?'

'Hardly.' He paused for a moment, as if he was giving the matter some thought. 'Look, Nurse, I think you might have got the wrong idea–'

'No, mate, it's you who's got the wrong idea, thinking you can sleep off your hangover in here.'

'Hangover? Oh, no.' He shook his head. 'You see, what happened is–'

'That's enough,' Dora cut him off. 'Just sling your hook. You're making the place look untidy.'

She watched him as he crammed his feet into his worn-out shoes. She wished she hadn't snapped at him. He seemed harmless enough, poor sod.

'Look,' she said, 'I'd let you stay if I could, but I can't. The Sister here is a right old cow, and she'd have my guts for garters.' She reached into her pocket and took out a coin. 'Here's threepence. That should buy you a cup of tea at the café on the corner. They'll probably let you shelter there for a bit, if you're lucky.'

'But–'

'It's all right, you don't have to pay me back. Just don't let me see your face around here again, all right?'

He stared down at the coin nestling in his giant paw. 'I – I truly don't know what to say, Nurse.'

Dora smiled as she watched him shambling out through the double doors. She felt very pleased with herself for her good deed, not to mention for averting another drama with Sister Percival.

No sooner had he shambled off across the courtyard than Penny Willard arrived.

'Oh, my, is that the time?' She made a big pretence of looking at the clock above the booking-in counter. 'My alarm clock must be slow.'

Dora sent her a sceptical look as she wrote that day's date on a fresh page in the booking-in ledger. 'It's a good thing Percival's not coming in until late this morning.'

'Isn't she? I'd forgotten all about that.' Penny didn't meet her eye as she pulled her copy of the *Daily Express* from under her cloak. She sat behind the desk, calmly flicking through the newspaper.

Dora stared at her. 'What are you doing?'

'I have to read my stars every morning before I can start my day.'

'What about the patients?'

Penny's heavy-lidded gaze moved slowly across the empty waiting room. 'I don't think we'll be overwhelmed by the rush, do you?'

'If we don't have any patients in Casualty we could always make a start on today's Outpatients list?'

Penny gave her a lazy smile. 'Do calm down, Doyle. We might as well make the most of it, since Percy's not here to crack the whip.'

She consulted her horoscope and then insisted on consulting Dora's, too. A couple of patients arrived, but Penny took their names and sent them off to wait on the benches until she was ready to receive them.

'You're going to have an unexpected encounter today. Ooh, that sounds interesting, doesn't it?' Penny read out.

'Not really,' Dora replied. 'Every day's an unexpected encounter in this place. You never know
what you're going to see.'

As if to prove her point, the double doors suddenly flew open and a young policeman came
through them, hauling a man with him. From the
firm grip he had on the man's arm, it was hard to
tell if the policeman was holding him up or
stopping him from escaping.

Penny Willard sat up straighter behind the
counter and pulled a strand of blonde hair from
her cap. 'Hello, who's this? He looks rather nice.'

Dora recognised the policeman immediately.
She watched as he strode up to the desk, dragging the man behind him.

'We arrested this one trying to break into a
warehouse this morning,' he said. 'Funny thing
is, as soon as we got him to the station he started
complaining of a bellyache.'

'I've got appendicitis, I know I have.' The man
tried to wriggle free from the policeman's grasp,
but he held on grimly.

'You'll have a broken arm, too, if you don't
pack it in.' The policeman looked up and noticed
her. 'Dora?'

'Hello, Joe.'

'I didn't know you were working in Casualty?'

'I started a couple of weeks ago.'

Penny looked from one to the other. 'Do you
two know each other?'

'I should say.' Joe gave Dora a warm smile.
'Dora and me are courting. Ain't that right?'

'I–' She was aware of Penny's interested look.
But before she could say any more, Sister Percival

90

arrived and threw herself into the middle of the situation like a fizzing ball of perpetual motion.

'You two. What are you doing?' The words came out short and sharp, too fast for Dora and Penny to defend themselves. 'I hope you're not flirting when there are patients waiting? I know what you young nurses are like. Man mad, the lot of you.' Her eyes darted to Joe and the man. 'Can I help you?'

'PC Armstrong has brought in a prisoner, complaining of abdominal pains.' Dora stepped in quickly while Penny was still trying to slide her copy of the *Daily Express* under the counter.

'Then you'd better get him attended to, hadn't you?' Sister Percival replied sharply. 'Take him to Consulting Room Three at once, and inform Dr McKay. Not you,' she added, as Joe went to follow them. 'Patients and medical staff only in the consulting rooms.'

'But he's under arrest...'

'I said, patients and medical staff only.' Sister Percival drew herself up to her full height, which barely reached Joe's shoulder. 'Don't worry, Constable, we'll make sure he doesn't escape through a window.'

Dr McKay took a long time examining the man, palpating his stomach, listening to his heart and asking all kinds of questions.

'I'm sorry, young man, but I'm afraid I can't find anything wrong with you,' he said finally. 'But that doesn't mean you're not ill,' he went on, as the man's face fell. 'We should probably admit you to the ward for further tests.' He turned to Dora. 'Arrange for this patient to be transferred up to Judd, would you?' He looked at the man, who was fighting to keep the grin off his face. 'I hope that's all right with you, Mr Treddle?'

'Fine by me, ta, Doctor. I reckon I can put off going to jug for a few days!'

When Dora returned to the waiting room, Joe Armstrong was standing at the counter talking to Penny Willard. Dora heard her laughter carrying down the corridor.

He saw Dora and headed towards her.

'Where is he?'

'Dr McKay wants to admit him for tests.'

Joe's face fell. 'You're having a laugh, ain't you? There's nothing wrong with him.'

'We don't know that until we've done the tests.'

He sighed. 'My sergeant won't be happy about this.'

'Then he'd better have a word with Dr McKay.' Dora went to the counter and picked up the next patient's notes. Joe followed her.

'Can I talk to you?' he asked.

'Sorry, I'm working.'

Just her luck, Sister Percival appeared at that moment. 'I want you to go for first lunch, Doyle,' she said.

She was aware of Joe standing beside her, listening. 'Do you mean now, Sister?'

Sister Percival consulted her watch. 'Unless someone has rearranged the timetable in the dining room without informing me,' she said. 'Go along, Nurse. And I want you back here not a moment later than half-past ten.'

Joe trailed after Dora and out into the courtyard. 'I haven't seen you in ages,' he said.

'I haven't had much time off lately.'

'I've phoned that nurses' home of yours so often, I reckon that old dragon of a Sister must be sick of me!' He reached for her hand, but Dora pulled away.

'Matron's office is right over there,' she hissed. 'Do you want to get me the sack?'

'But I've missed you.'

She turned her head to look at him properly for the first time. She could understand why Penny Willard had been flirting with him outrageously. Joe Armstrong looked so handsome in his policeman's uniform. He had tucked his helmet under his arm and his fair hair glinted in the spring sunshine.

He was everything she could have wanted in a boyfriend. And yet...

And yet he wasn't Nick Riley. She was angry with herself for even thinking it, but it was the truth.

They had been out together on a couple of occasions over the past few weeks, and in that time Dora had desperately tried to make herself love Joe. She'd hoped that if she spent enough time with him then sooner or later something would click. But it hadn't happened, and she had begun to give up hope that it ever would.

'So when am I going to see you again?' he asked.

'I'm not sure when I'll get my next night off.'

'You must have some idea, surely?'

Dora took a deep breath. She was going to tell him that she thought it might be better if they didn't see each other any more, but his green eyes were so full of appeal she couldn't bring herself to do it.

'Next Thursday,' she said. 'If I can get the time off.'

He grinned. 'That's my girl! I'll take you dancing.'

'Do we have to?' Dora pleaded. 'I don't really feel like dancing after fourteen hours on my feet!'

'The pictures, then. I'll even let you sit in the back row with me, if you're good.'

Before she could stop him, he swooped down and gave her a long, hard kiss on the lips.

'Joe!' She pushed him off. 'What are you doing?'

'Something I've wanted to do for a long time.'

'Did you have to do it here? Heaven knows who could be watching...'

She glanced around nervously – and spotted Nick, smoking outside the Porters' Lodge. Dora wasn't even sure he'd seen them, but still felt as if she'd been caught doing something she shouldn't.

'You'd better go,' she said, giving Joe a little shove in the direction of the gates.

'I'll see you next Thursday.'

'If I can get the time off,' she reminded him.

'You'd better!' He grinned.

Penny Willard was waiting for Dora when she returned from lunch. 'I suppose that was your unexpected encounter, like it said in your stars,' she said. 'You kept *him* quiet. Why didn't you tell me you had a boyfriend?'

Dora shrugged. 'We've only been out a few times.'

'All the same, I'd hold on to him if I were you. He seems really nice. And you can tell he's keen on you.'

'Yes,' Dora sighed, her gaze drifting towards the double doors. 'Yes, he is, isn't he?'

That was the problem. She didn't want to lead Joe on and hurt him. But he was so persistent, it was hard to say no.

Perhaps she wouldn't want to say no after next week, she told herself bracingly. One more date, and she would know whether or not to end it.

Sister Percival appeared again, springing up out of nowhere like a jack-in-the-box, as usual.

'There you are,' she said. 'Dr Adler wants you to help him with a poisoning in Consulting Room Two.'

'Dr Adler?' Dora frowned.

'Yes. He's back, didn't anyone tell you? He arrived from Switzerland early this morning. Poor man, I expect he's utterly exhausted. But he's so dedicated, he came straight back to work.' She beamed her approval of Dr Adler's selfless-ness.

At last I get to meet him, Dora thought, as she made her way down the corridor. She had heard so much about the famous and brilliant Jonathan Adler, she wondered if the reality could ever match up.

But then she pushed open the door to the consulting room and realised they had already met, as she found herself staring at a young man bent double, retching into a bowl – and the man she had thrown out of the department first thing that morning.

He had swapped his shabby black coat for a white one, but she would have known him anywhere.

'Ah, Nurse Doyle.' Dr Adler's face was impassive under his shaggy mane of dark curls. 'Mr Creasey here thinks he may have accidentally ingested some rat poison. Let's see if we can't wash him out, shall we?'

Chapter Eight

Shoreditch Working Men's Club was packed for the Thursday night fight. A pall of cigarette smoke mingled with the smell of sweat and stale beer. Men gathered around the ring, pints in their hands, jeering and yelling encouragement.

'Come on, Nicky boy! Give him your right!'

'Stop dancing about, this ain't the bloody Royal Ballet!'

Nick was barely aware of the sea of faces around him, all his attention fixed on his opponent. Little Billy Brown barely came up to his chin, but he was strong, stocky and as tough as teak. Nick had had him on the ropes several times but he kept coming back for more. He'd landed a few good blows, too: Nick could feel the drip of blood down his temple from where Little Billy had caught him on the brow, but his body was too tense to feel pain. That would come later, when the fight was over.

Little Billy grinned at him, his teeth red from a

split lip. 'Show us what you've got, big lad,' he taunted.

Nick kept his focus, shutting out the banter. Billy was trying to rile him, but Nick had the measure of his opponent now. Little Billy might be tough, but he didn't have a payoff punch.

'Don't let him get too close,' Nick's trainer Jimmy had warned after the fourth round. 'See those short arms of his? He has to move in to drive the blows home. Once he gets in, he's dangerous.'

Little Billy was tiring, too. He was in his late-thirties, he'd been in the game since he was Nick's age, and all those years were beginning to tell on his stamina. That bloodied grin of his was all show. He could barely keep up as Nick sidestepped around him, drawing him in circles, playing a cat-and-mouse game.

Nick respected Little Billy too much to want to humiliate him, and he needed to put on a good show for the crowd. But it was getting late, he'd been working hard today, and all he wanted to do was go home and get some kip.

He timed it to the second. He lowered his guard for a moment, tempting Little Billy in. A wiser fighter might not have taken the bait, but Billy was greedy. As he moved in closer, Nick was ready for him. With deadly accuracy, he drove an uppercut to the other man's chin that lifted him off the ground and sent him flying across the ring.

The referee stood over him, counting him out, but Nick knew it was all over. Little Billy made no attempt to haul himself off the canvas as the crowd roared.

Afterwards the two fighters made their way

down the narrow, darkened passageway that led to the boxers' changing room. Jimmy, Nick's trainer, followed them.

'Good fight tonight,' Billy said, voice muffled by his swollen mouth. 'You did well, mate.'

'You too. Sorry about that last jab.'

'I asked for it. Got a bit greedy, didn't I?' Billy ruefully nursed his jaw. 'Still, it was a fair fight.'

'I just hope Terry pays up.' Terry Willis, the local promoter, had been known to sneak off without paying his fighters in the past.

'I don't think he'd dare pull a fast one on you!' Billy grinned.

The door to the changing room was stuck as usual. Nick put his shoulder against it and gave it a shove. Inside the poky back room, the bare light-bulb cast a sickly light on paintwork yellowed with nicotine. Crates of empty ale bottles took up most of the room, filling the air with a stale beer smell.

Joe Armstrong was perched on one of the crates, his kit bag at his feet. He jumped up when the door opened, then sat back down.

'What you doing here?' Little Billy asked.

'I'm waiting to see Terry.'

'Don't reckon he'll want to see you, after what you did to Johnny Jago.'

Joe's chin lifted. 'I beat him fair and square.'

'Nothing fair or square about that fight.' Little Billy turned to Nick. 'Did you hear about it? Disqualified for elbowing, he was. Caught him full in the face. Smashed his nose to a pulp and put him in hospital.'

Nick looked at Joe's smirking face and felt the urge to land his fist in it. He knew Johnny Jago well. He wasn't the greatest boxer in the world, but his family relied on the money he brought in from his fights. Everyone knew to go easy on him, to make him look good so Terry would keep booking him.

Everyone except Joe Armstrong.

Nick unlaced his gloves. 'I expect Terry's still in the bar, counting his takings, if you want him.'

'I'll wait here for him.'

'No, you won't.' Nick kept his voice calm, his eyes fixed on Joe. 'We've got no room for dirty fighters in here.'

They stared at each other, like feral cats meeting in an alleyway. It was Joe who looked away first.

'I ain't got time for this,' he muttered, snatching up his kit bag. 'Tell Terry I was looking for him.'

'Well done, mate,' Little Bily said, as the door slammed behind him. 'We don't need blokes like him in this game.'

But Nick wasn't thinking about boxing. His mind was fixed on Dora, and the picture that still burned in his brain of her and Joe kissing at the hospital. He knew he had no right to be jealous, but when he'd seen them together it was all he could do not to march straight over and tear the other man off her. Dora deserved better than Joe Armstrong.

He stopped himself. The truth was, he wouldn't have been happy if Dora had started courting King Edward himself. But she was entitled to a life of her own, and he had to keep out of it.

Terry Willis came to the changing room after the

fight to give Nick his money. He fancied himself a bit of a gangster in his pin-stripe suit, with a homburg hat tilted low over a narrow, foxy face.

'Easy money, eh, Nicky boy?' He leered at Nick as if he knew what it felt like to win a fight.

'You weren't the one getting belted.' Nick winced as his trainer Jimmy massaged his tense shoulders.

Terry sniggered. 'True enough, lad.' He counted out two pound notes into Nick's hand. 'And there's more where that came from, if you fancy a few more fights?'

'He's already doing enough,' Jimmy put in. 'It won't do to wear himself out if he wants a shot at a title fight.'

'Still got your eye on making it big in America, then? Want to go over there and show the big boys what an East End lad can do?'

'Something like that.' Nick wasn't interested in fame or glory. All he wanted was to find a doctor who could make his brother better again. He'd heard they were achieving all kinds of medical miracles in America, and if there was a chance they could make Danny right, he had to take it.

'Shame,' Terry said. 'You're already one of the best fighters in London. I could put you in the ring twice a week, if you were interested.'

Nick thought about it. He'd been putting away all the money he'd earned from his fights, and after four years he had a tidy sum saved – enough to get him and Danny to America at least. But he still had a long way to go.

And it wasn't just Danny he had to think about now.

'I'm interested,' he said.

Terry flashed him a gold-toothed grin. 'That's my boy. You wait and see, I'll make us both rich.'

'If he don't kill you first!' Jimmy muttered when Terry had gone. He glared at Nick as he packed up his bag. 'Are you daft or what? You'll be knackered in three months.'

'I'll be all right.'

'We agreed only title fights, remember? You'll be in no fit state to go to America by the time Terry Willis has finished putting you through the mill.'

'I'm going to America, don't you worry about that.' Nick threw his battered leather gloves into his bag. 'But I've got a family to look after, too, don't forget.'

Ruby had been on at him to buy new furniture for the flat ever since they'd moved in four weeks earlier. And the nagging had got worse since she'd found out about his savings.

'Think of what we could do with that money,' she said. 'We could buy a new three-piece suite ... a new bed. I'm sick of sleeping on that old mattress, aren't you?'

'We'll get a new bed soon,' Nick promised. 'But I already told you, that money is to take Danny to America.'

'And what do you think they're going to do to him?' Ruby's voice was harsh. 'Let's face it, it would take a miracle, not medicine, to set that boy straight!'

'All the same, I've got to try. If there's the slightest chance...'

Ruby had sighed. 'It's just a pipe dream, Nick. Besides, you've got a wife now. You should be thinking about me and our future, putting us first.'

'I do,' he insisted. 'But I have to look out for Danny, too. You don't understand, Rube. I'm the only one he's got—'

But nothing he said made any difference. Ruby had cold shouldered him, turning away from him in bed that night. By morning the storm had blown over and she was back to her old self, laughing and joking as she fried up bacon for his breakfast. But her words had hit home. She was right, Nick thought. He had to start providing for his baby as well as his brother.

He trudged home down the narrow dark backstreets. It was nearly closing time, and drunks fell out of pubs on every street corner, weaving across his path, laughing and singing and squaring up to each other. Workers cycled past, wending their weary way home after their factory shift.

It was nearly eleven when he let himself into the flat. As Nick dumped his bag by the front door, Ruby came out of the kitchen to greet him.

'Well? How did it go? Did you knock him—' Her smile turned to a wince when she saw his eye. 'Blimey, that's a nasty cut.'

She moved closer and reached up, but Nick jerked his head away. 'Don't touch it, you'll open it up again. It'll be all right once I've bathed it.'

'I'll do it for you.' She took his hand and led him into the kitchen. 'You do know you're going to have a right shiner by tomorrow morning? God only knows what that Head Porter of yours is going to say. You'll need salt water on it, to stop it getting infected...'

But Nick wasn't listening. He stopped dead in

the doorway and stared at the contraption squatting in the middle of the kitchen. It looked like a white barrel on three legs, with a lid in the top.

'Where did that come from?'

Ruby beamed at him. 'It's a washing machine. It arrived this morning. Isn't it smashing? It's the latest thing.'

'I can see what it is. Where did you get the money to pay for it?'

'Oh, you don't have to worry about that. I got it on HP. Half a crown a week.' She was reaching up into a cupboard for the salt packet, so Nick didn't see her face.

He felt his anger rising, making his swollen eye socket throb. 'I told you I didn't want anything on tick in this house!'

'It's too late, I've already signed the forms,' Ruby said calmly. She couldn't meet his gaze as she filled a bowl with water.

'We'll see about that! You're going straight down to that shop tomorrow and you're going to tell them you've made a mistake.'

'I will not! Now sit down and let me bathe your eye. It's bleeding again.'

'Never mind that! You had no right to start running up debts without talking to me first.'

'I did talk to you, remember?'

'And I said no!'

Ruby rolled her eyes. 'Oh, for heaven's sake, Nick, it's only a washing machine. And they're easy instalments.'

'Easy for who? We've still got to pay it back.'

'Yes, but only two and six a week. Mr Wallis says—'

'And who's Mr Wallis, when he's at home?'

'He's the bloke from Parker's. The loan company.'

'A tallyman!' Nick's lip curled.

'It's not like that. He helps young couples like us–'

'By getting us into debt? That's a big help!' Nick sank down into a chair at the kitchen table. The pain of the fight was beginning to flow through his body. Every muscle seemed to ache at the same time. 'We ain't made of money, Ruby. We don't want to run up debts, especially not with the baby on the way–'

'And I don't want people thinking we're poor as church mice, either!' Ruby shot back. 'I'm ashamed to let anyone into this place, with all these shabby old bits and pieces. I don't want people looking down their noses at us, thinking we're not good enough...'

'They'll be looking down their noses at us when the bailiffs come round!'

'Don't be daft. No one's going to send the bailiffs round. We'll manage.'

'If we live on fresh air.'

Ruby paused for a moment, then the anger seemed to leave her. When she turned to face Nick again, she was smiling.

'Let's not fight, Nick,' she said softly. She dipped the cotton wool in the bowl and gently dabbed his eye. Nick flinched at the sting of the salt water. 'I know I should have talked to you about it. But don't you think it's a smashing washing machine?' she coaxed. 'And won't it be nice that I don't have to do all that laundry by hand? You wouldn't want me heaving wet washing about, would you? All that heavy lifting ... scrubbing and rinsing sheets under the tap?'

Nick met her gaze and realised he was being played. Ruby knew just what to say, and just how to flash those blue eyes at him to get him to do what she wanted.

But not this time. 'It's got to go back,' he said. 'I told you, we'll buy one when—'

But Ruby wasn't listening. Her eyes immediately lost their softness, turning to hard chips of ice. 'When, Nick? When the cows come home? I want one now!' She stamped her foot. 'Why do I have to live like my mum, scrimping and making do because her husband's too tight to do anything about it?' She threw down the cotton wool and knocked the bowl off the table with an angry sweep of her arm. It shattered on the floor, sending shards of china and water everywhere.

'Now look what you've made me do!' she screeched. 'I don't suppose I'll get a new bowl, either!' Then she burst into tears.

'Ruby—'

'Bugger off, Nick. I don't want to talk to you.'

She fled out of the kitchen and he heard the bedroom door slam. He hauled himself wearily to his feet and started to clean up. His sides ached painfully as he bent down to pick up the broken shards. He thought about leaving them, but he knew Ruby wouldn't pick them up. She could be a stubborn little cow when she wanted to be.

He couldn't be doing with this, he thought. He'd had a long day, his whole body was sore with bruises, and all he wanted to do was rest.

He staggered painfully into the bathroom, kneeled down and eased back a corner of the lino. He'd found a loose floorboard when they first moved in, which made a perfect hiding place for his savings.

He groped around in the narrow space under the boards and pulled out the rusty biscuit tin. He opened it and took out two five-pound notes, then slipped them into his pocket.

Ruby had locked him out of the bedroom.

'Ruby?' He rattled the doorknob. 'Ruby, let me in.'

'Go away.' Her voice was muffled on the other side of the door.

He felt his temper spark, molten heat rising through his veins. 'If you don't open this door, I'm going to kick it down,' he threatened.

Silence. Nick braced his shoulder against the door, ready to splinter the wood.

Then, suddenly, the door opened and Ruby stood there, her face puffy with tears. Without her usual mask of make-up she looked like a vulnerable child, her blonde hair falling in delicate tendrils around her pale face.

'What?' she said sulkily. 'If you're going to have another go at me—'

'I'm not.' He held out his hand. Ruby stared down at the cash.

'What's that?'

'The money to pay for that contraption. Since you're so set on keeping it, I want you to go down to the shop tomorrow and pay for it.'

'Oh, Nick!' She looked up at him, her face full

of hope. 'Do you really mean it?'

'Just this once. And no more debts, all right?'

She threw her arms around his neck, nearly knocking him off his feet.

'No more debts, I promise,' she said.

Chapter Nine

'Have you heard about that gypsy woman, Nurse? She reckons she can tell your future!'

Millie stifled a sigh. News of Mary Ann Lovell's so-called powers had spread since she'd arrived on the ward a few weeks earlier. Now everywhere she went, the patients seemed to be talking about her.

Florrie Hibbert was more animated than Millie had seen her in a long time. The poor woman had been through so many tests since she'd been admitted with haematemesis, but as yet no one could tell her what was wrong with her. She'd spent days lying on her back, desperate with worry and unable to eat for vomiting up blood.

Millie smiled as she dipped a swab in the small pot of glycol-thymol, ready to clean her mouth. 'You don't really believe that, do you?'

'Well, you know, normally I'd say it was nonsense. But she seems to know such a lot. She's a Romany, so she says. Makes her living telling fortunes with a travelling fair.'

'So I've heard.'

'She told that woman in the corner she could see a journey over water, and her sister's just moved to

Greenwich.' Florrie Hibbert looked impressed. 'How do you think she knew that?'

'How indeed? Open wide for me, please, Mrs Hibbert.'

She finished swabbing out the woman's bald pink gums, and then carefully replaced her false teeth. 'There, all done. That feels better, doesn't it? I must say you're looking a lot brighter, Mrs Hibbert.'

'Oh, I am, Nurse.' Florrie Hibbert beamed at her. 'Mary Ann told me I'm going to be going home soon. That's good news, isn't it?'

Millie frowned. Harmless predictions were one thing, but telling Mrs Hibbert she was going home when her chances of getting better were so slim seemed almost cruel.

But then she looked at the woman's shining, eager face, with more colour in her cheeks than she'd had in a long time, and she wondered whether there was really any harm in it. If it cheered her up and stopped her fretting, then perhaps a bit of hope wasn't so bad after all.

It wasn't just the patients who were discussing Mrs Lovell's powers.

'There must be something to it, don't you think?' Katie O'Hara said, as they polished spoons in the kitchen ready for inspection. Every Tuesday morning, every piece of cutlery, plate, cup and saucer had to be taken out of the cupboards, washed, dried and set out on the table in the middle of the ward for Sister Everett to check. She would then inspect each piece closely, count them all and note the figure on a list which remained locked in her desk drawer, never to be referred to again.

No one could work out why the inspection had to be done, but no one dared question it either. It was just put down as one of Sister Everett's Little Ways, like her pet parrot and her custom of leading the patients in rousing spirituals on her harmonica every Sunday morning.

'She definitely has powers,' Katie went on. 'I don't like the way she looks at me, as if she can see right in here.' She tapped her temple.

'I'm surprised she can find anything going on between *your* ears!' Amy Hollins snorted. She and the other third-year Sheila Walsh were emptying the cupboards, arranging cups and saucers on a tray. 'Honestly, O'Hara, you should listen to yourself. You're so silly and superstitious. I expect it's that backward little village you come from.'

'Take no notice of her,' Millie whispered, seeing Katie's hurt expression. 'I suppose it would be nice to know what the future holds, wouldn't it? I'd love to know when Seb is coming home from Berlin.'

'I'd like to know if my Tom is going to propose to me,' Katie said.

Millie laughed. 'Steady on! You've only been courting five minutes!'

'Two months, actually,' Katie replied primly. 'And it doesn't matter how long you've been together, if you know it's true love.'

Millie sent her a sideways smile. She wondered if Katie's boyfriend Tom knew that she was planning their future so seriously. Millie had only met him once but he didn't strike her as the type to settle down.

'What about you, Hollins?' Sheila asked. 'Don't you want to know if your mystery man is going to pop the question?'

Hollins smiled enigmatically but said nothing. She picked up the tray and carried it out of the kitchen.

'I wonder who he is?' Katie whispered, as the door closed behind her. 'It's not like her to be so mysterious, is it? I've heard he's a millionaire.'

'I really don't care,' Millie shrugged. 'She's so spiteful, I'm surprised she's even got a boyfriend.'

Mary Ann Lovell was at it again that afternoon. As Millie finished the tea round, she was annoyed to see one of the other patients, Mrs Penning, perched on the edge of her bed, hand outstretched. Mary Ann's neighbour, Mrs Wilson, leaned forward listening eagerly.

'Never!' she was saying. 'Go on, what else does it say?'

'It says you'll soon be coming into money,' Mary Ann Lovell intoned gravely, drawing Mrs Penning's palm closer to her face.

'Ooh, did you hear that? Coming into money, eh? Maybe you'll come up on the football pools.'

'If my husband don't get his hands on it and spend it all before I get home!' Mrs Penning said gloomily.

Millie glanced around the ward. Amy Hollins and Sheila Walsh had sneaked off to the kitchen for a gossip, while Sister and Staff Nurse Crockett were tending to a patient behind some screens at the far end of the ward. All hell would break loose if they found patients wandering about.

'What are you doing? Get back into bed at

once.' Millie tried to give her voice the right note of stern authority. None of the women took any notice of her. 'You'll catch a chill,' she tried again. 'And you know Sister doesn't like you out of bed.'

'Oh, never mind Sister. She's not here, is she?' said Mrs Penning carelessly over her shoulder.

'Have you had your palm read yet, Nurse?' Mrs Wilson asked, turning to her.

Millie caught Mary Ann's challenging gaze. She looked every inch a gypsy, her grey-streaked hair framing a weatherbeaten face.

She held out her hand. 'How about it, my wench?' she invited.

'No, thank you.'

'Go on, where's the harm?' Her voice was as low as a man's, throaty from too many cigarettes.

'She's right,' Mrs Wilson said. 'It's only a laugh. Gawd knows we could do with it in this place!'

Mary Ann trapped Millie in her gaze. 'You never know, I might have good news for you,' she rasped. 'Here, let me look–'

'What on earth is going on here?'

Millie froze at the sound of Sister Everett's footsteps advancing briskly towards them.

'Why are these women out of bed, Benedict?' she demanded. 'Did you give them permission to wander around the ward?'

'No, Sister.' Millie studied the polished toes of her shoes.

'I'm surprised at you,' Sister Everett scolded. 'I turn my back for five minutes, and you allow my ward to descend into chaos. Explain yourself, Nurse!'

'I – I–'

'It wasn't her fault, Sister,' Mrs Penning broke in. 'I wanted to get my palm read, that's all.'

'Not this nonsense again?' Sister Everett turned to Mary Ann. 'Does this look like a fairground? Do you see any gypsy caravans? Any sideshows?'

'No, but–'

'No, this is a hospital ward, full of sick patients. And I'll thank you to treat it as such. I will not have you reading palms or consulting tea leaves or gazing into crystal balls, or whatever other mumbo-jumbo nonsense it is you carry out. Is that quite clear?'

She and Mary Ann glared at each other for a moment.

'Ain't my fault if they want my dukkering,' the gypsy mumbled, her expression truculent. 'I got the gift, see.'

'Well, I'd rather you didn't use it on my ward.' Sister turned to Millie. 'Get Mrs Penning back into bed at once. And then you can go and give Mrs Allen her liniment.'

'I wouldn't bother,' Mary Ann said carelessly, examining her fingernails. 'She'll be dead before sunrise.'

There was a shocked silence, broken only by the distant sound of a pro rattling bedpans about in the sluice.

Sister Everett recovered her composure first. 'What utter codswallop! This has gone too far. It's bad enough that you persist in this silly fortune-telling, but to upset my patients...'

'I know what I know,' Mary Ann insisted stubbornly. 'The fates don't lie.'

'I don't know about the fates, but our consultant seems to think she is doing very well,' Sister Everett retorted. 'And I would put modern medicine over your hocus-pocus any day of the week. She turned to Millie. 'Well? What are you standing there for? Stop gawping and go and fetch that liniment, girl, or you won't need a fortune-teller to tell you what lies in store for you!'

'Excuse me, Nurse, I'm just about to take my break. I don't suppose you could spare three-pence for a cuppa?'

Dora managed a weary smile at Dr McKay's joke. Two weeks on, and the doctors still hadn't tired of making fun of her.

Word had quickly spread around the Casualty department about the case of mistaken identity, and everyone had thought it hilarious. Even Sister Percival had cracked a smile. Dora didn't think she would ever live it down.

'How was I to know Dr Adler had come back from Switzerland on the night train?' she said to Penny Willard. 'He didn't even look like a doctor.'

'I know,' Penny replied with a sigh. 'That's because he doesn't have a woman to look after him.'

There was something about Dr Adler that brought out all the nurses' maternal instincts. Penny could often be found sewing buttons on his shirts, while Sister Percival turned a blind eye whenever he spent the night stretched out on a wooden bench after a late shift because he was too exhausted to go home.

'He's so dedicated,' she explained. 'And brilliant, too. He could have been an eminent professor in any medical school in the world, but he chose to stay here and care for our patients.'

Brilliant and dedicated he might be, but he also had a wicked sense of humour. And he'd found the right partner in Dr McKay. The pair of them could often be found plotting mischief together.

And Dora seemed to be their particular target. Only that morning, she had spent five minutes calling across the waiting room for a patient called Buttock, until she'd seen Penny Willard with her head down behind the counter, doing her best not to laugh, and realised that the doctors had filled the emergency treatment list with a lot of fake notes featuring silly names.

'Sorry, Nurse,' Dr Adler chuckled, his big shoulders shaking. 'We couldn't resist it.'

'You're like a couple of schoolboys,' Dora sniffed. 'And you wouldn't do it if Sister Percival was here.'

'Now there's an idea.' Dr McKay's brown eyes gleamed behind his spectacles. 'I'd like to see Percy standing in the middle of the waiting room, calling out for Mr Bighead.'

'You wouldn't dare!'

Dr Adler and Dr McKay looked at each other.

'Is that a challenge? We love a challenge, don't we, David?' Dr Adler said.

'We do indeed, Jonathan.'

'Then why don't you take on the challenge of looking after some of these patients, instead of wasting time playing silly beggars?' Dora said.

'Ooh,' Dr Adler pulled a face. 'I think Nurse Doyle has just issued us with a reprimand, Dr McKay.'

114

'I think Nurse Doyle has been spending too much time around Sister Percival,' Dr McKay agreed.

Dora sighed and shook her head. 'You two are the giddy limit.' She started to search through the notes for the next patient. 'How are we supposed to know who's who, with all these daft names you've put in? And you could have made up better names than some of these,' she added, waving a piece of paper at them. 'I mean, who would ever believe someone was called Pearl Button?'

'Did you call, Nurse?' came a timid voice from the other side of the waiting room.

Dora flushed bright red, but Dr McKay kept a completely straight face as he called out, 'I'll see you now, Miss Button.'

Dr Adler waited until the door of the consulting room had closed before he roared with laughter. 'Oh, Nurse Doyle, your face! That will teach you, won't it?'

Dora turned away, just as the doors opened and Nick came in, half carrying her brother Peter who was limping badly, his teeth clenched in pain.

Dora rushed over to them. 'Pete? What's happened?'

'He took a tumble down the basement steps when he was taking some rubbish down to the stoke hole,' Nick explained. 'Mr Hopkins reckons he might have broken his ankle.'

'Sit him down.'

Peter gave a yelp of pain as Nick lowered him on to the bench. Dora bent down and rolled up his trouser leg. 'It looks swollen. Does it hurt when I touch it?'

115

'Jesus!' Peter jerked away. 'What do you think?' he hissed.

'All right, Nurse. What seems to be the problem?' Dr Adler stood behind them.

'This is my brother, Doctor. He's a porter here. He thinks he might have broken his ankle.'

'Let's take a quick look, shall we?' Dr Adler kneeled down, but Peter moved his foot away.

'S'all right,' he said stiffly. 'I can wait, if you've got other patients to see?'

'It won't take me a minute to check you over. If it's a simple sprain, your sister can bandage you up and send you on your way–'

'I said, I'll wait!' Peter's green eyes flared. He shared Dora's colouring and features: a freckled face, wide, obstinate mouth, and ginger hair flattened under his hospital porter's cap. 'Besides, I'd rather see the other doctor.'

'Pete?' Dora frowned.

Dr Adler's smile became tense. 'I can assure you, Mr Doyle, I am as adequately qualified as my colleague to diagnose a sprained ankle.'

'All the same, I'd rather see Dr McKay.'

'And why's that, Mr Doyle?' Dr Adler asked softly.

Peter shot him a filthy look. 'Because I don't want your dirty Jew hands on me,' he said in a low voice.

'Peter!' Dora gasped. 'You apologise to Dr Adler at once–'

'It's all right, Nurse Doyle.' Dr Adler slowly straightened up to his full height. 'I'm sure Dr McKay will be available shortly,' he said. His expression gave nothing away, but Dora could only

116

guess how hurt and humiliated he must be feeling.

As he walked away, she turned on Peter. 'How dare you say that to him? Dr Adler is a good doctor, one of the best in this hospital.'

'He's still a yid though, ain't he? I'm not having him touching me.'

Dora looked at Nick. His mouth curled with the same disgust she felt.

'What's happened to you, Pete? You're not like my brother any more. When did you get so full of hate?'

But she already knew the answer to that one. It was the day he'd joined the Blackshirts.

He wasn't the only one to get sucked in by Sir Oswald Mosley and his British Union of Fascists. They had started to creep into the East End a few years earlier, recruiting their members from working-class men who had no jobs, no hope and no future. Somehow they managed to convince them that it was immigrants, especially the Jews, who were responsible for their plight. Before long many had joined the ranks of Mosley's black-shirted army. They handed out leaflets, held raffles and marches, made speeches and sold *The Blackshirt* newspaper on street corners.

More worryingly, many of them had taken to harassing Jews on the streets, attacking innocent people, smashing their windows and setting fire to their shops.

Dora hoped Peter had more sense than to get lured into those kind of activities. But looking at him now, his pond-water green eyes full of malevolence behind their ginger lashes, she wasn't so sure.

'I don't need a lecture from you,' he muttered.

'No, you'd rather listen to those Blackshirt mates of yours!' Dora shook her head. 'What would Mum say if she heard you talking like this? It's not how she brought you up, Peter Doyle, and you know it!'

'Nurse Doyle?'

She looked round. Sister Percival had returned from her break and was bearing down on her.

'There are other patients to attend to, when you've quite finished?' she reminded her severely.

'Yes, Sister.' Dora shot a look back at her brother. 'I'll deal with you later,' she promised.

She was so mortified, she could hardly face Dr Adler for the rest of the day. It wasn't until they were together in the consulting room treating a delivery boy with a dog bite that he said, 'How was your brother's ankle? Was it fractured?'

Dora shook her head, eyes fixed on the patient as she cleansed the wound. 'Just a sprain.'

'I thought as much.' Dr Adler nodded wisely. 'I daresay he'll be relieved he doesn't have to miss out on any of those marches the Blackshirts are so fond of.'

Embarrassed heat flooded Dora's face. 'Oh, Doctor, I'm so sorry.' She blurted out the words she had been practising in her head all day. 'He should never have said those terrible things to you.'

'Don't worry, Nurse, I don't hold you responsible for your brother's opinions.' Dr Adler gave her a weary smile. 'And he didn't say anything I haven't heard before. Living in the East End these days, you get used to people spitting at you and calling you names in the street.'

Dora stared at him in disbelief. 'But you're a doctor!'

'In here, I am. Out there, I'm just another – how did your brother put it? – dirty Jew.' His mouth twisted. 'To them we're all the same. People to hate. People who don't belong.'

'But you do belong here!' Dora said.

'I used to think so, but now I'm not so sure.' Dr Adler's dark eyes were serious as they held hers. 'Look around you, Nurse Doyle. Look at your brother. I'm telling you, the East End is changing. And if Oswald Mosley and his Blackshirt thugs get their way, soon there won't be any room for the likes of me.'

Chapter Ten

Every morning Sister Sutton planted her bulky frame beside the front door of the nurses' home, her Jack Russell terrier Sparky at her side, inspecting the girls like troops going off to battle.

'Is that lipstick you're wearing, Hollins? Take it off immediately, you're a nurse, not a showgirl. Doyle, do something about your hair. If you can't get those curls inside your cap I'll cut them off for you myself.'

Of course Millie didn't escape her gimlet-eyed attention.

'Benedict, your cap is crooked,' she pronounced, swooping on her as she hurried past. Sister pulled it off Millie's head and stuffed it back into her hand. 'Go back upstairs and do it again. You'd think after nearly two years you'd be able to get it right.'

'Yes, Sister.'

As a result, Millie was late for breakfast and barely had time to manage a crust of bread before she had to rush off to the ward for seven o'clock.

The night staff were still serving breakfast when she arrived on duty with Katie O'Hara and Amy Hollins.

'It's been pandemonium,' Pritchard, the student who had been looking after the ward overnight, skimmed past them carrying a plate of bread and butter. 'We lost one last night.'

'Who?' Amy asked. But Millie's eyes were already drawn to the corner bed, hidden behind its tell-tale screens.

'Mrs Allen,' she said.

Pritchard frowned at her. 'How did you know?'

Millie and the others exchanged worried glances.

'She had a heart attack in the early hours,' Pritchard went on. 'It was so unexpected.'

'I'll tell you who did expect it,' Katie muttered, nodding towards Mary Ann Lovell. She was sitting up in bed, sipping her tea and chatting to Mrs Wilson in the next bed, completely unconcerned.

'It's just a coincidence, that's all,' Millie said.

'Or that woman put a hex on her.' Katie shuddered. 'I'm telling you, I'm not going anywhere near her again!'

But Amy Hollins had a different view. 'I want

her to tell my fortune,' she declared, cornering Millie as she filled hot water bottles later. 'And we've all got to do it, so we don't get into trouble.'

Millie thought about Katie. 'That's not fair,' she said. 'What if we don't want to?'

'You've got to. I'd ask Walsh, but it's her day off.'

Millie sighed. 'All right, I'll do it,' she agreed. 'As long as you leave O'Hara out of this. She's terrified of Mrs Lovell, poor thing.'

Sister Everett had the afternoon off. They waited until Staff Nurse Crockett had gone off for her dinner at twelve, then Amy nodded to Millie and they both made their way to Mary Ann Lovell's bedside.

She didn't seem at all surprised to see them. 'Afternoon, my wenches.' She grinned toothlessly at them as Amy pulled the screens around her bed. 'What can I do for you?'

Millie glanced sidelong at Amy, who straightened her shoulders and said, 'We want you to tell our fortunes.'

'Do you now?' Mary Ann settled back against her pillows and regarded them with shrewd eyes. 'And what will your Sister say about that? She's already given me a mouthful for dukkering on her ward.'

'She doesn't have to know.'

'Is that right?' Mary Ann's gaze settled on Amy for so long, even Millie began to feel uncomfortable next to her.

'Will you do it or not?' Amy snapped.

'That depends, doesn't it?'

'On what?'

'Whether you cross my palm with silver.'

121

Amy gasped. 'That's unfair! You didn't charge anyone else.'

'Happen I don't like your face, young lady.' Mary Ann stared down her hooked nose at her. 'Besides, it ain't as if *she's* a pauper, is it?' She whipped round to look at Millie. 'That's right, ain't it, my wench? Got a bit of money in your family.'

Millie fought the urge to run away. It's just a bit of fun, she told herself. Nothing but harmless, silly nonsense.

She stood rooted to the spot while Amy and the gypsy woman haggled over a price. Finally, it was settled, and Amy fetched the coins.

'I'll go first,' she announced.

'You'll wait your turn.' Mary Ann pointed a bony finger at Millie. 'I'll tell her fortune first. Or I won't tell any at all,' she added, as Amy opened her mouth to protest.

Amy's mouth dosed again, setting in a frustrated line. 'All right,' she agreed. 'But don't take all day about it,' she warned Millie.

'She's a bad 'un, ain't she?' Mary Ann murmured in her low, gravelly voice, as they watched Hollins strutting away down the ward. 'Not like you, eh, my wench?' She turned her gaze back to Millie. 'You've got a kind heart. A good soul. I can see it shining out of you, like a golden light.'

'Um ... thank you.' Millie shuffled her feet.

She tried not to flinch as Mary Ann seized her hand and turned it over to examine the palm. The woman's own skin was hard, like worn leather.

'I see a great fortune coming your way in the future.'

So Cousin Robert might not be getting his hands on the estate after all, thought Millie. Grandmother will be pleased. She had been fretting for years about Billinghurst passing into a distant branch of the family if Millie didn't produce an heir in time.

'And I see a wedding, too. To a fair-haired man.'

Millie smiled, thinking about Seb. 'Will I be seeing him soon?' she asked.

'Soon enough, my wench. Before the summer is out, at any rate.' She drew Millie's hand closer to her face, so close she could feel Mary Ann's warm breath against her skin. The woman's brows drew together in a frown.

'What is it?' Millie asked. 'What do you see?'

The woman raised her head. The bleakness in her dark eyes shocked Millie.

'You'll be wearing mourning black when you see him again.'

Before Millie had a chance to react, Amy stuck her head through the screens. 'Are you finished yet?' she hissed. 'Crockett will be back soon, and I don't want to miss my turn.'

'Yes. Yes, I'm finished.' Mary Ann didn't resist as Millie slipped her hand out of her grasp. She pushed past Amy Hollins through the screens and walked back down the ward on legs that suddenly felt as if they didn't belong to her.

Katie O'Hara abandoned her TPRs on the other side of the ward and followed her into the kitchen.

'What did she say?' she asked, closing the door behind her.

'Nothing.' Millie picked up the kettle and went

123

to fill it at the sink. 'I'll start the tea round, shall I?'

Katie came closer, studying her face with earnest blue eyes. 'She must have said something?'

'Just a lot of nonsense, that's all.' Millie fought to keep her hands steady as she lit the gas.

'There's something you're not telling me, I know it.'

Millie managed a light laugh. 'You're imagining things!'

No sooner had she put the kettle on the hob than the door flew open and Amy stormed in, making them both jump.

'That was quick!' Katie said.

'It was a complete waste of time.' Amy's face was taut. 'She's a fraud.' She threw open the cupboard and started slamming cups down on the tray. 'Aren't you supposed to be finishing those TPRs?' she snapped, turning on Katie.

'I'm going.' Katie pulled a face. 'But I think you're both mean to keep secrets,' she added.

Neither of them spoke after Katie had gone. Millie stared at her blurred reflection in the tiled wall as she waited for the kettle to boil.

It was all nonsense, she told herself. Nothing to worry about.

She looked around. Amy Hollins was standing on the other side of the kitchen, staring down into the teacups. And from the look of her face, she was thinking exactly the same thing.

On Thursday afternoon, Dora joined the other second-year students in the teaching block for Sister Parker's weekly lecture. All the students were given time off from their wards to attend, although some sisters gave it more grudgingly than others. To listen to Sister Percival go on, anyone would think Dora was going off to Clacton for the day, instead of sitting for two hours in a cramped, airless classroom, scribbling notes until her hand ached.

But at least she didn't have to keep up with Sister Parker's machine-gun dictation on this particular afternoon as the lecture was being delivered by Mr Cooper, the Chief Gynae Consultant. He was a lot nicer to look at than Sister Parker, too. He was more like a film star than a doctor, with his piercing blue eyes and black hair that gleamed like polished patent leather. All along the front row, Dora could see students sitting up straighter, fiddling with their hair and readjusting their apron bibs in an effort to make themselves more alluring.

Not that Mr Cooper seemed to notice, as he gave his lecture on the treatment of inevitable abortion.

'It may be taken as a general rule that there is no such thing as a complete abortion,' he intoned, in his deep, well-educated voice. 'Even when the pregnancy has reached the placental stage it is rarely expelled completely, small pieces of placenta or more commonly large pieces of chorion being retained *in utero.*'

He could even make the gruesome details of a late miscarriage sound charming, Dora thought. All around her, pens scratched on paper as the students struggled to get down every word he uttered.

125

'For the sake of the patients, the uterus must therefore be emptied with the fingers, sponge forceps and curette. In the first eight to ten weeks of pregnancy, it is very easy to complete the evacuation of the uterus, but after the twelfth to fourteenth week, the difficulty is much greater and requires considerably more cervical dilatation. Are there any questions so far?'

He looked around the classroom expectantly. Not a single hand went up. Dora caught Sister Parker's forbidding look as she stood on the dais behind the consultant, her hands folded in front of her. Not that anyone would dare to question a consultant in any case.

'Very well, then.' Mr Cooper looked down at his notes. 'I will now describe the curettage procedure...'

As Dora picked up her pen again, she realised there was silence beside her. Millie had stopped writing and was staring into space, her pen still in her hand.

Dora glanced at Sister Parker. Thankfully, her eagle gaze was turned on the other side of the classroom.

'Are you all right?' Dora gave Millie a quick nudge. Her friend turned to smile vacantly at her.

'Sorry, I was miles away.'

'So I see. Why aren't you making notes?'

Millie stared down at the half-empty page in front of her, as if seeing it for the first time. But before she could reply, Sister Parker's voice rang out.

'Are you quite finished, Nurses?'

Dora looked around, realising for the first time

that the classroom had fallen ominously silent. All eyes were turned in their direction – including Mr Cooper's.

Hot colour flooded her face. 'Sorry, Sister,' she mumbled.

'It isn't me you should be apologising to, is it?' Sister Parker's Scottish accent was sharp. 'May I remind you, Mr Cooper is a very busy man. He has generously given up his time to offer the benefit of his wisdom to you, and all you can do is chatter throughout his lecture. Really, Nurse Doyle, you have shown an appalling lack of respect.'

'Yes, Sister.' Dora cleared her throat. 'I'm very sorry, Mr Cooper.'

'Please, Sister, it was my fault,' Millie piped up beside her.

'I don't doubt that, Benedict, since you seem to be the source of a great deal of mischief in this set.' Sister Parker eyed her severely. 'Very well, since you are so keen to share the punishment, you and Nurse Doyle can both stay behind and clean the classroom after the lecture has finished.'

Dora heard Millie's gasp of outrage, quickly stifled.

Sister Parker heard it too. 'Yes, Benedict?' She swung round to face her, her eyes glacial behind her pebble glasses. 'Is there something you wish to say?'

Please don't make it worse, Dora prayed silently. Thankfully for once even Millie had the good sense to know when she was beaten.

'No, Sister,' she whispered humbly.

Afterwards, when all the others had gone, they got out the brooms and the dusters and started on the cleaning.

'I'm so sorry about this,' Millie said, as she flicked dust from the skeleton's collarbone. 'It's my fault that you're having to stay behind.'

'I was the one Sister Parker caught talking.'

'Only because you were trying to stop me getting into trouble.' Millie's large blue eyes were filled with dejection. 'Now you're having to do this on your night off.'

'It doesn't matter.' Dora kept her head down as she damp dusted the skirting board.

'But you're meant to be meeting Joe, aren't you?'

'We'll be finished soon enough.'

If she was really honest with herself, Dora wasn't looking forward to her night out. But she didn't want to admit it because then she would seem ungrateful.

She changed the subject. 'Why were you so quiet in class? You looked as if you had the weight of the world on your shoulders.'

Millie sighed. 'Oh, it's nothing. Just something that happened on the ward.'

'Oh, yes? What was that, then?'

Millie opened her mouth to reply, then closed it again. 'It doesn't matter,' she said. 'Just me being silly.'

But as she went back to her sweeping, Dora could see that her friend was troubled.

And I reckoned I was the one who kept my problems to myself, she thought.

Dora was twenty minutes late for her date with Joe. She'd been half expecting him not to wait for her, but as she turned the corner she saw him pacing the pavement outside the picture house, a box of chocolates in one hand.

His scowl turned to a smile when he saw her running towards him.

'There you are. I thought you'd stood me up.'

'Sorry I'm late.' Dora stopped running, fighting to get her breath back 'Benedict and I were caught talking in class and had to stay behind.'

'At least you're here now.' He handed her the chocolates. 'I bought these for you.'

'You shouldn't have.' She admired the padded silk box, finished off with a big red bow. 'They must have cost a fortune.'

'Only the best for my girl.'

She winced. 'Look, Joe—'

'I'd better hurry up and get those tickets,' he cut her off before she had time to finish her sentence. 'The film's about to start.'

'I'll get them—' Dora started to fumble in her bag, but Joe stopped her.

'You put your purse away. It's my treat.'

'At least let me pay my share?'

'You can get them next time, how about that?'

She opened her mouth to argue, but he was already sauntering off to join the end of the queue at the ticket booth. Dora watched him, standing so tall and handsome, smiling as he gallantly allowed an older couple to go before him. Any girl would be proud to be with him.

It must be her, she decided. She was too prickly and difficult to allow herself to be loved. If only she was as sweet-natured as Katie O'Hara, she could be blissfully happy by now.

'Nurse Doyle?'

She turned to face the man who had approached her. There was something familiar about his smiling face, but Dora couldn't quite place it. 'I'm sorry...?'

'You don't recognise me, do you?' he grinned. 'I'm not surprised. The last time you saw me I was flat on my back with half my arm hanging off!'

As Dora peered at him, a mental picture began to slide into place. 'Of course, I remember you now. It's Mr Gannon, isn't it?'

'That's right!' He beamed, delighted. 'Blimey, Nurse, you must have a good memory!'

'It was my first day in Casualty. I'm not going to forget that in a hurry!' She grimaced. 'How is your arm now?'

'As good as new, thanks to you and Dr McKay.' He flexed his arm, clenching and unclenching his fist to prove his point.

'I don't think I had much to do with it,' Dora said ruefully. 'It was all I could do to stop myself fainting on the spot!'

'You and me both!' Mr Gannon said. He glanced towards the doors. 'Oops, my missus is giving me a funny look. I reckon I'm going to have some explaining to do, stopping to chat to a young lady!' He shook Dora's hand. 'It was nice to see you, again, Nurse. You'll thank Dr McKay for me, won't you?'

'I will, Mr Gannon. And I'm glad your arm's on the mend.'

Dora was still smiling when Joe came over.

'Who was that you were talking to?' he demanded.

Dora blinked at him, taken aback by the bluntness of his question. 'He was my first patient on Casualty.'

Joe glared after him. 'You seemed very friendly.'

Dora laughed, until she saw the muscles clenching in Joe's jaw. 'So what if we were?' she replied tartly.

'I just don't like strange men getting over-familiar with my girl, that's all.'

'I'm not your girl,' Dora snapped. 'And you certainly can't tell me who I can and can't speak to!'

A shadow passed across Joe's handsome face, and then his smile was suddenly back in place. 'You're right. Sorry.' He shrugged. 'Let's go in before the film starts, shall we?'

The cinema was crowded, but the usherette found them two seats on the back row. Couples disentangled themselves hastily as they found themselves caught in the roving beam of her torch.

The film started and Joe's arm snaked around her shoulders. Dora kept her eyes fixed on the screen, where Max Miller was playing a cheeky racing tipster. Everyone was laughing at his antics, but all she could think about was the weight of Joe's arm, and the way his hand dangled limply over her shoulder, almost brushing her breast through her jumper.

Suddenly Max Miller disappeared and all she could see was her stepfather Alf's leering face looming at her, his slobbering mouth and the smell of beer on his breath...

She jumped, just catching the box of chocolates as it slid off her lap. Joe leaned closer to her. 'Are

131

you all right?' he whispered.

'I'm fine.' She shifted position slightly to loosen his grip on her shoulders.

She was fine, she told herself. Alf had been gone for a while now, and as the days went by she thought of him less and less. But sometimes, when Joe came too close, the dark memories would come creeping back and the old fear would engulf her.

After the pictures, he insisted on walking her back to the Nightingale. It was a mild May night. The cherry trees in the park were heavy with blossom, and the scent of mown grass filled the air.

It seemed too nice an evening to spoil, but Dora knew she had to set Joe straight. She took a deep breath. 'Look, Joe—'

'Before you say anything, there's something I need to tell you,' he cut her off. 'It's about your brother.'

She stared up at him, all other thoughts forgotten. 'Peter? What about him?'

Joe paused, choosing his words carefully. 'There was a bit of trouble at a British Union of Fascists' meeting last night in Whitechapel. Someone started heckling, and a few of the Blackshirts turned on him and gave him a hiding.'

Her blood turned to ice. 'And Peter was involved?'

'I'm not saying he started it,' Joe said. 'But he was in there with the rest of them, throwing punches. Broke the other bloke's nose.'

'The silly sod.' Dora ran her hand wearily over her eyes. 'That's all we need, for him to end up in jail.'

'It's all right, I didn't arrest him. I just gave him a warning and frightened him a bit. But if we see him causing trouble again, I might not be able to let him off. And I don't want to see him up in front of the judge on account of those thugs.'

'Me neither,' said Dora.

Joe looked anxious. 'Sorry to be the bearer of bad news. I wasn't sure if I should tell you?'

'I'm glad you did. And thanks for looking out for him.'

'I did it for you, not him.' Joe wrapped his fingers tighter around hers. 'I'd do anything for you, Dora.'

He moved in to kiss her again, but she pressed her hand against his chest, keeping him at a distance. 'Look, Joe, I don't want you getting the wrong idea.'

He frowned. 'What about?'

'Us.' She looked up into his face. His eyes were narrowed, wary. 'I really like you, but I meant what I said. I'm not your girl.'

'What are you, then?'

'I dunno. Your friend, I suppose.'

His mouth curled. 'I don't usually take my friends to the pictures, or buy them expensive boxes of chocolates.'

'I didn't ask you to buy me chocolates.'

'You didn't turn them down, either!' His hand tightened around hers, squeezing her fingers. 'What is it you want, Dora? One minute you're keen on me, the next you're giving me the cold shoulder.' His gaze sharpened, suddenly hostile. 'Is there someone else? Is that it?'

His question took her by surprise. She looked

up into his eyes, glittering in the light from the street lamp.

'No, there's no one else,' she said, pulling free from his grasp. 'But even if there were, it wouldn't be any of your business.'

Joe glared at her and then suddenly the darkness cleared from his face, just as it had in the cinema earlier.

'You're right, I'm sorry,' he said. 'If you want to stay friends, then that's all right by me.'

'I'm pleased to hear it,' she said, relieved.

'But don't think I'm giving up on you,' he went on. 'You might not want to be my girl now, but one day you will.' He smiled down at her, his handsome face full of confidence. 'You wait, Dora Doyle. I'm going to win you over in the end!'

Chapter Eleven

Helen stood back and admired her reflection in the changing-room mirror. In all her twenty-two years she had never worn a ballgown before, and she was startled at the transformation in herself. The deep raspberry pink perfectly suited her dark colouring, and the elegant drape of the bias cut made her feel sophisticated and grown up.

She did a half-turn, enjoying the swish of the satin fabric against her skin – and then she caught her mother's reflection in the edge of the mirror. Constance Tremayne was perched on a gilt chair, gloved hands clasped tightly in her lap, mouth pursed in objection.

'No, no, that simply won't do. You can't wear that décolletage with your long neck, it makes you look like a giraffe.'

Helen turned back to look at herself. She no longer saw an elegant princess but the gawky girl she really was.

'Where is that wretched assistant? How long does it take someone to look for a dress, I wonder?' Constance looked around, frowning.

She's probably hiding, Helen thought. Her mother had had the poor salesgirl running around for the past hour.

'Must you slouch so, Helen? Stand up straight, and put your shoulders back. I know you're far too tall, but you'll just have to make the best of it ... ah, here she is,' said Constance as the salesgirl appeared, staggering under the weight of another armful of dresses. 'About time, too. Have you brought the blue one I asked for? No, not that one. I meant the other blue one. Does that look blue to you? It looks distinctly eau de nil to me.' Constance tutted. 'Well, I suppose she might as well try it on. But go and fetch that blue one. Run along, girl, we don't have all day.'

'She's doing her best, Mother,' Helen said, as the girl scuttled off.

'I'm sure she is, but it's simply not good enough.' Constance gave a heavy sigh. 'Honestly, you would think a place like Selfridges would have more experienced people to assist customers, wouldn't you?'

'Perhaps there aren't any more dresses left for me to try on?' Helen gazed in despair at the rows of gowns hanging up on the rail in front of her. They had been in the ladies' evening wear department for almost two hours, and so far nothing had been to her mother's satisfaction. Helen was beginning to think there wasn't a dress in existence that would disguise all her faults.

'Nonsense, I'm sure we'll find something,' Constance dismissed briskly. 'We just have to keep looking until we find one. It's a good thing you have a half-day's holiday.'

Helen glanced at the clock. She had planned to spend her precious afternoon off with Charlie, until her mother had informed her they would be shopping for a dress for the Founder's Day Ball instead. Luckily, Charlie had come up with the idea of meeting her up west and having tea at Lyons in the Strand.

The salesgirl returned with more dresses, and Helen was bundled into the changing room to try on the next of her mother's selections.

'I don't understand why I need a new dress anyway,' she said, as the salesgirl fastened her into a green crepe creation. 'I'm sure Benedict has a gown she would let me borrow.'

'Go to the Founder's Day Ball in a borrowed dress? I wouldn't hear of it.' Her mother's outraged voice rang out from the other side of the changing-room curtain. 'This is a very important occasion, and as the daughter of a member of the Board of Trustees, you need to look your best. There will be some very important people attending, and I do not want you to let me or yourself down. Remember, everything you do and say reflects on me.'

Helen caught the salesgirl's eye in the mirror, and saw her look of silent sympathy.

'But no one will be looking at me.'

'Of course they will. As I said, there are some very important people attending this event. You must make a good impression on them, for the sake of your future career.'

I'd rather have fun, Helen thought.

They had never had a ball at the hospital before. Founder's Day was in July and so far the most exciting thing to happen on it was a garden party held two years ago. But this year the Trustees had decided to hold a fundraising ball instead. Or rather, Constance Tremayne had decided and the other Trustees had followed meekly in her wake, as usual.

It was to be the social highlight of the year. It was still two months away, but the other nurses were already excitedly planning what they were going to wear, and how many bottles of gin they could smuggle in tucked into their stocking tops.

Helen pulled back the curtain and emerged from the changing room to present herself before her mother. She could hardly bring herself to look at her own reflection. The dress was made of a stiff fabric that scratched her skin. It was matronly, long-sleeved, and fastened up to the neck with an unbecoming ruffle. The drab, muddy green colour made her pale face look sallow. It was the ugliest dress Helen had ever seen.

She already knew what her mother would say before she opened her mouth.

'Well, I suppose it's the best we've seen so far.'

Helen caught the salesgirl's appalled look.

'Don't you think it might be a bit – old for me, Mother?' she ventured.

'Nonsense, it's entirely appropriate. You young girls dress far too indecently these days,' Constance dismissed this.

Appropriate. Helen smiled at the word. She couldn't remember her mother ever telling her she looked beautiful. The only one who told her that was Charlie.

She glanced at the clock. Not long to go now, and she would be meeting him.

'Under Nelson's column at four o'clock. Don't be late!' he'd warned her.

'Helen? Are you listening to me?'

She turned to her mother, still smiling. 'Sorry?'

'I said, I'm buying this dress. Unless you want to try on some of the others again?'

'No!' Helen said. 'It's all right, honestly. We'll take this one.'

'Very good. But we will have to have it altered, of course. If only you weren't so thin...' Constance shrugged. 'Oh, well, I suppose it can't be helped.' She nodded to the salesgirl, who hurried off to fetch her pins.

As Helen stood there patiently, being tucked and darted and hemmed into place, Constance opened her capacious crocodile-skin handbag, took out her diary and consulted it. 'Now, I have a number of errands to do in town, and then I have to go to the hospital. I have a meeting with Matron about some new equipment she has insisted we order.' Helen recognised the light of battle in her eyes. 'We can take a taxi to the Nightingale together.'

'Oh, there's no need. I'm meeting Charlie in town.'

Constance looked up sharply. 'But I'd planned for us to have tea in Fortnum's.'

Helen twisted round to look at her. Constance was already consulting her diary again, ticking things off as if that was an end to the matter.

'I'm sorry, Mother, but Charlie will already be on his way. I can't put him off.' Not that Helen would want to, even if she could. 'Why don't we all have tea together?' she suggested.

Constance's mouth lifted at the corner. 'In Fortnum's? I don't think so, my dear.'

Helen bristled. 'Why not?'

'Because it's not really what he's used to, is it?'

He's not going to drink his tea out of his saucer, if that's what you're worried about, Helen thought. 'We could go to Lyons instead?'

'But I want to go to Fortnum's.'

Helen sighed. 'I wish you'd give Charlie a chance, Mother,' she said. 'You'd like him if you got to know him.'

'I'm sure he's a pleasant enough young man, in his way.' Constance turned her attention to the salesgirl instead. 'Are you sure that hem is quite straight?' she said. 'It looks rather lopsided to me.'

Helen turned back to the mirror, frustration welling up inside her. As usual, her mother had closed the subject. But this time Helen was determined to get her point across.

'You'll have to meet him at the ball,' she said.

'Oh, no, I don't think so, dear.' Constance didn't lift her gaze from the hem of the dress.

'What do you mean?'

139

'I mean he's not coming to the ball.' Her mother looked at Helen. 'You didn't really think he was invited, did you?' she said with a quizzical smile.

'But he's my boyfriend! All the other girls are taking theirs.'

Constance shot a look at the salesgirl crouching at their feet. 'This is not the time to discuss it,' she said. 'We'll talk about it later.'

'No, Mother, we'll talk about it now.' Helen fought to keep her voice from shaking. 'I'm not letting you sweep this under the carpet again. You're always doing this, pretending Charlie doesn't exist. Why don't you want him to come to the ball?'

Constance went white to her lips. 'Really, Helen, I don't know why you're taking this tone with me,' she snapped. 'As a matter of fact, I'm only doing it because I'm concerned for him. I don't want him to feel embarrassed or out of place.'

'Who says he'd be out of place?'

Her mother smiled condescendingly. 'It's not a world he's used to, is it? Mixing with important and influential people, he'd be like a fish out of water. I'm sure he'd be far happier staying with his own kind.'

'His own kind?'

'You know what I mean.' Her mother pursed her lips. 'Working-class people.'

Helen gasped. 'This isn't about Charlie at all. You don't want him there because you're worried he'll embarrass you.'

'No, I'm worried he'll embarrass *you*.' Constance's dark eyes flared with anger.

'He won't,' Helen said. 'Because I'm not a snob like you.'

'If being a snob means I don't think he's good enough for you, then perhaps I am.' Constance bristled. 'Anyway, I've made up my mind. He's not coming to the ball, and that's final.'

'Very well. If he's not coming then neither am I.' Helen looked down at the salesgirl, who was clearly enjoying every word. 'Help me take this off, please. We won't be buying it after all.'

The girl started to pull out the pins, but Constance stopped her. 'Please continue,' she instructed. 'Really, Helen, do you have to be so dramatic? You're making yourself look foolish.'

'I mean it, Mother. I'd rather stay at home than go to this wretched ball without Charlie.'

Their eyes clashed and held for a moment, both waiting for the other to yield.

'You're being very childish,' her mother said in a low voice.

'We'll see, shall we?' Helen turned to the girl. 'Are you going to help me with this horrible dress or do I have to tear it off?' she snapped, surprising herself with her sharp tone. Usually she would be all apologetic politeness, but her mother had enraged her too much.

Without waiting for a reply, Helen gathered up the dress and headed back to the changing room, trailing pins behind her.

'Helen, wait! Put that dress back on at once, you're making an exhibition of yourself!' Her mother's sharp voice followed her into the changing room. 'Are you listening to me?'

'Not until you're ready to listen to me.' She

141

swished the changing-room curtain across, shutting out her mother's livid face.

Constance Tremayne poured herself a cup of tea. She was so upset, she didn't even check if the pot was warmed properly.

Having tea in Fortnum & Mason was one of her little treats whenever she came up to town from Richmond. But now Helen had ruined it all with her silly temper tantrum.

The mere fact that her daughter had spoken to her like that was proof to Constance that Charlie Dawson was not a good influence. Helen would never have defied her like that before she met him, and she certainly wouldn't have flounced out of the shop, leaving her humiliated in front of the salesgirl. Helen used to be such a respectful, well-mannered girl, and *he* was turning her into a hoyden. She would be eating pease pudding and swearing like a docker soon.

Constance pursed her lips, remembering how rude Helen had been. Why couldn't she see her mother was only doing this for her own good? Everything Constance Tremayne did was for Helen's benefit, to help her to rise as far as she could in the world and never sink into ignominy.

Because Constance Tremayne had been there, and she never, ever wanted that for her daughter.

She shuddered to remember the mistakes she had made when she was a young girl like Helen. The man she had fallen in love with had far more wealth and power than Charlie Dawson, but he'd still brought about her downfall. Constance had been so besotted, she hadn't seen the danger until it was too late and her reputation was ruined.

Marriage to Timothy Tremayne, a young curate, had saved her and helped restore her to her rightful place in respectable society. But no matter how many charitable committees she sat on, how many flower shows she judged and how blameless a life she led, the memory of her earlier disgrace was like a stain on her character that she could never wash off.

The only thing she could do was to make sure her daughter never made the same mistake. From the moment Helen was born, Constance had exercised ruthless control over her daughter's life. She chose her clothes, her friends, dictated where she went to school and what her career should be. She knew she could be overbearing at times, but she was acting out of love.

And then Charlie Dawson had come along, and twenty years of careful management had gone out of the window.

Helen thought she was in love, but Constance knew better. She understood how that kind of infatuation could ruin a life. And she wasn't prepared to sit back and watch her daughter brought low by an East End stallholder's son.

Constance Tremayne had come too far for that.

Chapter Twelve

'Oi! Keep your hands off the merchandise.'

Ruby grinned at the stallholder, a potato in her, hand. 'Ain't I allowed to know what I'm buying?'

'As long as you are buying.'

''Course I am.' Ruby tossed him the potato. 'I'll have two pounds, and half a pound of carrots, to go with them.'

'Cooking a nice roast for your husband, are you?' The costermonger smiled. 'That's the way to a man's heart, so they say.'

'I can think of a better way!' Ruby winked at him, then caught his wife's fierce glare.

'Take no notice of her,' the man whispered as he tipped the potatoes into Ruby's bag. 'I've put you a few extra spuds in, just for brightening up my day.'

'Ta, love.'

As Ruby walked off, the stallholder shouted after her, 'I hope you brighten your husband's day, too.'

So do I, Ruby thought. Because she needed all the help she could get.

After six weeks of marriage, she had finally decided to tell Nick the truth about the baby.

'The longer you leave it, the worse it'll be,' her mother had warned her that morning when Ruby called in to Griffin Street for a cup of tea. 'I dunno why you didn't just tell him straight off, get it over and done with.'

'I couldn't.' The past six weeks had been the happiest of Ruby's life. She couldn't bring herself to spoil things.

'Well, you've got yourself in a right old mess now, haven't you? He's got eyes in his head, girl. He's going to wonder why you're not showing, when you're meant to be nearly four months gone!'

Ruby put her hand over her stomach, flat under her fitted skirt. 'He won't notice.'

'Nick Riley ain't a fool. So you'd best not treat him like one if you know what's good for you.'

'Bit late for that, ain't I?'

Ruby had been silly, she knew it. Her mother was right, she should never have put it off. Now she'd made everything ten times worse.

'He's going to kill me when he finds out,' she whispered.

'He ain't going to be shouting from the rooftops, that's for sure.' Lettie Pike's thin face took on a rare expression of sympathy. 'I know it ain't going to be easy. But you'll get round him, love. You always do. Look at that washing machine. Only you could pull a trick like that and get away with it!' She smiled with grudging admiration.

'This is a kid we're talking about, not a flaming washing machine!' Panic washed over Ruby. 'What if he leaves me, Mum?'

'He won't. Not if he knows what's good for him. You've been a smashing wife to him, and you've made a lovely home. I daresay he's got no complaints. Where's he going to find another girl like you?'

'I suppose you're right.' Ruby picked at the

145

chipped remains of her pink nail polish.

'You get yourself home, make him a nice dinner. Get him in the mood.' Lettie grinned. 'He'll be putty in your hands by the time you've finished with him!'

Ruby wished she was as confident as her mother. Underneath the bright and breezy front she put on for the rest of the world, she was quaking with nerves. She had been practising what she was going to say for days, trying to get the words exactly right. But every time she played out the scene in her head it ended in the same way, with Nick walking out on her for ever.

Somewhere in the back of her mind, Ruby had hoped that by the time she made her confession Nick would be so besotted with her he wouldn't care that she wasn't pregnant. But however much she tried to convince herself she had won him over, she knew he didn't really love her yet. He cared about her, did everything a loving husband should, but she always had the feeling he was making the best of a bad situation. Without the baby, there would be nothing to hold him to her.

She hadn't banked on how much he was looking forward to being a father, either. He didn't say much about it, but she could see the way his eyes lit up whenever he talked about the baby.

It was strange, she had never imagined Nick Riley with a kid on his knee. And yet it was enough to bring on one of his rare smiles. Sometimes Ruby found herself feeling jealous of a child who didn't even exist.

Nick had the afternoon off but he was supposed to be going to the gym on his way home from work, so she had plenty of time to prepare. She was in such a daydream as she let herself into the flat, she almost walked straight into the figure standing in the kitchen doorway.

'Jesus, Nick!' She dropped her shopping bag and put a hand to her fluttering chest. 'You scared the life out of me. What are you doing here? I thought you were training?'

'Sparring partner didn't turn up.' Something about the way he stared at her made Ruby uneasy.

'You spoiled my surprise,' she said, bending down to pick up the carrots that had rolled over the floor.

'You like surprises, don't you?'

She straightened up. 'What's that supposed to mean?'

'Don't act innocent with me, Rube. I've found out your little secret.'

Blood rushed to her head, and the room started to spin.

He knew.

'How did you find out?' she whispered.

'I'm not stupid, Ruby. I can see what's in front of my face.' His blue eyes blazed with anger. 'How long did you think you could go on lying to me?'

Her mouth was suddenly so dry she could barely get the words out. 'I was going to tell you,' she stammered. 'It just never seemed to be the right time—'

'So you thought you'd just go on pretending instead?'

'I'm sorry Nick, truly I am.' She couldn't bear to see the contempt in his face. 'I swear, I wanted to tell you. I tried so many times...'

147

'So why didn't you?'

'I don't know – I was scared, I suppose. I knew you'd leave me...'

'Leave you?' His frown deepened. 'Why would I leave you over a few bills?'

It took a moment to register with her what he'd said. 'Bills?' she heard herself say faintly.

He nodded. 'I found them stashed under the bed. Where you'd hidden them,' he accused.

Ruby leaned against the wall, her legs too weak to hold her up.

He'd found the bills. She'd been so worried about the baby, she hadn't given them a second thought.

She had kept her promise at first, after he'd paid off what they owed for the washing machine. For a week or two there had been no more debts. But then she got so bored in the flat by herself, she'd taken herself off to look round the furniture shops, just to see what she might be able to buy if she had the money. The sight of all those lovely things was too much for her, and before she knew what she was doing she had signed another loan agreement with Bert Wallis, and taken out credit in the local drapers.

She'd learned her lesson after the washing machine, so she made sure she only bought small things, just bits and pieces to brighten up the place and make it nice. Some new sheets and blankets, fluffy towels for the bathroom, a butter dish to go with her wedding china. But even odds and ends added up, and soon she was behind with the repayments.

Which was when she'd started hiding the

148

reminder notes under the mattress. Out of sight, out of mind.

'Ruby?' Nick frowned at her. 'Are you all right?'

She opened her mouth to speak but started to cry instead.

'Ruby!' He came forward and put his arms around her. 'Come on, girl, it's not the end of the world. I just don't want you to run up any more bills we can't pay, all right?' He pulled her closer, against the hard muscled wall of his chest. It felt so safe, so secure. 'Promise me you won't do that?'

She nodded, sniffing back her tears. 'I won't,' she mumbled into his shirt. But she wasn't even thinking about money. Relief was like a bright white light, flooding her brain and leaving no room for anything else.

'Come here, you daft cow.' He pulled her closer. 'Why did you think I was going to leave you?'

Tell him, a voice inside her head urged.

'I – I don't know,' she sniffed.

'I told you, I'm not going anywhere. I'm going to look after you and our baby, whatever happens.'

Whatever happens. The grim determination in his voice scared her. Ruby pulled away from him.

'You do love me, don't you, Nick?' She searched his face, desperately beseeching.

He looked down at her, his dark brows drawn together in a frown. 'You're my wife, Ruby.'

'That's no answer, is it? I can think of a lot of husbands who don't love their wives. Look at my dad. Him and my mum had to get married, and they've spent the last twenty odd years making each other suffer for it.'

Nick's mouth curved. 'You think I'm like your dad?'

Ruby thought about her father, fat and slovenly in his stained vest, his thinning hair spread across his gleaming pink scalp, and a reluctant smile came to her lips. 'I suppose not.'

'That's a relief, at any rate.' Nick looked down at her, his eyes suddenly serious. 'Listen, there's no reason why we should end up like your mum and dad, or mine for that matter. I know it wasn't the best start to a marriage, but we've still got a lot going for us. I want this to work out, Ruby. I don't want our baby growing up in an unhappy home, any more than you do.'

And what if there were no baby? The question hovered on her lips, but she couldn't bring herself to say it.

'But you've got to understand, I don't like lies, Ruby,' Nick went on. 'I've grown up around too many of them to want to listen to any more.' He pressed his lips into her hair. 'You know there's nothing you can't tell me. As long as we're honest with each other, we can get through anything.'

Tell him.

'Nick...'

He held her at arm's length. 'Blimey, don't tell me you've got something else to get off your chest already?' His eyes lit up with amusement. 'Let me guess ... your mum's moving in?'

'It's about the baby...'

She saw his face fall. 'What about it?' he said. 'Is there something wrong? Has something happened?' His gaze immediately dropped to her belly.

'No, it's just–' She couldn't tell him. She desperately wanted to, but the words dried in her throat.

She pressed her face to his chest. She could feel his heart beating steadily against her cheek. She breathed in the warm, male smell of his skin. It was like a drug to her, she couldn't imagine living without it.

'Everything's fine,' she said. 'That's all I wanted to tell you.'

He grinned. 'That's a relief! You had me worried for a minute there.'

Ruby pulled herself out of his embrace, picked up her shopping bag and headed for the kitchen. 'I'd better get on with our tea, or we'll be eating at midnight.'

'Before you do, I've got a little present for you.'

Her heart lifted. 'For me? What is it?'

'Wait there.' He disappeared into the bedroom and returned a moment later with a brown paper package. 'Here,' he said, handing it to her.

Her fingers fumbled with the string. 'What is it?' The package felt soft. Perhaps it was a new blouse, or that gorgeous cornflower blue jumper she'd had her eye on? Although she couldn't really imagine Nick going anywhere near a ladies' wear shop, let alone knowing what to ask for...

Impatient, she gave up trying to untie the string and ripped at the brown paper, instead. But it wasn't a new blouse inside, or a jumper.

'One of the porters at work gave them to me,' Nick said. 'His nipper's grown out of them so his missus wondered if we could make use of them.' He beamed with pride. 'Lovely, ain't they?'

151

Ruby stared down at the pile of matinee jackets and bootees in her hands. The delicate, lacy knitting and tiny ribbons seemed to be taunting her.

He frowned at her. 'You all right, Ruby?'

Tell him, the voice said again.

'Look, I know you've set your heart on having everything new, but I didn't think it would hurt to have them,' he said. 'Every little helps, eh? Besides, Arthur reckons they've hardly been worn. Turned out his baby was a right bruiser when he was born, hardly fitted any of his newborn clothes.' He picked up one of the matinee jackets and held it up. 'I reckon our baby's going to be the best-dressed kid in Bethnal Green, don't you?'

Chapter Thirteen

A tide of indignation had carried Helen all the way down Regent Street, across Piccadilly Circus and down Haymarket. By the time she'd stomped her way to Trafalgar Square, she was worn out but still fuming.

How dare her mother look down her nose at Charlie? She hadn't even taken the time to get to know him before she'd condemned him. It was so typical of her.

Helen plonked herself down on the steps under Nelson's column. It was a fine May day, and the fountains in Trafalgar Square sparkled in the late afternoon sunshine. People milled around, tourists and street vendors and newspaper sellers, their cries filling the air.

Helen watched a woman in a headscarf feeding pigeons from a brown paper bag. They gathered around her in a grey swarm, nudging and pecking each other to get closer. Every so often the rumble of a passing bus would send them fluttering up into the air, only to settle again a moment later. One even flew up to perch on top of the woman's head.

Usually Helen would have enjoyed watching the world go by, but today she could hardly bring herself to smile at the birds' antics. Her mother had cast a shadow over her whole day, taking away the last shred of happiness as she always did.

Then Helen saw Charlie crossing the road towards her, and her heart lifted. She ran towards him and hugged him fiercely.

'Steady on!' he laughed, straightening his hat. 'Blimey, I should be late more often.' He leaned down and kissed her. 'What's all this in aid of?'

'I'm just happy to see you, that's all.'

'I'm happy to see you, too.' He held her at arm's length. 'You look beautiful.'

'So do you.' He looked different, dressed in a raincoat, a rakish trilby on his golden head.

'I dunno about that!' An embarrassed blush rose in his cheeks. 'But I thought I'd smarten myself up a bit, since we're up west. What do you reckon? Do I look like a proper gent?'

His words touched a nerve with her. 'You're always a gentleman to me,' Helen replied, tight-lipped.

Charlie's smile turned quizzical. 'You all right, love?'

153

'I'm fine.' She took his arm. 'Do you mind if we don't have tea just yet? I'd rather do something else for a while.'

'What's the matter? Has shopping with your mum taken away your appetite?'

'Just a bit.' Helen looked away so he wouldn't see her grim expression.

They crossed the road to the National Gallery. It was an oasis of peace after the bustle of traffic and people in the square. Helen wandered from one vast echoing room to another, hand in hand with Charlie, quietly lost in the beautiful paintings.

'When are you going to tell me what's wrong?' he whispered, as they stood in the Impressionists room.

'There's nothing wrong.'

'Come off it. You've been staring at that vase of flowers for ten minutes.' He sent her a shrewd sidelong look. 'It's your mum, ain't it? Have you two had another falling out?'

'You could say that.' Helen was still tight-lipped. 'I told her I wasn't going to the ball.'

Charlie's laughter earned him a stern look from the curator sitting by the door. 'Blimey, was the dress that horrible?'

'It was nothing to do with the dress.'

'What was it, then?' He paused. 'Was it about me?'

'No,' she said. But her quick, unguarded glance gave her away.

'Yes, it was. I can see it in your face.' He sighed. 'What's this all about, Helen?'

'I don't want to talk about it. I'd rather forget

154

my mother, if you don't mind. We haven't got long together, and I don't want her to ruin it.'

'I reckon she's already done that, don't you?' Charlie reached out, turning her chin so she had no choice but to look into his smiling blue eyes. 'You can't hide anything from me, Helen. I know you too well. So you might as well tell me about it.'

They sat down on a bench in the middle of the hushed gallery, and in a whisper Helen explained what had happened.

'It was awful,' she said, unable to control her anger any longer. 'She made it sound as if she was doing you a favour by not inviting you.'

'She might be right,' Charlie agreed. 'Let's face it, I'm not the kind to get dressed up in a monkey suit. And it's not as if I can dance, is it?' he said wryly.

'It's not right at all! She's just being a bully as usual, trying to control everyone around her.' Helen's mouth set in defiance. 'Well, she needn't think she can control me. I've already told her I'm not going to her stupid ball, and that's final.'

Charlie was silent for a moment.

'And what good will that do?' he said at last.

Helen stole a glance at his profile. 'What do you mean?'

'It won't help the situation, will it? If you don't go, your mother will blame me. She'll say that I'm a bad influence, that I've turned you against her.'

'But that's not true! This is all her doing, not yours.'

'That doesn't matter. It's what she'll think, and

155

you know it.'

Helen buried her face in her hands. 'I don't know what to do,' she said helplessly. 'I've spent my whole life trying to please her, and now it feels as if she's asking me to choose between the two of you. How am I supposed to do that?'

'Shh, don't get upset.' She felt Charlie's arm around her, strong and reassuring. 'It'll all be all right. You wait and see.'

'How? How can it be all right?'

'These things have a habit of working themselves out.' He kissed her head. 'Now you need to swallow your pride and tell your mum you will go to her ball after all.'

'But–'

'No, listen to me. You go and enjoy yourself. You deserve a good night out.'

'It won't be a good night out without you.'

''Course it will. All your friends will be there, so you'll have fun. And I bet you'll be the belle of the ball, too.'

'Not if my mother has anything to do with it!'

'You'd look beautiful in anything.'

Helen looked at him through a blur of tears. If only her mother could hear Charlie now, she thought, surely she would realise how wonderful he was? 'Are you sure I should go? Because I'd really rather stay with you...'

'I told you, didn't I?' He kissed her. 'Now can we go and have some tea? You might have lost your appetite, but all this looking at pictures has got me gasping for a cuppa!'

Dora barely recognised her brother at first.

156

A small crowd had gathered around the corner of Columbia Road market, where a man stood on a soap box making a speech. In his well-pressed military uniform, with his polished boots, neatly clipped moustache and slicked-back hair, he could have been Sir Oswald Mosley himself.

'People of the East End,' he addressed the crowd in a powerful voice, 'we have lived under the yoke of the Jews for too long. English properties ... our very livelihoods ... have fallen into their hands.'

Dora let the speaker's words wash over her. Her attention was fixed on Peter. He stood with a dozen other men, forming a guard around the man who spoke. His black uniform gave him a menacing air she had never seen in him before. It was hard to remind herself that this stern-faced stranger was her beloved big brother, who had chalked a wicket on the wall and taught her how to play cricket, laughing as he caught her out time and time again.

'Over the years, the Jews have obtained a monopoly of the businesses in East London,' the orator continued. 'Unless the workers accept the terms offered to them, they get no job. And the labour of the relatives of Jewish bosses from Germany – the cheapest labour in London today – is used as a weapon to force down our wages to the lowest possible level.'

'Funny, I don't remember seeing him queuing up at the dock gates with the rest of us every morning!' a man in the crowd quipped.

'Look at him, in his fancy uniform. He don't look like he's had to do a day's work in his life,' another added. But Dora noticed the crowd had grown, as more and more people drifted away from the market stalls to listen to what the speaker had to say.

'We must rise up and reclaim what is rightfully ours,' he boomed. 'I urge you to take up the struggle against Jews and communists, otherwise you will witness your churches pulled down, your children's eyes torn out and nuns carried through the streets and raped!'

A shocked hush fell over the crowd. A few people cheered, while others looked at each other in horror. Peter and the other men scanned the crowd with narrowed, hostile eyes.

'Down with the Blackshirt troublemakers! Fascism means war!' a young man suddenly cried out from the other side of the crowd. Immediately, three or four of the Blackshirts plunged into the crowd after him. There was a scuffle, lots of shoving and shouting. A woman screamed out, 'Leave him alone! Don't hurt him!' Dora tried to go forward but the surging crowd held her back.

And then it was all over. The orator had stepped down from the soapbox and moved through the crowd shaking hands, his guard following him, handing out pamphlets.

She pushed her way to the front of the crowd as Peter approached. As he handed her a piece of paper, she said, 'No, thanks. I don't want your Fascist filth.'

He stopped dead, his scowl deepening. Then he recognised her. 'Dora? What are you doing here?'

'Well, I didn't come to listen to *him!*' She nodded towards the speaker who was moving away swiftly through the crowd. He seemed smaller and less imposing off his soapbox. Just a funny little man in a fancy uniform.

Peter glanced over his shoulder, then back at her. 'You ain't got no business being here.'

'It's a public place, ain't it? I can go where I like. Or do you and your bully-boy mates decide that too now?'

Peter's mouth tightened. 'What do you want, Dora?'

'For a start, I want to know what happened to that bloke who just shouted out.' She looked around her, searching for him. 'Did your mates beat him up?'

'He shouldn't have come here starting trouble.' Peter's chin lifted stubbornly. 'He was asking for it.'

'What about the people who came to your meeting the other night? Were they asking for it too?'

Peter paused for a moment. 'I suppose Joe Armstrong told you?' he said finally. 'He had no right to go running to you.'

'I'm glad he did,' Dora said. 'Because now I can put a stop to it.'

Peter's lip curled. 'And what are you going to do?'

'Try to talk some sense into you, make you see what's right.'

'This is right,' her brother insisted. 'And you're not going to stop me, because this is something I believe in.'

Dora was shocked. 'You mean, you believe in stirring up trouble, and hurting innocent people?'

'You heard what Mick Clarke said. We need to rise up, reclaim the East End.' Peter's green eyes

159

glittered with fervour. 'The government has been too weak, they're not going to do anything for us. We need to help ourselves.'

Dora stared at him in disgust. 'Listen to yourself, this isn't you. What's happened to you, Pete?'

Before he could answer, they were interrupted by another of the men. He towered head and shoulders over Peter, his black shirt taut against his burly frame. The silvery remains of a jagged scar ran from his ear to his chin.

'Aye-aye, Pete,' he greeted him. 'What would your missus say about you chatting up other women?'

'She's my sister,' Peter replied in a low voice.

'Oh, yeah?' He turned to Dora. Even when he was smiling, there was still a chill in his beady eyes. 'Come to join us, have you?'

'I'd rather die.'

The man reeled back as if she'd slapped him.

'Take no notice of her, Del.' Peter stepped in hastily. 'She didn't mean anything by it.'

'Yes, I did,' Dora said. 'I think you're a bunch of bullies and troublemakers. If you ask me, *you're* the ones ruining the East End, not the Jews!'

She was aware of Peter shifting uncomfortably to one side of her, but her unflinching gaze was fixed on the bigger man, Del.

He smiled nastily. 'I didn't know your family were a bunch of Jew-lovers, Pete?' he said softly.

'At least the Jews don't go round breaking people's windows and burning down their businesses.'

'You've got it all wrong, Dora,' Peter said. 'We're just taking back what's rightfully ours, protecting

160

our families—'

'I don't need protecting, thanks very much,' she retorted.

'I dunno about that, love,' Del growled, flexing his fingers into a fist. 'The East End can be a dangerous place for a young girl on her own.'

Dora faced him. 'Are you threatening me?'

'That's enough.' Peter stepped between them. 'Please, Dora, go home,' he pleaded. 'This is no place for you.'

'It's no place for you, either. Think of Mum ... think of your wife,' she begged. 'If you carry on like this you'll lose your job, and then where will you be?'

A shadow fell over them. Some other men had joined them.

'So what's it going to be, Pete?' Del challenged him. 'Are you going to do what your sister says, and run along like a good boy?'

Peter squared his shoulders, his pride wounded. 'You'd best go, Dora,' he muttered.

'But Pete—'

'You heard me. I told you to go.'

'And don't come back if you know what's good for you,' Del added.

Dora looked at him. 'I'll go where I please, thanks very much,' she said. 'These are my streets, not yours.'

Del sent her a level look. 'I wouldn't be so sure of that, love.'

Chapter Fourteen

'Honestly, Mum, I thought I'd had it for sure!'

Ruby leaned against the mangle in the Pikes' narrow, sunless strip of back yard, watching her mother hang sheets on the drooping washing line.

'What did I tell you?' Lettie replied through a mouthful of pegs. 'You should have come clean a long time ago. And as for getting into debt again–'

'Tell me something I don't know!' Ruby chewed on her thumbnail. 'The question is, what am I going to do now? I can't tell him I lied about the baby.'

'Shh!' Lettie shot a quick glance over her shoulder at Danny Riley, hunched on top of the coal bunker. 'You don't know who's listening.'

'Oh, take no notice of him,' Ruby dismissed. 'You know he's got no more sense than a cabbage. He can't understand half what's being said to him at the best of times.' She folded her arms across her body, shivering in spite of the warm May day. 'Nick will go mad,' she said. 'He made me promise I wasn't hiding anything else from him. I can't very well tell him I pretended to be pregnant, can I?'

Lettie bent down stiffly to pull a pillowcase from the basket at her feet. 'Can't you tell him it was a false alarm?'

'For four months! Don't make me laugh!'

'It can happen. We had a woman come into Gynae, swore she was six months gone. Size of a house, she was. Turned out it was what they call a phantom pregnancy.'

'That's no use to me, is it?' Ruby snapped. Usually she liked hearing her mum's stories about life as a ward maid at the Nightingale, especially when there was some juicy gossip involved. But today she wasn't in the mood. 'I need something a bit better than a phantom pregnancy if I'm going to stop Nick packing his bags.' A sudden breeze caught the sheet, slapping it wetly in her face. She pushed it away impatiently. 'You should have seen him with those clothes, Mum. Pleased as punch, he was. He held those mittens like he was holding his baby's hand.'

'I dunno what he was thinking of, bringing them home in the first place,' Lettie grumbled, passing her the end of a sheet to fold. 'Everyone knows it's bad luck.'

A train rumbled overhead, shaking the ground under their feet. Danny Riley curled up, arms covering his face.

'Look at him, the daft sod!' Lettie laughed. 'What's the matter, Danny? Worried the train's going to fall on your head?'

'Leave him alone.' Ruby was pensive as she helped her mother peg the sheet on the line. 'What was that you were saying about bad luck?'

'It's bad luck to bring anything for the baby into the house before it's born. I thought everyone knew that?'

'Nick doesn't,' Ruby said slowly.

'Well, I daresay it's just an old wives' tale, but

163

Mrs Prosser's eldest brought a pram into the house and one of her twins was born dead.' She shook her head. 'Such a shame, it was.'

'I'll bet,' Ruby said, her thoughts already elsewhere.

Her mother stopped pegging and turned to look at her. 'Come on, then. Out with it,' she said.

'Out with what?'

'I know that look, my girl. You're up to something.' Lettie regarded her through narrowed eyes. 'If you're having another one of your ideas, I only hope it's better than the last one.'

'Oh, it is.' Ruby smiled. 'But I'm going to need your help...'

Dora was surprised to see Esther Gold in Dr Adler's consulting room first thing in the morning.

'It's just a cut really,' she explained apologetically as he unwound the bloodsoaked strip of sheeting. 'I tried to sort it out myself, but I can't seem to stop the bleeding.'

'Miss Gold?' Dora said.

She looked up. 'Dora! How lovely to see you.'

Dr Adler glanced from one to the other. 'Do you two know each other?'

'I used to work at Miss Gold's clothing factory before I came here,' Dora explained.

'My father's clothing factory. I'm just the supervisor.' Esther smiled affectionately at her. 'Dora used to be one of our best machinists. But I always knew she was too good for factory life.'

'It was you who talked me into applying to be a nurse.' If it hadn't been for Esther encouraging her, Dora would never have found the courage to take that first step.

'Yes, and my father hasn't let me forget it since!' Esther looked rueful. She was in her late-thirties, big-boned and solid. Her untidy mass of black curls did nothing to soften her strong features, but her dark brown eyes twinkled with kindness.

Dr Adler finished unwinding the bandage, and Dora had to bite her lip to stop herself crying out. The cut was painfully deep, exposing raw, glistening tissue.

'That looks nasty.' He sounded calm and professional as always. 'You're lucky you didn't sever a ligament.' He turned to Dora. 'Clean this up for me, Nurse.'

Dora quickly set about preparing the warm carbolic lotion. 'I'm afraid this might sting a bit,' she said.

Esther gave a hiss of pain as Dora touched the cotton-wool swab to her wound. 'Sorry,' she said. 'I'll try to be quick. How did you cut yourself so badly?'

'Broken glass.' Esther kept her eyes fixed on the wound. 'It was all over the factory floor when I opened up this morning. I wanted to get rid of it quickly, before my father saw it. More haste, less speed.' She looked rueful.

'Someone smashed your windows? Who'd want to do a thing like that?'

She saw the quick glance that passed between Esther and Dr Adler.

'The same people who tried to set fire to our neighbour's shop, I expect,' Esther said.

Dora finished cleaning her wound and took the

165

bowl over to the sink while Dr Adler set to work stitching. She had a sudden, awful vision of Peter, roaming the streets. Surely he would never do such a thing?

She shut out the thought from her mind and listened to them talking instead. It turned out Esther and Dr Adler had several friends in common, and they were soon gossiping over who'd died and who'd just got married.

He finished stitching her up and sat back. 'There,' he said. 'All done. And a beautiful job too, if I say so myself.'

Esther inspected her hand. 'Very nice,' she agreed. 'With stitching like that, you can have a job at our factory any time.'

'Did you hear that, Nurse? Miss Gold says I could be a machinist.'

'You should be honoured,' Dora smiled back.

'I might even put you on embroidery,' Esther said.

As she started to get off the bed, Dr Adler stepped forward and grasped her arm. 'Take it steady,' he advised. 'You have lost a lot of blood. Perhaps you'd like to lie down and rest for a while?'

'Thank you, but I need to get back to my father. I don't like to leave him on his own for too long.' Esther's dark eyes were troubled.

'You'll need to come back in eight days to have the stitches removed,' Dr Adler said. 'And if there are any signs of infection, come back and see me straight away.'

'I will. And thank you again.'

'You're most welcome.'

There was a long pause while they stood staring at each other. As Dora busied herself tidying the consulting room, she noticed the look Esther gave Dr Adler from under her lashes. If Dora didn't know better, she would have sworn her former boss was flirting.

After Esther left, Dr Adler sat on the bed for a moment, staring at the door.

'She seems like a nice woman,' he commented, a bit too casually.

'She is. Like I said, I would never have been brave enough to apply here if she hadn't pushed me into it. She even gave me her *hamsa* for good luck when I came for my interview.'

Dora still had the tiny silver hand charm tucked in her drawer at the nurses' home. It was her most treasured possession.

'Is that right?' Dr Adler said. 'In that case, she must be a very nice woman indeed.'

The waiting-room benches had filled by the time Dora had finished cleaning up. A couple with a young child stood at the booking-in counter, but Penny Willard was on the other side of the room, serving cups of tea to two policemen. Dora's heart sank when she saw that one of them was Joe Armstrong.

She hurried to the booking-in counter, hoping he wouldn't see her. But he was there before she had picked up the next patient's set of notes.

'Hello, stranger,' he grinned at her.

'Hello, Joe.'

She went to move past him, but he stepped in front of her. 'We had to bring another prisoner

167

in. He's with the doctor now.'

'Not another suspected appendicitis?'

Joe shook his head. 'This one fell over in the cell.'

'Must have been a bad fall.'

'It was. Very nasty.'

'I'm surprised it took two of you to bring him in?'

Joe grinned sheepishly. 'You're right, he was Tom's prisoner really. I just tagged along, hoping to see you.'

He moved closer. Dora stepped out of his reach, glancing around the crowded waiting room. 'Look Joe, we're a bit busy, so—'

'Nurse Willard's been telling me all about the Founder's Day Ball. Between you and me, I think she was hinting for me to take her.'

'Maybe you should.'

He frowned. 'I'd rather go with you.'

Dora sighed. 'I've already told you—'

'You're not ready to start courting. Yes, I know.' He nodded. 'But we could still go dancing, couldn't we? What's the harm in that?'

She looked up into his clear green eyes. The harm was that he might get the wrong idea. 'I probably won't even go,' she said. 'It's just a do for the bigwigs, anyway.'

'That's not what Nurse Willard says. She reckons all the nurses are going. She made it sound like the social event of the year. And Tom says Katie's asked him to go with her.' Joe cocked his head. 'Go on, it'll be a laugh. You deserve a good night out.'

'I'll see,' Dora said.

'So is that a date, then?'

'I said, I'll see.'

'I'll get us two tickets.'

'Joe, I don't want–'

'When you've quite finished, Doyle, Dr Adler needs assistance with his next patient.' Sister Percival interrupted before she had a chance to finish.

'Oops, looks like you're wanted.' Joe grinned. 'I'll let you know when I've got those tickets.'

'Joe, listen–'

'Doyle!' Sister Percival cut her off. 'Really, it's bad enough that Willard spends half her time flirting with anything in trousers, without you joining in! I expected more sense from you, I really did.'

'But I wasn't...'

'I hope you're not arguing with me, Doyle?' Sister Percival eyed her severely. 'Now go and help Dr Adler with his projectile vomiting.'

She sighed. 'Yes, Nurse.'

Dora stared at Joe in frustration as he sauntered off. He turned and winked at her over his shoulder. How much more did she have to do to convince him she wasn't interested?

'Dislocated shoulder,' Tom said as they left hospital later without their prisoner. The man had been admitted to the ward for treatment. 'It was bloody lucky he didn't break his arm or fracture his skull.'

'Lucky for him, you mean?'

'And for you. If he tells the doctor how he got injured like that...'

'Who's going to believe the word of a tea leaf against mine?' Joe sneered. 'Besides, he deserved it. That'll teach him to get lippy with me.' He

169

caught his friend's wary look. 'Oh, come on! What are you staring at me like that for? We all give them a dig now and then. How else are we meant to get any respect?'

'There's getting respect and there's laying into someone for no reason,' Tom said. 'You go too far sometimes, and you know it.'

'Yeah, well, it's done now, ain't it?'

Joe strode off. Tom hurried to catch up with him. 'What's got into you? You've had the hump ever since we left the hospital.'

'I'm all right.'

'No, you ain't.' Tom sent him a sideways look. 'It's that girl Dora, ain't it? What's the matter? Did she give you the brush off again?'

'She was busy,' Joe mumbled.

'Avoiding you, more like!' Tom gave him a friendly nudge. 'You must be losing your touch, mate!'

'And you're fighting the girls off, aren't you?' Joe snarled back.

'At least Katie's keen.'

'A bit too keen, if you ask me,' Joe muttered under his breath.

Tom stopped. 'And what's that supposed to mean?'

'Nothing.'

'Come on, out with it. Are you saying my Katie's easy?'

'Why not? You've said it yourself often enough.'

'That's different. I ain't having you insulting my girl.'

Joe swung round, squaring up to him, pent-up tension scorching through his veins.

170

'Go on,' Tom taunted softly. 'What are you going to do, lay me out like you did that poor bloke in the cells? I don't reckon the sergeant would buy two accidents in one day, do you?'

Joe looked at his friend's scowling face and felt his anger ebbing away. What was he doing? Another second and he would have taken a swing at his best mate.

'Sorry,' he mumbled, turning away. 'Take no notice of me. I'm just fed up, that's all.'

That was what Dora Doyle did to him. She got under his skin like no other girl he'd ever met.

'Frustrated, more like,' Tom said wisely.

'You could be right.' Joe couldn't understand it. He wasn't bad-looking, he tried to treat her right – better than Tommy treated Katie, anyway – and yet Dora wouldn't let him anywhere near her. It was driving him mad.

'When are you going to give up, pal? Just admit she ain't interested?'

'I can't.' That was the problem. Joe didn't like to lose. That was what made him such a mean fighter in the ring, because he couldn't stand the idea of being beaten. He would do whatever it took to win, even if it earned him a bad reputation.

And that was how he felt about Dora, too. The thought of not having her, of Tom and the other lads at the station all knowing he'd failed, was too humiliating for Joe to contemplate.

'What you need is someone to take your mind off her. Like that Nurse Willard, for instance. She's a good-looking girl. And she definitely likes you,' Tom told him.

'I'm not interested.' Joe shrugged. Without being

vain, he knew girls like Nurse Willard were two a penny, especially for a good-looking bloke like him. But Dora was a real challenge. And the more she pushed him away, the more he wanted her.

He wasn't ready to give up on her. Not without a fight.

Chapter Fifteen

It was a sunny Saturday afternoon in June, and Helen should have been spending it with Charlie. But that morning he'd telephoned the nurses' home and left a message to say that something had happened and he wouldn't be able to see her after all.

She then planned to spend the afternoon catching up with her revision, but Dora and Millie both had a few hours off and had persuaded her to join them for a walk in Victoria Park.

'It's such a lovely afternoon, it's a shame to waste it locked up indoors,' Millie had said.

Helen eyed the textbooks, teetering in a pile beside her bed. 'I really should get on with some studying...'

'You know what Miss Hanley always says. Fresh air is good for the brain!' Dora reminded her.

Helen was glad they had persuaded her. It was a gloriously sunny day and the park was full of families and couples strolling arm in arm. The rose bushes were in full bloom, their exquisite fragrance filling the air. The happy clamour of children playing mingled with distant sounds from the brass band on the bandstand.

Charlie would have loved it, Helen thought. She couldn't imagine what might be so important that he would miss out on spending time with her.

But at least she had Millie and Dora for company. She had been so busy in Theatre and studying for her Finals, she had hardly spent any time with her room mates recently.

They turned away from the bandstand and headed towards a grove of tall poplar trees, their dark spikes reaching up into the cloudless blue sky. To their right, on the field, an army of women, all dressed in white vests and black shorts, stood in regimented lines, swinging Indian clubs above their heads. Every eye was fixed on a woman who stood in front of them, barking instructions like a sergeant major.

'What on earth is going on there?' Helen asked.

'The Women's League of Health and Beauty,' Dora replied. 'Sister Percival from Casualty told us about it. She and her friend Marjorie often come over here to exercise. She's ever so keen.'

'Rather her than me,' Helen said. 'After heaving patients around all day, the last thing I'd want to do is spend my time off flinging clubs about.'

'What do you reckon, Benedict?' Dora grinned. 'Shall we join in?'

Millie looked up vaguely. 'I'm sorry?'

'Blimey, you were miles away!' Dora laughed.

'I suppose I must have been.' Millie smiled back, but Helen could see her blue eyes were troubled.

173

'Are you all right?' she said. 'You've been very quiet.'

Millie hesitated. 'It's nothing.'

'You've been saying that for ages, but we can tell you've got something on your mind,' Dora said. 'Come on, out with it.'

'Promise not to laugh?' Millie regarded them apprehensively.

'Just spit it out!'

She took a deep breath, and they could see her gathering her thoughts. 'We had a patient on Everett a few weeks ago, a gypsy. She said she could tell people's fortunes...'

'O'Hara told me about her,' Dora put in. 'Didn't she say a patient was going to die?'

'That's right.' Millie nodded. 'Everyone was in a frightful state about it.'

Helen guessed what was coming next. 'Please don't tell me you let her tell your fortune?' she sighed.

'I didn't want to. Hollins made me do it.'

'I might have known she'd be involved!' Dora muttered.

'So what did the gypsy tell you?' Helen asked Millie.

'She told me ... Sebastian was going to die.'

'What?' Helen and Dora both stopped in their tracks at the same time.

'Those weren't her exact words. But she did say the next time I saw him, I'd be wearing mourning black. And that's the same thing, isn't it?'

Millie looked from one to the other, her blue eyes huge with apprehension. Helen glanced across at Dora's grim expression.

'And you've been worrying about that all this time?'

'Wouldn't you?'

Helen shook her head. 'You mustn't take any notice of her. It's all a load of nonsense.'

'Tremayne's right,' Dora added. 'It's all made up.'

'Are you sure?' Millie's voice was tremulous with hope. 'She seemed awfully convincing.'

'They always do,' Dora said. 'Half the women in my street used to say they could read tea leaves, but most of what they said was a load of old twaddle.'

Millie bit her lip. 'I wish I could believe that,' she said. 'But she predicted Mrs Allen was going to die...'

'It's a hospital,' Helen pointed out. 'Someone's bound to die occasionally, aren't they? She probably overheard the doctors talking.'

Millie looked pensive, taking this in. 'Do you really think she might have made it all up?'

'I'd bet my next week's wages on it,' Dora said firmly.

'You mustn't worry about it any more,' Helen said. 'Sebastian will come home safe and sound, you'll see.'

'I hope you're right.' Millie looked at them, shame-faced.

'I suppose I have been a bit silly, haven't I?'

'You, silly? Never!' Helen grinned at Dora.

'No suppose about it,' Dora said. 'Right, now we've sorted that out, let's have an ice cream to celebrate.'

They bought cornets from the hokey-pokey

man on his bicycle. Then they skirted the boating lake while they ate them, and Helen told them about her mother not wanting Charlie to go to the Founder's Day Ball.

They were both suitably outraged.

'That's awful! Why would she do such a thing?' Millie said.

'Because she doesn't think he's good enough for me.'

'But he's an absolute angel, everyone knows that.'

'Try telling my mother,' Helen said. 'She won't give Charlie a chance. She barely speaks to him if she can help it.'

'You could try locking them in a broom cupboard together, and not let her out until they've made friends?' Millie suggested.

Helen and Dora looked at each other, neither of them quite sure if she was serious. There was no telling with Millie Benedict.

'I suppose that's an idea,' Helen said slowly. 'But somehow I don't think it would work.'

'Dora! Dora!'

She stopped, her ice cream halfway to her mouth.

It was Millie who turned around to see where the voice was coming from. 'I think someone's trying to get your attention,' she said.

Helen looked over her shoulder, squinting into the sunshine. Two young men were approaching them. She recognised the taller one with dark curly hair, but not the pale, slight boy shambling along beside him. 'Isn't that Nick Riley, from the hospital?' she said.

'So it is,' Millie said. 'But who's that with him?'

'His brother Danny.' Dora's voice was flat.

'Do you know them?' Millie asked.

'I used to live next door to them.' Dora started to walk on, but Helen and Millie stayed put.

'Don't you want to talk to your friends?' Millie asked.

Before Dora had a chance to reply, the pale-haired boy rushed up to her. His brother held back, slowing his steps.

'All right, Danny?' Dora's smile was forced. 'How are you?'

'Nick's t-taking me on the boat!' The young man's eager smile lit up his face, transforming his odd features.

'That's nice for you, love.'

Nick Riley caught up with them. He nodded a curt greeting to Millie and Helen, but barely spared a glance for Dora.

'Come on, Dan, we'd best go. They're letting all the passengers on, and we don't want to get left behind.' He took hold of his brother's sleeve, but Danny held back.

'W-Why don't you come with us?' he asked Dora.

'No, love, I can't. I'm here with my friends.'

'Th-They can c-come too, can't they, Nick?'

'I don't think so, mate.'

'Oh, but I'd love to!' Millie chimed in. 'I haven't been on a pleasure cruiser for ages. And it's such a lovely day. Oh, do let's!'

Helen caught Dora's tense expression. 'We really should be getting back,' she ventured, but Millie was having none of it.

177

'Nonsense, we have lots of time! Now, where do we buy the tickets?' She had already turned and was picking her way down the path towards the boat house.

Helen glanced back at Nick. 'Looks like we don't have any choice,' she said apologetically. 'I hope you don't mind?'

He shrugged his broad shoulders. 'It's a free country,' he muttered, his expression as tight as Dora's.

The only ones who seemed happy about the trip were Millie and Nick's brother. After clinging to Dora's hand shyly for a minute or two after they set sail, Danny had slowly shuffled towards Helen and Millie as they stood at the rail, looking out over the lake.

'Hello, young man,' Millie greeted him cheerfully. 'Come to look at the ducks with us, have you?'

She chatted easily to him, pointing out the various birds as they bobbed along beside the boat and making up stories about them. Danny listened avidly to her every word, gazing up at her enchanted, as if he had never seen such a glorious creature in his whole life. Helen smiled to herself. It looked as if Millie Benedict had won another admirer.

But Danny's brother wasn't so easily won over. Helen watched him as he sat on the narrow bench, his gaze fixed on the far horizon. Dora sat at the other end of the bench, her hands folded in her lap, gazing in the opposite direction. Both still as statues, both of them looking at anything and everything except each other.

178

And yet even from the other side of the deck, Helen could feel the tension crackling between them, like a ribbon of electricity binding them together.

As soon as the boat docked, Nick was on his feet, springing across the gap between the side of the boat and dry land, even before the crew had a chance to lay down the gangplank. He waited on the bank to help his brother off, guiding his unsteady steps across the narrow strip of wood.

'You're all right, mate. I've got you,' he said.

Millie stepped up next, putting out her gloved hand for him to help her.

'Would you mind?' she asked.

Nick hesitated for a moment, then took her hand and guided her across. Helen followed, grateful for his strong, steady grip as she tottered down the gangplank.

Then it was Dora's turn. 'It's all right, I can manage,' she said shortly.

Nick didn't need telling twice. He dropped his hand to his side and stepped back to let her pass.

Helen watched them. They were doing everything in their power not to touch or look at each other. Which could only mean they had something to hide.

'We're h-having tea now,' Danny stammered, breaking into her troubled thoughts. 'C-can you come?'

Millie's face brightened, but Helen got in before her. 'We really must get back,' she said.

Danny's slack mouth turned down in disappointment.

'Tell you what,' Millie said, 'why don't I buy

you a toffee apple instead? Come on, let's go to the kiosk.'

'Looks like she's won him over!' Helen smiled as Millie took the young man's arm and marched him down the path.

'I'd best go with them, make sure they don't get back on that boat!' Nick muttered.

'Thanks again for letting us come on your excursion,' Helen called out, but he was already striding away from them, catching up with Millie and his brother.

Helen watched him go. She didn't need to look at Dora to know she was watching Nick too, her gaze fixed on him as if she couldn't drag her eyes away.

Helen wondered if she should say something, but one look at her friend's wretched expression and she knew it would be wiser to stay silent. Private as she was, the last thing Dora would want was anyone to guess her secret.

Chapter Sixteen

On Saturday afternoon Constance Tremayne was in her rose garden, inspecting the blooms with her husband.

'What a marvellous display we have this year.' Timothy Tremayne bent to breathe in their scent. 'I think all the rain we had earlier has done the garden good.'

'And brought out the greenfly.' Frowning,

Constance examined the underside of a leaf.

'This is my particular favourite. It's called Rambling Rector – rather appropriate, don't you think?' Timothy chuckled. 'I'm sure it must be Morley's little joke.'

'Morley takes advantage of your good nature,' Constance snapped. 'He clearly hasn't kept up with the dead heading at all. I sometimes wonder what we pay him for, apart from pulling up the odd weed and drinking tea in the kitchen with the maid.' She took out her secateurs and savagely snipped at a wilting bloom, then looked up and caught her husband's eye. 'What?'

Timothy Tremayne gazed at her with affectionate amusement. 'You know, my dear, sometimes I think if you reached the gates of heaven themselves, all you would probably notice is that they needed a lick of paint.'

Constance bristled. 'I just like to see a job done properly, that's all.' She straightened up, and caught sight of a lone figure in the distance, coming down the lane towards them.

'Now who's this?' She frowned with irritation. They must be coming to the Vicarage because it was at the end of a country lane and no one ventured that way unless it was on church business. 'I do hope it isn't Mr Gregory again,' she sighed. The elderly churchwarden always kept Timothy talking for ages. 'His visits are so tiresome.'

'Mr Gregory is very lonely since he lost his wife,' her husband pointed out. 'He likes the company.'

But it wasn't Mr Gregory. The man walked with a limp, leaning heavily on a stick. As he approached, he took off his cap and Constance caught a flash of red-gold hair. She let out a gasp of dismay.

'What's *he* doing here?' she murmured. But her husband was already ambling down to the gate to meet the visitor.

'Charlie, what a delightful surprise! Is Helen with you?'

'I'm afraid not, Sir.' Charlie shot Constance a glance. 'I hope you don't mind me dropping in like this?'

'Of course not, old chap, we're very happy to see you.'

'Although you might have telephoned first to let us know you were coming?' Constance put in.

Charlie's smile faltered. 'If it isn't convenient, I can always come back...'

'Of course it's convenient,' Timothy interrupted before Constance could reply. 'Come in, come in.' He pulled open the gate. 'I'm just sorry we couldn't order you a taxi from the station. Surely you didn't walk all the way?'

'It wasn't too far,' Charlie assured him cheerfully as he walked up the path. 'Besides it's such a glorious day, and it's not often I get to breathe in country air.'

Constance pulled off her gardening gloves, her afternoon ruined. 'I hope he's not going to stay long,' she hissed to her husband.

'My dear, he is a guest. At least let him take his coat off,' Timothy replied mildly.

'It's very poor form for a guest to invite themselves unannounced,' Constance whispered. 'What if we'd been entertaining?'

Her husband looked amused. 'We rarely do.'

'Nevertheless, it might have been very embarrassing,' Constance insisted.

She was still in a bitter mood as she instructed Mary, their maid of all work, to make some tea. 'Doesn't he realise this is not the East End?' she muttered, as much to herself as to the maid. 'We don't just drop in and out of each other's houses without an invitation. It's simply not good manners. Don't use the best cups, Mary. Where are the ones we'd put aside for the church rummage sale?'

She tarried in the kitchen for as long as possible on the pretence of making sure Mary made the tea properly, until she couldn't put off seeing Charlie any longer.

She was shocked when she joined the men in the drawing room to find Charlie with a screwdriver in his hand, adjusting the lid of the piano.

'What are you doing?' she demanded, horrified.

Timothy looked up at her. 'Charlie is fixing the piano lid for us, my dear. You've been saying for weeks we should do something about it before it crashed down on someone's fingers.'

'I meant we should call in a local carpenter,' Constance said tightly.

'No need, it's a quick enough job.' Charlie put down the screwdriver and stepped back. 'There, that should do it. Try it now.'

Timothy opened and closed the lid a few times to test it. 'Perfect,' he said. 'Look, Constance, you can practise your Chopin without fear now.'

'Marvellous.' Her tense smile made her jaw ache.

'I'll take a look at that desk drawer of yours too, if you like?' Charlie offered. 'The one you said

183

keeps sticking?'

'Would you?' Timothy's eyes shone with gratitude. 'I say, Constance, isn't it grand to have a useful chap in the family?'

Family! Constance bristled silently. Not if she could help it.

'Really, Charlie, we shall be asking you to use the tradesmen's entrance soon!' She said it lightly, but knew her barb had hit its mark when she saw the hurt look in his eyes. 'Now, shall we have some tea?' she offered. 'Or would you rather have it in the kitchen, with the other staff?'

'Let's have it here.' Her husband spoke hastily. 'Then Charlie can tell us why he's come to see us.'

'As a matter of fact, it's Mrs Tremayne I've come to see. I wondered if we might have a word in private?'

'I hardly think...' Constance was about to refuse but Timothy cut her off.

'Of course, dear boy,' he said. 'It's quite all right, I have a sermon to finish.'

'You don't have to leave.' Constance shot her husband a beseeching look, but either he didn't notice or he chose to ignore it.

Then she was alone with Charlie. Constance busied herself pouring the tea and planning her tactics. She already had a notion of why he had come, and wanted to be ready for him.

'I suppose Helen sent you?' she said, handing him his cup.

'She doesn't know I'm here.'

That was something, at any rate. Constance didn't like to think of her daughter being involved in anything so ill-mannered.

184

She dropped a lump of sugar into her cup and stirred it. 'Well, I can't think what on earth you would want to talk to me about.'

'Are you sure about that, Mrs Tremayne?'

His direct blue gaze flustered her. Her spoon rattled against the side of her cup. 'If you're talking about the ball...'

'I don't care about the ball,' he dismissed. 'But I do care about Helen. She's very upset.'

Constance stared at him, sitting there in his shabby suit, clutching one of her second-best teacups in his work-roughened hands. 'And so she should be.' She pulled herself upright. 'She said some very unkind things.'

'So did you, from what I hear.'

She coloured under his frank gaze. 'I stand by everything I said.'

'I daresay you do.' Charlie smiled. 'But I haven't come to pick a fight with you, Mrs Tremayne. I know you've got your opinion of me, same as I've got my opinion of you. But it's Helen I'm worried about. Your behaviour is hurting her, and I want it to stop.'

'My behaviour? How dare you!' Anger scorched through her veins. 'You've known my daughter for all of five minutes, and now you come in here and lay the law down to me?' She set her cup down. 'I think you should leave.'

'I'm not going anywhere until I've said my piece. Sorry, Mrs Tremayne, but you can't order me about like you do everyone else.'

Constance gasped. 'And you wonder why I want my daughter to have nothing to do with you?' she spluttered. 'You are rude, ill bred...'

185

'...and *you* never listen to anyone else!' Charlie cut her off. Constance stared at him, shocked into silence. She couldn't remember anyone ever daring to raise their voice to her.

She could see him fighting for control, trying to calm himself down. 'I haven't come to argue with you,' Charlie said quietly. 'That's the last thing I want. I actually came here to see if we could sort it out between us, try to get along for Helen's sake.' He put down his teacup carefully. 'I know you've got a good heart, and that you love your daughter. And I know you don't mean to hurt her, but that's what's happening. All Helen wants to do is to please you, and you making her choose between us is tearing her apart. It's just not fair on her.'

Constance winced. Charlie had touched a nerve, but she was determined not to show it.

'Surely my daughter should be the one to say all this?' she said coldly.

'She's tried, but you won't listen. You always cut her off because it's not what you want to hear.'

'That's not true!'

'You see? You're doing it now.'

She looked at him, as if seeing him for the first time. Charlie was handsome, with his golden hair, firm chin and candid blue eyes. She didn't blame Helen for falling for him. But that didn't change the fact that he was eminently unsuitable for her.

Constance had fallen for a handsome face herself once, and looked how that had turned out.

'It was Helen who walked out on me, the last time we met,' she pointed out.

'I'm not surprised, from what she told me.'

'I was buying her a dress. I thought it would be a treat for her.'

'No, you were choosing one for her. Just like you've chosen everything else. But Helen's over twenty-one now. She's a grown woman, and entitled to make her own decisions.'

'And what if she makes the wrong one?'

Charlie smiled wryly. 'Like choosing me for a boyfriend, you mean?'

If he'd expected her to deny it, he had another think coming. 'I'm sure you're a very nice young man, but you're not right for my daughter. Helen could do a lot better.'

'I daresay you're right.' Charlie sounded resigned, almost weary. 'But I love your daughter with all my heart. Surely that counts for as much as knowing which knife and fork to use?' He leaned forward, appealing to her. 'Please, Mrs Tremayne, I'm begging you. I know we'll never be the best of friends, but can't you find it in your heart to get along with me, for Helen's sake?'

Constance turned her gaze towards the French windows and out over the rose garden. The June sunshine was disappearing behind a cloud, turning the garden grey.

'It will rain soon,' she said. 'You'd best be getting back to the station, if you don't want to be caught in the downpour. I'll get Mary to see you out.' She reached for the bell.

'So that's it?' Charlie said. 'There's nothing I can do to build bridges between us?'

'Yes, there is something you can do.' She turned back to him, steely-eyed. 'You can stay away from

187

my daughter. If you really love Helen, you'll walk away from her and stop dragging her down.'

Charlie's mouth firmed. 'That's not going to happen.'

'In that case, there is nothing more to say.' Constance turned her face away again. The first drops of rain were already pattering against the windows.

There was a soft knock on the door and Mary appeared. 'You rang, Madam?'

'Our guest is leaving.'

Constance held herself rigid as she heard him stand up. Charlie reached the door and she was about to let out her indrawn breath when he turned and said, 'You know what's so sad, Mrs Tremayne? That you always have to be right. That's what's going to come between you and Helen in the end, not me. As far as I'm concerned, there's room for all of us in her life. And Helen needs you as much as she needs me.'

Constance laced her fingers tightly in her lap; 'And you can tell my daughter I will be waiting for an apology for her behaviour,' she called after him.

Charlie gave a sad little laugh. 'Typical, Mrs T. You always have to have the last word, don't you?'

Timothy returned to the drawing room just as the front door banged shut. 'Has Charlie gone?' He looked disappointed.

'He had to catch his train.'

'Surely you didn't let him go out in this weather? We could have telephoned for a taxi.'

'You heard what he said. He appreciates the fresh air.' Constance looked at the rain, which

188

was falling steadily now.

'What a pity it was such a flying visit.' Timothy shook his head. 'He's such a nice young man.'

'If you say so.' Constance's lips tightened. She changed the subject. 'How are you getting on with your sermon?'

'Oh, very well, thank you. I thought I would tackle the subject of courage, using the example of Daniel.' He smiled. 'Such a wonderful story, don't you think? A young man who walks into a den of lions for what he believes in.'

Constance looked sharply at her husband, but Timothy Tremayne's blandly smiling expression gave nothing away.

Chapter Seventeen

'Five pounds,' the woman in the shop said.

Nick whistled. 'You sure about that, missus? It's a pram I'm after, not a Bentley!'

The woman pursed her painted lips. She had pearl-grey hair piled like candy floss on top of her head, and a hoity-toity accent that was as false as the pearls around her throat.

'It's a Silver Cross, the best pram you can buy,' she said. 'The Duchess of York herself used this one for the little princesses. But if it's too expensive, we do have cheaper models. Or sir could always find something secondhand in the market...'

'No, thanks.' Nick stiffened at the insult. No

kid of his was going anywhere in a secondhand pram. Only the best for his son or daughter, even if it did cost a bomb.

He crouched down and spun one of the wheels. He wasn't an expert on prams, but this one looked all right. Handsome, in fact. He could just imagine Ruby pushing it around Victoria Park on a sunny Sunday afternoon, with him at her side. They would stroll by the lake, so their little one could look at the ducks. He'd buy them ice creams from the hokey-pokey man, and feed it to the baby bit by bit...

'So is sir interested or what?' The woman interrupted his daydream, her accent slipping a fraction.

Nick straightened up. 'Well, if it's good enough for royalty, I s'pose it'll be good enough for us.' He reached into his pocket and pulled out his wallet. 'A fiver, you say?'

'Plus two shillings for storage and delivery.'

'I don't want storage or delivery. I'll take it with me.'

The woman's pencilled eyebrows rose. 'Are you sure? Most of our customers prefer to have their pram delivered after the baby's born.'

'I said, I'll take it with me,' Nick insisted firmly. He couldn't wait to see Ruby's face when he showed it to her.

Shafts of pain shot down his back as he pushed the pram along Mile End Road. He'd had two fights that week, and he was feeling it in his bruised muscles.

'I warned you, didn't I?' Nick's trainer Jimmy had been unsympathetic as he'd cleaned him up

190

after last night's bout. 'Carry on like this and you'll be in no shape for a title fight, you mark my words.'

'I need the money.' Nick pressed on a wet towel to staunch the blood flowing from his nose. He would never have let a blow like that touch him if he hadn't been so worn out. Jimmy was right, he was beginning to lose his edge.

Kids were playing Tin Can Copper on the green in front of the flats. Nick smiled as he passed them. One day it would be his nipper playing out here. He was glad Ruby had dug her heels in and insisted they should move. Victory House was a much better place to bring up a child than the mucky tenements of Griffin Street.

Every muscle in his body protested as he lugged the heavy pram all the way up to the third floor, bumping it up each stair. A group of women gossiping on the stairwell of the second floor stopped to smile at him.

'New pram, love? That's a beauty, that is.'

As he walked away, he heard one of them say, 'I bet his wife's a happy woman.'

'I bet she is,' her friend agreed. 'Those prams cost a fortune.'

'I wasn't talking about the pram!' the woman cackled.

Smiling to himself, Nick parked the pram in the walkway outside the flat and let himself in. There was a strong smell of carbolic in the air. Ruby must have had a right old spring clean, he thought.

'Ruby?' he called again. 'Are you in? I've got something to show you.'

The bedroom door opened. Nick turned, his

191

smile fading when he saw his mother-in-law standing there.

His heart sank. Trust Lettie to be round, sticking her nose in and spoiling his surprise. Ruby saw more of her mum now than she had when they lived under the same roof.

'You here again?' he said, shrugging off his jacket. 'I dunno why you don't just move in and save yourself the shoe leather.'

He waited for the biting retort, but it didn't come.

'Are you going to put the kettle on, or what? You might as well make yourself useful while you're–' He saw her stricken expression and broke off. 'What is it? What's happened?'

Lettie stepped towards him, wringing her bony hands. 'Oh, Nick, it's Ruby,' she whimpered. 'She's lost the baby!'

She lay curled up like a child on top of the bedspread.

'Ruby!' He sank down to his knees beside the bed, all the strength suddenly gone out of him. 'Are you all right? What's happened?'

She turned her head to face him, and he was shocked by how pale she looked. Her make-up was streaked in dark rivulets down her ashen cheeks.

He went numb inside. 'When did it...'

'This afternoon,' Lettie answered for her. 'She'd been having pains all day, so she said. She was in a right old state when I came round. Then she went to the lav, and – it happened.' She turned away, covering her mouth with her hand.

192

'Oh, Rube.' He reached for her hand. Her fingers felt so small and limp in his. 'Why didn't you call an ambulance, get yourself to hospital?'

'What would be the point?' Lettie spoke up behind him, harsh and practical. 'It was already over and done with. Terrible mess it was, too. Blood everywhere. I've cleaned it all up now. We didn't want you to come home to all that. Did we, love?'

Ruby opened her mouth, but no sound came from her pale lips.

Guilt stung him. 'I'm so sorry, Ruby. I should have been here.'

'You're here now.' She found her voice, but it was barely a whisper. Her eyes met his, huge pools of misery. 'I'm sorry, Nick. I know how much you were looking forward to being a dad...'

She started to cry. Nick put his arms around her, holding her close to him as the huge, shuddering sobs racked her body. 'Shhh, it's all right, Ruby. Don't cry, girl, it's all right.'

'But ... but I let you down,' she sobbed.

'Don't talk like that. You haven't let anyone down.' He patted her back automatically. He wanted to weep with her, but he couldn't allow himself to give in. 'We'd best call for a doctor,' he said.

'No!' She came to life in his arms, no longer the limp rag doll she had been a moment before.

'She's right,' Lettie said. 'There's no need. It's over.'

'But you should get examined, make sure you're all right...'

'She don't want no more fuss. Not after what she's been through. Ain't that right, girl?' Lettie

193

turned to Ruby, who nodded dumbly. 'She just needs some rest, that's all.'

'If you say so.' Nick frowned, still doubtful. It didn't seem right to him, but Ruby looked so beaten and worn out, he didn't want to argue. 'Anything you want, Ruby.'

She gave him a wan smile. 'Thank you.'

He stood up and looked around him. 'Is there anything I can do for you?'

She shook her head. 'Mum's looking after me.'

'Right.' He met Lettie's grim expression with one of his own. He didn't like her, but he understood Ruby needed her mum.

He started for the door, but Ruby reached for his hand again. 'Nick?' she whispered. 'You won't ... leave me, will you?'

The pleading note in her voice caught him by surprise. 'What are you talking about?'

'I know you only married me because I was expecting. But now the baby's ... gone.' She swallowed hard. 'I mean, I know there's no reason for you to stay...'

He stared at her, genuinely shocked. 'Do you really think I'd walk out on you after something like this? Bloody hell, what kind of a bloke do you think I am?'

'I – I don't know,' she whispered. 'I wasn't sure–'

'Well, I ain't going anywhere.' He bent down, pulling her close. 'We're going to get through this, Ruby. You and me.'

'You and me,' she sighed, her arms closing around him.

He left Lettie fussing over her daughter, and went into the sitting room. He found the

194

medicinal bottle of brandy in the sideboard and splashed some into a glass, his hand shaking. Poor Ruby. She looked so pale and fragile, curled up on the bed. He couldn't bear to think of what she'd gone through.

He crossed over to the window and stared out. The first thing he saw was the pram, parked on the walkway outside.

How could he ever have thought it was beautiful? It was nothing but a huge hunk of metal, taunting him. It took all his self-control not to throw the damn thing off the walkway. All he wanted was to see it smashed on the ground below, its gleaming bodywork crushed and twisted, wheels spinning uselessly in the air.

He sank back down on the settee and gulped his brandy. The burning in his throat briefly numbed the pain he felt. His limbs were so heavy, he couldn't move. He wanted to stay there for ever, staring into nothing.

In the middle of his despair, he suddenly thought of Dora. He desperately wanted to talk to her. Somehow he knew she would understand, be able to take his pain away...

He stopped himself. It was wicked of him to be thinking of another woman when Ruby had been through something so terrible, had just lost their baby. He had to be strong for her. She needed him, now more than ever, and he had made a promise to her.

He refilled his glass and downed it in one. Then he sank his head in his hands and, in the gathering darkness of the sitting room, where no one could see him, Nick Riley cried.

Chapter Eighteen

'Dr Adler's looking very spruced up these days, don't you think?' Penny Willard commented.

Dora squinted across the waiting room at the doctor, who was crouching down to reassure a crying child. There was certainly something different about him. He'd trimmed his shaggy mane of dark curls and his white coat was well pressed for once.

'I can't remember the last time he asked me to sew a button on for him,' Penny said.

'Maybe he's got someone else to sew them on for him?'

He'd certainly had a spring in his step since Esther Gold came in to have her stitches taken out. He'd also stopped working late into the night and sleeping on benches. He hadn't said anything, but everyone knew he and Miss Gold were walking out together.

'Do you think he'll bring her to the ball?' Penny asked.

Dora rolled her eyes. With the Founder's Day Ball only a matter of weeks away, it was all Penny seemed to talk about.

'At least he's got someone to go with,' Penny sighed, her chin in her hand. 'I still can't find anyone to take me.'

'You could always go on your own? Lots of the other girls are.' She'd heard some of her set making plans to go together. They made it sound so much fun, Dora wished she could go with them. But Joe had already bought their tickets.

'Doesn't look as if I've got much choice, does it?' Penny said. 'It's all right for you, you've got a boyfriend to take you. You're one of the lucky ones.'

'Aren't I just?' Dora muttered.

At that moment, Nick emerged from the corridor behind them, pushing an empty wheelchair. His expression was even surlier than usual.

'He looks happy,' Penny remarked. 'I wonder if he's coming to the ball?' She smiled. 'I'll ask him, shall I?'

'I wouldn't–' Dora started to say, but Penny was already calling out to him as he passed.

'Will you be bringing your wife to the ball, Mr Riley?'

He whipped round to scowl at them. 'What?'

'The Founder's Day Ball. I wondered if we'd be meeting Mrs Riley there? Or are you thinking of going by yourself?' Penny gave him a slow, lazy smile. 'Because if you are…'

'I don't know anything about a ball, and I don't want to know either!'

He barrelled past them, pushing the empty wheelchair as if it was a battering ram.

'Well!' Penny watched him go, eyes wide with astonishment. 'I didn't think he could get any more bad-tempered, but he's managed it. What do you suppose that was about?'

'I haven't got a clue.' Dora frowned. But she understood him well enough to know when he was angry, and when he was upset. And Nick Riley was definitely upset.

Before Nick had reached the double doors, they crashed open and a heavily pregnant woman staggered in, on the arm of a middle-aged man. He looked so sick and white-faced, it was hard to tell which of them needed treatment.

'Help me, please!' he begged. 'My wife's having a baby!'

'Well, she can't have it here!' Sister Percival appeared, brisk as ever. 'You need the Maternity ward. It's out of the doors, turn right–'

She started to direct him, but the man cut her off. 'You don't understand,' he cried. 'It isn't due for at least another month. But she fell down the stairs and now her waters have broken. That's not right, is it? It shouldn't have happened now.'

Sister Percival took a step back, assessing the situation. Then she turned to Penny. 'Ring the bell,' she ordered, in a clipped voice. 'And you,' she called to Nick. 'Bring that wheelchair over here immediately.'

Suddenly the whole room was galvanised into action. Dr McKay appeared, and within moments Dora found herself in the consulting room with him and the woman.

'I – I tripped and took a tumble down the stairs,' she stammered as Dora helped her on to the bed. She was older than Dora had first thought, in her late-thirties. Her eyes were wide with terror in her thin face. 'I blacked out for a couple of minutes, and when I came to...'

'Shh, try to calm down, love.' Dora held the woman's hand. 'The doctor is just going to have a listen to the baby's heart, see what's going on.'

But one glance at Dr McKay's face as he listened with his ear trumpet to the woman's distended abdomen told her that all was not well.

'The heartbeat is very slow,' he said. He gently pressed the woman's belly, feeling around for the baby's position. 'How long have you been having contractions?'

'I'm not sure... Quite a while, I think. My waters broke an hour ago.' The women looked from one to the other. 'Is my baby all right?'

'I'll have a better idea about that when I've examined you properly.' Dr McKay was already scrubbing his hands under the tap.

The woman whimpered softly, her mouth moving in silent prayer as he examined her. She clung to Dora's hand, her nails digging into the soft flesh of her palm so hard it was all Dora could do not to cry out.

'It seems as if the baby's brow presentation,' Dr McKay said, when he'd finished. 'We're going to have to operate immediately.'

'Noooo!' The woman let out a wail that echoed around the consulting room. 'My baby can't be born now, it's too soon!'

She struggled to get up, fighting Dora off as she tried to hold her down.

'It's our only chance, Mrs Edgar,' Dr McKay said. 'Your baby is on its way whether we like it or not. The best we can do is give it a helping hand.' He forced lightness into his voice, but Dora could see from his face how serious the situation really was. 'Prep her for surgery,' he instructed in a low voice. 'I'll get Sister Percival to telephone down to Theatre.'

They rattled down the corridors to Theatre, Nick pushing the wheelchair, Dora at his side. Mrs Edgar sobbed all the way.

'Will they save my baby?' she begged Dora. 'Please, Nurse, will they save him?'

'They'll do their best, Mrs Edgar.' She gave the woman's hand a reassuring squeeze. It felt inadequate in the face of such cataclysmic grief.

'It's our first,' she sobbed. 'We've been trying for so long, we started to think we couldn't have kids. And then it happened. We ... we called it our little miracle–'

Dora shot a sidelong look at Nick. He was gritting his teeth so hard, she could see the muscles knotting in his jaw.

Helen emerged from the scrub room as they came through the double doors, very businesslike in her Theatre dress, her dark hair completely hidden by a cotton cap.

'Has she been prepped?' Dora nodded. 'What about her stomach?'

'She says she hasn't eaten for at least five hours.'

'Urine?'

'I've already taken a sample.'

'Very good.' Helen gave Dora a warm smile, suddenly more like her room mate again. 'I'll take over now, thank you.'

The rattle of the empty wheelchair was muffled by the thick white-painted stone walls as they made their way back to the lift.

'Will it be all right?' Nick asked suddenly. 'The baby, I mean. Will it survive?'

Dora glanced sideways at him. His knuckles

were white as they gripped the handles of the wheelchair.

'I don't know,' she admitted. 'There was a heartbeat, so hopefully if the baby is delivered soon...'

Nick took a packet of cigarettes out of the pocket of his brown overalls, shook one out and stuck it between his lips.

'Ruby lost ours,' he said flatly.

His words were like a punch in the stomach, knocking the air out of her. Dora swung round to face him. 'When?'

'Yesterday.' His voice was calm but his hands were shaking so much he could hardly hold the lighted match still. 'I thought you'd want to know, being her friend.'

'I'm so sorry,' Dora whispered.

He nodded, blowing a stream of smoke towards the ceiling. His eyes were fixed on the lift doors.

'She's taken it hard.'

'And what about you?'

He drew in a deep breath. 'Ruby's the one who matters, not me.'

The lift rattled above them, on its way down.

'I'd appreciate it if you'd go and see her,' Nick said. 'She needs a friend.'

She's not the only one, Dora thought, staring at his rigid profile. It looked as if it was taking him every ounce of his strength not to fall apart in front of her.

Seeing him hurting so much made her lose control. Before she knew what she was doing, Dora had reached out to touch him. 'Nick—'

He jerked away from her, as if snatching his arm away from a flame. 'No!' He looked almost fearful. 'I can't,' he said, his voice ragged with emotion. 'I can't do it to Ruby, not now...'

The loud ping of the lift doors broke the silence. Dora stole a glance at Nick's grim profile as he stepped forward and wrenched open the grille.

They travelled up in the lift together, standing apart like strangers, not looking at each other. Dora ached to reach out to him, to kiss away his pain and wretchedness.

But Nick was right, she thought. They couldn't do it to Ruby, not after what she'd been through.

Chapter Nineteen

Helen was making sure the unconscious woman was positioned correctly on the table when Miss Feehan the Theatre Sister arrived. Helen waited tensely as she looked about her, searching for faults. Finally she seemed satisfied.

'Very good,' she said. 'You'll be assisting today, so get yourself ready.'

Helen glanced around to make sure it was really her who was being addressed. 'Me, Sister?'

'Yes, Nurse.' Miss Feehan smiled at her bemused expression. 'Don't look so shocked, you've been here nearly three months, you've seen how things are done. It's high time you put your training into action.'

'But what if I get it wrong?' Helen blurted out the words without thinking.

Miss Feehan lifted one eyebrow. 'I hope you aren't questioning me, Nurse?'

'No, Sister. I apologise, Sister.' Helen lowered her eyes. 'It's just ... I don't want to make a mistake...'

'You won't.' There was a touch of warmth in Miss Feehan's voice that Helen hadn't heard before. 'Just remember to stay within the sterile field, keep close to the surgeon and do as you're told. And if you can do everything before you're told to, all the better. Don't look so terrified, Nurse Tremayne. I wouldn't suggest it if I didn't think you were more than capable.'

Helen's mind was still whirling as she headed off to scrub up. Surgeons generally preferred to work with scrubbed nurses they knew well. How would this one take to having a mere student thrust on him?

She realised the answer to that one when she found her brother William up to his elbows in carbolic soap. He was flanked by Alec Little and a nervous-looking junior houseman.

Suddenly it all made sense. If William were the senior doctor on duty then he would have to deal with any emergency surgery. Helen had no doubt he'd asked for her to assist him.

'Ah, there you are, Nurse Tremayne.' He greeted her with a grin. 'I understand we're working together today? Hurry up and get scrubbed, please. Dr Little has already put the patient to sleep and we don't want to keep her waiting.'

Moments later she was at the operating table beside him, the tray of instruments in front of her. Helen had never been allowed so close to an operation before, and was terrified she might faint at the first sight of blood. She winced when William's scalpel pierced the woman's flesh, but after that everything happened quickly, and Helen was so intent on handing him the correct instruments at the right time she barely had time to register what was happening.

She stole a few nervous glances at him as he worked. He was so precise and calm and in control it was hard to remember he was her brother, once a gawky twelve year old who had built secret dens with her in the garden and skinned his knees while scrambling up trees.

'Scissors.' Remembering Sister's words, Helen was ready with the instrument before he'd had time to put out his hand. 'Right, here we go.' William looked up, addressing his assistant. 'I have cut the tissues down to the peritoneum, which I will now open with scissors. You'd better stand by with those towels,' he instructed Helen.

A second later a geyser of warm blood gushed out of the hole in the woman's abdomen, flowing over their hands and instruments and soaking the carefully placed sheets. As Helen made a grab for a handful of fresh towels to mop it up, William reached in and eased the baby out. A lump rose in Helen's throat as he lifted the tiny creature, bluish-grey and blotched with blood, still attached by a thick, glistening rope.

'A baby boy,' William announced.

'Is he all right?' Helen whispered. 'He seems so small...'

At that moment, the baby let out a thin, reedy cry, its tiny birdlike limbs flailing.

'There's your answer.' William grinned at her, his eyes warm above his mask. He turned to Alec. 'Do you think the grateful mother will name him after you or me?'

'You,' Alec sighed. 'You always get the credit.'

'Quite right, too.'

Helen watched through a blur of tears as he clamped and snipped the cord. She automatically reached for the baby then, but William shook his head. 'Not you, Nurse Tremayne,' he said, as one of the other nurses stepped forward with a towel to receive the child. 'Have you forgotten, you still have work to do?'

She had forgotten, she was so used to being the one who did the fetching and carrying. But this time she could only watch as the runners washed the baby and wrapped him up in warm blankets. Meanwhile, William went to work to remove the placenta, delivering it with a heavy plop into the enamel receiving dish his assistant was holding out for him.

'All done,' he announced with satisfaction, then nodded to the junior doctor. 'Close up for me, would you?'

Soon the operation was over, and mother and baby were on their way back up to the Maternity ward. William and Alec joined Helen as she was instructing the junior in the best way to clean and sterilise the instruments.

'You did very well, Nurse Tremayne,' William said.

'Thank you, Sir,' Helen replied, equally formal.

He reached over to turn on the tap over the sink. 'So what's this nonsense I hear about you

205

not going to the Founder's Day Ball?'

'What's this?' Alec interrupted them. 'You're not going? Why not?'

Helen stared at her brother, taken aback. 'Who told you?'

'I'll give you three guesses.' His mouth lifted at the corners. 'Mother is terribly upset.'

'And I expect you've been asked to try and change my mind?'

'Something like that. Although I would probably say "instructed" rather than asked.'

'How typical of her.' Helen tightened her lips.

William regarded his sister consideringly, his head on one side. 'I know Mother can be an old battleaxe sometimes, but this ball is terribly important to her. I think she's rather nervous about it, to be honest.'

'Our mother, nervous? Never!' Helen said scornfully. 'Mother has never been nervous of anything in her life.'

'All the same, she's anxious the evening should go well. Couldn't you just come along for half an hour? Let her know we're all behind her? It would mean so much to her.'

Helen saw the appeal in her brother's brown eyes, and hesitated. With Charlie and William both urging her to go, she wasn't sure how long she could refuse. 'I'll think about it,' she murmured. 'But I'm not promising anything.'

'Good girl!' William's face broke into a grin. 'Mother will be delighted.'

'I told you, I'm not promising anything...' Helen called after him, but he was already sauntering out of the room.

'Typical William, never takes no for an answer,' Alec remarked.

'I think it's the secret of his success,' Helen agreed with a sigh.

Alec turned to her, his expression serious. 'I hope you do decide to come to the Founder's Day Ball. I was looking forward to our first dance.'

Helen frowned. 'What do you mean?'

'Didn't your mother tell you? She asked if I would partner you. Not that I needed to be asked,' he added hastily, his cheeks turning pink. 'As a matter of fact, I was going to ask you anyway–'

Helen stared at him, shocked. 'When did this happen?'

'About a week ago. Why?'

'I'd already told her I wasn't going by then.' Helen's mouth firmed. How typical of her mother, to take no notice of her wishes.

Alec looked confused. 'I'm sorry, have I put my foot in it?'

Helen saw his bemused expression and felt sorry for him. 'It's not your fault,' she assured him. 'But for your information, I have a boyfriend.'

'Oh!' He blinked owlishly. 'I'm sorry, I didn't realise. Your mother didn't mention it.'

'I'm sure she didn't.' Helen picked up a towel to dry her hands.

Alec watched her carefully. 'I take it this means you don't need a partner for the ball?'

'No, Dr Little, I don't.' She threw down the towel. 'I don't need a partner because I'm not going.'

'Oh! But I thought you told William–'

'I told William I would think about it,' she said.

207

'Now I have thought about it. And wild horses wouldn't drag me to that ball!'

'What about this one?'

Hundreds of tiny mint green pleats fanned out from Lucy Lane's narrow hips as she did a neat little pirouette in front of them.

'It's Fortuny,' she said. 'Mummy ordered it from Paris.'

Dora stifled a yawn with the back of her hand. She and Millie were supposed to be helping Katie O'Hara with her dress for the ball, but Katie's room mate Lucy Lane had taken over. She'd spent the last half hour parading around their room, showing off her latest couture gowns. Every time Dora thought her wardrobe couldn't possibly hold any more, another came out, more expensive and extravagant than the last.

The only one who seemed remotely impressed was Katie.

'It's beautiful,' she sighed enviously. 'We're all going to look like carthorses next to you in all your finery.'

Lucy Lane smirked. 'It's so hard to choose, isn't it? I have so many gowns I could wear, it's difficult to pick one.'

'You're lucky,' Katie said. 'I've only got one, and I'm not sure even that will do. Mammy didn't think to pack a ballgown when she sent me over from Ireland!'

'I can't think why not,' Lucy sniffed, her nose turned up to the ceiling. 'Every sophisticated woman needs at least one ballgown.'

Or in your case, a dozen, Dora thought. 'Let's

see your dress,' she encouraged Katie.

She hesitated. 'I'm really not sure it will do...'

'We won't know till we see it, will we?' Millie joined in. 'Go on, show us.'

'All right. If you promise not to laugh?'

It took ten minutes for Katie to inch the pink satin over her wide hips. 'What do you think?' she asked.

'Well...' Dora searched for something tactful to say. It was hardly the most flattering dress she'd ever seen. The short puffy sleeves cut into the plump white flesh of Katie's upper arms, while the thick shiny fabric clung unforgivingly to every bulge.

'I think I must have put a bit of weight on since I last wore it,' Katie sighed.

'A bit?' Lucy shrieked with laughter. 'You look six months pregnant!'

Dora shot her a dirty look. 'If you can't say something nice, don't say anything.'

'Well, I think it looks delightful,' Millie said loyally. 'Although perhaps if you wore a foundation garment of some kind...'

'She'll need two corsets in that thing,' Lucy put in.

'She's right. It looks horrible.' Katie's voice was choked. 'That's it. I can't go to the ball like this. I look like ... a shiny pink pig!'

'Don't get upset, I'm sure we can sort it out. Let me see.' Dora crouched in front of her to examine the dress more closely. 'I could let out the side seams a bit. That would give you more room.'

Katie turned to her, tears glistening on her

thick black lashes. 'Do you really think you could do that?'

'Of course she can,' Lucy put in. 'Don't you remember? Doyle used to stitch knickers in a sweat shop before she came here.'

Dora opened her mouth to reply, but Millie shook her head. 'Don't,' she warned. 'She's not worth it.'

'True.' Dora gritted her teeth and turned around so she didn't have to see Lucy's smirking face. Lucy Lane got her down sometimes. She never let Dora forget her humble origins.

She never let anyone forget where she came from, either. Her father had made a fortune manufacturing lightbulbs and Lucy was his privileged only child.

'There's plenty of allowance in these seams,' Dora went on, looking up at Katie. 'If you've got some scissors I'll take them apart and repin it so it fits you.'

'And there you were, thinking you'd left the sweat shop behind.' Lucy's voice grated across her nerves. 'I bet you never thought you'd need to use your sewing skills again?'

'I'd like to sew your mouth up!' Dora muttered in an undertone.

Katie wriggled out of the dress with much huffing and puffing and handed it to Dora to unpick.

'Perhaps I should join the League of Health and Beauty,' she said ruefully. 'That might help slim me down.'

'Unless you really are pregnant,' Lane said, standing sideways to admire her own slender shape. 'What?' She looked around at the others' shocked faces. 'She could be, you know. Irish girls are always getting themselves into trouble.'

Dora and Millie glared at her, but Katie O'Hara just shrugged. 'She's right,' she said. Then added mischievously, 'Maybe I should tell Tom I'm in the family way. That would give him a shock, wouldn't it? He might even marry me!'

'Run away, more likely!' Lucy said.

'It worked for my cousin Imelda,' Katie said. 'Five years she was with her man, but he never gave a hint about wanting to put a ring on her finger until she told him she was in the family way. They were married a month later.'

'And what did he say when he found out she'd lied to him?' Millie asked.

'What could he say?' Katie shrugged. 'She just told him it was a false alarm. Besides, she was pregnant before they'd been married a month, so what did it matter?' She looked down at her bare left hand. 'Maybe I should try it,' she mused. 'We could have a double wedding, me and my Tom and you and Joe,' she said to Dora. 'Just think, they'd probably give us a police guard of honour!'

Dora kept her head down, unpicking the tiny stitches with the point of her scissors. 'I'm not marrying Joe.'

'That's what you think.' Katie gave her a knowing smile. 'My Tom reckons Joe's got his heart set on you.'

'But we hardly know each other!'

'Must have been love at first sight,' Katie said.

'More like love is blind,' Lucy muttered unkindly.

Dora went back to her unpicking, panic fluttering in her chest. She shouldn't have agreed to go to this stupid ball with Joe, she thought. She had tried to let him down gently, but the more time she spent with him, the more of a chance he seemed to think he had.

She finished unpicking the seams of Katie's dress and repinned it so it fitted her better. She'd just put in the last pin when Sister Sutton's voice boomed down the passage, announcing it was nearly time for lights out, so Dora took the dress back to her room, promising to finish sewing it before the ball.

'I feel sorry for O'Hara,' Millie said, as they climbed the attic stairs.

'Having to share a room with Lane, you mean?' Dora said.

Millie laughed. 'She is awful, isn't she? No, I mean because of that boyfriend of hers. I've heard all kinds of rumours about him. He's got quite a reputation.'

'I've heard a few stories too.' Dora had even seen him flirting with Penny Willard. 'Poor O'Hara. She really wears her heart on her sleeve, doesn't she? She's just asking to get it broken.'

'Not like you.' Millie sent her a sidelong smile. 'Sounds as if you've got the right idea, playing hard to get with your boyfriend. He sounds well and truly smitten!'

'He's not my boyfriend!' Dora insisted.

Millie arched her eyebrows. 'Maybe you should tell him that?'

'Oh, I intend to. Don't you worry,' Dora said firmly.

Chapter Twenty

The following morning Dora was off duty from nine until one, so she decided to pay Ruby a visit.

She had been putting it off for a few days, not knowing what to say to her friend. What words of comfort could she hope to offer to someone who had been through such an ordeal? Dora could see every day how much Nick was suffering. He hadn't spoken to her again since that moment in the lift, but she didn't need to hear from him to understand how he felt. Pain seemed to radiate through every inch of him. He moved as stiffly as an automaton, as if even the effort of putting one foot in front of the other was too much for him.

If he was in so much agony, she couldn't imagine how wretched Ruby must be feeling. Dora had seen and heard about the mechanics of late miscarriage in Gynae lectures, but she could only guess what it must feel like to lose a child.

She had never been to Victory House before, and it took her a while to find the right flat on the third floor. She could hear gramophone music playing as she approached Ruby's front door. A lively swing number, the kind she knew her friend always loved to dance to.

She knocked, and the music stopped abruptly. A moment later Ruby came to the door, smoothing down her blonde curls. Dora was taken aback by how bright and summery she looked in her yellow cotton dress patterned with sprigs of cornflowers.

'Oh, hello.' Ruby's smile of greeting faded when she saw Dora. 'What are you doing here?'

'Nick told me what happened. Oh, Rube, I'm so sorry!' Emotion overcame Dora and she stepped forward and gathered Ruby in her arms. Whatever wrong she had done in the past, Ruby was still Dora's oldest friend and she didn't deserve what she was going through. 'It's so cruel, it really is…'

'These things happen.' Ruby's body was rigid in Dora's arms. 'You just have to get on with it, don't you?'

Dora pulled away from Ruby, holding her at arm's length. 'You don't have to put on a front for my sake, you know. I'm your mate, remember?'

'Yes well, like I said. You just have to get on with it.' Ruby stepped out of her embrace, her downcast gaze fixed on the linoleum floor.

Dora frowned. She knew it was the East End women's way to paint a brave face over their troubles. She had seen her mother and grandmother do it, and she had done it herself over Nick enough times.

But not Ruby. Dora had known her friend wail for hours over a broken fingernail. Perhaps her heartache went so deep she couldn't even express it?

'Why don't we stick the kettle on?' Dora suggested. 'Then we can have a good catch up over a brew.'

Ruby pursed her lips. 'As a matter of fact, I was just about to go out when you knocked. I promised my mum I'd call round.'

'Oh. Oh, right. Sorry, I should have warned you I was coming.' Dora frowned as a thought struck her. 'Are you sure you're all right to be up and about? I thought you'd still be resting in bed.'

'Oh, I don't need to bother with all that. I'm as right as rain,' Ruby said briskly, putting her hat on in front of the hall mirror.

'All the same, you need time to recover–'

'I don't want to mope about in bed,' Ruby said firmly.

Dora caught her friend's defiant look reflected in the mirror. Perhaps Ruby was just putting a brave face on after all?

'I'll walk back to Griffin Street with you,' Dora offered.

'Oh, no, you don't have to.'

'I want to. I can call in and see my mum too. Then we can have a chat on the way, can't we?'

Ruby's smile stiffened. 'That'll be nice.'

It was a bright, sunny June morning, but Victory House and all the blocks around it were silent. Their footsteps echoed along the concrete walkway as they walked past the line of closed front doors.

'Where is everyone?' Dora asked. 'You'd think they would have their doors open to enjoy the sunshine, wouldn't you?'

Ruby pulled a face. 'Everyone likes to keep themself to themself round here.'

'It ain't like Griffin Street, then?' Dora grinned. 'Everyone in and out of each other's houses all day long?'

'No,' Ruby said. 'It ain't nothing like Griffin Street.'

She looked so wistful when she said it. 'You sound as if you miss it?' Dora remarked.

'Sometimes.'

Dora sent her a sidelong look. Under her thick mask of make-up, Ruby's face was pale and strained. Poor girl, she could probably do with her friends around her after going through such an ordeal.

Dora tucked her arm in Ruby's, trying to jolly her along. 'Cheer up,' she said. 'It'll all be all right, you'll see.'

'Will it?' Ruby said bleakly.

''Course it will. You'll get through it, I promise.' Dora paused, trying to choose her words carefully. 'Did the doctor say why it might have happened?' she ventured. Ruby was silent. 'Ruby? You have seen the doctor, haven't you?'

'I don't need to see a doctor.'

'Ruby!' Dora was horrified. 'You have to go and see him. He needs to check everything's all right.'

'Everything's fine.' Ruby's face was shuttered.

'But we had a lecture on it. Mr Cooper the consultant said it was important to make sure–'

'I'm not interested in what the bloody consultant said!' Splotches of angry colour were splashed like red paint up Ruby's throat and across her cheekbones. 'Stop acting like you know everything, Dora Doyle!'

Dora flinched before her friend's anger. 'I was only trying to help.'

'Well, don't. I don't need your help. It's over, it's finished, and I'm sick of talking about it. I just want to forget it ever happened, all right?'

'If that's what you want.' But Dora was still

216

troubled. Surely Ruby's mother should have told her to go to the hospital? Lettie worked on Gynae, she would have seen what happened to women who didn't get proper medical attention.

They walked on, down by the canal. Ruby was so prickly, Dora hardly knew what to say to her.

Finally, it was Ruby who changed the subject. 'Don't let's fall out,' she said. 'You're my mate, and I don't want to argue with you.'

'Me neither.'

'That's all right, then.' Ruby beamed at her, suddenly more like her old self. 'Can we talk about something else? I'm fed up with feeling sorry for myself.'

'Of course.' That would explain the music and the dancing, Dora thought. No matter how heartbreaking the situation, there was a limit to how much misery a young girl could stand. 'What shall we talk about?'

'I dunno – anything.' Ruby turned to her. 'What's been going on with you? How's that boyfriend of yours? Joe, ain't it?'

Dora sighed. 'He's not my boyfriend.'

'Ooh, have I touched a nerve?' Ruby teased. 'Don't tell me he ain't interested?'

'Far from it. I'm the one who ain't interested, although I can't seem to get him to believe that.'

'Why not? He seemed like a bit of all right to me.'

Dora gazed across the flat brown water of the canal. 'It just doesn't feel right. He's gone and bought us tickets for the hospital ball, even though I told him I didn't want to go with him.' She turned back to Ruby. 'How do I make him

217

understand I don't want to start courting?'

But Ruby wasn't listening. 'What ball is that, then?'

'The Founder's Day Ball, next month.'

'Nick's never mentioned it.'

'He probably didn't think you'd be feeling up to it.'

Ruby's mouth firmed. 'I reckon a night out's just what I need. I can't stay cooped up for ever.'

'Then maybe he's the one who's not feeling up to it?' Dora suggested. 'He's been ever so upset since–' She didn't finish the sentence, afraid of upsetting Ruby again.

'Then he wants to buck up like the rest of us!' Her friend sounded dismissive. 'I'm fed up with seeing him walking about with a face like a wet weekend!'

Dora stared at her, shocked. 'You can't blame him for being upset, Ruby. He was looking forward to this baby...'

'You think I don't know that?' she snapped. 'If I'd known he was going to be like this, I would never have told him–' She stopped dead, her mouth shutting like a steel trap.

Dora regarded her curiously. 'Would never have told him what, Rube?'

'Nothing,' she said, tight-lipped.

Dora searched her friend's face. 'Ruby?'

'Come on, Mum will be wondering where I am.' She turned and marched off down the street, leaving Dora standing on the pavement.

Dora stared after her. Then it started to dawn on her, like a speck of light on the dark horizon. Surely she hadn't...

218

No. She dismissed the thought. It was too wicked, even for Ruby. And yet suddenly, once she'd allowed the idea to creep into her mind, it all started to add up. Why Ruby was so determined she didn't need to see a doctor. And that flash of yellow dress, twirling to music behind the net curtains. Perhaps it was nothing to do with wanting to get over her heartache. Perhaps there was no heartache to begin with...

A sudden image of Katie O'Hara flashed across Dora's mind. Posing in her pink dress, the shiny satin tight across her bulging tummy, laughing about the trick her clever cousin Imelda had played on her boyfriend.

'Ruby?' she called out. 'Wait, I want to ask you something...'

'There was no baby, was there?'

Ruby stopped dead, but she didn't turn round. Dora instantly knew she was right.

'That's a wicked thing to say.' Ruby's voice was flat.

'Then tell me it's not true.' Dora stared at the back of her friend's blonde head. 'You can't, can you? You can't even look at me.' She was too stunned even to feel angry. 'Why did you do it? Why did you lie to everyone?'

Ruby turned around slowly. Dora saw the way her eyes darted and wondered if the next words that came from her mouth were going to be another lie.

But then her shoulders sank in defeat. 'He was going to leave me,' she said flatly. 'I couldn't let that happen. I didn't even know what I was saying until the words came out,' she looked up at Dora, her eyes appealing for understanding. 'You know me, always opening my mouth before I stop to think!' She smiled weakly.

'Oh, Ruby!' Dora couldn't think of anything else to say. Her mind was a jumble of thoughts and emotions – anger, disbelief, pain – all tumbling over themselves. 'But you let him marry you...'

Ruby shrugged. 'I wanted to marry him.'

And what about us? a voice inside Dora's head screamed. What about what Nick and I wanted?

'Anyway, it's done now, ain't it?'

Yes, it's done now, Dora thought. One lie had taken Nick away from her for ever.

She thought about the wedding day: how she'd stood and watched Ruby marry the man she loved. It had hurt so badly Dora thought she would die from the pain, but she had endured it because she thought it was the right thing to do, for the sake of Ruby and the baby she was carrying.

And all the time Ruby had been lying, stringing them along. She had destroyed Dora's happiness, and all so she could get what she wanted.

Dora stared at her. Ruby looked so casual, as if she had been caught out in a silly fib. Dora thought she saw a faint gleam of satisfaction in her eyes, and clutched her hands together to stop herself from slapping that smug face.

'How could you do it?' she whispered.

'There's no need to look at me like that,' Ruby snapped. 'All right, so I wasn't straight with him. But so what? We're happy together now. I've been a good wife to Nick, I've given him everything he could want. You ask him, if you don't believe me.'

Dora shook her head in wonder. 'You don't understand, do you? You're that selfish, you just can't see it. He's mourning for a baby who never existed. You broke his heart, Ruby.'

The other girl turned her face away, her mouth set in an obstinate line. 'He'll get over it.'

'You need to tell him the truth.'

Ruby gave a squawk of disbelieving laughter. 'Are you joking?'

'If you don't tell him, I will.'

The colour drained from Ruby's face. 'You wouldn't!'

'He should know the truth.'

'He'd leave me.'

'Maybe that's what you deserve.'

Ruby stared at her for a moment. Then a slow, knowing smile spread across her face. 'You'd like that, wouldn't you?' she said. 'And I suppose you'd be there to welcome him with open arms? Good old Dora, always ready with a shoulder to cry on. Or maybe you'd like to offer him more than that?' she suggested slyly.

Dora felt her face flaming. 'I dunno what you mean.'

'Don't give me that!' Ruby's lip curled. 'Do you really think I'm that daft? I know you're in love with my husband. I've always known it. You think you're so clever, but for all your brains you can't hide your feelings.' She shook her head pityingly. 'All this talk about Nick needing to know the truth, as if you're doing him a favour. When all the time you're thinking about yourself, looking for your chance to take him away from me.'

221

'That's not true...'

'Isn't it?' There was a taunting edge to Ruby's voice. 'You sure about that, Dora? Because from where I'm standing, you're the one who's selfish, not me.'

Dora could hardly believe what she was hearing. 'How do you work that out?'

'Think about it,' Ruby said. 'We're married. Maybe Nick wouldn't have wed me in the first place unless he'd thought I was expecting, but we're happy now. If you tell him about the baby, what good would it do? All right, he might walk out on me. But he could never divorce me, not unless I gave him grounds. And whatever else I've been, I've never been unfaithful to him. So he could never really be yours, could he? And I don't suppose that Matron of yours would like the idea of you taking up with a married man, do you?'

Dora stared at Ruby's face, twisted with spite. She barely recognised the hard-faced girl standing before her as her friend.

She hated to admit it but Ruby was right. Telling Nick the truth would surely break up his marriage, but it wouldn't bring Dora any happiness. He would still be a married man, and she would be disgraced if she had anything to do with him.

And if he stuck to his vows and stayed with Ruby, they would be unhappy for ever. Did she really want to condemn him to a lifetime of misery and mistrust?

Ignorance is bliss, so her Nanna Winnie always said.

Ruby must have seen the doubt in Dora's face. She smiled.

'You can tell Nick if it makes you feel better,' she said. 'But it won't change anything. He was mine the minute he put this ring on my finger. And nothing you can do or say is going to change that!'

Chapter Twenty-One

It was the night of the Founder's Day Ball, and the attic room was in chaos. Helen sat on her bed, with a heavy textbook propped on her knee, and tried to read as discarded shoes, aprons, collars and cuffs flew through the air around her.

Katie O'Hara hopped around the bedroom, pulling on a stocking. 'We'll be so late, we might as well not bother going.'

'The sooner you stop complaining, the sooner we'll be ready,' Lucy Lane snapped, jostling with Millie for space in the mirror over the chest of drawers.

'I hope my Tom doesn't think I've stood him up.' Katie stepped into her dress and wriggled it over her hips.

'I'm sure he'll find someone to keep him entertained,' Lucy muttered as she applied her lipstick.

'I heard that!' Katie looked up, hurt. 'I know what everyone thinks, but my Tom isn't like that. Not any more, anyway. He says he's a changed man since he met me – oh, no! Now look what I've done!'

Helen looked up from her textbook. White flesh poked through a rip in the seam of Katie's dress.

'That's your fault!' she accused Lucy.

'Me? What have I done?'

'You made me agitated, talking about my Tom.'

'I did not!'

'You did!'

'If anything it's your fault for putting on more weight.'

'Calm down, both of you. I can easily stitch it up again.' Dora cast Helen a long-suffering look as she reached on top of her wardrobe for her sewing kit.

'Have a drink, it'll make you feel better.' Millie pulled a bottle of gin out from under her mattress and passed it to Katie.

'Do you have to drink that in here?' Helen cast a panicked glance at the door as Katie opened the bottle and took a long swig. 'If Sister Sutton comes in...'

'She won't,' Millie said, taking the bottle back and swigging some herself. 'She's too busy downstairs, ordering everyone to take their make-up off.'

'If she tells me to take my make-up off, I'll – I'll kick her dog!' Katie declared.

Helen smiled to herself as she went back to her reading. 'Are you sure you don't want to come with us, Tremayne?' Dora asked.

'Quite sure,' Helen said, keeping her eyes fixed on a diagram of the digestive system.

She wasn't sure she could trust herself to see her mother, after what Constance had done. How dare she ask Alec Little to take Helen to the ball? And after she had said she wasn't going, too.

Constance was probably expecting Helen to turn up with her tail between her legs, to fall in with her plans as usual. But not this time. Helen was determined to make a stand.

'I'll probably go and visit Charlie later anyway,' she said, flicking over a page of her book.

Ten minutes later they were gone and a welcome hush fell over the room. Helen listened to them stumbling down the stairs, trying to be as quiet as possible so as not to rouse Sister Sutton. She smiled when she heard Sparky yapping, followed by Sister Sutton's voice roaring, 'You girls! Where do you think you're going in such a hurry? What have you been told about running?'

Helen smiled to herself. She hoped Sister Sutton didn't find the hip flask of gin Millie had tucked into her evening bag.

After they'd gone, she quickly tidied up everything they'd left behind, folding up uniforms, smoothing out collars and cuffs and tucking discarded shoes under the bed. Then she put on her coat and hat and went out to visit Charlie.

She'd reached the landing downstairs when she heard a sound coming from Amy Hollins' room at the far end of the passage. Helen hesitated, listening. It sounded like someone crying.

She paused for a moment, her hand on the banister. It was none of her business, she told herself. She started down the next flight of stairs, but had barely taken two steps before the sound of muffled sobbing stopped her in her tracks again.

She went back up the stairs and crept along the

225

passageway towards Amy's room. As she breathed in, she caught the scent of roses. It seemed oddly familiar, but she couldn't place where she'd smelled it before. Probably on one of the girls who had just gone out, she decided.

'Hollins?' she called out softly. 'Are you all right?'

The crying stopped abruptly. Helen waited, then tapped on the door. 'Hollins?'

'Go away!' a voice clotted with tears called out from the other side of the door.

Helen stepped back as if she'd been slapped. Every ounce of good sense she had told her to walk away, but somehow she couldn't.

'You sound upset,' she said. 'I just wondered if there was anything I could do–'

'I said, go away!' Amy's voice was harsh.

Helen didn't need to be told again. Gathering her coat around her, she hurried down the stairs.

'Scarlet Fever?'

Helen stood on the doorstep of the Dawsons' narrow terraced house. It had just started to rain, but she barely noticed the big fat drops that splashed off the end of her nose. She could scarcely believe what she was hearing.

'He's been poorly for a couple of days now,' Nellie Dawson said. 'Sorry, love, I did leave a note up at the hospital for you. Charlie will be so cross you've had a wasted journey.'

But that was the last thing on her mind. 'How bad is he?' Helen asked.

'Well, he's in a right old state with himself. Hasn't been able to do anything the past couple of days, and you know that's not like our Charlie.' Nellie Dawson smiled on seeing Helen's stricken expression. 'There's nothing to worry about, ducks,' she assured her. 'He'll be right as rain by the end of the week. I've nursed most of mine through Scarlet Fever, and it always looks worse than it is.'

'Can I see him?'

Nellie frowned. 'Are you sure that's a good idea, love? We wouldn't want you catching it, would we?'

'I suppose not.' Helen bit her lip, fighting the sudden urge to cry

Nellie Dawson sighed. 'Look, since you're here, why don't you come in for a cuppa? It's all right, none of us are infectious or we would have shown symptoms by now. I've scrubbed the house from top to bottom, and Charlie's tucked away up-stairs. You're quite safe.'

'All the same, I wouldn't want to intrude–'

'Bless you, love, you couldn't intrude if you tried. Come on in, before you catch your death in that rain.'

Helen sat at the table in the Dawsons' cosy kitchen and watched Nellie bustling around, pre-paring the tea on the big, old-fashioned range. Whenever Helen had visited before, Nellie had always insisted on her going into the front parlour, their 'best' room, as she called it.

'It's because she thinks you're posh!' Charlie always laughed.

But Helen much preferred the kitchen. It felt like the heart of the house, full of warmth and noise. Charlie's dad snored softly in the chair beside the fire, his stockinged feet up on the range, the evening paper still open on his lap. Charlie's younger brothers and sisters played cards at the other end of the table, smiling shyly at Helen as if she was some exotic creature. Band music came from the crackling wireless in the corner and Nellie hummed along as she filled the teapot. She was a big, comfortable-looking woman, with the same red-gold hair, bright blue eyes and rosy cheeks as her son.

Nellie put the enormous brown teapot on the table, followed by a plate holding big slabs of cake.

'It's only a bit of seed cake,' she said apologetically. 'I would have got something better in if I'd known you were coming.'

She dislodged a fat ginger cat snoozing on a kitchen chair. As it left in a huff, Helen noticed the book it had been perched on. It was a copy of *Great Expectations*.

'What's this?' She reached for it. 'Is this yours, Mrs Dawson?'

'Bless you, love, can you imagine me reading all them long words?' A blush crept up Mrs Dawson's plump cheeks. 'Our Charlie got it out of the library last week.' She took it from Helen and dusted the cat hairs off it. 'He was asking for it this morning. I wondered where it had got to.'

'I didn't know Charlie liked Dickens?'

Mrs Dawson leaned forward confidingly. 'Between you and me, he's decided to go back to night school, get some exams,' she said. 'And I reckon we've got you to thank for that.'

'Me?'

Nellie nodded. 'Now he's stepping out with such

a clever young lady, I think he wants to improve himself.'

Helen had a sudden mental image of her mother. 'He doesn't have to improve himself for my sake,' she said.

'I realise that, love, but you know what Charlie's like.'

Helen turned her eyes to the ceiling. 'I wish I could see him.'

Nellie thought for a moment. 'Perhaps it wouldn't hurt for you to just take a peep at him, through the door?' she suggested. 'If you kept a long way away from him, I'm sure you wouldn't catch anything.'

Charlie was sleeping when she cautiously pushed open the door and looked inside. She could see immediately the tell-tale flush on his face, deep pink against the whiteness of his pillow. He was bundled under a pile of quilts.

Helen watched him for a moment. He looked like a sleeping angel with his burnished golden hair tousled, lashes curling on his cheeks. He looked so peaceful she didn't want to wake him, but as she was stepping away he suddenly spoke her name.

She looked back around the edge of the door. Charlie's blue eyes were staring straight at her, his mouth curved in a sleepy smile.

'I didn't want to disturb you,' she whispered.

'I would have been upset if you'd gone without saying hello.' He rolled over on to his back and stretched. 'What are you doing here? Why aren't you at the ball?'

'I couldn't face it. How are you feeling?'

'Blooming awful, since you ask. I ache all over, and my head's pounding. And I can't get warm, no matter how many blankets I sling on.'

'You'll feel better soon.' Helen smiled. 'The rash will probably get worse in the next day or two, but it should start to subside by the end of the week – what?' She stopped talking on seeing his amused expression. 'What's so funny?'

'You. You're like a walking textbook, aren't you?'

She smiled reluctantly. 'That's what comes of too much studying, I suppose.'

They gazed at each other longingly. The small bedroom seemed a mile wide when they were unable to touch. Helen didn't think she would ever take holding his hand for granted again.

'You should have gone to the ball, you know,' Charlie said. 'It's not right for you to fall out with your mum.'

'I don't want to talk about her,' Helen said flatly.

'I know, but promise me you'll make it up with her?' He looked at Helen appealingly, his head tilted to one side. 'Go on,' he urged. 'For me?'

'I'll think about it,' she promised. 'Now I'd best get back downstairs. Is there anything you need before I go?'

'I wouldn't mind a kiss, but I can't have that.'

Helen laughed and blew him one. 'You'll just have to make do with that, I'm afraid. I'll kiss you properly next time I see you.'

He winked at her. 'I'll hold you to that.'

Chapter Twenty-Two

'You look gorgeous,' Joe said, as they climbed the broad marble staircase of Bethnal Green Town Hall, where the Founder's Day Ball was being held.

'I don't know about that.' Dora blushed at the compliment. 'I don't remember ever wearing anything this fancy, though. I borrowed it off Benedict. It's proper silk chiffon, so heaven knows how much it cost.'

She had been reluctant to wear the emerald green gown at first. 'What if I tear a hole in it, or spill something down the front?' she had wailed.

'It doesn't matter,' Millie had insisted. 'And anyway, what else are you going to wear? The only long dress you have is your nightgown, and you can't go to the ball in that!'

'It's not the dress that's fancy. It's you.' Joe's gaze was so intense it made Dora's skin prickle. 'I must be the luckiest bloke in the room.'

They'd reached the top of the stairs. Before she knew what was happening, he pulled her to him and kissed her.

'Stop it!' Dora pushed him away. 'Everyone's looking at us!'

The wide sweeping landing was crowded with people waiting to go into the ballroom. Nurses, ward sisters, doctors and consultants, all turned to look at them.

'So? Let them look. I want everyone to know you belong to me.'

'I don't belong to anyone,' Dora replied, tight-lipped.

Joe looked down at her hands braced against his chest. 'You think you can keep me at arm's length for ever?' He grinned at her. 'I told you, I'm going to get you in the end, Dora Doyle. You see if I don't!'

There was a reckless glint in Joe's eyes that made her feel uneasy. She frowned. 'Have you been drinking?'

'Tommy and I might have stopped for a couple of pints on the way, just to get us in the mood.' He laughed. 'Don't look so disapproving! We're meant to be having fun, ain't we?' Joe slipped one arm around her waist, pulling her to him. 'You could do with a drink yourself, loosen you up a bit.'

'We've been given orders to stick to the fruit punch.'

His brows rose. 'Since when did you nurses ever do as you're told?'

Dora glanced towards the double doors leading to the ballroom. Miss Fox the Matron was standing just inside them, tall and elegant in a gown of midnight blue crepe. She was smiling, but her gaze was everywhere, missing nothing. Dora wondered how many of the nurses would be lining up outside her office the following morning, feeling very sorry for themselves.

Inside, the ballroom resembled a magical wonderland. The enormous chandelier showered sparkling diamonds of light over the marble and mirrored walls. Dora couldn't help gawping around at it all. She had never seen anything so grand in all her life. The room was filled with people, alive with the sound of laughter, voices, and the muted chink of glasses. Waiters circulated with silver trays of drinks, and at the far end of the room an orchestra played. Some couples had already taken to the floor, twirling and whirling about. A row of disconsolate unaccompanied nurses in their best dresses sat around the edge of the room, clutching glasses of fruit punch and pretending they didn't want to dance anyway.

She caught sight of Dr Adler with Esther. She looked so much younger and more beautiful than Dora ever remembered seeing her, dressed in deep plum velvet, her dark hair falling in soft curls around her radiant face.

'Let's dance,' Joe said, taking Dora's hand.

'But we've only just got here!'

'I don't care. I can't wait to have you in my arms.'

He pulled her towards the floor but she hung back. 'I want to say hello to my friends first.'

Joe pulled a face. 'You see them every day.'

'Not all of them. I haven't seen Willard at all since I moved to Female Medical last week.' She waved at Penny, who was sitting with the other wallflowers, sulkily biting into a sausage roll. She dropped it at once and came over, looking very striking in a dazzling peacock blue dress.

'You look lovely,' Dora said.

'Thanks, but I don't think Miss Hanley approves. She's already told me I look indecent.'

'Why?' Dora looked Penny up and down. The dress clung to her slender curves, but the neckline was modest enough, cutting across the hollows of her collarbone. 'You look covered up enough to me.'

'You haven't seen the back.' Nurse Willard spun around and Dora gasped. The dress plunged daringly to the base of her spine, revealing a bare expanse of skin.

'I see what she means.'

'I think she's just being an old fuddy-duddy.' Penny Willard glared across the room at the Assistant Matron. 'How dare she lecture me? Have you seen that awful thing she's wearing?'

Miss Hanley couldn't have been more covered up if she'd tried. Every inch of her square, mannish frame was covered in burgundy velvet. A trim of gold brocade around her neck only emphasised the uncompromising squareness of her jaw.

'It looks like the old curtains from the Rialto,' Joe observed. Penny screamed with laughter.

'Yes, that's exactly what it looks like! Oh, Joe, you are funny.' She batted her eyelashes at him. 'Isn't he a hoot, Doyle?'

Dora tried to smile, but she couldn't help feeling sorry for Miss Hanley. The poor thing looked like a fish out of water, gazing about her in bewilderment at the other women in their glamorous dresses. Dora knew exactly how she felt.

Joe drifted off to fetch them some drinks, leaving Dora to chat to Penny.

'It's strange to see everyone dressed up like this,' she remarked. 'I hardly recognise them.'

Penny nodded in agreement. 'I know, isn't it odd? You get so used to seeing them in uniform, it gives you quite a fright when you see them in anything else. Some of the men look quite dashing, don't they? Who would have thought our Dr Adler would scrub up so well?' She nodded to him as he whirled past with Esther in his arms.

'That's what love does for you.' Dora smiled.

'And have you seen Mr Latimer's wife?' Penny nodded over to where the consultant was standing with a dumpy, cross-faced little woman, talking to Mrs Tremayne. 'She doesn't look like much of a match for him, does she? But I've heard she's rich, which I suppose explains a lot...'

But Dora wasn't listening. She was staring across the room at another couple, standing on the far side talking to a group of porters.

'Now there's a couple who go together, don't you think?' Penny followed her gaze. 'But I suppose someone like Nick Riley was always going to have a pretty wife, wasn't he?' She sighed. 'Not that I could ever see myself marrying a hospital porter,' she said. 'But he does look like he would be rather fun for a fling...'

Dora tried to tear her gaze away, but she couldn't. The sight of Nick in a suit brought back all kinds of painful memories of his wedding. And there was Ruby, bold as brass in brilliant scarlet, her blonde curls piled on top of her head, clinging to his arm as she threw back her head and laughed.

'I thought they weren't coming,' Dora said.

'Looks like they changed their mind.' Penny shrugged. 'Oh, here comes Joe with the drinks.' She teased a tendril of hair around her finger. 'He's such a gentleman, isn't he? Gosh, Doyle, you don't know how lucky you are.'

Joe handed Penny her drink and then turned to Dora. 'Can we have that dance now?' he asked, an edge to his voice.

She let him lead her on to the floor as the band started playing 'The Way You Look Tonight'. Joe pulled her into his arms, crooning the words of the song softly into her hair, as he pressed the length of his body against hers.

Dora closed her eyes and tried to lose herself in the music, but when she opened them again she found herself staring straight at Nick Riley.

He was watching her across the crowded dance floor, his face expressionless. When he caught Dora looking back at him, he turned abruptly towards Ruby.

The song ended and Dora went to walk away, but Joe pulled her back. 'Another dance, please?' he begged. 'I've been waiting all night for this.'

'Do you mind if I sit this one out?' she said. 'My feet are killing me.'

A shadow crossed his face as he released her. 'If that's what you want.'

He followed her off the dance floor. 'Where are you going?' he asked as she headed for the door.

'Only to the Ladies' to powder my nose. Is that all right?' She looked back at him challengingly.

For a moment he actually looked as if he might argue. 'Don't be too long,' he muttered.

When she was sure he wasn't watching her, Dora walked straight past the door to the Ladies' cloakroom, down the stairs and out into the warm evening air. The sun was starting to sink behind the rooftops, streaking the coppery sky with pink and violet. Even the ugly black smoke belching from the factory chimneys couldn't take away from the beauty of the night.

Dora sank down on the Town Hall steps, relieved to be alone. Joe seemed to close in on her so tightly, she barely had a chance to breathe. Everywhere she looked, he was there, pressing against her, telling her he loved her, his intense gaze on her, urging her to love him back.

But she couldn't. No matter how hard she tried, she knew she would never have those kind of feelings for him. It was time to make that clear, she decided, before he wasted any more of his time on her.

A long dark shadow fell across her, and she realised she was no longer alone. Thinking Joe must have come looking for her again, she said, 'Look, please leave me alone. I just need to be on my own for a minute.'

The shadow didn't move. Dora swung round and saw Nick looking down at her.

'I'm sorry.' he mumbled. 'I didn't know you were out here. I'll go somewhere else...'

He started up the steps, but Dora called him back.

'It's all right,' she said. 'I thought you were someone else. You can stay, if you want?'

He hesitated, then sat down a few feet away from her.

They stared out over the street together, both lost in their own thoughts. Guests wandered up and down the steps around them, but neither of them seemed to notice.

'Where's Ruby?' Dora broke the silence finally.

'Having a dance with Harry Fishman. I'm not really one for dancing.'

'Me neither.'

She felt his sidelong glance. 'You were dancing earlier?'

'Only because Joe wanted to.'

The silence stretched between them. 'Thanks for going to see Ruby.' Nick's voice was gruff. 'It really perked her up.'

Dora felt a pang of guilt, remembering her secret. 'She looks a lot brighter.'

'She is. It was her idea to come tonight. She thought it would do us both good to get out.'

Dora risked a glance at him. He was gazing up at the sky, and his profile looked as if it had been carved from stone. 'And is it doing you good?' she asked.

Nick turned his head slowly to look at her. Dora was shocked to see the raw wretchedness in his eyes.

'I can't stand it,' he said.

Anger rose up inside Dora. If she could have got hold of Ruby at that moment, she would have wrung her neck.

'I suppose it might be a bit too much, what with all the people and the music and everything...'

'I'm not talking about that,' he dismissed. 'What I can't stand is seeing you with *him*.'

This was so completely unexpected, it took her breath away. Dora stared at him, unable to speak. But before she could find her voice, Nick said, 'I'm sorry, I had no right to say that. It's not fair on you or Ruby.' His words came out in a rush, tumbling over each other. 'Forget I said it, I'm

238

not thinking straight.' He stumbled to his feet. 'I should be getting back, Ruby will be wondering where I am...'

'Nick, wait!'

He stopped, his back still turned to her. Dora could see the muscles in his broad shoulders tensing under his suit jacket.

'What?' he said.

Tell him, a voice inside her head urged. Tell him the truth about Ruby and you can change everything.

'You're right,' she said. 'You should get back to Ruby.'

She watched him as he climbed the steps without looking back.

Penny Willard had had too much to drink. So much for sticking to the fruit punch, Joe thought as he disentangled himself yet again from her grasping fingers.

'Dora's been gone a while,' he said, his eyes fixed on the doors. 'I hope she's all right?'

'Oh, she'll be fine,' Penny dismissed. She smiled at him, her smudged lipstick blurring the edges of her wide mouth. 'She must be very sure of herself, to leave a handsome young man like you alone among all these single women?' she teased.

'She knows I love her.'

'And does she love you?'

Joe frowned. 'What's that supposed to mean?'

'Oh, nothing. It's just she never talks about you, not like the other girls talk about their boyfriends.' Penny cocked her head, listening as the band struck up again. 'I love this tune. "Pennies from Heaven".' She started to hum to herself, swaying from side to side. 'Funny, isn't it? That's my name … Penny. Penny's from Heaven.'

'And are you?' Joe asked absently, his gaze fixed on the doors.

'That's for you to find out, isn't it?' She tapped his chest playfully. 'Dance with me and I might show you.'

'Thanks, love, but I'd better go and see what's keeping Dora.'

'I'll come with you.' Penny tottered unsteadily after him. 'I can check in the Ladies' cloakroom, make sure she hasn't fainted or anything!'

But Dora wasn't in the cloakroom. 'Perhaps she's run away?' Penny giggled.

'She'd better not have.' Joe tried to smile, but inside he was burning with humiliation. 'She's probably just gone outside for a smoke. I'll take a look.'

He ran down the staircase, taking the steps two at a time. He could hear Penny clattering behind, unsteady in her heels, but he didn't wait for her. He was at the door before she had even reached the last step.

He was about to go outside when he spotted Dora through the frosted glass. And she wasn't alone.

Joe pulled in a sharp, jerky breath, as if someone had thrown a bucket of cold water over him.

Dora and Nick were sitting on opposite sides of the steps, not touching, not even looking at each other. But somehow he knew they were together. It was as if there was an invisible rope binding them.

Penny caught up with him. 'Well? Is she out there – oh!' She peered through the etched glass, tilting her head to get a better view. 'Well, I never! Nick Riley. I knew it.' She smirked. 'There was always something about the way she looked at him…'

Joe turned away and paced across the foyer, fighting down his anger. He was so blinded by rage, the black-and-white floor tiles blurred in front of his eyes.

'He's coming back!' Penny rushed over to him, quivering with excitement, just as the doors flew open and Nick appeared. He strode straight past them, not even looking Joe's way as he lurked in the shadows.

'Well?' Penny's face fell into a pout of disappointment. 'Aren't you going to go after him and punch him on the nose?'

Joe watched Nick stomping up the stairs. He could feel a slow burn of rage creeping like molten lava through his veins. 'He ain't worth it.'

'Neither is she.' Penny shot a filthy look towards the doors. 'To be honest, I don't know why you bother with her. You could do a lot better for yourself.'

But I don't want to do a lot better, he thought. He wanted Dora, simple as that. And the fact that she plainly didn't want him only made him more determined to have her.

'Why don't you come back inside?' Penny coaxed. 'I bet I know how to cheer you up.'

'Some other time,' he said, heading for the doors.

Dora was still sitting on the steps, her face

241

buried in her hands. She turned at the sound of his footsteps. Joe pretended not to notice the hope dying in her eyes when she saw it was him.

'There you are.' He forced lightness into his voice. 'I wondered where you'd got to.'

She gave him a weary smile. 'Sorry, Joe. I didn't mean to abandon you like that.'

'Are you coming back inside?'

She shook her head. 'Would you mind if I went home? I've got a headache and I don't really feel like dancing.'

'Neither do I,' he admitted heavily. The thought of going back into that ballroom and pretending everything was fine was beyond him. 'I'll walk you home.'

'There's no need. I don't want to ruin your evening?'

He sent her a long, steady look. 'I think it's too late for that, don't you?'

Chapter Twenty-Three

There was something different about Joe as they walked home. He slouched along beside her, his hands thrust deep into his pockets. Dora was grateful not to have to fend off his wandering arm, but the quiet anger vibrating off him made her wary.

'I'm sorry we had to leave early,' she said again.

''S'all right,' he muttered.

She glanced at his sulky profile. 'You didn't

have to come with me, you know. I could have walked home by myself.'

'Are you sure you just don't want me out of the way so you can sneak off and meet him?'

She frowned. 'What are you talking about?'

'Don't look so innocent,' snarled Joe. 'I saw you two together. How long has it been going on with you and that porter?'

The truth dawned. 'You mean Nick?'

'Of course I mean Nick! Why, who else are you playing about with?' The harshness in his voice shocked her.

'I'm not playing about with anyone.'

'That's not how it seemed to me. I saw the way you looked at each other. Does his missus know?'

Dora caught the angry glint in Joe's eye and knew there would be no reasoning with him. 'You don't know anything about it.'

She started to walk away but he snatched at her arm, swinging her round to face him. 'Oh, no, you don't. You don't walk away from me!'

Dora looked down at his hand gripping her arm. 'Let go of me.'

'That's all you ever say to me, isn't it? Don't touch me ... stay away.' His lip curled. 'I thought it was because you were such a nice girl. But I was wrong, wasn't I? You were just stringing me along, while all the time you were having it off with a married man.' Joe's handsome face was flushed with temper. 'I bet you were having a right laugh at me, weren't you? What a mug I've been, thinking you were so different from the other girls. When all the time you were the biggest slut of them all...'

243

Dora's stinging slap stopped him mid-sentence. 'How dare you! Don't you ever call me that.'

'What else would you call a girl who goes with married men?'

'I don't have to listen to this.' She wrenched her arm free but he grabbed her shoulders, slamming her back against the wall.

'I told you, you don't walk away from me,' he hissed.

'Get off, you're hurting me.' She tried to struggle free but he pinned her, his full weight against her. She could feel the hardness of him, pressing into her.

'Not until you've given me a taste of what Nick Riley's been having all this time.' Joe's eyes were mad with malice, his mouth twisted into a terrifying leer. She barely recognised the man she thought she knew.

She suddenly remembered her stepfather Alf and the way he used to force himself on her. Her heart was crashing against her ribs, but she forced herself to stay calm.

'Let me go and we'll forget this ever happened,' she whispered.

'Forget it? Oh, no, love. I want to make this a night to remember.'

Joe's mouth came down on hers before Dora could make a move to stop him. There was no tenderness in his kiss. His mouth was fierce and possessive, grinding against hers, his tongue invading. Dora couldn't breathe, couldn't even cry out in pain as her lips were crushed against her teeth. She tried to jerk her head away but his hand came up, clamping around her chin so she couldn't move, couldn't breathe. She felt the damp, rough brickwork grazing her bare skin as he rammed the length of his body against hers, his hand fumbling in the folds of her skirt.

No. A single thought, as clear and piercing as a beam of light, penetrated her fear. Not this time. Not again.

She brought her knee up with all her strength between Joe's legs. He buckled instantly, doubling up, gurgling with shock and pain.

He let her go to clutch at his groin and Dora seized her chance to get away, kicking off her heels and sprinting down the road towards the hospital.

Helen was sitting up in bed studying when Dora burst in.

'You're early, I didn't expect–' Her smile died when she looked up and saw the state her friend was in. Dora's dress was smeared with dirt, one strap hanging loosely off her freckled shoulder. Her shoes were missing and her stockings were shredded and bloody. 'Oh my God, Doyle, what happened to you?'

'I fell over.'

Helen threw down her pen and scrambled off the bed. 'You're shaking like a leaf.'

'I'm just a bit c-cold, that's all.' Dora sank down on her bed. She didn't resist as Helen pulled the quilt up around her shoulders, fussing over her.

'What really happened?' she asked.

'I told you, I fell over.'

Helen looked at the fingertip-shaped bruises blossoming on the plump flesh of Dora's arms. 'And did you get these falling over, too?' Dora stared at the ground. 'You can tell me. I'm your friend.'

Dora was silent, her jaw obstinately set.

'Very well,' Helen sighed. 'At least let me help get you cleaned up.'

'I can manage.'

'I'm sure you can, but I want to help. You get undressed while I run you a bath.'

At least with everyone out at the ball there was enough hot water for a decent bath. Helen filled the tub to the brim. All the time she couldn't stop thinking about those bruises on her friend's arms, or the bloody grazes down her back.

She had just finished running the bath when Dora came in, huddled in her old dressing gown.

'There you are,' said Helen. 'You'll feel better after a nice hot soak.'

'Thank you.' Dora's lips were so swollen and bruised, she could barely manage a smile.

'I wish I could do more.' Helen hesitated. 'Are you sure there's nothing you want to tell me?'

Dora shook her head. 'I already said—'

'You fell over. Yes, I know,' Helen sighed.

She went back to their room. Dora's clothes were abandoned in a heap beside her bed. Helen picked up her shredded, blood-stained stockings and threw them away, then folded up the dress and stuffed it to the back of the wardrobe.

Dora returned half an hour later, her red hair hanging in damp corkscrew curls around her face.

'Do you feel better?' Helen asked.

'Much better, thanks.' But Helen noticed how carefully Dora eased off her dressing gown, wincing with pain. She was wearing her flannel nightgown underneath, feet rammed into her old slippers.

Helen watched her out of the corner of her eye as she turned off her bedside lamp and slipped into bed, pulling the sheets up to her chin. There was no point in trying to talk to her any more, she decided. Once Dora had made her mind up she wasn't going to speak, wild horses wouldn't have dragged a word out of her.

Helen went back to making her notes, and a moment later she heard Dora's deep, even breathing, telling her she had drifted off to sleep.

'Describe the complications of Scarlet Fever.' Helen shuddered as she read the sample exam question, thinking of Charlie.

Seeing him so ill had frightened her. But she forced herself to be practical. His mother was right: Scarlet Fever might be nasty but in a week or two he would be as right as rain.

She picked up her pen and began to write. 'Complications of Scarlet Fever include otitis medea, hyperpyrexia, kidney failure—'

'No!' Dora's sudden cry made Helen jump, splotching ink on the virgin whiteness of her new page. 'Get off me! Don't touch me!'

'Doyle?' Helen put down her pen, slipped out of bed and crossed the room. 'Doyle, wake up!' She held Dora's thrashing arms, trying to still her. 'It's all right, you're safe.'

Dora's eyes shot open. Her body was rigid. 'Where ... what happened?'

'You had a nightmare,' Helen soothed her. 'But it's all right now, you're quite safe.'

She put out her hand to stroke the curls off

247

Dora's face. She felt Dora flinch under her touch, then the fight seemed to go out of her and she relaxed. A few moments later, she drifted back to sleep.

Helen was still writing by torchlight when Millie crept in just after midnight. She tiptoed exaggeratedly across the room, her shoes in her hand.

'How did you get in?' Helen whispered.

'We climbed through O'Hara's window.' Millie hiccuped loudly. 'It was safer than climbing all the way up here.'

'You're lucky you didn't break your neck, the state you're in.'

'Don't be silly, we've done it lots of times. It's perfectly safe ... ouch!' Millie tripped over her bedframe and stumbled headlong across the room.

Helen watched her climbing to her feet, and tried not to smile. 'Did you have fun?'

'Rather! Our gin ran out quite quickly, but luckily we met a couple of very sweet med students who sneaked us drinks. We were all terribly merry, but then one of the boys was sick all over Mr Latimer's Bentley. Such larks! His chauffeur was utterly furious. Chased us for miles.' She shrieked with laughter, then quickly covered her mouth.

She flopped backwards on to her bed, her arms outspread. 'How was your evening?'

'Charlie has Scarlet Fever.'

'Really?' Millie catapulted upright, instantly alert.. 'Oh, bad luck How is he?'

'Feeling very sorry for himself, so his mother says.'

'I'm not surprised. Scarlet Fever is beastly. But I'm sure he'll be up and about in no time.'

Dora stirred. Millie squinted into the darkness. 'Is that Doyle? What's she doing back so early?'

Helen hesitated, wondering whether to tell Millie about the state Dora was in when she returned home. She doubted if their room mate would thank her for sharing the secret.

'I think she wanted an early night,' she said, and glanced back at Dora's hunched shape under the sheets. 'She had another nightmare.'

'Really? She hasn't had one of those in months.' Millie turned to look at Dora, frowning. 'I wonder what brought that on?'

Helen looked at the girl, fast asleep again. 'I wonder,' she said.

Chapter Twenty-Four

'But Joe's said he's sorry,' Katie O'Hara protested.

Dora looked down at the plate of greasy grey stew in front of her. 'Sorry isn't good enough.'

'He couldn't help it. He was a bit tipsy.'

'A bit tipsy!' Dora caught Sister Sutton's sharp glance from the other end of the dining table, and lowered her voice. 'He was pie-eyed!'

'All the more reason why you should forgive him,' Katie said through a mouthful of food. 'He didn't know what he was doing.'

He knew what he was doing, all right, Dora thought. Two weeks after the ball, and she was still reliving what had happened that night. God only knew how far Joe would have gone if she

249

hadn't fought him off.

But he was sorry for it now. The day after the ball he had turned up at the hospital gates to see her, but Mr Hopkins had turned him away at the Porters' Lodge. Since then Joe had sent her notes and telephoned the nurses' home so many times that Dora had started to jump every time she heard the jangle of the bell in the hall.

And now he'd appealed to Katie for help.

'I don't understand what all the fuss is about.' O'Hara shrugged. 'All he did was get a bit fresh with you. All men try it on.'

Dora felt herself blushing as several pairs of interested eyes turned in her direction.

She put down her fork. 'Look, I know Tom's asked you to put in a good word for Joe, but you're wasting your time. As far as I'm concerned, it's over. So do me a favour and stop discussing my private business in front of everyone!'

Katie looked hurt. 'You'll regret it,' she mumbled. 'Joe Armstrong's a good catch.' Dora kept her head down and didn't reply. 'I'm only saying–'

'Well, don't,' Millie cut in. 'Could we talk about something else, please? I don't know about you, but I'm finding this constant talk about Doyle's love life rather tedious.' She skewered a lump of gristle on the end of her fork and held it up for closer inspection. 'Could someone tell me what this meat we're eating is supposed to be?'

'Beef,' someone said.

'Rabbit?' suggested another.

'One of old Latimer's patients!' someone else chimed in, and soon there was a lively debate around the table.

Dora shot a quick, grateful look at Millie. She might seem a bit flighty at times, but she knew how to smooth ruffled feathers.

'Which drugs or agents could be locally applied to check haemorrhage?'

'Let's see ... there's adrenalin, tannic acid, gallic acid, turpentine, hamamelis...' Helen took the dripping flannel out of the bowl of iced water and wrung it out. 'Cautery, of course, then heat, cold, and...' she paused for a moment to think, then it came to her '...hydrogen peroxide,' she finished. 'There. How did I do?'

'Word perfect, as usual.' Charlie looked up admiringly from the textbook. 'How do you remember all those complicated words?'

'I've had three years of practice. And I study a lot.'

'I'm surprised you have any time, what with working nights and spending all day with me. I hope you're not wearing yourself out?'

'Don't be silly. I want to be here.'

'All the same, I'd hate to think I was keeping you from your revision...'

'What do you think we're doing now?' Helen nodded towards the textbook. 'Now hold still while I put this on for you.'

He submitted meekly, lifting his chest for her to apply the cold compress to his swollen throat.

She didn't tell him about the telephone call she'd had with her mother the previous day. Constance had telephoned the nurses' home because she had heard Charlie was unwell.

251

At first Helen thought she might have called because she was worried about him. But Constance's first words had soon dismissed that hope.

'I trust you're not neglecting your studies to spend time with him?' Her voice was sharp with reproof. 'May I remind you, Helen, you have your Finals coming up in October. I wouldn't like to think of three years' study going to waste because you have your mind on other things.'

It had taken all Helen's forbearance for her to make the right noises and assure her mother that she was glued to her books, when deep inside she felt a slow burn of resentment. Not once had Constance asked how Charlie was feeling.

'Helen?' She came back to the present to find him watching her. 'You're looking very serious all of a sudden. What's the matter?'

'Nothing.' She forced a smile and took away the compress. 'There, how does that feel now?'

'Better, thank you. But you really don't have to nurse me, you know. My mum's bad enough, flapping around like a headless hen!'

'Oi! I heard that!' Nellie Dawson bustled into the room carrying a fresh jug of water. 'Any more lip from you, young man, and I'll pack you off back to your bedroom.'

'Don't do that!' Charlie groaned. 'I don't think I could stand looking at those four walls any longer!'

Since he was no longer infectious, Nellie had moved her son down to sleep on the settee in the front parlour. At least he could feel part of the family again, although Helen knew he was restless to be up and about.

'How is the patient?' Nellie asked Helen.

'He's doing well,' Helen replied. 'His temperature is normal, and the swelling seems to be going down, doesn't it?'

His mother nodded. 'And I've been using that antiseptic lotion for the rash, like you said.'

'Will you two stop talking about me as if I wasn't here?' Charlie glared from one to the other. 'I told you, I'm fine. Anyway, I've got to be up and about by August Bank Holiday, because I've got a surprise planned,' he went on.

Helen and Nellie looked at each other. 'What kind of surprise?' Helen asked.

'We're going on an outing.' Charlie beamed at them both. 'I've booked us all on the works charabanc to Southend. I thought Dad could mind the stall, and you could bring the kids, Mum. You deserve a treat, what with me being laid up and everything.'

'Ooh, lovely! I haven't had a trip to Southend in years.' Nellie sighed with pleasure. 'The kids will be pleased an' all.'

Charlie looked at Helen. 'I reckoned you could do with a break, too. You've been working so hard lately. You'll be able to come, won't you?'

Helen hesitated. Her mother would absolutely forbid it.

'Try and stop me!' she grinned.

'That's settled, then.' Charlie looked pleased with himself. 'Right, we'd best get back to work.' He picked up the textbook. 'We've got a lot to do, if you're going to pass these exams.'

Chapter Twenty-Five

Dora had never been to the ballet before. She had never wanted to go, either, but a theatre up west had sent a batch of free tickets to the hospital, and Katie O'Hara had badgered her into going.

Not that Dora had seen much of the show. She was so tired that as soon as the lights dimmed she had sunk down in her seat and fallen asleep. She only meant to close her eyes for a moment to rest them, but the next thing she was waking up with a start to rapturous applause. Katie was on her feet and joining in so enthusiastically, Dora guessed she must have missed a wonderful show.

'Wasn't it grand?' Katie sighed as they sat on the top desk of the bus, heading back to Bethnal Green.

'Yes,' Dora lied, turning her head to stare out of the window at the lights of the city.

'Lane will be sorry she missed it. She's always going to the ballet with her mother. I expect she'll want to know all about it.'

'I expect so.'

Katie hesitated. 'So ... could you work out what was going on, exactly?' she asked.

Dora pretended to think. 'Well ... I know there was a lot of dancing,' she invented. 'People jumping about, kicking their legs in the air.'

'And there was that man in the tights,' Katie put in helpfully. 'He was quite an eyeful, wasn't he?'

'He was indeed.' Dora racked her brains for something to else to say, then gave up. 'I'm sorry,' she sighed. 'To be honest I nodded off as soon as the flaming thing started.'

To her surprise, Katie laughed. 'Me too! I was dead to the world from the minute the curtain went up.'

Dora stared at her in astonishment. 'But you were clapping?'

'Only because everyone else was!' They looked at each other and laughed. 'I still enjoyed it,' Katie added. 'It was the best sleep I've had in ages.'

'Me too!' Dora agreed. 'Best not tell Lane that, though, eh?'

'Oh, Jesus!' Katie rolled her eyes heavenwards. 'She's going to ask me all about it. She's going to want to know every detail!'

'You'll have to make it up.'

St Peter's church clock was striking ten when they got off the bus on Hackney Road.

'Gawd, we're so late!' Dora started to run but Katie didn't move. She stood at the bus stop, looking around her.

Dora turned back 'What are you waiting for?'

'You'll see.' Katie glanced up and down the street. 'It shouldn't be long ... ah, here he is now.'

Dora heard a man's footsteps striding up the street towards them. She didn't need to look round to know who it was.

She turned on Katie furiously. 'You did this deliberately! No wonder you were so keen for me to come out with you tonight.'

'I'm sorry, but he begged me to do it.' Katie's face was full of anguish. 'He was so upset when

255

you wouldn't talk to him...'

'*He's* upset? What about me?' She quivered with rage, every nerve on alert as Joe approached.

'Hello, Dora.'

She turned slowly to look at him. He stood there in his police uniform, his head bent. He looked contrite, like a kicked puppy.

'I'll leave you to it,' Katie said, but Dora stopped her.

'Oh, no, you don't! You're staying here with me, O'Hara.'

Katie's eyes flew to Joe. 'But–'

'I'm not being left alone with *him*.'

Joe sighed impatiently. 'You'll be quite safe. I ain't going to hurt you. All I want to do is apologise.'

'At least hear him out,' Katie pleaded. 'You owe him that much.'

'I don't owe him anything!' Dora thought about telling Katie what he had done, but she probably wouldn't believe it. Joe Armstrong could do no wrong in her eyes.

'Please, Dora?' Joe begged. 'Just five minutes, that's all I'm asking.'

She sighed. 'If I listen to you that long, will you promise to leave me alone afterwards?'

'If that's what you want.'

'But I'm warning you, if you try anything–'

'I won't,' he promised. He looked sick with nerves. Or perhaps he was just remembering that knee she'd delivered to his privates, Dora thought with grim amusement.

'Thank you,' he said quietly, after Katie had gone.

'Don't get any ideas. I only did it to stop you sending me notes and calling the nurses' home. The Home Sister's getting as fed up of it as I am.' Dora confronted him. 'It was a low trick, getting O'Hara to do your dirty work for you, though. You ought to know by now I don't like being forced into anything.'

He winced. 'I know. I'm sorry.' He lowered his gaze. 'I feel so ashamed of the way I behaved that night. I've thought of nothing else since.'

'Me neither,' Dora muttered.

She started to walk back towards the hospital, and Joe fell into step beside her.

'It's not like me.' The words came out in a rush. 'I'm not that sort of bloke, honestly. I would never have done something like that if you hadn't pushed me into it–'

Dora faced him. 'Are you saying I *asked* to be attacked?'

'No, no, of course not.' A blush swept up his face. 'I'm not saying that. I was just so jealous when I saw you with him...'

'You had no right to get angry. I'm not your property.'

His chin lifted and she caught a glint in his eyes, shadowed by the brim of his helmet. 'You're my girl.'

'No, I'm not. I never was. That's what I kept trying to tell you, but you wouldn't listen to me.'

Joe flinched as if she'd slapped him hard around the face. 'I'm sorry,' he mumbled.

As they crossed the street he went to take her arm and then thought better of it.

'Can we start again?' he said. 'I'm truly sorry

257

about what happened, Dora. I know I don't deserve it, but I'm asking for another chance to prove how much I love you.'

Dora suppressed a sigh. 'No, Joe.'

'Just because of one night?' There was a sudden, sharp edge to his voice.

'Not just because of that night.' Dora paused for a moment, searching for the right words. Whatever she said, he chose not to understand her. She had no option but to be blunt, no matter how cruel it might seem. 'Look, Joe, I don't want to see you again.'

'You don't mean that.' He stared at her blankly. 'I love you. I want us to be together.'

'But I don't.'

He seemed genuinely confused, as if such a thought had never occurred to him. 'I can make you happy...'

'You can't, Joe. That's what I'm trying to tell you.'

He looked hurt, like a lost little boy. 'There's someone else, isn't there?'

'No,' she sighed. 'Why can't you just accept that I just don't want to be with you?'

He was silent for a moment. She could see rage like thunderclouds rolling in, darkening his face. Her eyes darted around, looking for places to run.

'You're confused,' he said finally. 'It's because of the other night, I'm sure of it. But if you just give me another chance–'

'For God's sake, Joe, how many more times do I have to spell it out?' She stopped talking for a moment. 'Did you hear that?'

'What?' Joe sounded sulky.

'That noise. It sounded like someone crying out.'

'It's probably just someone mucking about.' No sooner had he said it than a scream tore through the air.

'That doesn't sound like mucking about to me.' Dora lifted her face and began turning slowly to pick up the sound. 'It came from over there, I think. Near the railway arches.'

'Dora, wait!' She heard Joe calling to her as she sprinted in the direction of the sound. A second later he was running too, his footsteps pounding behind her, catching her easily.

She turned the corner and froze. At the other end of the street a gang of men, illuminated by a pool of lamplight, were kicking at something on the ground.

'Dora, don't!' Joe snatched at her sleeve but she shook him off and ran towards them.

'Oi! What do you think you're doing?'

They stopped for a moment, all turning towards her, five figures silhouetted against the lamplight. Then they took off and disappeared into the railway arches.

Dora stopped and bent double, fighting for breath. 'They went that way,' she panted to Joe, pointing up the street. 'If you go after them, you'll corner them under the arches.'

He didn't move. 'Joe?' She frowned at him. 'Did you hear what I said? Go after them.'

'It's too late, they're long gone.'

'But there's no way out through...' she started to say. He was already walking towards the bundle on the ground. She watched as Joe bent down,

259

put out a hand towards it, then stood straight up again.

'Find a telephone box and call an ambulance,' he ordered, fighting to keep his voice level.

'Why, what is it?' She took a step towards him, but he put his hand out, barring her way.

'Just go and call that ambulance, Dora. Please?' The bundle moved slightly and she realised it was actually a person, cowering and covered in blood. Dora's hand flew to her mouth. 'Oh, God! No!'

She tried to push past his restraining arm, but Joe held her back. 'You don't want to look, it's too nasty.'

'But you don't understand,' Dora said, fighting to get past. 'I know her. It's Esther Gold!'

Dora barely recognised the bloody pulp of a face, hidden under a carapace of clotted blood. Ugly purplish swelling had distorted Esther's eyes to slits. Her swollen mouth hung open limply, revealing bloody gaps where her teeth had been smashed. Her hair was matted and stuck to her face by blood.

'Is she ... dead?' Joe whispered.

'I don't know.' Dora held her breath, then released it when she felt the feeble jump of a pulse under her fingers. 'No, she's alive, thank God. But her pulse is very weak, and her respiration is shallow. She's in a very bad way.' Dora took charge then. 'Go down to that pub up on the corner and see if they've got any brandy and blankets. Get them to call for the ambulance.'

She sat alone in the middle of the empty street,

cradling Esther's head in her lap. Dora took out her handkerchief and tried to clean off some of the blood that caked the wounded woman's face, but her hands were shaking so badly she couldn't manage it.

She saw the lights go on in the pub on the corner, and shortly afterwards Joe came running back up the street with his arms full of blankets.

'How is she?'

'Hanging on, just about.' Dora took the blankets from him and tucked them around Esther's body as best she could. Esther had gone very still, her breathing ominously shallow. Dora could hardly bring herself to look at her. 'Did you telephone for an ambulance?'

'The landlord's doing it now.' He looked down at Esther. 'Should we try to get her to the pub, keep her warm?'

Dora shook her head. 'Best not to move her, we don't know how bad her injuries are.' She lifted her gaze to meet Joe's. 'Why didn't you go after those men?'

'I couldn't catch them.'

'But you didn't even try.' She saw his grim expression and realisation dawned. 'You let them go,' she said with disbelief.

Joe's jaw clenched. 'We've got our orders.'

'What orders?' Dora said scornfully. 'To turn a blind eye? To let thugs walk the streets?'

'If we went round arresting every trouble-making Blackshirt, the cells would be full by the end of the night.'

'So what? That's your job, isn't it? To protect the rest of us from scum like that?'

'I told you, we've got our orders,' Joe insisted stubbornly. 'I don't make the rules, do I?'

'No, but you're happy enough to carry them out!'

Dora looked down at Esther's bloody, ravaged face. Her shallow breath was gurgling in her throat.

The ambulance came hurtling round the corner, bell ringing. As the driver got out and ran round to the back to throw open the doors, Dora turned to Joe.

'I'm going with her.'

'We'll both go.'

Dora shook her head. 'I don't want you to come.'

'But I'm a policeman. I should be there...'

'No, Joe, what you *should* be doing is looking for the swine who did this to Esther.' Dora stood back, brushing down her dress as the ambulance men set to work lifting Esther's limp body on to the stretcher.

'Don't you blame me for this!' she heard Joe's voice calling after her as she followed them towards the ambulance.

Dora looked back at him. 'Why shouldn't I blame you?' she said. 'From where I'm standing, you're every bit as guilty as those Blackshirt thugs!'

Chapter Twenty-Six

'Still no change, Nurse?'

Dora read the despair in Dr Adler's face. There were deep grooves around his mouth, and dark shadows under his eyes. It was hard to believe this was the same man whose booming laughter could so often be heard around the Casualty department. He had aged ten years since Esther Gold had been admitted to a private room off the Female Medical ward.

Dora felt as if she had aged, too. She hadn't been able to sleep all night, and in the morning she was almost too afraid to face the night nurse's ward report, convinced that it would be bad news.

'No, Doctor. I'm sorry.'

'At least you're here to keep an eye on her.' Dr Adler's smile was strained. 'It's a blessing she was sent to your new ward, isn't it, Nurse Doyle?'

'Yes, Sir.'

'It will mean a lot to Esther to see a familiar face when she wakes up,' he said bracingly.

If she wakes up. Dora read the unspoken message in his bleak eyes.

Dr Adler consulted the pulse and respiration Dora had carefully noted on Esther's chart, then put his finger to the artery in her neck, as if to reassure himself she was still alive. Her breath was shallow and her face, where it wasn't distended and purple, was the colour of marble.

It wasn't just her face, either. Under her starched hospital gown her body was a mass of bruises where she had been kicked and punched.

'So all we can do now is wait,' Dr Adler said. 'We won't know the extent of the damage until she regains consciousness...' The catch in his voice betrayed him. He took a deep, steadying breath and thrust Esther's chart back into Dora's hands. 'Keep a close eye on her,' he said. 'And I want you to send for me the moment she wakes up. Immediately, Nurse. Do you understand?'

Dora nodded. 'Yes, Doctor.'

He gave her a weary smile. 'I know she's in good hands, Nurse Doyle.'

As he left, Dora said, 'Excuse me, Doctor? I just wondered ... has anyone spoken to her father?'

Dr Adler nodded, his expression grave. 'The police have been to visit him, I believe.'

Dora looked away so he wouldn't see the disgust on her face. The police hadn't done enough for Esther. 'Poor man,' she said. 'Esther is all he has.'

'I know,' Dr Adler said heavily. 'I'll go and see him later. Hopefully by then we'll have some good news.'

But from the look on his face Dora could tell he didn't expect it any more than she did.

It was a long day. As she went about her work, Dora kept her eyes fixed on Esther's door, constantly alert for any sign of panic, of screens being hastily pulled around her bed, anything to show that she had taken a turn for the worse.

When she wasn't kept away with other jobs, Dora attended to Esther constantly: taking her temperature, checking her pulse, refilling her hot water bottles or just holding her hand.

Sister Everett caught her watching over the patient shortly after Dora had been sent for her break.

'Aren't you supposed to be off duty until five?'

'Yes, Sister. Sorry, Sister. I just wanted to make sure Miss Gold was all right...'

Sister Everett's brows rose. 'I assure you she will be in perfectly good hands until you return, Nurse Doyle.'

'Yes, of course, Sister.' Dora lowered her gaze.

'It's quite all right, Doyle, I understand she is a friend of yours. It's only natural for you to be concerned about her.' Sister consulted the chart. 'She has been unconscious for some hours, I see?'

'Yes, Sister.'

'But at least her pulse and respiration are steady, if weak.' Sister Everett replaced the chart. 'You know, it may be a good sign that she hasn't woken up yet,' she said. 'The body sometimes needs to conserve all its energy to repair and recover.'

'I hope so, Sister.' Dora rubbed eyes that felt gritty from lack of sleep.

'Talking of recovering, I suggest you rest now,' Sister Everett said. 'You will be no use to anyone, least of all your friend Miss Gold, if you're half asleep.'

'Yes, Sister.'

'Have something to eat, then go back to the nurses' home, wash and change into a clean uniform. It will make you feel much fresher.'

'Thank you, Sister.'

Dora obeyed Sister Everett, and returned to the nurses' home. She moved slowly, her limbs heavy, aching for sleep. But as soon as she lay down on her bed all trace of tiredness vanished. She could feel every lump in the horsehair mattress under her spine as she stared at the ceiling, waiting for five o'clock to come round.

It was just striking the hour when Dora hurried back to Everett ward. She held her breath as she turned down the passage towards the double doors, then released it in a sigh of relief when she saw Esther's door was still half-open.

A figure in brown overalls was sitting at her bedside.

'Pete?' Her brother jumped guiltily to his feet. 'You know you're not supposed to be up here. What are you doing?'

He glanced down at Esther. 'I heard she'd been brought in. How is she?'

Dora frowned. 'Not good.'

'But she'll get better, won't she?'

'I don't know. We're not sure whether she'll wake up, or what state she'll be in if she does. A blow to the head like that can do all kinds of damage. She might be paralysed, lose her sight or hearing ... Pete?' She stared at her brother. He had sunk down on to the chair beside Esther's bed, his face buried in his hands. 'Are you crying? Why are you so upset? You hardly know her–'

Realisation hit Dora. She tasted bile rising in her throat and covered her mouth. 'Oh, God, no! Pete, please tell me it wasn't you–'

'No!' His face was pale under his shock of ginger hair. 'I never laid a finger on her, I swear.'

'But you know who did?' Dora watched him mopping his eyes with the sleeve of his brown overall. Her insides turned to ice. 'You were there, weren't you? When those men set about her?' She looked down at Esther's heavily bandaged face. 'You ... you stood by and watched them do that to her.'

'There was nothing I could do!' Peter whined. 'I didn't know what they were going to do, did I? I thought they were just going to push her around a bit, have a bit of fun. But then she started fighting back, and they didn't like that, so...' He shuddered.

'Why didn't you help her?'

'I tried. I was trying to pull them off when you and Joe arrived, and they all scarpered. You've got to believe me,' he pleaded. 'I did my best.'

'Yeah, you were a right hero,' Dora said coldly. Her heart felt like stone in her chest. She looked at Peter, snivelling with tears of self-pity. She hadn't thought it was possible to hate her own brother, but he didn't feel like her flesh and blood any more. He was a vicious stranger, turned feral by hate.

'You don't know what they're like. Dora, please, you've got to understand. I didn't mean this to happen...' He reached out to her, but she snatched her hand away.

'Don't,' she said. 'Don't you dare touch me.' She shook her head. 'I don't know you any more, Peter Doyle.'

He stared at her, stricken faced. 'Don't say that! I'm still your brother—'

'My brother wouldn't have stood by and watched an innocent woman nearly killed by a bunch of thugs. But you're one of them now, aren't you?'

'I'm not!'

'You wear that uniform, don't you? You go to their meetings, pass around their pamphlets on the street, help spread their filth...'

'I thought I was doing some good!'

'Good?' Dora lunged forward and grabbed his hair, yanking his head up. 'Look at the *good* you and your mates have done. Go on, take a look at her!' He struggled to free himself but she held him fast. 'I want you to remember her face, Peter Doyle. I want it to haunt you every bloody day of your life. And next time you and your pals are strutting around in your black shirts, I want you to see her staring back at you!'

'Stop it!' Peter jerked himself out of her grasp. 'Do you think I don't know what I've done? It was all right at first, but some of the things they say and do – it turns my stomach, Dora, I swear!'

'Then go to the police. Turn them in for what they did.'

Peter shook his head. 'I can't.' He looked up at her with fear-filled eyes. 'You don't know them, Dora. You don't just hand in your uniform and walk away. And you certainly don't rat on them. Once you're in with them, that's it. There's no getting out.'

She stared at him in contempt. 'You're frightened they'll come after you?'

'Not me.' He lifted his eyes to look at Esther. 'You've seen what they can do. What if it was Lily or Mum lying there?'

'They wouldn't do that.'

'Wouldn't they? You don't know them, Dora.

The last time I tried to stand up to them ... it was when they were planning to set fire to a shop. I told them I wanted no part of it, that I'd had enough. Two days later, a couple of blokes followed Bea home from school. Our little sister, Dor!' He knotted his hands together to stop them from shaking. 'They frightened her. Got her up against the wall and said they were going to do all kinds to her. Mum says she hasn't been able to sleep since.' He glanced at Esther. 'I'm sorry this has happened, I really am. But I've got to protect our family.'

Dora looked at his hopeless, desperate expression, and for the first time felt a twinge of compassion for her brother. In his own way he was trying to protect their family, just as she would. 'But surely if you told the police, they could do something...'

'The police?' Peter laughed harshly. 'What good would they do? They've been told to give them a wide berth, just like everyone else.'

Dora remembered what Joe had said. They had orders to turn a blind eye. No wonder the Blackshirts thought they could do as they liked.

'What are you going to do?' she asked.

'Nothing I can do,' he said. 'I'm in this up to my neck, Dora. I have to go along with them, whether I like it or not.'

'Even if someone gets killed?'

Peter didn't reply.

The sound of Sister Everett's voice ringing out from beyond the double doors brought Dora back to the present.

'You'd better go,' she said, 'Sister will be here in

a minute.'

She pushed him towards the doors. 'There was something else,' Peter said.

She stopped abruptly. 'What?'

He glanced towards Esther's bed. 'I ... I think she saw me,' he whispered.

'You mean, she recognised you?'

He nodded. 'I can't be sure, but I think so.' He turned to Dora, his face desperate. 'What if she wakes up and tells the police, Dor?'

Dora looked back at him steadily and said, 'I hope she does.'

Chapter Twenty-Seven

Ruby tried to smile fondly across the kitchen table at Danny as he struggled to cut up his sausages. His eating habits were truly disgusting, even worse than her brothers'. She could hardly bear to lift her gaze from her own plate, he made her feel so sick.

'Would you like me to help cut that up for you, ducks?' she offered through gritted teeth.

Danny stared at her, his strange pale eyes wary. Did he have to jump like that every time she spoke to him? He was so jittery she wanted to slap him. How was she ever supposed to impress Nick when Danny acted as if he was terrified of her?

'Ruby asked you a question, Dan,' Nick prompted him gently. 'You have to answer people when they talk to you.'

'It's all right, Nick.' Ruby reached over and took the knife and fork out of Dan's hands. She vented her frustration on his plate of food, hacking his sausages into tiny pieces. 'There you are, love,' she said, handing the fork back to him. 'You can manage now, can't you?'

'Look at him.' Nick nodded at Danny as he started to eat. 'He doesn't often get a decent meal.'

'It's only a few sausages!'

'All the same, it's more than my mum ever does for him.' He turned his gaze to her. 'Thank you,' he said.

Ruby felt herself blushing, warmed by his gratitude. She couldn't remember the last time Nick had looked at her so lovingly.

She had felt as if she was losing him over the past few weeks. Their day-to-day life hadn't changed – Nick went to work, came home for his tea, put his pay packet on the table every Friday and acted like the dutiful husband – but she could feel him slipping away, growing more and more remote from her every day.

The thought of losing him made her desperate. Which was why she'd come up with her new plan.

'It's not fair, the way your mum treats Danny,' she said. 'I worry about him.'

'Me too.' Nick's face darkened. He'd always worried about Danny. Tough as he was, his brother was his weak spot.

'I was thinking,' Ruby ventured. 'Perhaps he would be better off coming to live with us after all?'

271

Nick flashed a glance at her. 'Do you mean it?'

'Of course I mean it.' She toyed with her food. 'I know I said I didn't want him to move in before, but that was only because I didn't think we'd have room with the baby. But now...' She let the words trail off, gazing down at her plate.

Nick said nothing. Ruby flicked a quick look at him from under her lashes. His face was expressionless but she could see the sadness in his eyes. She wished she hadn't mentioned the baby.

She had never anticipated how much it would affect him. Her pregnancy had not been real to her, but it had to Nick. He tried to hide it for her sake, but his misery weighed down on them, and would sink them if she weren't careful.

'I just want to make sure Danny has a good home,' Ruby continued. 'Somewhere he's loved and looked after.'

She didn't look at Danny as she said it. The thought of him being under her roof actually made her feel sick. She could imagine him lolloping about, being clumsy, and breaking her precious things. And the thought of his strange eyes watching her wherever she went gave her the creeps. But she was desperate.

Nick turned to his brother. 'What do you reckon, Dan? Would you like to come and live with me and Ruby?'

'No,' Danny's voice was firm, for once with no trace of a stammer. 'I don't want to live with her.'

Ruby looked up sharply. Danny was staring straight at her across the kitchen table.

'Charming!' She tried to laugh.

'That's not a very nice thing to say, Danny,'

Nick said.

'She d-didn't say nice things about m-me.'

Ruby saw Nick's dark frown and laughed to cover her dismay. 'Oh, Danny, that's a wicked lie. I never said anything bad!'

'You d-did. I heard you. You told your m-mum I was a c-cabbage.'

She blushed, feeling Nick's eyes on her. 'You must have got that wrong, love,' she said kindly.

Danny nodded violently, his head loose on his spindly neck. 'You w-were talking to your mum. About the l-lady who was having a baby and then she wasn't. You said about pretending–'

'Well, I can't say as I remember it.' Ruby jumped up, gathering the plates. 'I'll clear these away and get the pudding. It's jam roly-poly, your favourite.'

She took her time lifting the muslin-wrapped pudding out of the saucepan, gripping the edge of the stove to stop herself from shaking. Trust Danny to remember that conversation! He couldn't remember his own name most of the time.

She was tense as they ate their pudding. Her eyes kept going to Danny, waiting for him to say something else. He only had to open his stupid mouth and he could blow her whole world apart.

After tea, Nick said he was taking his brother home.

'I'll come with you,' Ruby said, rushing to fetch her coat. 'I fancy a walk,' she added, seeing Nick's quizzical look.

'But it's raining?'

'I can still get some fresh air, can't I?'

'Suit yourself.' He shrugged.

June Riley was at home for once. She was asleep in the armchair by the empty kitchen grate, her feet up on the fender, cigarette hanging out of her mouth. In the corner, Cab Calloway sang about Minnie the Moocher on the wireless.

June opened one eye as they let themselves in the back door.

'You're late.' She took the cigarette out of her mouth and flicked ash into the grate. 'I thought you'd kidnapped the little sod.'

'As if you'd care,' Nick sneered back.

'I hope you haven't over-excited him?' June glared at her eldest son and then at Danny who ducked back outside. Ruby watched him clamber up to his perch on top of the coal bunker. She glanced back at Nick and June, still arguing, and went outside.

Danny was staring up at the grey sky. Ruby picked her way across the yard and sat down on an upturned tin bath, heedless of the damp that seeped through her coat. Rain pattered down around them.

'What are you looking at, Danny?' she asked.

'The stars.'

Ruby gazed up. It wasn't yet seven in the evening, and the sun was still high in the August sky, though presently it was hidden behind a pewter cloud. 'It ain't even dark yet!'

Danny shot her a quick, scornful look 'The stars are st-still out there, even when it ain't d-dark.'

'Is that right? You learn something new every day.' Ruby patted her hair. The rain would ruin her curls if she stayed out much longer. 'I bet you know all the stars' names, too. You remember a lot of things, don't you, Dan? Things we don't give you credit for.'

He turned his face back up to the sky. Ruby searched for the right words. What she said next was so important, it had to be exactly right.

'Look, Danny. What you heard me and my mum saying – about babies and stuff – none of it was true. We were just having a laugh, that's all.'

He didn't look at her. She couldn't even be sure he was listening.

Ruby took a deep breath. 'The thing is, Nick would be upset if he heard what we'd been saying. He'd be upset with me ... and with you, too. He might even not want to see you for a while. You wouldn't want that, would you?'

He still didn't look at her, but she caught the slightest shake of his head. 'It would upset me, too. And Frank and Dennis might want to know why I was upset, and then I'd have to tell them it was you who'd caused all the trouble. Can you imagine how angry they'd be with you then?'

She saw the flash of fear in his eyes. He'd understood that all right.

'I don't want to have to tell them anything,' Ruby went on. 'So let's just keep this our little secret, shall we?'

Before Danny had a chance to reply, Nick came out of the house. 'Right, we're off.' His sharp gaze moved from her to Danny. 'Is everything all right?'

'Everything's fine.' Ruby stood up, brushing the rain off her coat. 'We were just having a little chat. Ain't that right, Danny?' She sent him a meaningful look.

Nick took her hand as they walked home. It was

the first time he'd touched her in weeks.

'Thank you,' he said.

'What for?'

'For trying so hard with Danny.' His eyes met hers in the darkness. 'I know it's not easy for you.'

Ruby smiled at him. 'Don't be daft, he's family. Besides, you've put up with my mum often enough!'

'All the same, I really appreciate it.'

'Show me how much.' She turned, winding her arms around his neck, willing his rigid body to respond.

And it did. Slowly but surely, she felt his muscles relax as he melted against her, his strong arms slipping around her waist.

Chapter Twenty-Eight

'Spain,' Millie said flatly.

'There's a conflict over there. A group of army officers started a revolution against the government in the Canary Islands, and it's spread to the mainland.' She could hear the excitement in Seb's voice, crackling down the telephone line even though he was thousands of miles away. 'The newspaper wants me to go out to Madrid for when it starts.'

'It sounds dangerous.'

'It's a terrific assignment, and a great chance for me. And the bureau must think a lot of me, if they think I'm up to it...'

But Millie didn't hear the rest of his sentence. Her head was suddenly filled with the sound of gunfire, exploding bombs – and the gypsy woman's voice.

You'll be wearing mourning black next time you see him...

'I don't want you to go,' she blurted out.

She heard Seb sigh. 'Look, I know you're disappointed I'm not coming home straight away, Mil. I'm disappointed too. But this is a marvellous opportunity...'

'What if you're killed?'

He laughed. 'I've stayed out of trouble so far, haven't I?'

'They weren't firing bullets in Berlin, were they? I mean it, Seb. Please come home,' she begged.

'I will, darling. I just need to do this first...'

'And what about what I need?'

'What about it?' His voice turned cold. 'I seem to recall supporting your decision to be a nurse.'

There it was again, the old argument. Seb had been so good about her training, even when everyone else had been against it. He had even agreed to put off their wedding until after she had qualified. It was only fair that she should offer him the same kind of support. But she was too afraid.

'That's different,' she said.

'How is it different?'

'Nurses don't get shot at, for one thing.'

She heard his heavy sigh. 'You're just being silly.'

'And you're being selfish!' Millie slammed down the phone and immediately felt wretched. She snatched up the receiver again, but all she heard was silence.

The following morning brought a new admission to Judd, the Male Medical ward.

'Bed seven. Acute nephritis,' Sister Judd whispered when she gathered her nurses around the table to hand out the worklists. How she had ever become a ward sister Millie had no idea. Her shyness was almost painful. 'Mr Latimer has already been in to see him. The patient must be kept very warm, so I want you to make sure his hot water bottles are topped up regularly.' She addressed the bib of Millie's apron, unable to meet her eye. 'It is very important that they must not be allowed to cool.'

'Yes, Sister.'

'You must also be sure to check for oedema whenever you do his TPRs,' she added, her gaze sweeping the floor at their feet. 'If there are any signs of swelling, tell me at once.'

She handed out the worklists, and the nurses quickly dispersed to carry out their various jobs. Millie headed straight to the kitchen to prepare the hot water bottles for the new patient.

It wasn't long before her thoughts strayed back to Seb. She knew she was being unfair. Seb had backed her all the way when she'd decided to defy her family and train as a nurse. She didn't blame him for expecting her to do the same for him. He'd finally found something he was good at, something he felt as passionately about as she did about her nursing. She was proud of him for doing so well. And yet...

It was that wretched fortune-teller's fault. If she hadn't put those stupid thoughts in her head, Millie would never have lost her temper.

'Have you finished making those hot water bottles yet, Benedict?'

Staff Nurse Strickland stood in the doorway. If Sister Judd was a mouse, then Strickland was a rhinoceros. She had no difficulty throwing her considerable weight about on the ward, her voice as loud as Sister's was inaudible.

'Yes, Staff.' Millie felt Strickland peering over her shoulder, waiting to pounce as she screwed the stopper on the rubber bottle.

'Is that on securely? Are you sure you've expelled all the air from the bottle?'

'Yes, Staff.'

'And you've inspected the washer and screw for leaks?'

'Yes, Staff.' Millie suppressed a sigh as she wrapped the bottle in its flannel cover.

She left the kitchen and headed down the ward, Strickland following her. 'Remember, Nurse, the bottle must not touch the patient,' she boomed. 'A burn or a bruise is a disgrace to you and this ward, do you understand?'

'Yes, Staff.' Millie rolled her eyes heavenwards. She had been on the ward for nearly six weeks, and Strickland still treated her like a dirty pro.

'Honestly,' Millie muttered to herself, 'if I can't manage something as simple as filling a hot water bottle by now, it's a pretty poor show...'

'Goes on a bit, doesn't she?' said a familiar voice.

Millie looked up and found herself looking into

the cheeky, smiling face of the new patient in bed seven.

It was early afternoon and Helen sat at the third-year dining table, still groggy with sleep after waking up from her night shift. She could hardly face her plate of mince and potatoes. She pushed the food around her plate, listening to Brenda Bevan as she chatted to Amy Hollins at the far end of the table about her wedding plans.

'I've just chosen my dress,' she enthused, her eyes sparkling. 'Oh, you should see it, it's absolutely beautiful. Such a pretty neckline, and the lace...'

Helen caught Amy's glance from the other end of the table. For once, she didn't seem to be listening very keenly to her friend, her eyes glazed, chin propped on one hand. Helen wondered if it was because she was feeling tired and groggy too. For the past six weeks they had been working nights on adjoining Female Medical wards.

Not that they'd exchanged a single word in all that time. While the other night nurses kept each other company, Amy was always more interested in entertaining her boyfriend than talking to Helen.

'Now all I have to do is decide what jewellery I'm going to wear,' Brenda droned on, oblivious to Amy's lack of interest. 'I was thinking of pearls...'

Before she could finish her sentence, Millie appeared in the doorway to the dining room. She spotted Helen and came hurrying over.

'Thank goodness you're awake, Tremayne. I was hoping to catch you—'

'What do you think you're doing?' The sight of a second-year at their table galvanised Amy into life. 'You can't just stroll over here, you know. Get back to your own table at once!'

'Oh, do shut up, Hollins!'

'What did you just say to me? I could report you, you know.' Amy Hollins' mouth opened and closed like a stranded fish, but Millie ignored her, turning straight back to Helen.

'I have something very important I need to say to you...'

Helen sighed. 'Don't tell me you've left your cigarettes out in the room again and you want me to hide them before Sister Sutton finds them?'

'It's more serious than that.' Something in Millie's sombre face made Helen's skin prickle. 'Now I want you to promise me to stay very calm...'

All the way up to Judd ward, Helen kept telling herself that it must be a mistake. Yet as soon as she walked through the double doors, she knew it was him. His bed was at the far end of the ward, but Helen would have known him anywhere.

She started towards him, but Staff Nurse Strickland stepped in her path.

'And where do you think you're going?' she boomed.

'Please, Staff ... my boyfriend has just been admitted. Mr Dawson?'

Nurse Strickland looked over her shoulder towards Charlie's bed, then back at Helen. 'That doesn't give you the right to wander into this ward at will, you know. It's not a free-for-all.'

'I know, Staff.' Helen planted herself firmly in

front of her, not moving. Nurse Strickland glared at her for a moment.

'Wait there,' she instructed.

As she went off to consult Sister Judd, Helen kept her eyes fixed on Charlie's bed. She was going to see him, whatever Strickland or Sister Judd said.

She was all ready to run to him when Nurse Strickland returned. 'Sister says you can have five minutes,' she said. 'Five minutes, Nurse. Do you understand?'

Charlie's face lit up when he saw Helen.

'Surprise.' He smiled weakly. 'Bet you didn't expect to see me, did you?'

'No, I didn't.' Helen fought to keep her voice steady. 'How are you, Charlie?'

'Well, I feel as if I've been kicked in the side by a donkey, but apart from that...'

She sank down on the chair beside his bed. 'What happened?'

'I dunno, love. I was doing all right till yesterday. All ready to get up and about, I was. But then I took a turn for the worse and Mum sent for the doctor and here I am.' He struggled to lean closer to her. 'To be honest, I was hoping you could tell me what's going on. That consultant bloke who came this morning used that many long words, I didn't have a clue what he was talking about!'

Helen reached for his hand. His skin felt clammy in hers. 'You have nephritis,' she explained. 'It's a kidney infection. It can be a side effect of Scarlet Fever.'

Charlie nodded. 'And this infection ... is it serious?'

Helen hesitated. She wanted to lie to him, but she couldn't. 'Infections are always serious,' she chose her words carefully. 'But they can be treated. And you're young and strong enough to fight it.'

'Then I reckon that's what I'll do.' He leaned back against the pillows. 'I'm in good hands, anyway. Although I'd thank your mate not to keep piling me up with blankets and hot water bottles!' He tugged at the collar of his pyjamas. 'I'm sweltering in here. Doesn't she know it's flaming August?'

Helen smiled. 'That's part of the treatment, I'm afraid.'

'Talk about kill or cure!'

Out of the corner of her eye, Helen saw Staff Nurse Strickland advancing up the ward towards her.

'I've got to go. Can I get you anything?'

'A couple of new kidneys might be nice.'

'I was thinking more of a newspaper!' she laughed.

'As a matter of fact, there is something you can do for me, if you don't mind?' Charlie's face was suddenly serious. 'Can you have a word with my mum, let her know what's going on? She's bound to be in a state, and I know she won't make head nor tail of anything the doctor says to her. Can you let her know I'm alive and in good hands?'

'I'll go and see her before I go back on duty,' Helen said. 'I'm not due back on until nine, so I've plenty of time.'

'Thanks, love. You'll let her know I'm all right, won't you?'

She read the unspoken message in his blue eyes.

'I'll put her mind at rest,' Helen promised.

Chapter Twenty-Nine

On Sunday morning, Dora had to go to church with the other students who weren't on duty until the afternoon. She had never been much of a churchgoer until she came to the Nightingale, but this morning she kneeled in the dusty pew and prayed as hard as she could for God to deliver Esther Gold.

She didn't know if she was doing the right thing, or whether He would even listen.

'Does God mind if you pray for Jews in church?' she had asked Helen when they met briefly at supper the previous evening. She knew Helen of all people wouldn't laugh at her for asking such a thing and besides, her father was a vicar.

Helen considered it seriously for a moment. 'I don't think it matters,' she said. 'We are all God's children, after all. And don't forget, Jesus himself was a Jew,' she added.

Dora also prayed for Helen's boyfriend Charlie, and for her own brother Peter, that he would finally see sense and leave the Blackshirts. Although she wasn't sure he deserved her prayers; they had hardly spoken since that day at Esther's bedside. If they passed in the hospital corridor, he refused even to meet her eye.

After church, she missed dinner and rushed straight back to Everett. She nearly fainted when she saw the door to Esther's room firmly closed.

As she was dithering outside, wondering what to do, the door opened and Sister Everett appeared.

'Ah, Doyle, there you are.' She greeted her with a smile. 'Don't look so worried, girl, it's good news. Your friend has woken up at last.'

Dora felt her legs buckle with relief. 'Is – is she all right?' She hardly dared to ask the question.

'The consultant is with her now. But so far it seems very promising.' Sister gave Dora a severe look. 'You needn't think I can spare you to go visiting just yet,' she warned. 'There are the bathrooms to clean first. If I can see my face in the taps, then I might allow you to spend a few minutes with Miss Gold.'

Knowing Esther was awake was such a relief Dora would have happily cleaned a hundred bathrooms. She scrubbed and wiped and polished until the gritty Vim powder turned her hands raw.

An hour later, Sister Everett inspected her distorted reflection in the taps and then pronounced herself satisfied.

'Very well,' she said. 'You may go and see your friend. But be sure not to overtax her,' she warned.

Esther was still very groggy. Dora watched her as she drifted in and out of sleep.

'Miss Gold?' she said softly. 'Esther?'

She turned her head slowly. 'Dora?' She winced as she tried to smile through stiff, swollen lips. 'What are you doing here?'

'You're on my ward,' Dora said.

'Am I?' Esther looked around her vaguely. Her

dark brows drew together as she tried to think. 'How long have I been asleep?'

'A couple of days. You had us all worried!' Dora smiled shakily.

'I – I can't remember what happened. It was dark... I was walking home...' Her eyes suddenly opened wide, full of fear and panic. 'My father! Has anyone seen him? He'll be so worried...'

'Shhh, it's all right.' Dora quietened her. 'You don't have to worry. Dr Adler is looking after him.'

'Dr Adler?' Esther relaxed back against the pillow. 'That's very kind of him.'

'He thinks a lot of you,' Dora said. 'He's been by your bedside every day.'

'Has he?' Esther started to smile then closed her eyes, flinching with pain.

Dora leaned over her. 'Miss Gold? Are you all right?'

'I have a terrible headache. Everything is such a jumble in my mind...'

'It will all sort itself out in the end. You just need to rest now, and try to get better.'

'Thank you. I'm glad you're here.' As Esther reached out her hand to Dora, something dropped on to the blanket. 'What's this?'

Dora blushed. 'It's the *hamsa*,' she said, pressing it back into Esther's hand. 'It belonged to you once, but you gave it to me for luck when I first came here for my interview. I – I thought you should have it back.'

It seemed like a silly gesture now, but at the time it was the only thing she could think of.

'I remember it.' Esther's fingers closed around it. 'You're very kind.'

She tried to hand it back, but Dora shook her head. 'You keep it,' she said, adding silently, You need a bit of luck more than I do.

Ruby tipped the tin of charred roast potatoes into the dustbin and replaced the lid with a crash. She was in a rage, and didn't care who knew it. It was all she could do to stop herself from kicking the dustbin down the concrete stairwell.

'All right?' Nick came out of the sitting room as she slammed the front door shut.

'What do you think?' She pushed past him into the kitchen. Nick followed her.

'What's the matter?'

'If you must know, I've just chucked our Sunday dinner in the bin.'

He stared at her. 'What for?'

'Because the stupid oven burned it all. The Yorkshire puddings have gone flat, the potatoes are like bits of coal, and you could probably mend your boots on this horrible lump of beef.' She thrust the tin under his nose. The beef sat in the middle of it, shrivelled and congealing. 'You see? Everything's ruined.'

'Are you sure you didn't just leave it in the oven and forget it again?' Nick smirked.

'That's right! Blame me. It's always my bloody fault, ain't it?' Ruby dropped the roasting tin with a crash, then burst into tears.

Nick's smile dropped. 'Jesus, Ruby, what's wrong with you? You've been in a rotten mood all day.'

She sank to the floor, her face buried in her hands. Now the tears had started, she couldn't

287

stop them.

She heard Nick cross the room and crouch down beside her, then his arms came round her shuddering shoulders. 'Ruby, what is it? What's the matter?' he soothed.

'I – I'm not pregnant!'

Nick sighed. 'Is that all? Blimey, I thought it was something serious!'

'It *is* serious.' She had been bitterly disappointed when her monthlies arrived that morning. Especially as they had been late. For the past three days she had nursed the secret, allowing herself to hope, only for it all to come crashing cruelly down.

'Come here, you daft thing.' Nick pulled her closer. 'So what if you didn't get pregnant straight away? We've got plenty of time, ain't we?'

Have we? Ruby thought, resting her head against the broad wall of his chest. With every month that went by, it felt as if her time was running out. If she didn't get pregnant soon, she was going to lose Nick. She was sure of it.

'What if it doesn't happen?' she whispered.

'Why shouldn't it happen? You got pregnant easily enough first time round, didn't you? A bit too easily, some might say!' His hand smoothed her hair, rocking her like a baby. 'It's just taking a bit longer this time, that's all. But you can't hurry these things. You've got to let nature take its course.'

And what if it doesn't? She couldn't help wondering if this was a punishment for all the lies she'd told. What if she turned out to be one of those women who could never have kids? She didn't know how she would explain that to Nick.

She sagged against him, all the fight gone out of her. She didn't want to explain any more. She was sick and tired of making up lies, watching every word that came out of her mouth in case she accidentally gave herself away.

'Cheer up,' Nick's arms tightened around her. 'We'll just have to keep trying, won't we?'

She looked up at him, tears drying on her cheeks. 'Do you mean that? You're not going to leave me?'

The look in his eyes was unreadable. 'We're married, ain't we? Till death do us part, and all that.'

Before she could reply, there was a loud knock on the front door.

Nick looked up sharply. 'Who's that, I wonder?'

'Ignore them,' Ruby clung to him, needing the reassurance of his arms around her. 'They'll go away.'

The knock sounded again, louder this time.

'Doesn't look like they're going away, does it? I'd better answer it.' Nick released her and got to his feet.

Ruby was scraping the remains of the beef joint off the floor when she heard Nick's voice raised in anger.

'Look, mate, I dunno who you are, but you've got the wrong house. We don't owe anything to anyone.'

'I think you do, Mr Riley.' Bert Wallis' voice, nasal and insinuating, drifted down the passageway. 'Now if I could just have a word with your missus–'

'You ain't having a word with anyone. Now

clear off!'

Ruby's head shot up, panic surging through her. It was Sunday, she'd thought she was safe from the tallyman. But Bert Wallis must have got wise to her and decided to catch her unawares.

She pressed herself against the kitchen door, her heart fluttering, looking for a way to escape. But there was no way out.

'Ruby!' she heard Nick shout. 'Come here a minute.' She crept into the hall, hunched with fear, trying to make herself as small as possible.

'Hello, Mrs Riley.' Bert Wallis smiled nastily. 'Long time no see. Anyone would think you've been avoiding me or summat?'

Nick turned to her. 'This bloke reckons you owe him money. Tell him he's got it wrong, and then he can sling his hook.' He eyed Bert Wallis as if he wanted to make him do just that.

But Mr Walls stood his ground. 'I'll sling my hook when I've got my money,' he said. 'I'm sick and tired of knocking on this door and getting no answer. It's been over a month since you last paid me anything.'

Ruby fixed her gaze beyond Bert's shoulder, towards the distant rooftops. The thudding of her heartbeat in her ears drowned out the excited voices of the children playing on the green below.

'Ruby?' Nick's voice was uneasy. 'You don't owe him anything, do you?'

She bit her lip. Suddenly all she wanted to do was to run away and never stop running.

'Told you.' Bert Wallis' smile was tinged with malice.

'But we paid it all off months ago. Didn't we,

Ruby? D'you remember, I gave you that money?'

She opened her mouth to reply, but no sound came out.

'I'm afraid your wife has taken out two further loans since then, Mr Riley,' Bert Wallis said.

'Ruby?' She could feel Nick's gaze on her, but she didn't dare look at him. She didn't want to see the hurt and anger in his eyes. 'Ruby, answer me. What's going on?'

She stared down at her wedding band, gleaming dully on her finger.

'How much?' Nick asked in a cold voice.

'Let's see, shall we?' Bert Wallis consulted his big leather book. 'With all the interest on the payments you've missed ten guineas, six shillings and fourpence.'

'Ten guineas!' Ruby found her voice. 'It can't be … I never borrowed that much, I swear I didn't!'

'That's what happens when you miss as many payments as you have, Mrs Riley. It all adds up.'

Ruby turned to Nick. His face was a blank mask. 'Nick, you've got to believe me. I never thought–'

He turned and stomped off down the hall, slamming the bathroom door behind him, leaving Ruby alone to face Bert Wallis.

'Happy chap, your old man, ain't he?' Bert said.

'You shouldn't have come,' she whispered.

'You would have had to face me sometime.'

'Yes, but not now. Not in front of him…'

Before Bert could reply, Nick had returned. 'Here,' he said, stuffing a handful of notes into the tallyman's hands. Bert Wallis stared. 'What's this?'

'Your money, what does it look like? Paid in

291

full, so we don't want to see your face round here again, all right?'

'No need to be like that, Mr Riley.'

'And if I do see your face on my doorstep again, I'll sling you off that balcony, understood?'

Bert Wallis' insinuating smile faded. 'I didn't ask your missus to get herself in debt,' he started to say, but Nick slammed the door in his face.

The atmosphere in the sitting room was tense. Ruby sat on the couch, her hands folded in her lap, eyes fixed on the rug, unable to look at her husband.

She might have felt better if he'd raged, or shouted, or called her all the names under the sun. But the way he sat very still beside her frightened her even more. She could feel his quiet fury vibrating through every inch of him, as taut as a bowstring.

'You shouldn't have done it. You shouldn't have gone behind my back like that. I told you I didn't want any debts, and you just went ahead and did it anyway.'

'I'm sorry,' she whispered. 'I won't do it again, I promise.'

'You promised last time, too.' His voice was filled with resignation.

'I know.' She didn't have to look into Nick's face to know she had destroyed his trust. And this time she would never get it back. 'Thank you,' she whispered.

He sighed raggedly. 'If it happens again, I can't bail you out. All the money's gone.'

She looked up at him. 'Not your savings? What about America?'

His mouth twisted. 'Doesn't look like I'll be going, does it?'

The bleak expression in his blue eyes shook her. 'But you've got to go! We'll get the money back, you'll see.'

'What's the point? You were right, it was just a pipe dream.'

'But it was your dream.'

And now she'd taken it away from him, just as she'd taken away all his other dreams.

Chapter Thirty

First thing in the morning the porter brought the morning papers up to the ward.

Millie kept her face averted as she went about her work so she didn't catch sight of the morning headlines. Every day brought fresh news from Spain, of bombs exploding, buildings being burned to the ground and hostages being shot. One morning she knew she would see a headline saying that a young reporter had been caught in crossfire and killed.

But try as she might to avoid it, the bad news still managed to get to her.

'I see Franco's lot have gained more ground,' a young patient called Alan Cornish commented, scanning the front page. 'Well, that's it, then. Looks like they've got a full-scale war on their hands.'

'More fool them,' another patient, Mr Tucker,

mumbled from behind his *Daily Sketch*. 'Let's hope they don't try and get the rest of us involved.'

'But we're already involved,' Alan argued, his face full of emotion. 'Don't you see? This is just the start of it. If the Fascists are allowed to defeat the government in Spain, what's to stop them spreading through the whole of Europe?'

'It won't come to that.' Mr Tucker shook his head. 'No one wants another war, not after what we all went through the last time.'

'We've got a fight on our hands, whether we like it or not. I just wish I were fit enough to go over there myself. I'd give bloody Franco and his lot what for!'

'Oh, do shut up, Mr Cornish. You have no idea what you're talking about!'

They both looked round, astonished by Millie's outburst. Alan Cornish's face flushed. 'I'd welcome the chance to do my bit! As soon as I'm out of here I'm going to go over there and–'

'Then I don't know why we're bothering to nurse you at all, if you're just planning to go and get yourself killed!'

'You tell him, Nurse!' Mr Tucker chuckled. 'He wouldn't be so quick to say that if he knew what war was really like. I served for two years on the Western Front, and I'm telling you, it wasn't all beer and skittles!'

Alan Cornish looked affronted. He opened his mouth to argue, but Millie stuck a thermometer in, shutting him up.

At least Charlie Dawson didn't want to discuss the war. He greeted her with his usual bright smile when she arrived at his bedside.

294

'How are you feeling this morning?' she asked.

'Oh, can't complain. I woke up with a bit of a headache, but I'm not too bad, considering.'

'Let's take a look, shall we?'

She popped the thermometer into his mouth and went to take his pulse. His wrist felt spongy under her fingers. 'Your pulse is a little bit faster this morning.'

'That must be you holding my hand!'

'Careful, I'll tell your girlfriend you're flirting with me!'

'Helen knows I only have eyes for her.'

'She's a lucky girl.'

Charlie eyed Millie sympathetically. 'No word of your young man yet?'

'Not yet.'

She pulled back the bedcover to check Charlie's legs for signs of oedema. As she rolled up the leg of his pyjamas, she could see at once that his skin was stretched and waxy-looking under the sprinkling of golden hairs. His solid flesh didn't yield under her finger.

'I'm sure he'll be home soon,' Charlie said, his mouth still clamped around the thermometer. 'Nurse...?'

Millie looked up, distracted. 'Hmm?'

'I said, he'll be home soon.'

'I expect he will.' She smiled bracingly, took the thermometer out of Charlie's mouth and checked it. At least that was normal.

He watched her as she wrote the figures on the chart. 'What do you reckon, Nurse? Am I on the mend?'

For once Millie tried to think before she spoke.

'These things take time, Charlie.' She hung the chart back on the end of his bed. 'Now, I'll see about getting you something for that headache.'

She turned to go, but he called her back. 'Nurse?'

'Yes, Charlie?'

'Everything is all right, isn't it?'

His trusting smile was like a knife in her heart. 'Of course.'

'I mean, I'm not getting any worse, am I?'

She couldn't stop thinking about the solidity of his flesh under her fingers. 'I told you, Charlie. These things take time.'

'Yes ... yes, of course.' His smile flickered. 'Sorry, Nurse. I'm just being daft.'

Millie hurried away, hoping her expression hadn't given away her real concerns.

Nick was hauling a sack of rubbish down the stone steps to the basement when he spotted Joe Armstrong with Nurse Willard.

They were lurking in the shadow of the Porters' Lodge, out of sight of the wards and Matron's office, talking. As Nick watched, Nurse Willard smiled shyly up from under her lashes, then Joe reached out and brushed a stray lock of hair away from her face.

Nick stared at the arrogant, handsome profile, and blood sang in his ears. It was all he could do not to march straight over and knock Joe down.

He forced himself to wait until Nurse Willard was heading back towards the Casualty department. Joe turned away and was walking towards the gates, smiling to himself. But his self-satisfied smirk disappeared when Nick stepped out in front of him.

'I want a word with you.'

Joe looked down at the rubbish sack and then back up at Nick's face. 'Don't you have work to do?' he jeered.

Nick ignored the jibe. 'What's going on with you and that nurse?'

'What nurse?'

'Don't play games with me. I just saw you talking to that blonde from Casualty.'

'You mean Nurse Willard?' Joe shrugged. 'What about her?'

'Does Dora know you're messing about behind her back?'

A slow sneer crossed Joe's face. 'You're a fine one to talk about messing about! What about you and your missus?'

Nick took a step towards him. 'You'd better not hurt Dora,' he warned.

'Or what? What are you going to do about it?' Joe sent him a scathing look. 'You'd better not be threatening a policeman, or you could find yourself in big trouble, pal.'

'I'm not your pal. And I'm not frightened of you, either.'

'You should be.'

'Is that right?'

Joe squared up to him. 'See this uniform? It means I've got the power to make your life a misery if I want to.'

'Your uniform don't scare me.'

'More fool you, then.'

'All right, Nick?' He heard Harry Fishman's

297

voice behind him. The argument had brought him and a couple of the other porters out of the lodge to investigate. 'What's going on?'

'Nothing. I was just having a chat with the constable here.'

Joe's lip curled. 'You're brave when you've got your mates behind you, ain't you?'

'I don't need any mates to help me deal with the likes of you, believe me.'

'You want to get on your way,' Harry said, moving to stand beside Nick. 'Ain't you got any criminals to catch?'

'I've got better things to do with my time than hang around here, that's for sure.' Joe turned back to Nick. 'By the way, you've got it wrong. I ain't with Dora any more.'

Nick stared at him. 'What?'

'You heard.' Joe gave him a disgusted look. 'She ditched me. And I reckon I know why, too.' He stepped closer to Nick. 'You'd better watch yourself, pal. Because next time I see you, you might not have your mates around to back you up!'

Chapter Thirty-One

'How's your boyfriend?'

The question came out of the blue. Helen wasn't even sure it was directed at her until she glanced up and caught Amy Hollins looking at her. They had both just come off their respective night shifts and were sitting awkwardly together at an otherwise empty breakfast table.

'It's Charlie, isn't it?' said Amy.

'Yes, that's right.' Helen tensed, waiting for the sharp remark to follow. But there was genuine sympathy in Amy Hollins' face instead.

'I heard he was on Judd. How's he getting on?'

'He's – getting better, thanks.'

'That's good. It must be a real worry for you?' Again, Helen waited for the sting in the tail, but it didn't come. Amy gazed back at her, her pretty face full of concern.

'We were both on Male Surgical when you first met him, do you remember? After his accident?' Helen nodded. 'He was such a nice chap,' Amy recalled. 'Always so friendly and polite. Not like some of the grumpy old so-and-sos you meet in this job.' She leaned across the table and patted Helen's hand. 'Give him my best wishes, won't you? And if there's ever anything you need, you only have to ask...'

'Thanks.' Helen stared down at Amy's hand, covering hers. She wanted to pinch it, just to make sure she hadn't fallen asleep at the table after her busy night shift.

It wasn't until she returned to her room in the night nurses' corridor after breakfast that she realised why Amy had been so sympathetic. Helen saw that she looked a wreck. Ever since Charlie had been admitted she had tried to get by on the minimum of sleep. Nurses on night duty were forbidden to get up before noon at the earliest, and many liked to sleep in later. But Helen found it hard to sleep at all, and would usually be sitting up on her bed, waiting for the clock to strike twelve so she could get up and visit Charlie.

But days without sleep had left deep purple hollows under her brown eyes, and when she removed her cap her hair fell in lank strands around her face. Her limbs felt heavy with tiredness, and yet she knew as soon as she put her head on the pillow she would be wide awake again.

She tried to tell herself that there was nothing she could do, that she needed to rest so she could be bright enough to face Charlie later. But even if she did drop off from sheer exhaustion, she would jerk awake a few minutes later, convinced she could hear him calling out to her.

At noon, after five hours of staring dry-eyed at the peeling plasterwork on the ceiling, Helen made her way straight to Male Medical.

Sister Judd nodded to her when she came in, but made no comment. Even Staff Nurse Strickland made no attempt to stop her any more. They had both accepted that Helen would come whether they liked it or not, and decided to put her to good use instead. While she was there watching over Charlie, it meant the other nurses on the ward had one less task to perform.

The screens were pulled around his bed. Helen's heart lurched with fear until she saw Millie emerging, pushing a trolley laden with a bowl, soap, flannels and towels.

She smiled when she saw Helen. 'Oh, hello. You're early.'

'I came as soon as I could.' She nodded towards the curtains. 'How is he?'

'I've just finished giving him a wash and brush up, so he's looking very respectable.'

Helen eyed her friend narrowly. 'And how is his illness? I noticed he was due to have a blood test this morning. Have the results come back yet?'

'You know you're not supposed to ask questions like that.' Millie's laugh was shrill with tension. 'And you're not to go snooping at his chart, either. Sister Judd will be furious if she catches you.'

'Is that you, Helen?' Charlie's voice came from the other side of the screen.

'Just a minute.' Helen turned back to Millie. 'How is he, really? What did the consultant say? Are they going to try serum treatment?'

'I don't know, do I? No one tells us students anything.'

'Benedict–'

'Is that Strickland calling me? I have to go.' Millie charged off down the ward, pushing the trolley ahead of her.

'Benedict was in rather a hurry,' Helen commented, as she slipped through the screens to Charlie.

'She's probably just busy.'

'Hmm.' Helen wasn't so sure. Millie had looked almost guilty as she darted away.

'Are you sure you haven't upset her?' she teased.

'No more than usual.' Charlie's smile was strained. He lay against the pillows, his face flushed against the snowy whiteness of the linen.

Automatically, Helen reached for the chart on the end of his bed. 'How are you feeling?' she asked.

'Do you have to?' There was an edge to his voice. 'I have enough people coming in here, staring at

301

that chart. I'm not your patient, Helen.'

'Of course. I'm sorry.' She replaced the chart and went to sit beside him. 'How are you, Charlie?'

'Better than you, I reckon.' He turned his face to look at her. 'When was the last time you got some sleep?'

'I'm on night duty. It's always hard to sleep on nights.'

'I bet you're not eating, either.'

She laughed. 'It's me who should be worrying about you, remember?' She searched in her bag. 'I've brought the *East London Observer* with me, I thought I could read it to you. I know you like the speedway results.' She pulled out the newspaper. 'There was racing on in the Harringay last night, so perhaps there'll be a report in here somewhere...'

'I mean it, Helen. You shouldn't spend so much time with me. You need to keep up with your studies.'

She laughed, still flicking through the newspaper, looking for the sports pages. 'Now you sound like my mother!'

Charlie put out his hand, his fingers closing round hers. It upset her to feel how little strength he had in his grasp. 'For God's sake, will you stop doing that and listen to me? I'm trying to tell you—'

She let the newspaper drop into her lap. She had never heard him speak to her so sharply before, and it made her nervous. 'What, Charlie?'

He was silent for a moment. Now he had her attention, he didn't seem to know what to say next. Finally, he took a deep breath and said, 'I've been thinking about it, and – I don't want you to come and see me any more.'

'Charlie!'

'I mean it, Helen. I don't think it's doing either of us any good, you being here all the time.' He turned his face away from hers.

'But I want to be here.'

'Well, I don't want you here!'

She stared at him, stunned. 'You don't mean that?'

'Yes, I do.' His hand slipped away from hers. 'Your mum's right. We don't belong together, we never have. It would be better for both of us if we parted.'

His face was still turned away from hers, so she couldn't see his eyes. This wasn't Charlie speaking, she thought. It couldn't be. 'Stop it, Charlie,' she pleaded. 'If this is your idea of a joke, then it's not very funny...'

'I'm not joking,' he said firmly. 'I want you to go, and don't come back.'

Outside the screens she could hear the sounds of ward life going on: the rattle of a trolley being pushed past the curtains, the sound of footsteps, of muted voices, people going about their business, oblivious to the fact that her world was collapsing.

And yet she still couldn't believe it. It all seemed too unreal.

'All right,' she said, fighting to stop the tremor in her voice. 'I'll go, if that's what you want. But first you have to tell me to my face.'

'Helen–'

'I'm serious, Charlie. If you're going to break

303

my heart then the least you can do is look me in the eye while you do it.'

He didn't move. 'Just go,' he said wearily. 'Please.'

Helen stared at his stubborn profile. 'I'm not going anywhere until you tell me why you're doing this,' she said. 'You can't lie to me, Charlie Dawson, I know you too well. That's why you can't look at me, isn't it? Because you're afraid I'll see the truth.'

'You want the truth?' Slowly, he rolled his head to face her, and she saw the tears glistening in his eyes. 'I'm dying, Helen.'

It was as if she had been plunged head-first into icy water. She gasped, desperately fighting for control. 'No, you're not!'

His mouth lifted at one corner. 'You know as well as I do, Helen Tremayne. I'm not getting any better, and I don't think I will.'

'But–' She stopped short. He was right. She had seen the figures on his chart, seen him struggling more every day, even though she had done her best to block the knowledge out. He wasn't responding to any treatment, and his limbs had started to swell as his kidneys failed to do their job. She didn't want to think about what would happen next, although she'd read it in her textbook many times. 'There's still hope,' she whispered. 'There are so many different treatments the doctors can try. And sometimes infections like yours just get better by themselves–'

'But more often than not they don't.' He managed a wry smile. 'Look, I might not have your education, Helen, but I'm no fool. I know what's happening to me, and I don't want you to have to go through that. I don't want you to watch me die.'

'I told you, you're not going to die.'

A single tear rolled down Charlie's cheek and soaked into the pillow. 'Please, Helen,' he begged. 'Don't make this any harder for me than it already is. It's taking everything I've got to say this. But I've got to do what's right.'

'How is it right to send me away when all I want to do is be with you?'

'What else can I do?'

'Marry me,' she blurted out. The words were spoken before she'd had time to think about them. But once she'd said it, she realised it was what she wanted.

'You what?' Charlie tried to lift his head from the pillow, his eyes wide with astonishment.

'Marry me. It's the right thing to do, Charlie,' she urged. 'I don't want us to be apart. Whatever happens, I want us to face it together.'

His blue gaze fixed on hers for a moment, then he shook his head. 'We can't.'

'We can. I'm not talking about a big church do or anything like that. We could even get a minister to marry us here, at your bedside—'

'I'm not talking about the wedding. I'm not going to marry you so I can leave you a widow.'

'That won't happen,' Helen said firmly. 'And even if it does,' she added, as he opened his mouth to argue, 'it's still what I want. I want to be with you, Charlie. For better or for worse.'

'In sickness and in health?' he said weakly.

She nodded. 'In sickness and in health.'

He looked at her for a long time. 'You do realise that even if I manage to survive this illness, your mother will kill me?'

Helen smiled. 'Is that a yes?'

He shook his head wonderingly. 'I never realised you could be so forceful, Helen Tremayne.'

'I am when I want something.'

'We don't even have a ring.'

'Wait there.' She slipped out through the screens and looked around the ward.

'Lost something, Miss?' The patient in the next bed, Mr Tucker, looked up from his newspaper.

'I won't know until I find it...' Helen caught sight of the ashtray beside his bed. 'Do you smoke, by any chance?'

Mr Tucker grinned guiltily. 'Only when Sister ain't looking! Why? Do you want one?'

'No, but I'd like to borrow your cigarette packet, if you don't mind?'

He reached into his locker and pulled out a packet of Kensitas. 'Here you are, love, help yourself. But don't let Sister catch you or she'll have your guts for garters!' He grinned.

'Thanks.' Helen opened the packet and tore out a strip of the silver paper, then handed it back. Mr Tucker watched her with interest.

'And what are you planning to do with that, then?'

Helen gave him a mischievous smile. 'You'll find out.'

Charlie turned to look at her as she slipped back inside the screens. 'You look pleased with yourself.'

'I've got my ring, look!' She twisted the silver

paper around her finger and held it up to show him.

Charlie looked at it, then back at her. 'It ain't much, is it?'

'It's all I need.' She pulled it off and handed it to him. 'But you've got to do it properly.'

He gave a dry laugh. 'There ain't nothing proper about this.'

'I don't care,' Helen declared. 'You've still got to ask me.'

'Helen–'

'Ask me. Please?'

He sighed and took the silver-paper ring from her. 'I can't get down on one knee.'

'That's all right. I'll just pretend.'

He paused. 'Are you sure?'

'Well, unless you think you can get out of bed?'

'I meant about the proposal. Are you sure you want to marry me?'

'I've never been more sure of anything in my life.'

'Very well, then,' he sighed. 'Helen Tremayne, will you marry me?'

'Yes, please!' She realised her hand was trembling as she held it out for Charlie to slip the ring on to her finger.

It was nowhere near as fancy as Millie's vintage emeralds, or Brenda Bevan's solitaire. But she still felt like the proudest, luckiest girl in the world as she held up her makeshift silver-paper band to the light.

'Just think,' she said. 'I'm going to be Mrs Charlie Dawson.'

Charlie shook his head. 'You do realise we

might not get as far as the wedding?'

Helen gave him a knowing look. 'Oh, yes, we will,' she said. 'You've made me a promise, and I'm not letting you go that easily!'

Chapter Thirty-Two

It was a relief to see Esther Gold sitting up in bed, looking so well again.

'I bet I look a fright, don't I?' she said to Dora. 'I haven't dared look at myself in a mirror yet.'

'You look lovely,' Dora reassured her. She looked a lot better than she had done a couple of weeks earlier, anyway. The bruises and swelling on her face had gone from ugly black and purple to a faded yellow, although the livid scar that ran down her cheek was a reminder of the ordeal she had suffered.

Esther gave a wry smile. 'I don't know about that. No one has ever said I looked lovely, even before all this. But I'm alive, and that's all that matters.'

'And you're doing very well, so the doctor says. He's ever so pleased with you,' Dora said. 'Your vision, hearing and speech are all normal, and you've recovered your memory, too.'

'I have, haven't I?' A shadow passed over her face, like a cloud over the sun. 'Although I've got to admit, there are some things I'd rather forget.'

Dora squeezed her hand in sympathy. The scars on Esther's face and body might be healing, but she knew there were other scars, ones that couldn't be seen, that the doctor could do nothing to heal. According to the night nurse's report, Esther often woke up screaming and had to be calmed down.

'I'll tell you something I haven't forgotten,' Esther said. 'To thank you for saving my life.'

Dora blushed. 'I didn't.'

'That's not what I heard. You were a heroine, Dora. If you hadn't found me that night and frightened off those men, I don't know what would have happened to me.'

'I'm just glad I was passing.'

'There are a lot who would have passed straight by and not got involved,' Esther said grimly. Then she added, 'The police came round to see me again this morning. Wanted to know all the details about what happened that night.'

Dora's throat went dry. 'And what did you tell them? '

'I told them I couldn't remember anything.'

She frowned. 'Are you sure? The doctors said there's nothing wrong with your memory...'

Esther's expression was firm. 'All the same, it was dark and I couldn't make out any of their faces.'

Dora hesitated. She wanted to protect her family, but she couldn't lie to Esther. Not if it meant her attackers went unpunished.

She took a deep breath. 'Miss Gold, there's something I've to tell you. It's about my brother Peter–'

'Anyway,' Esther cut her off, 'I just want to put it all behind me, forget about it. God works in mysterious ways, and I just pray that the people who did this will feel some remorse for what they did, and change their ways.'

A look passed between them, and Dora suddenly understood.

She nodded. 'I hope so too,' she said. 'Thank you,' she added quietly.

'No need to thank me, *bubele*. Just make sure something good comes of this, eh?'

'I will,' she promised.

Esther's gaze drifted to the enormous vase of flowers on her locker. No prizes for guessing who they were from, Dora thought.

'I notice Dr Adler has been in to see you again?'

A faint girlish blush rose in Esther's cheeks. 'He's been very kind,' she said. 'And it's such a relief that he's been staying with my father too, to make sure he's all right. That's been a real weight off my mind, I can tell you.'

'Dr Adler must be keen.'

Esther's gaze dropped. 'I don't know about that. I mean, I'm no oil painting at the best of times, but now...' Her hand rose to touch the scar. 'He could do a lot better than me,' she said.

'I don't think Dr Adler sees it that way.'

'Did I hear my name?'

They turned to see Dr Adler approaching them, all smiles. Dora noticed Sister Everett hurrying in his wake, issuing hasty orders to the junior nurses, clearly annoyed at being summoned from her duties to attend him. The presence of any doctor on the ward demanded a certain protocol, after all.

She seemed even more annoyed when Dr Adler

dismissed her with a cheery wave. 'It's perfectly all right, Sister, I've not come to check up on you. I've just come to visit Miss Gold.'

Dora and Esther exchanged amused glances.

'Really, Dr Adler, you must stop disturbing Sister's routine,' Esther chided him. 'Visiting hours are on a Sunday afternoon from two o'clock, as you well know.'

'This is not a visit,' he informed her loftily. 'I'm here to check up on a patient.'

'I don't remember seeing your name on my chart?'

'Former patient, then.'

'And do you make a habit of visiting all your former patients? It must take you rather a long time.'

'I can't help it if I'm dedicated, can I?' He smiled. 'How are you feeling today, Esther – I mean, Miss Gold?'

'Much better, thank you.'

'That's excellent news.' Dora glanced at Dr Adler. His smile was brisk and professional, but not quick enough to hide the look of relief that flashed across his face.

'I was just telling Dora how grateful I am to you for keeping an eye on my father,' Esther went on.

'I've enjoyed his company,' Dr Adler said. 'He's been teaching me to play backgammon. Although I gather I'm rather a poor student,' he added ruefully. 'Apparently you're a much more worthy opponent than I am.'

Esther laughed. 'I should be, I've been playing it since I was a child.' Then she ventured, 'Perhaps you'd like to continue your lessons after I get home? I'm sure my father would enjoy having

311

another man about the house. That is, if you'd like to?' she added quickly, her blush deepening. 'Of course, I understand if you're too busy. After all, you have lots of patients to see, and I know we've already taken up far too much of your time...'

'I would love to,' Dr Adler cut her off. 'But I wonder if you might take over the lessons? I suspect your father finds my lack of expertise rather tiresome.'

'It would be my pleasure.'

Dora edged away, leaving them lost in each other's company.

The blood test results arrived back from the pathology department just before lunch.

Millie watched from the end of the line of nurses as Mr Latimer the consultant examined Charlie. He was surrounded by eager-looking students, all craning over to get a better look.

Charlie glanced over at her and pulled a face. Millie forced herself to smile back. Her mouth was stretched so painfully her cheeks ached. But all she really wanted to do was cry.

'Patient was admitted with acute diffuse glomerulonephritis,' Mr Latimer announced to his students. 'In spite of treatment he has since developed oedema, his blood urea levels have gone up to 150 milligrams per hundred ccs and he is complaining of headaches and muscle weakness. What does that suggest to you?'

'Er ... uraemia, sir?' one of the young men suggested tentatively. Millie swallowed hard, trying not to let her face give anything away. She

312

knew Charlie was watching her.

'Precisely. And what is the recommended course of treatment?' Mr Latimer scanned the group impatiently. 'Come on, come on! Surely one of you must have an idea?'

'Sweating and purgation, sir?' someone said finally.

The consultant let out a loud sigh. 'What do you think these poor nurses have been doing since he was admitted? Holding his hand?' He shook back his leonine mane of hair. 'So no one can recommend a suitable course of treatment for poor Mr...' he consulted his notes '...Dawson here? Well, I must say I am rather disappointed. Not to mention dismayed for the future of our patients.'

An untidy-looking young man at the back of the group cleared his throat nervously. 'How about venesection, sir?'

'Venesection! Thank you, Mr Wilson. At last, someone who has bothered to read a textbook!'

Millie could see the young man's ears burning bright red with pride as the consultant turned to Sister Judd and instructed her to prepare the patient for surgery.

'What's happening now?' Charlie asked, as Millie set out the sterilised instruments, swabs, gauze and dressings at his bedside later. He eyed the scalpel and forceps nervously as they lay in their dish of carbolic. 'They're not going to take my arm off as well, are they?' he joked nervously.

'It's not as drastic as that, don't worry!' Millie smiled. 'They're just going to drain off some of your blood. It might help bring down your urea levels.'

'Might help? You don't sound too sure?' he laughed.

Millie busied herself arranging mackintoshes and towels over the bed, keeping her head down. 'It will make you feel better.'

She started as Charlie put out his hand to grasp hers. 'It isn't going to stop me dying though, is it?' he said, suddenly serious.

'I – I–' she stammered.

'I was watching your face when that doctor was in here. This isn't going to help. Nothing will.'

Millie glanced up at Charlie's face. He was smiling, but his blue eyes were full of fear.

'I'm not daft, Nurse. I realise you've done your best to hide it, but I've known for days I'm not going to get better.'

She wanted to say the right thing, to make him feel reassured. But the words had deserted her.

'Charlie, I – I don't–'

'It's all right, Nurse, you don't have to say anything. I didn't mean to put you on the spot.' He smiled kindly at her. 'How long do you think I've got?'

Millie hesitated. 'That's not for me to say,' she said. 'Anyway, you mustn't talk like that,' she went on. 'Even severe infections can suddenly just start to get better. The important thing is not to give up hope, Charlie.'

He nodded, taking it in. He looked so brave. Millie wondered if she could ever face her own fate as calmly or courageously.

'Just as long as I have time to marry Helen,' he said. 'I don't want to let her down.'

Chapter Thirty-Three

When Dora returned to their room after her duty was finished, she found the place in chaos. The wardrobe doors were flung open and there were dresses everywhere: draped over the beds and chair, heaped on the floor and hanging from the buckling curtain rail. The room was a riot of colourful silks, delicate georgettes and sumptuous velvets.

Helen stood in the middle of it, holding up a dress of oyster-coloured crepe de chine. 'What about this one?'

Millie kept her eyes fixed on the letter she was writing. 'It's very nice,' she said.

'You're supposed to be helping me, and you're not even looking!' Helen turned to Dora. 'What do you think? Will it do for a wedding dress?'

'It's lovely.' Dora glanced at Millie, who lay on her bed, chewing on the end of her pen. She was well known in the nurses' home for her expertise when it came to picking the right dress for the right occasion. Her couture wardrobe, especially selected by her aristocratic grandmother for Millie's London season, had seen many a student nurse through dinners, dances and dates.

'Don't ask her, she's being completely hopeless!' Helen sighed.

'I still can't believe Matron agreed to you getting married,' Dora said.

'She didn't have much choice.' Helen's face was determined as she added the crepe de chine to the growing heap on the bed. 'I told her I was going to marry Charlie even if it meant leaving the hospital. She said she could see my mind was made up and she didn't want me to give up my studies so close to the State Finals.'

'And what about when Charlie comes out of hospital?' Dora said.

'We'll cross that bridge when we come to it.' Helen pulled a blue velvet dress out of the wardrobe and held it up against herself.

'Too dark for a wedding,' Dora declared. 'It's meant to be a happy occasion. Isn't that right, Benedict?'

'I suppose so.' Millie still didn't look up.

'Now you're both here, I've got something to ask you,' Helen said, putting down the dress. 'It's a big favour, and you can say no if you like...'

'Spit it out!' Dora laughed.

Helen looked from her to Millie and back again. 'I wondered ... would you two be my bridesmaids?'

Dora pushed aside a heap of silk brocade and sat down on her bed. 'Do you mean it? You really want us to be your bridesmaids?'

'I know it's short notice,' Helen said. 'But you two are my best friends, and I'd feel a lot happier if you were with me.'

Dora stared at her. When she'd first met Helen Tremayne nearly two years ago in this very room, it had never occurred to her that they might even become friends, let alone anything else.

'If you really can't bear the idea, I don't mind.'

Helen's face was anxious. 'But I'd really appreciate it.'

'Of course we'll do it!' Dora grinned. 'We'd be dead chuffed, wouldn't we, Benedict? Benedict...'

She turned around. Millie was looking up from her letter, stony-faced. 'Of course,' she said in a flat voice. 'We'd be delighted.'

She put down her pen and got up, gathering her wash bag. 'If you'll excuse me, I'm going to get ready for bed.'

Dora followed her out on to the landing. 'What's the matter with you?' she hissed.

'I – I don't know what you mean.' Millie kept her head down, her towel and washbag clutched tightly under her arm.

'Your friend's getting married and you've got a face as long as a fiddle. You could at least try and look happy for her. Here, I'm talking to you!' Dora made a grab for her as she started down the stairs.

Millie swung round. Her face was stricken, blue eyes swimming with tears.

'What is it? What's wrong?'

'Oh, Doyle!' A fat tear escaped and rolled down her cheek. 'Charlie's dying.'

Dora released her abruptly, her hand dropping to her side. 'No!'

'The tests came back. He's developed uraemia. There's nothing more they can do for him.' Her voice was thick with emotion.

'Does Tremayne know?'

Millie shook her head. 'I don't think so. I mean, she knows he's ill, but I don't think she's worked out how serious it is. I feel so awful, listening to

317

her planning her wedding, knowing what's going to happen. It's just so horribly sad.'

'In that case I'm surprised at Charlie,' Dora said. 'Why would he let her go ahead with this wedding, knowing he's going to die? It seems so selfish, and not at all like him.'

'I'm the selfish one.'

Dora turned around. Helen stood in the doorway to their room, watching them. Her face was calm.

'He didn't want to marry me,' she said. 'I talked him into it when I found out how ill he was.'

'You – you knew?' Millie said.

'Really, did you think I wouldn't guess? I can read a chart, you know.' Helen gave a small, sad smile. 'Ever since he was admitted, I've been trying to tell myself it was going to be all right, but as time went by I could see he wasn't getting any better.'

Millie burst into tears. 'Oh, I'm so sorry,' she sobbed.

'Shh, don't cry.' Helen came over to them and put her arms around Millie. 'It's me who should be weeping, you silly thing.'

'Why didn't you say anything?' Dora fought to keep her voice steady.

'I didn't want a fuss,' Helen said. 'I just wanted to feel like any other girl who was about to get married. I couldn't bear the idea of people feeling sorry for me. Because I really don't need you to feel sorry for me,' she added, with a touch of defiance. 'I'm getting married to the man I love. And that makes me very happy.'

Dora looked at her face. She seemed so composed. Could she ever be as brave as Helen Tremayne, she wondered. 'That's why Matron gave her permission, isn't it?'

Helen nodded. 'We didn't talk about Charlie's illness directly, but I know she understands.'

I bet she does, Dora thought. Matron's wisdom was all-seeing and all-knowing.

Millie sobbed into Helen's shoulder. 'Look at me, I'm such a selfish idiot! I should be the one comforting you, not the other way round.'

'No one needs to comfort anyone.' Helen held Millie at arm's length. 'I told you, I want you to be happy for me. And besides, you never know, it may not turn out as badly as everyone seems to think. I've got to keep holding on to hope.'

As Millie mopped her face on her towel, Dora struggled to keep control of her own emotions. The last thing poor Helen needed were long faces all around her.

'Is there anything we can do for you?' she asked.

'You can be my bridesmaids. You can walk down that aisle with me and smile and make this a day for Charlie and me to remember.'

Millie sniffed back her tears. 'We'll do that. Won't we, Doyle?'

'And you can start by helping me to find something to wear. You know you're far better at choosing clothes than I am.'

Millie's face brightened. 'Leave it to me. I'll find you the best dress in the world.'

'You'd best hurry, you've only got three days to do it in!'

Dora braced herself. 'Is there anything else we can do?'

Helen smiled. 'Just be my friends.' She smiled then. 'Unless you want to help me break the news to my mother?'

Millie's mouth fell open. 'You mean, you haven't told her yet?'

Helen shook her head. 'I'm afraid I've been putting it off,' she admitted. 'I'm going down to Richmond tomorrow. And I don't think my mother is going to be quite so understanding as Matron!'

Chapter Thirty-Four

'No. I won't hear of it.'

Constance Tremayne kept herself rigidly under control, hands clenched in front of her. She reminded Helen of a tightly wound clock.

'Well, I think it's marvellous news.' Her father broke the tense silence. 'Congratulations, my dear. Charlie is a wonderful young man.'

'It's a perfectly ridiculous idea,' Constance snapped. 'And why do you have to get married so quickly, anyway?' The colour drained from her face. 'Oh, dear God. Don't tell me you're–'

'No!' Helen denied quickly. 'We – just love each other and want to be together, that's all.' She kept her eyes averted from her mother, certain she would be able to see straight through her lie.

'And I suppose this was all his idea?' Constance sniffed. 'Not content with dragging you down to his level, he now wants to ruin your future. Not to mention robbing you of a decent wedding.'

'It will be a decent wedding,' Helen defended. She turned to her father.

'Do you think you'll be able to give me away?' she asked.

Her father looked rueful. 'Well, I'm not sure about that.'

Her stomach turned over. 'Really? I know it's short notice, but I was hoping...'

Timothy Tremayne smiled. 'I didn't mean it in that way, Helen, don't look so worried! It's just, I rather hoped that you might ask me to conduct the marriage service. I quite understand if you've already made arrangements with the hospital chaplain, but ever since you were born I had imagined I might be allowed to marry you, so to speak?'

Helen grinned. 'Oh, Father, what a wonderful idea! I hadn't even thought about that. Would you really do that for us?'

'I would be honoured,' he said solemnly. 'And I'm sure your brother would be more than happy to take my place in giving you away.'

'Oh, for heaven's sake! Doesn't anyone care how I feel about this ... this farce?'

They both jumped as Constance stormed out of the room, slamming the door behind her. They heard the staccato rap of her footsteps heading down the hall.

Timothy looked at his daughter. 'I rather think we can guess, don't you?' he said dryly.

'I'd better go to her.' Helen stood up, but her father put out a hand to stop her.

'No, leave your mother for a moment,' he advised. 'Let's have a glass of sherry to celebrate your good news.'

Helen sipped her drink nervously. Her father was chatting to her about the ceremony, but she could hardly take in what he was saying. Her eyes were fixed nervously on the door. She was expecting her mother to come bursting back in at any moment.

Finally, Helen could stand it no longer. 'I had better go and see how Mother is,' she said, putting down her glass.

'Very well, my dear. But don't let her upset you,' her father advised. 'I'm sure she'll come round to the idea eventually. She just needs some time to adjust, that's all.' He frowned. 'Ignore her if she becomes too petulant, won't you?'

'Don't worry, I will!'

She found her mother pacing up and down in the kitchen, her arms folded tightly. As Helen crept in Constance turned on her, her face twisted with anger.

'How could you?' Cords of rage stood out on her thin neck. 'You stupid, stupid girl, how could you do such a thing after everything I've done for you? You do realise this is the end, don't you? There'll be no exams, no qualifications after this. You've thrown your whole career away, your whole future. You'll have to leave the hospital.'

Helen pressed her lips together to stop herself speaking. Apart from Millie, Dora and Matron, no one knew the real reason she was getting married so quickly, and she wanted to keep it that way. She couldn't stand the thought of all those long faces at her wedding.

'I won't,' Helen told her calmly. 'I've talked to Matron about it, and she's agreed that I can stay on until after the State Finals.'

'Oh, she's agreed, has she?' Constance's voice dripped pure acid. 'So you've spoken to Matron before you even consulted me?'

'I thought it would be for the best,' Helen faltered.

'For the best?' Constance gave a bitter laugh. 'If you were acting for the best you wouldn't be anywhere near that dreadful young man. I should have packed you off to Scotland while I had the chance,' she muttered to herself.

She started pacing again, and Helen braced herself for more rage and spite. She didn't have to wait long.

'And what about after your State Finals?' Constance spat out. 'Have you thought about what happens then? No, of course you haven't. You simply don't care, do you? You don't care that you're throwing away your future.'

'Charlie is my future,' Helen replied quietly, staying calm in the face of her mother's spitting rage.

'Your future!' Constance's face twisted. 'You stupid girl, you don't realise, do you? You don't *have* a future after you marry him. That will be the end of it all, the end of all your hopes and dreams, everything I've worked for...'

She closed her mouth like a trap, snapping back the words, but Helen caught them.

'Everything *you've* worked for?' she echoed. 'That's what all this is about, isn't it? It isn't my future you're worried about. You don't care about what I want. All you're interested in is how it reflects on you. Well, I'm sorry, Mother, but I'm not a pet dog you can teach to do tricks to impress people. This is my life and I'll do what I want.'

'You'll do as you're told!' Constance picked up a plate off the dresser and smashed it.

Helen stared at her. She had never seen her in such a rage. Her mother had lost all control.

'No, Mother, not any more,' Helen said calmly.

The door opened and her father burst in. 'What was that noise? I heard a crash...' He looked down at the china plate, shattered into fragments over the kitchen floor. 'What on earth has happened?'

'It was an accident,' Helen covered smoothly. 'Mother was picking it up, and it slipped out of her grasp. Isn't that right, Mother?'

Constance was silent and white-faced, though whether from rage or remorse Helen had no idea. Then it suddenly dawned on her that she didn't care. Like a weight lifting from her shoulders, she realised she didn't have to worry about her mother's moods any more.

Helen looked at her watch. 'I must be going,' she said. 'My train leaves in half an hour.'

'I'll telephone for a taxi,' her father offered.

Helen turned to her mother. 'The wedding is in two days, Mother,' she said. 'I hope you can come and see me get married?'

'I'd die first!' Constance snapped, her lips white with tension.

'I'm sorry you feel that way about it.' Helen took a deep, steadying breath. 'But you're not going to ruin my day for me. Charlie and I are getting married, whether you like it or not.'

After they'd served the evening cocoa that night, Helen and the pro did a last check on the patients, turning anyone who needed it, rubbing in liniments, applying poultices, plumping pillows and straightening bedclothes before they settled everyone down for the night. Then, while the pro carried all the vases of flowers out to the sluice, Helen sat down at the sister's desk, opened up the heavy leather ledger and started to make that night's ward report by the dim glow of the green-shaded light.

Within an hour, the muted chorus of wheezing and snoring told her that all the patients were sleeping soundly. She left the pro watching over them while she went into the kitchen to put the kettle on.

'I'll have one of those, if you're making it?'

She turned around, the kettle still in her hand, and was shocked to see Amy Hollins standing in the doorway.

Helen reached up into the cupboard and took out another cup. 'I didn't expect to see you here.'

Amy lifted her shoulders listlessly. 'I was bored.'

'Not seeing your boyfriend tonight?'

Amy looked up at her sharply. 'Why do you say that?'

'No reason. Only I heard that you meet up with him sometimes, after all the patients are asleep?'

'Oh, you heard that, did you? I suppose that sneaky little pro's been telling tales, has she?' Amy's face was full of spite, but for once Helen refused to be cowed.

'I didn't realise it was such a big secret.'

To Helen's utter shock, Amy's mood of anger

left her. 'I'm sorry,' she sighed. 'Take no notice of me, I'm just feeling fed-up tonight. I wanted some company.'

You must be desperate to seek me out, Helen thought. She stood at the stove and stared at the kettle, willing it to boil. The silence stretched between them.

It was Amy who finally spoke. 'I bet you're excited about the wedding?'

Helen smiled. 'Yes. Yes, I am.'

'Do you realise, you'll be the only married nurse in this hospital – maybe the whole of London. Or the whole country!'

'I never thought of that. I suppose I will, won't I?' Helen reflected as she lifted the heavy kettle off the hob and filled the teapot.

'Do you think there'll ever be a time when all nurses are allowed to get married?' Amy mused.

'I'm not sure many of them will want to.'

'Would you? I mean, if things had been different, would you want to go on working as a married woman?'

Helen considered it for a moment. 'I don't know,' she said. 'It does seem a shame to let all that training go to waste, I suppose.'

'I wouldn't,' Amy declared firmly. 'I'd tell Matron where to stick her rules and regulations, not to mention her bloody uncomfortable shoes, like a shot!' She looked at Helen consideringly. 'But I suppose it's different for you, isn't it?'

'In what way?'

'Well, you're born to it, aren't you? It's in your blood.'

'Is it?' Helen said. 'Actually, I always wanted to

be a teacher.'

'Really?' Amy stared at her. 'Then why didn't you?'

'Because my mother wouldn't allow it.'

Helen could feel Amy's eyes on her as she filled the cups.

'You mean, your mother forced you to become a nurse?'

'That's about it, yes.' Helen glanced over her shoulder. 'Do you take sugar?'

'No, thanks. So does your mother often tell you what to do?'

Helen laughed. 'What do you think? Believe me, she treats me no differently from the way she treats everyone else. If anything, she's even worse with me.'

'I had no idea.' Amy's face was pensive as Helen handed her the cup.

They sat down at the table in the middle of the ward. The dim light cast long shadows across their faces.

'What are you wearing for the wedding?' Amy asked.

'I don't know,' Helen admitted. 'I think Benedict has something in mind. She usually comes to our rescue with the right clothes.'

Amy looked aghast. 'You mean, you don't have a proper wedding dress?'

'I haven't had time to buy one,' Helen sighed.

Amy sipped her tea, looking thoughtful. 'I could do your hair for you?' she offered.

Helen blinked in surprise. 'Thank you,' she said. 'That's very kind of you.'

'And make-up. You'll need make-up.'

'I daresay I will, if only to hide the bags under my eyes!' Helen grimaced.

'Don't be silly. You'll make a beautiful bride.'

Helen stared at her. Was this really the same girl who had made life a misery for her over the past three years?

As if she knew what Helen was thinking, Amy murmured, 'Look, I know we haven't always hit it off, but I want you to know I wish you well.'

'Thank you.'

'Actually, I envy you,' Amy sighed.

'Me? Why?'

'Because you're marrying the man you love.'

Helen smiled at her over the rim of her cup. 'I'm sure it will happen for you one day.'

'I don't think so.' Amy's voice was suddenly cold.

'Why not? Don't you think your boyfriend is the marrying kind?'

'It's not that...' Amy bit her lip. 'It doesn't matter.' She drained her cup, her cheerful smile suddenly back in place. 'Thanks for the tea. I'd better go back to the ward. My pro is so dozy she probably wouldn't think to warn me if the Night Sister's on her way!'

She put her cup in the sink. 'Toodlepip, anyway. Perhaps you could come to my ward tomorrow night for tea? Then we can plan what to do with your hair.'

'Thank you, I'd like that.'

Helen watched her saunter off. In spite of her bright smile, she couldn't help feeling there was something very sad about Amy Hollins.

Chapter Thirty-Five

'I demand you put a stop to this nonsense immediately!'

Kathleen Fox gazed calmly across the desk at the twitching ball of suppressed fury that was Constance Tremayne. They had had many such meetings in the two years she had been Matron of the Nightingale Hospital. In fact, she could barely remember a week when she didn't have Mrs Tremayne storming into her office demanding she either do something or desist from doing something else.

'And what particular nonsense are you referring to this time, Mrs Tremayne?' Matron smiled patiently.

Constance reared back in her seat, nostrils flaring like a startled thoroughbred. She was dressed for battle as usual, her tightly buttoned tweed suit perfectly reflecting her uncompromising character. 'I mean, Miss Fox, this utterly preposterous notion of my daughter getting married,' she bit out.

'I hardly think that's any of my business, do you?'

'It is if the marriage takes place in this hospital!' Constance's eyes blazed. 'You must forbid it.'

'On what grounds? I'll admit it is rather unusual, but it is not unheard of. Indeed, I understand that several marriages have taken place in the hospital chapel...'

'That's not the point, is it?' Constance Tremayne snapped. 'I'm not bothered about where the wedding is taking place, it's the fact that it is taking place at all!' Her thin mouth quivered. 'Really, Matron, I am surprised that you would so willingly allow a promising student like my daughter to slip through your fingers. Helen could have been an asset to the Nightingale. But you are allowing her to throw her future away.'

'Yes, but under the circumstances—'

'What circumstances? What possible excuse could there be for me to allow my daughter to make a mistake that will stay with her for the rest of her life?'

You don't know, Kathleen realised. For whatever reason, Helen Tremayne had not seen fit to tell her mother how grave Charlie Dawson's illness was.

'Your daughter is over twenty-one, Mrs Tremayne. Neither you nor I have any right to forbid this marriage,' Kathleen reminded her. Not that she would have forbidden it in any case. She had never seen a girl as happy and in love as Helen Tremayne.

She looked across at Constance's pinched face and tried to feel some understanding for the woman. They had had more than their fair share of confrontations, but underneath her busybody exterior there was a worried mother.

'Helen is not throwing away her future, Mrs Tremayne,' Kathleen said, more gently. 'I have already given her permission to stay on as a student here until after her State Finals.'

'And after that?' Mrs Tremayne snapped.

Kathleen stared down at the blotter in front of her. 'I think we should worry about that when the time comes,' she said gently.

Constance fumed. 'I might have known! It was thanks to your lacksadaisical approach that this — unfortunate liaison was allowed to happen in the first place. You should keep a tighter rein on your nurses, Matron, and then such improper conduct wouldn't occur.'

Kathleen forced herself to stay calm, but Mrs Tremayne had a way of getting under her skin. 'I can see nothing improper about two young people wanting to be married in the eyes of God, can you?' she said. 'On the contrary, I think it's wonderful that they are making such a commitment to each other.'

'Wonderful? You think it's wonderful, do you?' Constance stared at her, her skin tightly drawn across the bones of her face. Her gloved hands gripped the clasp of her crocodile-skin handbag. Kathleen had no doubt Mrs Tremayne would have fixed them around her neck, if good manners hadn't forbidden it. 'I might have known you would take such a sentimental view. I daresay that's why so many of the nurses here wander about with their heads in the clouds, instead of concentrating on their work!' She glared across the desk. 'I take it that's your last word on the subject?'

'I don't think there's much more to say, do you?'

'Very well then, you leave me no choice.' Constance rose stiffly to her feet, drawing herself up to her full height. 'We will see what the Board of Trustees has to say about this!'

'I do hope, Mrs Tremayne, you won't make things difficult for your daughter,' Kathleen advised. 'I would hate to see your relationship with Helen suffer in any way.' As if it hasn't suffered enough already, she added silently.

'I believe that is my business, Matron, not yours,' Constance bit out.

As she reached the door, Kathleen couldn't resist saying, 'So I expect I'll see you at the wedding?'

Every inch of Constance Tremayne seemed to quiver with rage. 'I can assure you if this – travesty – does take place, I will not be there to see it!'

She marched out, slamming the door behind her so hard the heavy books trembled on the shelves.

Then you're an even bigger fool than I thought you were, Kathleen thought.

'Have you got a minute, Doyle?'

Dora looked up from her sewing. She was in the students' sitting room, curled up in a corner of the battered Rexine sofa, letting down the hem of Helen's dress and listening to Katie O'Hara and Lucy Lane bickering over tuning in the ancient wireless.

She was surprised to see Penny Willard. They had barely seen each other in the last month, not since the night of the ball. Since Dora had moved to Female Medical, their paths rarely crossed.

Nurses rarely ventured into the students' home, either. Once they passed their State Finals, they moved into the nurses' block where they had their own rooms and lived in grand style, and never gave the poor students a second thought.

But here she was, standing in the doorway, looking decidedly out of place.

Dora put down her sewing. 'What can I do for you?'

'I'd like a word with you. In private, if you don't mind?' Penny cast a quick glance at Katie and Lucy, who had stopped twiddling the knob on the wireless and were pretending not to listen.

Dora followed her outside. It was a warm August evening, with barely a breath of breeze whispering through the plane trees. But Penny still hugged herself as she stood on the gravel drive.

'It's about Joe,' she said.

'Oh, yes?' Dora had a feeling she knew what was coming. It was written all over Penny's guilty face.

'The thing is, he's asked me to go to the pictures with him on Friday. But I said I wanted to talk to you about it first.' She scuffed the toe of her shoe in the gravel. 'I really like him, but you and I are friends and I don't want you to think I'd ever do anything behind your back...' Her words came out in a rush.

Dora frowned at her. 'Are you asking me if it's all right for you to go out with Joe Armstrong?'

'I suppose so.' Penny looked up at her. 'Is it?'

Dora shrugged. 'It's got nothing to do with me.'

'But you were his girlfriend. I know I'd hate if it one of my so-called friends started courting one of my boyfriends, even if I wasn't with him myself any more. It's just not right, is it?'

'I told you, it's got nothing to do with me. If you want to go out with him, then you've got my blessing.'

'Really?' Penny smiled hopefully. 'Only I really do like him. Not that I was ever interested in him while you two were still courting,' she added hastily.

'Heaven forbid.' Dora did her best to look serious. Did Penny not think she had eyes in her head? She'd seen the way the other girls had always looked at him, like a dog panting after the butcher's bike.

'I hope the two of you will be very happy,' Dora said sincerely.

Katie O'Hara was waiting for her in the hall when she came back inside.

'What a cow!' she hissed.

Dora laughed. 'You were listening, then? It was meant to be private.'

'I've got four sisters, I don't even know what private means!' Katie followed her into the sitting room. 'I'm surprised you didn't scratch her eyes out for her.'

'Why would I do that?'

'Well, it's obvious why she came round, isn't it? She came to crow. She wanted to rub it in that Joe had ditched you and asked her out.'

'That's not what it sounded like to me.' Dora settled herself back down on the sofa and picked up her sewing. 'Besides, he didn't ditch me, remember? I ditched him.'

'Yes, and look what a big mistake that was!' Katie flopped down on the settee next to her, upsetting her box of pins. 'Didn't I tell you he'd get snapped up by someone else if you weren't careful?'

'Yes, and I'm glad.' Dora bent down to pick her stray pins off the floor.

Katie stared at her. 'You really mean it, don't you? Jesus, I don't understand you, Doyle. I'd be beside myself if someone started courting my Tom.'

'That's because you're in love with your Tom, ain't it?'

All Dora could feel was relief that Joe was happy with someone else.

Chapter Thirty-Six

'Are you sure you won't change your mind, my dear?' Timothy Tremayne stood at the mirror, adjusting his collar. 'It seems such a shame that you won't be at your own daughter's wedding.'

'Someone has to take a stand against this travesty.' Constance sniffed, looking down at her sewing. 'It's bad enough that she insists on going through with this wedding, without me having to witness it. And I thought you might have supported me, Timothy,' she added, shooting him a quick look. She had certainly done her best to persuade him over the past couple of days, but for once he would not be budged.

'I'm sorry, Constance, but I have no intention of missing my daughter's wedding,' he said.

'Yes, well, Helen always has been a daddy's girl,'

Constance replied tartly. 'She had you twisted around her little finger from the moment she was born. It was left to me to discipline her, make sure she stayed on the right path.' She pursed her lips. No wonder she and Helen had such a difficult relationship. 'I don't suppose she'll even notice I'm not there,' she sighed.

'Don't be silly, my dear. Every girl wants her mother at her wedding. And you want to be there too, surely?'

Constance hesitated. 'I would if I approved of this match. But I simply can't allow myself to be party to something that is against my principles.'

Her husband turned away from the mirror and gave her an almost pitying look.

'You know, I've always admired your principles, Constance, but it must be very lonely up there sometimes, on that high horse of yours,' he sighed. 'I'm sure you would find life far more to your liking if you just allowed yourself to unbend a little occasionally.'

'Well, that's a fine thing for a vicar to say!' Constance retorted. 'I hope you don't tell that to your congregation on a Sunday morning.'

She pretended to dead head an urn of petunias as she watched him driving off in a taxi to the station. She felt a sudden, absurd urge to go after him. It was only the thought of what Mary the maid would say that stopped her from running down the drive.

But no. She had made her decision, and she was satisfied it was the right one, under the circumstances. Let Timothy do as he wished and indulge his daughter as usual; she would have nothing to do with such a farce.

It was a relief to have the house to herself, she decided as she returned to the drawing room. She could catch up with some sewing or some reading, listen to some soothing music. She might even go out into the garden later, if the weather stayed fine. The garden was starting to take on the burnished gold and russet colours of autumn, and she wanted to make sure Morley wasn't helping himself to all the early apples from their tree.

She ordered the maid to bring her tea, and settled down to read in her favourite chair by the French window. But she couldn't settle. Her eyes kept straying to the grandfather clock. The wedding was due to happen at three o'clock, and she could imagine Helen's growing excitement as she got ready...

Constance put down her book with a gesture of impatience. Really, this would not do at all! She prided herself on her single-mindedness, her ability to concentrate, but now her thoughts seemed to be scattered all over the place.

She rang the bell. After a moment Mary appeared, looking irritated. No doubt the wretched girl had supposed she might have the place to herself this afternoon, Constance thought.

'I want you to go up into the attic and fetch me down a box,' she instructed her.

'The attic, Madam?' Mary looked dismayed.

'Yes, Mary. The attic. You'll find the box in the far corner. It's clearly labelled with the date – May 1906. You should be able to find it easily enough.'

'Yes, Madam.' The girl didn't move.

'Well, get along with you!'

'Please, Madam, I'm scared of the dark.'

'Don't be absurd, girl!' Constance dismissed this. 'Go up there at once. Don't make a mess and see you don't break anything,' she called after her. 'I shall be up in five minutes and I expect you to have found my box by then.'

As she went up the stairs precisely five minutes later, she winced at the sound of crashing overhead. It sounded as if a wild boar had got loose among her belongings.

'I hope you didn't break anything?' she said, when Mary appeared down the ladder, her legs buckling under the weight of the box. She was pale-faced, her hair grey with dust.

'No, Madam.' She went to hand over the box, but Constance stepped back.

'Don't give it to me, girl. It's far too heavy, and dusty too. Put it down over there, in the bedroom.' She pointed towards the doorway. 'Then go and get cleaned up.' She frowned towards the small hatch that led to the attic. 'In fact, it might be a good idea for you to go up there for a day and give it a thorough cleaning,' she mused.

Mary's face drained of what little colour it had left. 'Go up there? For a whole day?' she blurted out.

'Oh, good gracious, girl. Don't make such a fuss!' Constance tutted. 'Now, I'm going to spend some time going through this box. I don't wish to be disturbed, do you understand?'

'Yes, Madam.'

Alone in her bedroom, Constance's hands trembled as she opened the box. On top lay a photograph. She paused for a moment to look at

338

it. She was twenty-six years old when she married Timothy Tremayne, but she still looked absurdly young. She clung to her new husband's arm, smiling shyly, eyes lowered modestly behind her veil.

She put the photograph to one side and took a deep breath as she carefully peeled away the layers of tissue paper, until she finally found what she was looking for.

Her wedding gown. Nothing showy or elaborate, she had deliberately chosen a very simple unadorned cream chiffon dress as if she wanted to prove to everyone how chaste and modest she was.

She held up the dress, running her hands over the soft fabric. She had always dreamed of Helen wearing it one day. She had imagined helping her to dress, fastening up the row of tiny pearl buttons at the back, helping to pin on her veil...

How dare Timothy suggest she didn't want to see her daughter getting married! It was supposed to be the happiest day of her life, seeing Helen safely wed to a respectable man, someone who would be able to look after her. It would be the pinnacle of her achievement, the proof that she had succeeded as a mother.

Downstairs, the grandfather clock struck three. Constance kneeled down on the floor of her bedroom, her unwanted wedding dress draped across her knees, and wept.

'I want you to have this.'

Helen hardly knew what she was seeing at first as Brenda Bevan stood before her in the doorway, her arms full of ivory silk and lace. And then it dawned on her.

'Your wedding dress?' She stared down at it, then up at Brenda. 'But I don't understand?'

'Hollins told me you didn't have time to find a dress for yourself, so I got my mother to bring it for you.'

Helen glanced at Amy, who was busy packing away her comb and pins after doing Helen's hair, then at Millie and Dora, her bridesmaids. 'I had planned to wear one of Benedict's old dresses,' she said. 'She was kind enough to lend it to me, and Doyle has spent ages altering it to fit...'

'Oh, never mind that,' Millie dismissed. 'This is far more beautiful than my old cast-off. And I'm sure Doyle doesn't mind, do you?'

'Not at all,' Dora agreed. 'I'd rather see you in a proper wedding dress.'

Helen gazed longingly at the dress. She had never seen anything so beautiful. It was so lovely she longed to reach out and touch it.

'I couldn't,' she said, drawing her hand back. 'It's your dress, Bevan. You haven't even worn it to your own wedding yet.'

'My wedding isn't for months. Honestly, I'd like you to wear it. Call it something borrowed, if you like?' She proffered the dress. 'At least try it on,' she said.

Helen tried on the dress. It could have been made for her, it fitted her so perfectly. And with her dark hair styled in soft waves around her face, even she had to admit she looked beautiful.

'Well?' Brenda asked. 'Will it do?'

'It's perfect.' Helen turned to her. 'I don't know how to thank you...' She was so choked she could barely say the words.

'There's no need.' Brenda looked down at the floor, embarrassed. 'It's the least I could do. I just wish I could be there to see you get married.'

'Oh!' Helen felt herself flushing. 'Well, you're welcome to come. I'm sorry I didn't invite you earlier, but I didn't think you'd want to.'

'It's all right.' Brenda waved away her apology. 'I'm due back on the ward in a minute. Sister will go mad if I'm late!' She reached out and grasped Helen's hand briefly. 'I hope it goes well for you, I really do.' She looked away, but not before Helen saw the tears glistening in her eyes.

She stared back at her reflection in the mirror. There were tears in her own eyes, too, blurring the vision of herself in her elegant dress.

'Now then, don't you dare start crying!' Dora stepped in bossily. 'This is meant to be the happiest day of your life, remember?'

'Besides, you'll ruin that make-up and we'll have to start all over again!' Amy Hollins added.

'It *is* the happiest day of my life,' Helen said. 'I just can't believe everyone has been so kind.'

'That's because you're our friend,' Millie said. She flapped her hand in front of her face to dry her own tears. 'Now come on, William will be waiting for you outside. And I daresay Sister Sutton will be standing guard, making sure he doesn't step over the threshold.'

'As if that ever kept him out!' Dora added, and they all laughed.

There was no sign of the Home Sister for once, but William still stood outside, looking as nervous as a groom himself in his smart suit.

341

'I didn't like to come in, just in case Sister Sutton was lurking around and–' He stopped talking abruptly when he saw Helen.

'Well?' she said, suddenly shy. 'Will I do?'

'I should say.' William's mouth trembled, and she could see he was fighting to keep control of his emotions. He proffered his arm. 'Shall we go?' he said softly.

As they crossed the courtyard, Helen could feel all eyes on them. Patients and nurses stood watching them from every window. Some patients had even been wheeled out into the courtyard to see them pass. Helen kept her gaze fixed on the cobbles, too self-conscious to look around.

'I'm not used to being the centre of attention,' she murmured.

William gave her arm a reassuring squeeze. 'You deserve it. It's about time everyone noticed how beautiful you are.'

'Is that really my brother talking?' she laughed.

'Your very proud brother.'

'And what about my mother? Is she proud too?' She glanced up at her brother's profile, and saw his smile slip a fraction. 'Too proud to be here, I imagine? It's all right, you don't have to answer that,' she said. 'I didn't really expect her to come.'

'It's her loss,' William said firmly.

Helen fixed her eyes on the chapel doors. 'Yes,' she said. 'Yes, it is. It's just a shame our side of the church will be rather empty though,' she sighed. 'Still, I daresay Charlie's family will be able to spread out a bit.'

'I wouldn't be too sure of that.'

Helen caught the glance that passed between

her brother and her bridesmaids. 'What?' she frowned. 'What aren't you telling me?'

Dora grinned. 'You'll see. It's another surprise.'

Two porters in brown overalls were standing outside the chapel. As she approached, they swung open the doors for her and Helen heard the rousing sound of the 'Wedding March' played on the piano.

'Sister Blake's idea,' William whispered. 'She said you can't have a wedding without music.'

But Helen wasn't listening. She was staring around the tiny chapel, which was festooned with flowers.

'That was Sister Sutton,' Millie chimed in. 'She picked them from the garden herself.'

Charlie's family sat on one side of the chapel, his mother, father, brothers, sisters, aunts and uncles, all smartly dressed, crowded into the narrow pews. On the other side the pews were filled with uniforms. Nurses, sisters, porters, even the cooks were there. Matron sat at the front, resplendent in her black dress and snowy white bonnet. Beside her sat Miss Hanley the Assistant Matron, the Night Sister Miss Tanner, Sister Sutton and Sister Parker.

'Anyone who could get the time off has come to wish you well,' William whispered.

Helen caught Amy Hollins' eye. She was standing at the back, with a few other girls from her set, all smiling at her.

And there was Charlie, waiting for her at the tiny altar with her father and his best man. He turned, his face lighting up at the sight of her. He was in a wheelchair, but as Helen approached he signalled to his father in the front row, who stepped forward and helped him to his feet.

'He insisted we dress him up in his best suit,' Millie whispered. 'You can't imagine the trouble it took, but he said he didn't want to get married in his pyjamas!'

Charlie smiled as Helen stood beside him at the altar. 'You look beautiful,' he said, reaching for her hand.

'So do you,' Helen replied.

Charlie nodded to his father, who helped him back into his wheelchair, and then they turned to her own father, standing before them with his prayer book poised, his face beaming with pride above his starched white surplice.

'Dearly beloved, we are here to witness the marriage of Helen Constance Tremayne to Charles Edward Dawson...'

Chapter Thirty-Seven

The wedding had tired Charlie out. By the time Helen had changed from her dress and back into her uniform he was fast asleep.

'Sister Judd said to give you some privacy,' Millie said, pulling the screens around the bed. 'She says you can stay as long as you like, since it's a special occasion.'

He went on sleeping for the rest of the afternoon and into the early evening while Helen sat at his bedside, holding his hand and admiring him with quiet pride. He even looked handsome when he was asleep, she thought. She tried not to notice the sheen of perspiration that made his pale skin glisten like a pearl. She knew he had been fighting off the progress of his illness, willing himself to get through their wedding day. But now the effort had finally exhausted him.

'My husband.' She tried the words out loud. It sounded so strange. But the whole afternoon had been so unreal. She felt as if she was drifting through the most magical dream, buoyed up by goodwill and kindness.

It was past eight o'clock when Charlie finally woke up. He stared about him in confusion and Helen's heart skipped, wondering if this might be the moment when it all started to go wrong. But then he saw her and smiled.

'How long have I been asleep?'

'About four hours.'

'That long?' He rubbed his eyes. 'Did everyone go home?'

'They've gone to the pub to celebrate.'

'You should have gone with them.'

'I'd rather stay here with you.'

He held up her hand. Her silver-paper ring was wrapped around her finger next to her new wedding band. 'You're not still wearing that, are you?'

'I like it.' It meant as much to her as any diamond.

He smiled wryly at her. 'Not much of a ring, is it? And not much of a honeymoon for you, stuck at my bedside.'

'Not much of a honeymoon for you, either.' She

smiled. 'Never mind, we'll have to have a proper honeymoon when you're better.'

His smile faded. 'Helen–'

'We'll go to Southend,' she gabbled on, determined to keep the shadows at bay. 'And we'll walk along the pier and the seafront. And you can show me the Planetarium, and the amusement park...'

She clung to Charlie's hand, silently begging him to keep up the fantasy with her. He seemed to understand.

'And cockling,' he said sleepily. 'Don't forget the cockling.'

'How could I forget that?' Helen leaned across him. 'Charlie? Don't go to sleep yet, I've only got a little while before I have to go on duty.'

But he had already drifted off, his breathing soft and shallow.

She hadn't meant to cry in front of him, but somehow the emotion of the day overcame her and the tears started to flow.

'Helen?' He groped for her hand on top of the bedcover.

'I thought you were asleep?'

'I was.' He half opened his eyes. It seemed to take all his strength. 'I'm sorry, love, I'm just so tired...'

'That's all right. You get some rest.'

'You're not going to cry, are you? Only tears of happiness on your wedding day, Helen Tremayne.'

She smiled shakily. 'It's Helen Dawson now, don't forget.'

'So it is.' His mouth curved. 'I like the sound of that.'

'Me too.'

Millie peeped through the screens. 'It's twenty to nine. Shouldn't you be getting ready to go on duty soon?'

'I've still got a few minutes.' Helen clung to Charlie's hand, her fingers curling into his. He tried to squeeze back but she could feel the strength ebbing out of his muscles. Slowly the strong young man she had once known was leaving her.

I'll just have to be strong for both of us, she thought.

With a roar of fury, Joe drove his fist into the sandbag, sinking every ounce of his rage into the punch.

'Watch it!' his friend Tom laughed, dodging it as it swung on its chain. 'Blimey, what's that poor old bag ever done to you?'

Joe didn't reply. He sank another furious punch into the sandbag, sending it swinging on its chain again. No matter how hard he hit out, his rage was still there, burning inside him. He could punch and punch until he was exhausted, sweat running down his body, and the rage would still be there, consuming him.

'You all right, mate?' Tom's face was worried.

'Fine,' Joe snapped back. 'Couldn't be better.'

He landed another punch in the centre of the sandbag, imagining Nick Riley doubling over in front of him.

Joe Armstrong didn't like to lose at anything. That was what made him such a formidable opponent in the ring. He knew he had a reputation for fighting dirty, but he didn't care. To him, winning was everything. The ends justified the means.

He bent closer to the sandbag, jabbing at it, left, right, left, right, until all his strength was spent.

'That's enough, mate.' He emerged from his fog of rage to see Tom watching him worriedly.

'You're right.' Joe smiled at his friend, stripping off his gloves. 'Sling us that towel, would you?'

Tom tossed it to him. 'Shall we stop off for a pint on the way home?'

'Why not? I've got to have a word with Maurice first, though.'

'What about?'

'My next fight.' He wiped the back of his neck with the towel. 'I'll meet you outside, all right?'

Maurice was just finishing putting a young boxer through his paces with a sparring partner in the ring.

'All right, Joe?' he greeted him. Maurice Jones' slight build led many people to misjudge him. He had been the undisputed featherweight champion of Whitechapel for more than twenty years. 'Saw you training just now. You looked like a bloke with a grudge!'

Joe didn't smile back. 'I want to talk to you about my next fight.'

'Of course, my boy, of course. I was talking to Terry Willis about you only the other day, as a matter of fact. He's got a bout next Tuesday that might interest you. Against Kid Lewis at the Whitechapel Working Men's Club?'

'I want to fight Nick Riley.'

'Do what?' Maurice laughed.

'What's so funny?' Joe frowned.

Maurice's smile dropped a fraction. 'You're serious, ain't you? You and Nick Riley?'

''S'right.' He caught Maurice's quick frown. 'What's the matter? Ain't I good enough?'

Maurice slipped between the ropes of the ring and jumped down to Joe's level. 'Look, lad, I'll be honest with you. You're a good fighter, one of the best I've got. But you're not in the same league as Nick Riley. He's – well, boxers like him don't come along very often. He's something special.'

Anger buzzed in Joe's ears, like a bee trapped inside his head.

You're not in the same league as Nick Riley. He's something special.

Everywhere he turned, that was all he seemed to hear. 'I want to fight him,' he said stubbornly. *I want to kill him*, a small voice in his head added.

Maurice seemed to understand. He patted him on the shoulder. 'Look, son. If this is personal between you two, I reckon it's better if you take him on outside the ring, all right? I know you got a temper on you, and I don't want you bringing no grudges with you when you fight.'

Joe stared at him for a moment. 'Maybe you're right,' he said.

Chapter Thirty-Eight

It was starting to rain as Nick lifted the latch on the back gate of number twenty-six Griffin Street. It was early afternoon but the pall of pewter-grey cloud seemed to press down on the narrow back-yard, making it feel like twilight.

'Danny?' he called. Usually his brother would be perched on top of the coal bunker waiting for him, but today the yard was empty.

He wiped the mud off his boots – he didn't know why, since his mum never cleaned – and let himself in through the back door.

'Dan? Where are you, mate?'

His voice echoed around the darkened, empty kitchen. His heart beat quickened.

'Danny?'

'Not so loud, you'll wake the flippin' dead!' June emerged from her bedroom, fastening the sash of her shabby dressing gown. 'Oh, it's you,' she said flatly.

'Been on another bender?' Nick looked at his mother, and a wave of revulsion hit him. June Riley looked half dead. Her eyes were smudged and traces of lipstick were smeared like jam around her mouth. 'I hope you didn't leave Danny on his own?'

'Oh, give it a rest. I'm entitled to a life, ain't I?'

A man's voice called out from the other side of the bedroom door, 'Who is it?'

'No one, Norm. Go back to sleep.' June reached for her cigarette packet and tipped one out. 'What?' she said, catching Nick's disapproving gaze. 'Aren't I allowed to have friends round either?'

His lip curled. 'I'm surprised you can remember his name, that's all.'

'I can't help it if I get lonely.' June lit her cigarette, took a deep drag and regarded him coldly through the rising plume of smoke. 'To what do we owe this pleasure, anyway? Have you come to check up on me?'

'I wouldn't even bother. I've come to see Danny.' He looked around. 'Where is he?'

'Out in the yard, sitting on top of that bloody coal bunker, where do you think?'

'No, he ain't.'

She looked at him sharply. 'He must be. He ain't here, is he?'

'I can see that!' Nick's heart started to hammer against his ribs.

June pulled her dressing gown more tightly around her and went to the back door.

'Danny?' she called out to the empty yard. 'Danny love, where are you?'

Silence. Nick and his mother looked at each other. He could see his own panic reflected in her eyes.

Danny wasn't safe out on his own. Crowds and traffic scared him, he didn't know how to cope. Nick tried to shut his mind to the awful visions that crowded into his head.

Behind them, the bedroom door opened and a man appeared looking bleary-eyed, pulling his

351

braces over his shoulders. 'What the hell's going on?'

June was already yanking on her shoes. 'Oh, Norm. My son's gone missing.'

Nick turned on her, his fear exploding into fury. 'Oh, you're worried now, are you? Maybe if you'd thought more about him and less about your fancy man, Danny wouldn't have run off!'

'Don't you have a go at me. Maybe if you hadn't gone off and left us on our own, he'd still be safe.'

'You're his mother, you're meant to look after him. You couldn't look after a cat, let alone your own son!'

'Now listen here,' Norm stepped forward, 'don't you speak to your mother like that!'

Nick turned on him. 'And what are you going to do about it?' he snarled.

The man took one look into Nick's blazing eyes and backed off straight away. 'All right, mate, calm down,' he said, holding up his hands. 'I didn't mean anything by it, boy.'

'I ain't your mate,' Nick said. 'And I certainly ain't no one's boy.'

'Belt up, you two. What are we going to do?' June asked. Nick turned to look at her. She suddenly looked very old, her face creased with fear. But he felt no pity for her. She'd wished both her sons dead too many times.

'N-Nick?'

Nick swung round. His brother stood in the back doorway. 'Blimey, Danny, you gave us a fright, going off like that.'

June turned on him. 'Where were you, you

little sod?'

'I was h-hiding.' Danny's eyes were fearful.

'Oh, yeah? Who from?' Nick flicked a hostile glance at Norm.

'Don't look at me, I ain't touched him!' Norm protested.

'You'd better not have,' Nick growled.

Norm shook his head. 'Stuff this,' he muttered. 'I'm off.'

'Norm, don't go. Wait!' June pleaded. He sent her a contemptuous look

'You ain't worth it, love.'

'Norm!'

But he was already gone, slamming the door behind him.

June faced Nick. 'Now see what you've done!' she accused. 'We had a good thing going, him and me. But you had to go and ruin it, didn't you?'

But Nick wasn't listening. All his attention was fixed on his brother.

'Go and put some clothes on while I talk to Dan,' he said to his mother.

'Don't you tell me what to do in my own house!'

'It's my house, in case you've forgotten. I pay the rent.'

June opened her mouth to argue, then shut it again. Snatching up her cigarette packet, she stormed out, slamming the door.

Nick ruffled Danny's hair. 'How about we go and get some chips, eh? I dunno about you, but I'm starving.'

They went down to the fish and chip shop, Nick bought them both saveloy and chips and they sat on the kerb to eat them.

'Where did you run off to?' Nick carefully un-wrapped the newspaper around his brother's food and handed it to him.

'I w-went for a walk. B-By the c-canal.'

Nick whipped round to look at him, all his senses instantly sharpened. 'The canal? Blimey, Danny, how many times have I told you you're not to go down there by yourself? It's not safe on that path, you could slip in or anything...' He saw the panic on his brother's face and forced himself to calm down. 'I'm sorry, mate, I didn't mean to shout. But I worry about you, see? If anything happened to you...'

If anything happened to Danny he would never, ever forgive himself.

'Who were you hiding from anyway?' He tried to keep his voice casual as he stared across the street at a rag and bone man trundling past, his wagon piled high with old bits of scrap metal.

Danny stared ahead of him. 'I mustn't say any-thing.'

'Mustn't say anything about what? You can tell me, Dan. I'm your big brother. We don't have any secrets, do we?' He nudged him, but Danny jerked away.

'She said she'd get her brothers on me if I told,' he said.

Nick stopped, a chip halfway to his mouth. 'Who told you that?' Danny fell very quiet, his mouth closing like a trap. 'Do you mean Ruby?' Nick saw the blush creeping up his brother's neck. 'What exactly did she say, Danny?'

'I c-can't tell you,' he mumbled. 'It's a s-secret.

354

I sh-shouldn't have been listening, but I c-couldn't help it. I was just sitting there when her and her m-mum were talking.'

'What were they talking about?'

'The b-baby.'

Nick drew in a deep breath. 'And what did they say about the baby?'

'I c-can't!' Danny turned anguished eyes to meet Nick's. 'She said you'd b-be angry with me if you f-found out.'

'You know I'd never get angry with you, Danny boy.'

'D-Dennis and Frank would. Sh-she said she'd set them on m-me.'

'Is that right?' Nick's jaw tightened. 'Don't you worry about Dennis and Frank, mate. You leave them to me,' he said grimly. 'Now just tell me what you heard. Right from the beginning.'

Chapter Thirty-Nine

Helen sat at the back of the classroom, lost in her thoughts. It wasn't like her to daydream through a lecture, but today she could only stare out of the window, her pen still in her hand.

Outside the summer was finally surrendering to autumn, which had blown in with a gusty wind that had almost stripped the trees of their burnished leaves overnight. Mr Hopkins was in the courtyard struggling with a wheelbarrow and shovel, trying to pick up the drifts. But every time he filled the barrow another gust of wind picked them up in a mini-whirlwind and tossed them through the air again.

Helen smiled to herself. Poor Mr Hopkins, he was fighting a losing battle but he refused to give up. She knew how he felt.

She stared at the clock. Was there still half an hour to go? She wished she hadn't listened to Charlie and come to the lecture. She would far rather be with him.

A whole week had passed since their wedding. And with every passing day, Helen began to feel as if the doctors had got it wrong. It made her smile to see the indignation on Mr Latimer's face every time he did his rounds. He seemed to take it as a personal affront that Charlie had dared to live beyond his prediction.

Helen knew Charlie was fighting back. She could feel him getting stronger every day. Only once had he woken up from one of his long sleeps and not known who she was, and that was just for a minute or two. And when she held his hand she could feel his fingers curling around hers.

She refused to listen to her brother William when he took her to one side and tried to explain how the disease would slowly claim Charlie.

'But he's getting better,' she insisted. 'There must be something else you can try to help him, surely? What about Prontosil, or lumbar puncture? It says in my textbook–'

But William only shook his head. 'I'm sorry, Hel, they won't do any good, and they'd only cause him more suffering. You wouldn't want to put him through that, would you?'

'I told you, he's improving. He just needs some help to fight it...'

But all William had done was look at her in that pitying way that drove her mad with frustration. And Helen had gone back to her books, looking for a new cure, something that might offer some hope. She spent more time researching than on her revision these days.

Sister Judd was even worse. It grated across Helen's nerves every time she talked in her hushed little voice about making Charlie 'comfortable'. Helen had used that word herself many times, and never realised how stupid and smug it sounded. She didn't want Charlie made comfortable, she wanted him made better.

Charlie's mum and dad had accepted that their son was going to die. Helen could see the raw pain in their eyes as they sat at Charlie's bedside. Even they frustrated her. Why weren't they fighting for him like she was, willing him on? Giving up on him felt like a betrayal.

'We talked for such a long time today,' she would tell them. 'Even Nurse Strickland said he was looking brighter...' But like William, all they did was look at her with sympathy.

'At least he's comfortable, love,' his mother would pat her hand and say.

If only Nellie had seen him earlier, Helen thought. When she'd visited him that morning – she had given up completely on any pretence of sleep now, and came straight from her night duty to his bedside – he had stayed awake for nearly an hour. She would have stayed at his bedside talking to him, but lunchtime had come and Charlie had insisted she should go to her afternoon lecture.

'Your Sister Parker will be on the warpath if you don't,' he'd warned.

'I don't care.'

'But your exams are important.'

'You sound like my mother!'

That made him laugh. When she'd left him he was chatting to Millie. Helen had smiled all the way to her class, knowing he had turned a corner. She couldn't wait to go back to the ward and see him again. She couldn't wait to see Dr Latimer's face the next day as he tried to explain to his medical students how he had managed to get a patient's prognosis so drastically wrong.

Finally the class was over. Helen quickly gathered up her books and hurried out of the dusty class-room into the fresh air. The sharp wind tugged at her cap, almost pulling it from its pins as she hurried across the courtyard.

She caught up with Mr Hopkins, pushing his wheelbarrow away from the teaching block.

'Good afternoon, Mr Hopkins,' she greeted him.

'Afternoon, Nurse.' Mr Hopkins set down his barrow and pulled off his cap. The elderly Welsh-man's sing-song tone was unusually sombre.

'Has the *Evening Standard* arrived yet? I want to take a copy up to the ward for Charlie. He likes me to read to him, and I've run out of...' She stopped as she saw Millie emerge from the ward block. William was with her. They both seemed to be looking around, searching for something.

As soon as she saw them together, Helen knew. They were looking for her. And she knew why, too.

'Charlie!'

Millie turned at the sound of her voice and Helen saw her stricken expression. For a second her heart stopped beating in her chest. And then suddenly it was going very fast, as if it would hammer itself out of her throat.

'Helen, wait!' She heard William calling her name but she pushed past him and Millie and sprinted through the door to the wards, taking the stairs two at a time. She could hear William and Millie behind her as she ran, her feet pounding along the passageway. The double doors of the Male Medical ward suddenly seemed a long way off, receding from her as she ran towards them. Voices and faces around her were distorted, as if everything was moving in slow motion...

William caught her as she reached the doors. His arms folded around her, pinning her, but she struggled against him.

'Let me go!' she screamed. 'I need to see him. I need to see Charlie!'

'He's gone, Helen. They've taken him away.'

She turned on him blindly. 'Where? Where have they taken him?'

She saw Millie behind her brother's shoulder, her head bent, shoulders shaking as she sobbed.

'I need to see him.' Helen fought to break free. 'You've made a mistake, Charlie's getting better, I know he is. Why won't anyone see that?'

'Helen, please, don't do this,' William pleaded with her, his dark eyes wretched.

'No! You've all given up on him, but I haven't. I told you, he's getting stronger every day–'

'He's dead, Helen.'

The shock of his words stopped the breath in her throat. She stared into her brother's face. 'You shouldn't have let them take him, not without me. You had no right. Why didn't you wait for me? Why didn't he wait...'

'I'm sorry,' William's arms cradled her, holding her tightly to him. 'Oh, Helen, I'm so, so sorry.'

She submitted rigidly to his embrace, her own arms by her sides, refusing to be comforted. She heard William's voice crooning in her ear, telling her over and over again that he was sorry, and Millie's muffled sobbing. But still she told herself they'd got it wrong, that there must be a mistake.

Charlie wouldn't go without her. Not without saying goodbye.

Chapter Forty

Kathleen Fox scarcely knew what to make of the young woman sitting opposite her.

She had expected Helen Dawson to be a sobbing, trembling ball of grief. It was less than four hours since her husband had died, and Sister Judd had reported how hysterical Helen had been, flinging herself at the doors, her screams echoing around the hospital corridors.

'That poor, poor girl,' she had whispered. 'I'm sorry, Matron, I know we should be used to death after all these years but this has really affected us all. We got to know and like Charlie – Mr Dawson – you see. And as for that poor girl – well, I simply can't imagine how she must be feeling. I think if she could have died herself at that moment, she would have.'

But the girl who sat before Matron was neither hysterical nor trembling. If anything she was unnaturally composed, smartly turned out in her uniform as usual, not a hairpin out of place. Only the way she kept twisting that ring of silver paper on her finger betrayed her inner agitation.

But it was as if all the life had gone out of her. Her cheeks were pale and sunken and she stared back at Kathleen with dead brown eyes. She wondered if the dose of sedative her brother had given Helen to make her sleep hadn't yet worn off.

'Nurse Tre– Nurse Dawson,' she corrected herself. 'I hope you do not intend to report for duty this evening?'

Helen glanced down at her pristine uniform. 'Yes, Matron. Of course.'

'No one would expect you to work under the circumstances.'

'Everett will be short staffed if I don't, Matron. The probationer is already finding it difficult to cope. If there is an emergency admission overnight–'

'I'm sure the Night Sister can deal with it,' Kathleen cut in. 'Really, Nurse, I think it would be far better for you if you went home.'

'No!' Helen came to life. The eyes that met Kathleen's were dark with panic.

'Just for a few days. You need some rest.'

'Please don't send me home, Matron.'

Kathleen raised her eyebrows but said nothing. She didn't need to be told why Helen didn't want to go home. The prospect of Constance Tremayne's tender mercies would be enough to deter anyone.

'Very well, Nurse. But you must rest. I will talk to Miss Tanner about finding another nurse to cover for you tonight. The new ward allocations are given out tomorrow, so it will be simple enough to take you off the rota.'

'If you please, Matron, I want to work. I – I want to keep busy.'

Kathleen looked at her steadily. She knew some people believed that ignoring grief was the best way to get through it. But she had always believed differently. She had the worrying feeling that under that unnaturally calm exterior, Helen Dawson was a churning mass of emotion. If she didn't allow herself time to mourn, those emotions would slowly but surely eat away at her until there was nothing left.

'I could force you to take time off, you know?'

Helen stared down at her hands. 'Yes, Matron.'

Kathleen sighed. 'Very well, Nurse. You will not report for duty tonight. But I want you to go to the sick bay and rest. That is my final word,' she said, as Helen opened her mouth to argue. 'You may report to your new ward for duty the day after tomorrow. But,' she added, as Helen let out her breath, 'if at any time you change your mind, or you feel your duties are too much for you, then you must tell me at once.'

'Yes, Matron.' Helen stood up, then paused. 'If you please, Matron?'

'Yes, Nurse?'

'I wondered ... may I have some time off next Wednesday? It's Charlie's – my husband's funeral.'

A lump rose in Kathleen's throat, almost choking her.

'Yes, Nurse. Of course,' she replied.

'Thank you, Matron.'

As she turned to go, Kathleen said, 'And don't forget, Dawson, my door is always open. If you want to talk about anything.'

'Yes, Matron. Thank you.'

Kathleen watched her as she walked to the door. Her steps were careful, measured, as if even the effort of putting one foot in front of the other was too much for her.

If there was anything troubling Helen Dawson, Kathleen had the feeling she would be the last to hear about it.

'That's the second day she hasn't eaten a thing,' Millie commented as they watched Helen across the dining room at supper time. She sat alone at the third-year table, her untouched plate of food in front of her. 'We should go over there, say something to her...'

'Like what?' Dora said. 'What could we possibly say that would make her feel better?'

'I don't know, do I?' Millie sighed. 'But I hate sitting here doing nothing. We're supposed to be her friends, aren't we?'

All the more reason why we should stay away, Dora thought. They could say sorry a hundred

363

times or more, and it wouldn't take away any of her pain.

As she watched, a group of third-years came into the dining room and sat down around Helen. She instantly came to life, smiling and talking to them. But Dora could see the strain on her face. All she really wanted was to be alone.

'She knows where we are, when she needs us.'

'I can't stop thinking about what happened.' Millie put her fork down and pushed her own plate away. 'She was completely hysterical, not like Helen at all. The way she screamed and fought, like a wild animal – I truly thought she was going to black her brother's eye, the way she lashed out at him. She kept saying it was a mistake, that Charlie was getting better. Poor girl, she'd been saying that for days, begging us to do more tests, telling us his oedema was going down when anyone could see it was getting worse...'

'She saw what she wanted to see, I suppose,' Dora said.

Millie nodded. 'I suppose so. I wish she'd been there when he died, then perhaps she would have accepted it. But to come back and find he'd been taken down to the mortuary like that ... well, it must have been a dreadful shock.'

'Death does funny things to people,' Katie O'Hara said gloomily, reaching across for Millie's plate. 'God, can you imagine being left a widow like that, barely a week after you were a bride? It's cruel, it really is.'

'It's hard to believe how happy we were on her wedding day,' Millie sighed.

'I wonder if she knew what was going to happen?' Lucy Lane mused. Dora shot Millie a look across the table but neither of them said anything.

'It doesn't sound like it, does it?' Katie replied through a mouth full of food. 'Besides, would you marry someone knowing they were going to die? I don't think I would.'

'Not even your Tommy?' Dora said.

Lucy grinned nastily. 'That's the only time he would marry her, over his dead body!'

Katie crossed herself. 'Don't even joke about it. I don't know what I'd do if he passed.'

'I can't believe she's going back to work tomorrow,' Millie said, her gaze still fixed on Helen. 'I'm sure that can't be a good idea.'

'It's her choice.' Dora shrugged. 'Maybe she feels like she has to keep herself busy? Besides, she's only been assigned to Male Orthopaedics. They're a lively lot there, it shouldn't be too depressing for her.'

'I don't know about that,' Katie said. 'My sister Bridget is a staff nurse there, don't forget. She'd be enough to get anyone down!'

Helen had already gone by the time they left the dining room after supper.

'When do you think she'll be moving back into our room?' Millie asked.

'If she's starting back on the wards tomorrow then she should be coming out of the sick bay tonight, I suppose,' Dora replied.

'Good.' Millie smiled. 'Perhaps she'll feel like talking to us then?'

'Perhaps,' Dora agreed. 'But we shouldn't push her, if she doesn't feel like it. We've got to give her time.'

Millie, Lucy and Katie were due back on the ward at nine o'clock, but Dora had already finished for the day. As she made her way back to the nurses' home in the fading evening light, she was so deep in thought about Helen she didn't notice the tall, broad-shouldered figure stepping into her path.

'I need to talk to you,' Nick said.

'Nick!' She glanced beyond him to the nurses' home. 'You're taking a chance, ain't you? What if Sister Sutton looked out of her window and caught us?'

'I don't care. I'm desperate.'

She peered at him. Even in the shadowy dusk, she could see the tension in the harsh planes of his face. 'What is it? What's wrong?'

'I'm leaving Ruby.'

'She lied to me,' said Nick. 'She was never pregnant. She made the whole thing up just so I'd marry her.'

Dora's mind raced, all kinds of thoughts crowding in on her at once. 'Who told you?'

'Danny heard her and her mum talking about it. Ruby was telling her about this plan she'd come up with, to pretend to lose it. And that old cow Lettie said she'd help make it look real, so I'd be none the wiser.'

He stopped speaking abruptly, and Dora saw the flash of pain cross his face.

'I'm sorry,' she murmured.

'She had me fooled,' Nick went on, his voice ragged. 'I felt so sorry for her. I thought if she was suffering half as much as I was...' He gulped in a steadying breath. 'She watched me breaking my heart, let me go on thinking our baby was dead. And all the time she was laughing at me!'

Dora kept her hands pinned to her sides, fighting the urge to reach out to him. 'I'm sure she wasn't laughing, Nick.'

He looked up at her sharply. 'You're not sticking up for Ruby, surely?'

'No, of course not. I just think she must have been really desperate to do something like that.'

'Conniving, more like!' Nick's lip curled with contempt. 'She's been lying to me the whole way through our marriage, right from the minute she walked into that church and said "I do". How she had the brass neck to make her vows before God, I've no idea. I'm surprised she didn't get struck by lightning!' His face was bitter. 'I should have known,' he said. 'I should have realised she'd pull a trick like this to get her own way. She never thinks about anyone else, not for a second. Why should she, as long as she gets her own way?'

Dora flinched from the raw anger in his voice. He was right, Ruby had been cruel and deceitful; she deserved his contempt, and a lot more besides.

But she'd drawn Dora into her lie too.

'Aren't you going to say something?' Nick was staring at her, his eyes hard and searching.

'I – I don't know what to say.'

'You don't seem very surprised. But then I suppose you know her better than anyone, don't you? You were her mate for a long time, you must know what she's capable of.' He eyed Dora narrowly. 'You didn't know anything about this, did you?'

'I–'

'No, of course you didn't. Forget I asked,' Nick dismissed his question. 'You're not like her, you'd never lie to me the way she has.'

Dora glanced behind him at the nurses' home. Light glowed in every window as the students started to return from their day's work. She wished she could be safely locked away with them.

'Have you talked to Ruby?' she asked.

Nick shook his head. 'I'm too angry to face her, I didn't want to do something I'd regret. Besides, I wanted to see you first. I just thought you could – I dunno, help me make sense of it all.'

He ran his hand through his dark curls. He looked more lost than angry, Dora thought. Like a man who'd had the stuffing kicked out of him and didn't know why.

'You need to talk to Ruby,' she said.

His mouth tightened. 'I've got nothing to say to her.'

'Then listen to what she's got to say.'

'Why? All I'll get out of her are more lies. She wouldn't know the truth if she fell over it. I just don't know what to believe or who to trust any more. Except for you.'

He reached for her hand, but Dora pulled away. She felt too dirty, too dishonest, to let him touch her.

'She took that away too, didn't she?' Nick said heavily. 'We could have been so happy together, and Ruby ruined it with her selfish lies. But it's not too late, is it? We could still be together...'

Dora could feel the tension coming off his body. 'Don't say it,' she pleaded. 'It's not right.'

'Why not? I love you. I've always loved you.'

'But you're married to her.'

Nick's eyes met hers, dark and direct. 'For now,' he said.

Dora felt sick. None of this should be happening, it was all wrong.

'Talk to Ruby,' she urged. 'See what she's got to say for herself.'

He sighed. 'All right, if you think that's best. But I'm telling you now, there isn't a damn thing she can say to make me change my mind.'

Chapter Forty-One

Charlie's funeral was a real East End affair, no expense spared. Two black-plumed horses pulled the elaborate hearse, heavy with banks of colourful flowers, through the narrow streets, followed by a procession of Charlie's friends and family. It felt as if the whole of Bethnal Green had turned out, lining the streets. As they passed Columbia Road market, the cries of the traders fell silent and everyone stood still, pulling off their hats and bowing their heads to show respect.

Helen kept her face stony as she followed the funeral cortege. She wished she could let her feelings out like Charlie's family were, but her mother always told her it was undignified to cry in front of other people.

Not that Charlie's family seemed to care. His mother, brothers and sisters were all sobbing.

Even his father, burly costermonger that he was, had tears streaming down his face. They put their arms around each other, holding each other up. But there was no one to support Helen as she walked alone behind her husband's coffin.

Dora and Millie had come, and Helen's father and brother. All four of them followed behind the procession, their heads bowed.

Of course, her mother hadn't come.

It was probably just as well, Helen thought bitterly. She could only imagine what Constance would have made of Charlie's family, howling with grief at the graveside. How she would have shuddered at the vulgarity of it all, the showiness of the flowers, the outpouring of emotion. Helen could just picture her, pursing her lips with distaste.

But at least Charlie's family were there to console his widow. After the service, Nellie Dawson came up to her. She was huddled in an astrakhan coat, her face bloated and blotchy with tears underneath her black hat.

'Oh, my poor little girl.' She drew Helen in her arms, enveloping her in a lavender-scented embrace. 'How you must be suffering I just don't know.' She held her at arm's length, scrutinising her face. 'How are you bearing up, love?'

Helen nodded, not trusting herself to speak.

'Well, you know, you mustn't be a stranger to us. You're family now, remember that.' She stroked a stray hair off Helen's face. 'Anything you want, anything you need, you come and see me, all right?'

'Thank you,' Helen managed to whisper.

'No need to thank me, my darling. Like I said, you're family now. That's what Charlie would have wanted.' Nellie sniffed back the tears that threatened to spill from her watery eyes. 'He loved you, you know. Loved you with all his heart, he did. I've never known him so happy as he was with you.' She pulled out her handkerchief. 'Why the Lord decided to take him away from us I've got no idea. They say He works in mysterious ways, don't they?' She gave a wobbly smile. 'Charlie's probably watching us now from up there and having a right old laugh at us carrying on, I shouldn't wonder.'

'I expect so.'

As Helen went to walk away, Nellie Dawson said, 'I almost forgot. Charlie asked me to give you something.'

Helen turned back to her, frowning, as Nellie rummaged in her bag.

'It's in here somewhere ... ah, here it is.' She pulled out a small velvet-covered box and held it out.

Helen stared down at it, her hands clenched at her sides, reluctant to take it. 'What is it?'

'You'd better look, hadn't you?'

But she already knew the answer before she had taken the box and opened it. Nestling inside was a beautiful diamond solitaire engagement ring.

'It belonged to his grandmother,' Nellie Dawson explained. 'Charlie said that you should have it ... if anything happened to him.' She managed a trembling smile. 'He wanted you to have a proper engagement ring, to replace that old bit of silver paper.'

'Thank you.' Helen stared numbly at the ring,

sparkling on its bed of black velvet. It was stunning. But as far as she was concerned it would never replace her paper ring. Nothing ever could.

Constance stood behind the tall iron railings on the far side of the churchyard. Pain lanced through her as she watched another woman comforting her daughter. She dearly wished she could make herself walk through the lych gate and down the path, but her pride stopped her. Just as it had stopped her from seeing her daughter married.

She hadn't realised how loved Charlie Dawson was until she stood among the well-wishers who crowded the roadside, and listened to them crying for him. Everyone praised his kindness, his generosity, the fact that he never had a bad word to say about anyone.

Not like her, Constance reflected. She felt ashamed of how harshly she had treated him, when all he'd done was to love her daughter.

But now it was too late to put things right. And it was too late to put things right with Helen, too.

Poor Helen. It had torn Constance's heart to see her daughter's slender figure walking behind the hearse, her head held high, expression impassive. Constance could only imagine what it must have taken for Helen to put on such a brave face. She had yearned to break free from the crowd and run to her. But she was afraid Helen might reject her, and she couldn't face that.

Matron had already told her that Helen did not wish to see her. As soon as she found out Charlie Dawson was dead, Constance had taken the first train up to London and gone to the Nightingale to bring her daughter home. But Matron had made it very clear: Helen did not wish either to see her or speak to her, and she certainly didn't want to leave the hospital.

'You don't need to worry, Mrs Tremayne. Your daughter is among friends here,' she had said. 'We will take care of her.'

Because you can't. She hadn't said as much, but her meaning was there, expressed clearly in those cool grey eyes of hers.

And perhaps she was right, Constance reflected. All these years, she had been so concerned with moulding Helen in her own image that she had allowed herself to be blinded to what her daughter really needed.

And now it was too late. She had lost Helen for ever.

After the funeral, Millie and Dora left Helen at the graveside and walked back from the churchyard together.

'Should we have stayed with her, do you think?' Millie asked anxiously. Dora shook her head.

'Charlie's family will look after her,' she said. 'Besides, we've got to get back. Matron only gave us two hours off.'

'I must say, I'll be glad to get out of these clothes,' Millie sighed. Even in the chill of the September air, her heavy black coat weighed her down. Dora looked just as gloomy, her freckled face covered by a thick black veil. 'Poor Tremayne, how on earth must she be feeling?'

'Don't you mean Dawson?'

'So I do.' Millie shook her head. 'I haven't had

time to get used to that name yet.'

'Nor has she, I bet.'

They trudged on, both lost in their own thoughts. The wind moaned mournfully through the trees of Victoria Park, and they had to keep their hands pinned to their hats.

'I can't believe she's gone straight back to work,' Millie said. 'I don't think I could bear it, do you?'

'I daresay she knows what she's doing.' Dora shrugged.

'Yes, but surely she'd feel better if she took time off to grieve?'

'And what good would that do? All the grieving in the world isn't going to bring him back, is it? She might feel she's better off trying to take her mind off it, if she can.'

Millie considered this for a moment. Dora was full of good sense, but she had a practical way of looking at the world that Millie sometimes found harsh.

But then Dora probably found Millie's wild optimism a bit too much to take at times, she thought.

As they reached the entrance to the park, a sudden gust of wind caught Millie's hat, tearing it off her head. She snatched at it but the wind had already whipped it out of her reach. It danced through the air and over the park gates.

'Quick, catch it!' She and Dora ran after it, dodging people, tripping over dogs and nearly colliding with trees. The hat twirled ahead of them, sinking tantalisingly within their grasp, only to bob upwards again when they lunged for it.

'It's going to get stuck in those trees, I know it

374

is!' Millie wailed.

'If it ends up in that lake, I'm not going in after it!' Dora panted back.

Finally the wind dropped and the hat drifted gracefully to the ground, landing at the feet of a man who was walking towards them. They caught up with him as he bent to pick it up.

'Yours, I believe?' he said, dusting it off and handing it over solemnly.

'Thank you. We've been chasing it all over the park.'

'Lucky I was here to catch it. Honestly, Mil, what would you do without me?'

She looked up sharply at the sound of her name, and saw the man's face properly for the first time. His fair hair was covered with a trilby, but she would have known those smiling blue eyes anywhere.

'Seb?' she whispered.

He grinned. 'Surprised to see me?'

'Flabbergasted, more like!' She stared at him, trying to take in this unexpected appearance. She still couldn't quite believe he was there, standing in front of her. 'But I don't understand – I thought you were in Spain?'

'I was, but the foreign desk seem to think I'd be better off back in Berlin. Apparently Herr Hitler and his cronies trust me more than the new chap. I'm still not sure if that's a compliment or not!' Seb grimaced. 'I persuaded them to let me have a few days back in England first. Told them I wanted to see if I still had a fiancée?' He sent her a quizzical look. 'I wasn't too sure after our last telephone conversation.'

'Oh, Seb!' Millie threw her arms around him, holding him close. 'I'm so sorry. I was just being silly. You see, I'd seen this fortune-teller–'

He held her at arm's length. 'A fortune-teller?'

'Yes, and she told me I'd be in–'

She stopped abruptly. She and Dora looked at each other. Dora's face was pale beneath her thick black veil.

'What did she tell you?' Seb laughed uneasily. 'Come on, you're making me nervous!'

'Nothing.' Millie took his hand. 'It doesn't matter now.'

Chapter Forty-Two

Nick sat on a bench on the moonlit patch of green below Victory House and tried to summon the energy to climb the stairs. The solid redbrick blocks reared up all around him, their rows of windows casting patches of light down on the empty green where he sat, smoking and brooding.

It was past nine o'clock and he had been walking the streets for more than three hours. He didn't want to go home, couldn't face dealing with any more of Ruby's lies. He wasn't sure he could trust himself, either. He had never raised his hand to a woman and despised any man who did. But the way he was feeling, if Ruby opened her mouth and another lie came out, he didn't know if he could be responsible for his actions.

He hated lies. He had been brought up with them, lived with them all his life. He had grown up always having to lie to someone: the rent man, the tallyman, the pawnbroker, the bloke in the corner shop when his mum needed cigarettes on tick. He had lied to his teachers about being sick when he had to take a day off school to work. He had lied to the neighbours when they demanded to know what his mum was doing in the pub when she'd sworn that tanner she borrowed was to feed her kids. He had even lied to the doctors who'd saved Danny's life, backing up his mum's story that his brother's injuries had been caused by a fall.

He lit another cigarette, the last in his packet, playing for time. His marriage was over, he knew that already. He had promised Dora he would give Ruby a chance to explain herself and that was the only reason he was there, sitting outside the flats, and not long gone. Not that he was interested in anything Ruby had to say. He couldn't imagine anything she could say that would make him want her again.

He had done his best to make a go of his marriage. For Ruby's sake and the sake of his baby, he had turned his back on the girl he loved. He had worked hard, handed over his pay packet every week and tried to be the best husband he knew how. He might have gone on doing it until his dying day, if he hadn't found out how she'd betrayed him.

Now he didn't owe her a damn thing.

It was almost ten o'clock when he finally let himself into the flat. Ruby came out of the sitting

377

room, dressed up to the nines as usual in a blue dress he hadn't seen before, topped off by a lacy cardigan. Her hair was done up in waves around her face, and she was wearing more make-up than usual. But the fresh coat of crimson lipstick only emphasised the sulky lines of her turned-down mouth.

'And what time do you call this?' she snapped.

He looked at her, standing in the doorway, arms folded across her bosom, and all the fight went out of him. He couldn't even summon up the energy to be angry with her any more.

He walked straight past her into the bedroom. Ruby followed him. 'That's it, is it? No apology, no excuse?' Her voice was shrill. 'Well, that's very nice, I must say. You go out until all hours, come in without a by your leave, and then you won't even tell me where you've been.' Her mouth firmed in frustration. 'And you needn't think I've kept any dinner for you, either, because that went in the bin hours ago.'

'I'm not hungry.'

'Oh, so you've still got a tongue in your head, have you? I thought you must have lost it the same place you left your manners...' She broke off at the sight of the battered suitcase Nick had pulled from on top of the wardrobe. 'What are you doing?'

'Packing, what does it look like?' He pulled open a chest of drawers, pulled out an armful of clothes and dumped them in the case.

It took her a second to react. 'Going some-where, are you?' She sounded brazen, but out of the corner of his eye Nick could see her regarding him warily.

'Anywhere, as long as it's away from you.'

She examined her fingernails. 'And am I allowed to know why?'

'You work it out.'

She sighed. 'If it's about the debts, I thought we'd sorted that out.'

'It's not about the debts!' He raised his voice and saw her flinch. 'Do you really think I care about a few stupid debts? You could have had us both turned out on the streets and it wouldn't have mattered as much as the lies you've told.'

Her face paled, but she recovered quickly. 'I really don't know what you're talking about.'

Nick pulled a shirt out of the wardrobe and dropped it into the suitcase. 'I talked to Danny.'

'Oh, yes?' Ruby smiled tightly. 'And what's that little rascal been saying now?'

'He heard you and your mum talking. About the baby.'

She frowned for a moment, as if she was seriously trying to recall it. Then she laughed. 'Oh, that! For heaven's sake, Nick, we were just talking about one of the women on her ward, that's all. Danny didn't really think I was talking about myself, did he?' She shook her head. 'That boy will get someone hung one of these days.' She chuckled. 'He must have got it all mixed up, you know what he's like...'

'Don't,' Nick said wearily, slamming down the lid of his suitcase. 'For Christ's sake, Ruby, can't you stop lying even now? Or have you forgotten what the truth sounds like?'

All kinds of emotions flitted across Ruby's face

before she settled on remorse. As Nick watched her, her lips trembled and her blue eyes filled with tears.

'Oh, Nick, I'm so sorry.' She sat down on the bed and buried her face in her hands. 'You're right, I've lied to you, said some terrible things. You don't know how much I've wished I could turn the clock back, start all over again.'

Nick watched her weeping. 'Why did you do it?' he asked.

'Because I love you!' She pulled a handkerchief from the sleeve of her cardigan and pressed it to her eyes. 'I was frightened you were going to leave me. I didn't mean to say those things, I didn't plan them or anything. It just happened. You've got to believe me, I'm telling the truth this time!' Her eyes searched his, pleading for understanding. 'I wanted to tell you, as soon as I'd said it. But then everything started happening at once, and I got caught up in the wedding, and I thought ... maybe once we're married it won't matter so much any more.'

'Won't matter?' He stared at her. Could she really be so naive, so utterly selfish? 'You lied to me, Ruby.'

'Yes, I know!' There was an edge of impatience to her voice. 'And I wanted to tell you the truth, as soon as we were married. I kept trying, but it never seemed to be the right time. And then I knew you'd leave me if you found out the truth, so–'

'So you told another lie,' he finished for her. 'Do you know how I felt when you told me you'd lost our baby? It broke my heart, Ruby. You watched me go through hell...'

'What else was I supposed to do?'

'You could have put me out of my misery. You could have told me the truth.'

'Yes, well, I didn't know you'd take it so badly, did I?'

'It was my child, my flesh and blood.' Even now, he couldn't bring himself to believe that it had all been a lie. 'But it was all a game to you, wasn't it? Just a big game.'

Ruby met his eyes defiantly. 'I've said I'm sorry,' she snapped. 'What more do you want?'

'Nothing,' Nick said wearily. 'I don't want anything from you.'

He closed his suitcase and snapped the lid shut. As he hauled it off the bed, Ruby jumped up and barred his way.

'Look, I know I've made a lot of mistakes, but we can make things right again,' she said eagerly.

'It's too late, Ruby.'

'Why? Why is it too late? We've been happy, ain't we? And I've been a good wife to you. You've got to admit that, ain't you?' He tried to move past her but she stepped into his path. 'I'm not expecting miracles, but if we give it time we can make our marriage work. All I'm asking for is another chance. Everyone deserves a second chance, don't you think?' She faced him, her eyes wide with appeal. 'Please, Nick? Give me a chance to prove I can be the wife you want?'

She looked so vulnerable, so full of childish hope, that Nick felt himself weaken.

'I don't want you any more, Ruby,' he said.

'You don't mean that!'

She made a wild grab for his suitcase. He

fended her off and suddenly she was attacking him, kicking, pummelling him with her fists and yanking at his hair. Nick dropped the suitcase and disentangled himself from her, pushing her back on the bed.

She lay there, breathing hard, staring up at him with hostile eyes.

'You bastard! I'll go to the police,' she threatened, brushing her disordered hair off her face. 'I'll tell them you attacked me.'

'If that's what you want.' Nick picked up his suitcase. 'I'll be staying at my mate Harry's, if they want to come and arrest me.'

'You mean, you're not going to *her?*'

Nick stopped dead, still facing the door. 'I dunno who you're talking about,' he said flatly.

'Now who's the liar?' Ruby laughed bitterly. 'Do you honestly think I didn't know about you and Dora Doyle?' Her voice dripped ice as she said the name. 'I've seen the way you look at her, panting after her like a bloody dog on heat. Although God knows why you'd want to make a fool of yourself over someone like her,' she mocked. 'Ugly Dora, dumpy little carrot top–'

'Don't you dare say that about her. She's been a good friend to you.'

'Some friend!' Ruby sneered. 'What kind of a friend sneaks around trying to steal someone's husband?'

'You can't steal something that belonged to you in the first place!' Nick shot back angrily. 'I love Dora, I always have. And I'll tell you something else. I would have run off with her on the morning of our wedding, baby or no baby, if only she'd said the word. But she wouldn't let me. She said I had to stay, do the right thing. She said I couldn't let you down, because you needed me. God help me, I wish I'd never done the right thing now!'

'Go, then. Go to her, if she's so bloody perfect!' Ruby spat.

'She might not be perfect, but at least she doesn't lie to me.'

'That's what you think.'

Nick paused, his hand on the doorknob. 'What's that supposed to mean?'

'That made you take notice, didn't it?' A slow smile spread across Ruby's face. 'Before you walk out of the door into the arms of Saint Dora, I reckon there are a couple of things you ought to know...'

Chapter Forty-Three

Helen was down on her hands and knees, scrubbing the wheels on the bed with a stiff brush and carbolic mixture. Since breakfast finished at seven, she and the other nurses had been cleaning. Even though it was tackled every day by the probationers and the ward maid, every week the ward had to undergo a thorough clean; beds were pulled into the middle, the floor was swept and polished, lampshades were taken down and washed in soapy water, lockers were turned out and damp dusted, windows were washed and paintwork scrubbed.

Even the springs on the beds were polished and the wheels cleaned.

Sister Blake walked up and down the ward supervising. Her lively brown gaze missed nothing.

'Watch out for those hidden corners, please... Make sure you dry inside the lockers thoroughly before you put the patients' things away, we don't want their belongings ruined... No, no, Nurse, use a clean duster, not that old rag.'

She reached Helen and stopped for a moment, watching her. 'Good gracious, Nurse,' she said finally. 'You'll wear those wheels away if you scrub them any harder!'

'I'm sorry, Sister.' Helen looked up in dismay. 'Have I done it wrong? I'll do them again–'

'Don't be silly, Nurse, they are spotless. But you don't have to put quite so much elbow grease into it,' said Sister. 'Save some energy for looking after the patients.'

'Now that's something you don't hear very often, a sister telling a student not to work so hard!' Brenda Bevan commented wryly, as she went past with an armful of vases. 'I bet you wouldn't hear O'Hara saying it.'

Brenda scowled at Staff Nurse O'Hara, who was watching a hapless first-year dusting a window ledge for the third time. She had the same dark Irish colouring as her younger sister Katie, but that was where the similarity ended. While Katie O'Hara was lively and full of mischief, Bridget looked as if she'd never cracked a smile in her life.

Helen plunged her hand into the bowl of scalding carbolic-scented water, and went on scrubbing. She didn't want to admit it to Brenda Bevan, but she was grateful for the mindless hard graft. If she was lucky, she could exhaust herself enough that she fell into a deep sleep the moment her head touched the pillow.

After the cleaning came the bedpan round. As Helen handed one of the young men a bottle, he gave her a cheeky wink and said, 'I don't suppose you could give me a hand, could you, Nurse?'

It was a request the nurses heard several times a day, especially on Male Orthopaedics where the patients were generally young and more bored than poorly. Helen was just about to smile sweetly and offer to fetch the rat-tooth forceps when the man in the next bed hissed, 'Have some respect, can't you? That's the young nurse that lost her husband!'

'I didn't know, did I?' The young man whispered back. 'She looked like a normal girl to me.'

I am normal, Helen wanted to scream as she walked away. She wished people wouldn't keep tiptoeing around her. She could feel the whispers and sympathetic stares following her wherever she went: in the ward, the dining room, the nurses' home, even when she was walking down the passageways. She knew they meant well and were only trying to be kind, but she was sick of it. She half wished that Staff Nurse O'Hara would take her to task for something, so at least she could feel that her life was normal. But even she avoided talking to Helen if she could.

Only that morning, the two pros had stopped laughing abruptly as she walked into the kitchen.

'What's the joke?' Helen had asked.

'Nothing,' one of them mumbled, as they exchanged embarrassed looks. The awkward silence had gone on until she walked out again, when she heard one of them whisper, 'Oh, God, I wish they hadn't put her on this ward. I never know what to say to her, do you?'

'It's awful, isn't it?' the other agreed. 'I was looking forward to Male Orthopaedics, but you don't feel as if you can have fun with her around.'

At least there was one person on the ward who treated her normally.

'Good morning, Mr Forster,' she greeted her favourite patient, pulling the screens around his bed. 'Are you ready for your bottle?'

'Go away.'

Marcus Forster glared at Helen from his traction prison. The other nurses nicknamed him the Mad Professor, and he was certainly odd-looking – over six feet tall, painfully thin, with a shock of light brown curls and disarming dark brown eyes. He was nineteen years old and eccentrically brilliant. He spoke four languages, translated Ancient Greek for amusement, and was studying physics at Cambridge. In fact, he had been trying to disprove a theory about gravity when he fractured his femur.

Now all his formidable intelligence was no use to him at all, as he was stuck in a Hodgsen Splint. This consisted of an iron frame over the bed, to which Mr Forster was attached by a complex series of pulleys and hooks. The lower end of the bed was raised on blocks, and a cover over his upper torso kept his arms firmly pinned to his sides.

Only his head was visible and unencumbered. And as Helen approached with his bottle, his face turned bright red.

'I don't need it,' he mumbled.

'Come along, Mr Forster. If you don't use it now you'll only be wanting it in ten minutes' time. And we can't be running up and down the ward with bedpans and bottles all day, can we?'

'I don't see what else you have to do.'

'You'd be surprised. Now let me help you...'

'No! I can manage.'

It was all she could do not to smile as she looked down at him, fastened securely into the splint, his legs raised above his head. 'Are you sure about that, Mr Forster? I know you're the one with the science degree, but from where I'm standing it looks like a physical impossibility.' His face turned a deeper shade of puce. 'Look, I can assure you it's no more embarrassing for me than combing your hair.'

'Bully for you. You're not the one lying here.' He turned his face away. 'You'd better get on with it, I suppose,' he sighed.

As she pulled back the screens afterwards, he said, 'Why do the other nurses keep looking at you?'

'Do they? I hadn't noticed.'

'I have. And they're whispering about you, too.'

Helen looked at him. If it had been anyone else, she might have thought they were being rude. But Marcus Forster's frankness disarmed her. 'Perhaps they have nothing better to do?'

He considered it for a moment, as if he was tackling a difficult mathematical problem. 'I don't think so,' he concluded. 'Less than five minutes ago you stated you have better things to do than wait for me. Ipso facto, those other nurses must have something better to do too. Which leads me to believe there is something about you they find particularly interesting.' He regarded her consideringly. 'Do you think it's because your husband is dead?'

'I—' Helen stared at him, taken aback. It was the first time anyone had asked her a question about Charlie.

But before she could answer, Staff Nurse O'Hara swept in. 'That's enough of that,' she said briskly. 'Nurse Dawson doesn't want to answer those kind of questions, Mr Forster.'

She turned to Helen, a steely brightness in her eyes. 'Go and get rid of that bottle, Nurse, if Mr Forster has finished with it?'

'Yes, Staff.' Helen rushed off, pleased to escape. For once she didn't find Mr Forster quite so entertaining.

She came off duty at nine o'clock and went straight back to the nurses' home, intending to get on with her studying. As she walked up the gravel drive, she noticed a car parked outside.

It was most unusual. Visitors seldom came to the nurses' home, mainly because guests were not allowed beyond the front step. As she drew alongside, Helen noticed a middle-aged man sitting behind the wheel, a woman at his side. They stared ahead of them, neither of them speaking, their faces drawn and sombre.

Helen's stomach plunged. If a nurse's parents came to the home, it usually meant bad news.

Sure enough, inside the home was an air of suppressed excitement. Students from Helen's set, who had spent the past three years in their rooms away from Sister Sutton's prying eyes, suddenly gathered in the sitting room, occupying the couches and staring out of the window.

Sister Sutton bustled up and down the passageway, Sparky at her heels, trying to regain order.

'Really, Nurses, your exams are four weeks away,' she chided. 'I'm sure you could find something more worthwhile to do with your time than gawping out of a window!'

Helen met Brenda Bevan as she came down the stairs.

'What is it?' she asked. 'What's happening, do you know?'

'Haven't you heard?' Brenda's eyes were round with dismay. 'Hollins has been dismissed!'

'Dismissed?' Helen stared at her, scarcely able to take in what she was hearing. 'I don't understand...'

'Apparently she's been having an affair with a married man!' Brenda's face was eager. 'Can you imagine? None of us had any idea, did you?'

'No, I didn't.' Helen had a sudden picture in her mind of Amy's wistful expression that night in the ward kitchen. 'How did they find out?'

'We've heard his wife discovered it and went to see Matron. Carson was working with Hollins on Casualty. She says Miss Hanley came storming in and dragged her straight out. No one saw her again.' Brenda shuddered. 'Can you imagine what Matron must have said to her? It doesn't bear thinking about.'

'Where is she now?'

'Upstairs packing, I think.'

'Is anyone with her?'

'I shouldn't think so.' Brenda frowned as if the thought hadn't even occurred to her. 'So who do you think it is?'

'Who?'

'Her mystery married man, of course! Carson's certain it must be someone at the hospital, but I don't think even Hollins would take a risk like that...'

'I don't know, and I don't really care,' Helen cut her off flatly. 'And I think it's pretty shabby that you lot would just stand by gossiping about her when she needs you,' she added, turning to face the others who were crowded around the bay window. 'I thought she was your friend?'

'Well, I–' Brenda's mouth opened and closed again.

Just then Amy came down the stairs, bumping her suitcase behind her. The other girls watched her struggling with her luggage, no one offering to help. It was as if Amy had become somehow untouchable.

Helen felt for her. She knew what it was like to be the girl everyone was talking about, the girl no one spoke to.

She stepped forward. 'Here, let me help you with that.'

She took hold of one end of the suitcase. Amy lifted her head briefly, long enough for Helen to see her red-rimmed eyes.

'Thank you,' she whispered.

Together, they carried the suitcase out to the car. As soon as she appeared, Amy's father got out and opened up the boot. He didn't look at his daughter as he loaded her suitcase inside, then slammed the boot shut, then opened the rear door for her. Amy didn't look at him either, her head hung in shame as she climbed inside.

Helen stood and watched until the car was out of sight. She waved, but Amy Hollins didn't look back.

Chapter Forty-Four

Rose Doyle was giving the front step a good going over with red Cardinal polish when Dora came home to Griffin Street. 'All right, Mum?' she said.

Rose sat back on her heels and smiled up at her daughter. Even in her polish-smeared pinnie, with her dark hair caught up in a headscarf, she still looked beautiful.

'Hello, stranger,' she said. 'To what do we owe this honour?'

'I had a couple of hours off, so I thought I'd come round and see you.'

It wasn't the only reason Dora had come back to Griffin Street. It had been three days since she had last spoken to Nick, and she was desperate to find out what had happened with him and Ruby.

She had seen him around the hospital, but only from a distance. Every time she tried to speak to him, he seemed to disappear. If she didn't know better, she would almost imagine he was avoiding her deliberately.

She couldn't very well turn up on Ruby's doorstep, which was why she'd come home. If anyone would know what was going on, it was her grandmother. Nanna Winnie made it her business to know everything that happened in Griffin Street.

'Who is it, Rosie?' Nanna's voice called out from the kitchen.

'And she reckons she's deaf!' Rose Doyle rolled her eyes. 'It's our Dora come to visit, Mum,' she called back.

'Is that right? I'm surprised she can still remember the way, it's been that long!'

Rose and her daughter exchanged wry smiles. 'Nice to see some things haven't changed!' said Dora.

'Oh, you know your nanna. She'll never change.' Rose wiped her hands on an old rag. 'Come in, love. I'll stick the kettle on. I dunno about you, but I'm gasping for a brew.'

The Doyles' kitchen was warm and comfortingly familiar. Nanna sat in her old rocking chair by the fire, a basket of mending by her side. Dora's youngest brother Little Alfie sat at her feet, playing with his wooden train set.

'Thought you were dead,' were her grandmother's first words.

'Don't be like that, Nanna.' Dora put down a fat brown paper bag on the table. 'Not when I've brought you a nice treat.'

'What's that, then?' Nanna craned her neck to see.

'Winkles. Got 'em off the market on my way here.'

'Lovely!' Nanna smacked her toothless jaws in anticipation. 'Bring us a bowl, Rose, I'll do 'em now.' She put down her mending and raised herself laboriously from her rocking chair. 'I suppose you've heard the news?'

Dora tried not to smile. She could always rely on Nanna Winnie. 'Heard what, Nanna?'

'About him and her. The happy couple.' Nanna nodded towards the wall that separated their house from the Rileys and the Pikes next door. 'He's left her.'

Rose came out of the scullery, a brown china bowl in her hands. 'Blimey, Mum, give Dora a chance to get her coat off before you start spreading gossip!'

'It ain't gossip. It's fact. Mrs Prosser told me.' Nanna arranged herself at the table and pulled out the pin she always kept fastened to the bosom of her pinnie. 'Don't just sit there, give me an 'and.' She nodded to Dora who sat down at the table and took the pin Nanna handed her. As she opened up the brown paper bag, she caught a whiff of salty sea air from the winkles.

'What happened?' she asked.

'Well, that's the mystery ain't it? Although there are some stories going round...' Nanna held the winkle shell at the end of her nose, stuck the pin in and deftly twisted out the blob of glistening grey-brown flesh. 'But the top and bottom of it is, he's packed his bags and moved out.'

Dora kept her eyes fixed on the small blue-black shell she held between her fingers. 'Has

393

Nick moved back next door?'

'Gawd love us, why would he want to do that?' Nanna cackled. 'Talk about out of the frying pan into the bleeding fire! Can you picture it, leaving your missus and moving under the same roof as her mother? And as for his own mum ... well, I reckon he'd want to stay as far away from her as he could.' She flicked another winkle into the bowl. She worked so fast, Dora had barely finished one before Nanna had got through half a dozen. 'No, no one knows where he's lodging. Only time we see him is when he drops round to see that brother of his.'

She sent Dora a shrewd look. 'We thought you might know more about it?'

'Me? Why should I know?'

'There's some who reckon you're the reason why they parted.'

'Me?' The shell Dora was holding slipped from her fingers and rolled across the table.

'I told you not to say anything, Mum!' Rose came in from the scullery again, this time with the tray of tea things. 'It's not going to do anyone any good, passing on gossip like that.' She set the tray down firmly on the table.

'It's not true, is it?' Nanna peered at Dora.

'No, Nanna, it's not true.'

'Told you!' Nanna turned to Rose in triumph. 'I said to you, didn't I, our Dora's got more sense than to get herself involved with a married man. Whatever Lettie Pike says.'

Dora caught her mother's eye as she handed over a cup of tea. There was something about the way Rose Doyle looked at her daughter that made her think she wasn't quite as convinced.

'I might have known Lettie would be behind it,' Dora muttered, spooning sugar into her cup. If Ruby's mother started spreading her nasty rumours at the hospital, who knew where it might end?

An image of Amy Hollins came into Dora's mind then. She'd heard all about her being ushered in shame from the nurses' home after her affair with a married man came to light. Now no one even dared speak about her. It was as if she had never existed.

'Let's talk about something else, shall we?' Rose said. 'There's enough unhappiness in the world without us making more. Tell us how you're getting on at that hospital. How are those girls you share a room with?'

'Oh, God, you haven't heard about poor Tremayne, have you?' Dora put down her cup. Nanna and her mother listened gravely as she told them about Charlie's death.

'That poor girl,' Rose sighed. 'Fancy losing your husband like that when you're still a bride. I'm surprised she hasn't gone home to her mother. She sounds as if she needs looking after, the little lamb.'

'I don't think her mother's the type to look after anyone,' Dora said grimly. 'You know, she didn't even come to the wedding or Charlie's funeral? Left Helen to go through it all by herself.'

'Well, that ain't right,' Rose declared. 'A mother's place is at her daughter's side. Even if she doesn't always agree with what she does.'

There it was again, that look over the rim of her teacup. Dora opened her mouth to ask why, but her mother shot a warning glance at Nanna Winnie.

'Let's clear these tea things away, shall we?'

They left Nanna Winnie still happily shelling winkles at the kitchen table, and Dora followed her mother into the curtained-off scullery. Rose tipped the dregs of the tea down the sink and ran the tap over the cups, then turned to face her.

'Now,' she said, her low voice muffled by the rush of running water, 'I want the truth, Dora. Have you and Nick Riley been carrying on behind Ruby's back?'

'No!' Blood rushed to her face.

'Are you sure? You look me in the eye and tell me, girl.'

Dora stared into her mother's steady dark brown gaze. 'I haven't, Mum, I swear.'

Rose held her gaze for a moment, then she nodded. 'I can see that now. I'm sorry for doubting you, love. I should have known you were better than that.' She turned off the tap. 'I reckon I know what's really been going on, anyway.'

'What ... do you mean?' Dora asked.

Rose turned to look at her. 'I ain't blind, ducks. I've seen the way Nick Riley used to look at you, and the way you looked at him, too. You two were made for each other, if you ask me. Until that vicious little cat Ruby came along and ruined it all.' She crashed the cups together in the sink in her agitation. 'I wouldn't have put it past her to get pregnant on purpose, just so he'd have to marry her.'

'Or to lie about being pregnant in the first place,' Dora said quietly.

Rose swung round to face her. 'Tell me you're having me on?'

Dora shook her head. 'It's the truth.'

'But she lost the baby...'

'She lied about that, too.'

'The wicked–' Rose trailed off, words failing her. 'And does her mother know?' Dora nodded.

Her mother turned away from Dora. 'I can't believe Ruby would stoop that low,' she murmured. 'When I think about all the poor women who lose babies every day ... she's making a mockery of them, that's what she's doing. A mockery.'

'You won't tell Nanna, will you?' Dora whispered. 'I don't want it spread all over Bethnal Green.'

'I don't see why not!' Two bright spots of colour blazed on Rose's high cheekbones. 'The Pikes are quick enough to spread gossip about you...' She paused, collecting herself. 'No, you're right,' she agreed. 'It wouldn't do any good to anyone. And it certainly won't make you feel any better, will it?'

'No,' Dora sighed. 'It won't.'

She pulled the teatowel off its nail beside the sink and dried the cups. Her mother watched her consideringly.

'I reckon you two will be together in the end,' she said.

Dora smiled sadly. 'How do you work that out?'

'Because you belong together.'

'It doesn't always work out like that though, does it? You said yourself, Nick's a married man.'

'Marriages can end.'

'Yes, but gossip doesn't.' Dora hung the teatowel back on the hook. 'Can you imagine what Lettie Pike would say if Nick left Ruby and we started courting? My name would be mud.'

'Take no notice of her.' Rose shrugged. 'No one else does. She's picked on this family before, and we've always come out the other side. Sticks and stones, as they say.'

'But I don't just mean round here,' Dora said. 'They've got rid of a nurse from the Nightingale for carrying on with a married man. If Lettie started spreading rumours like that about me...'

'If she starts spreading rumours about you, then we might start spreading a few of our own about her girl,' Rose replied.

'Mum!' Dora laughed, shocked. 'I thought you've always told us not to sink to her level?'

'You're right.' Rose's brown eyes twinkled. 'But I can't very well stop your nanna doing it, can I?'

'What's so funny?' Nanna Winnie's voice carried through from the other side of the curtain as they giggled together. 'What are you talking about?'

'Nothing, Mum.' Rose sobered quickly. 'I meant what I said, though,' she told Dora softly. 'If Nick divorces Ruby and you and him get the chance to be together, then you should do it, and never mind what anyone else says. Like I said, there's enough unhappiness in this world, so you might as well grab a bit of happiness while you can. You just look at your friend Tremayne if you don't believe me.'

Her mother's words stayed with Dora when she left the house ten minutes later, just in time to see Nick Riley letting himself out of next door's

398

back gate.

'Nick?' She saw him pause for a moment, his hand on the latch. Then, still keeping his head down, he slammed out of the gate.

'Nick, wait!' She followed him down the narrow, weed-covered alleyway that led back to the street. She had to run to catch up with his long strides. 'Why are you walking away from me?'

Dora put out her hand to stop him but he shrugged her off.

'Don't touch me!' he hissed. 'I've got nothing to say to you.'

She recoiled, bewildered. 'What have I done?'

He stopped abruptly and turned to face her. His eyes blazed with anger. 'You're good at playing the innocent, aren't you?' he sneered. 'Did you learn it off your mate Ruby?'

A stirring of unease began to uncurl inside her. 'Nick–'

'Just answer me one question. Did you know Ruby was lying about the baby?'

'I–' Dora opened her mouth to defend herself, but the words wouldn't come.

Nick's broad shoulders slumped. 'I knew it,' he said. He sounded more weary than angry. 'I can see it in your face. And there was me, trying to tell myself it was just another one of Ruby's lies.' His mouth twisted. 'You're not as good a liar as your friend,' he mocked. 'Your eyes give you away every time.'

'I – I was going to tell you,' she said. 'That's why I came round to see you. I couldn't live with myself...'

'So you say,' he sneered. 'But I didn't see you

rushing round to set me straight when you first found out.'

Dora stared down at the weeds pushing their way through the cracked paving slabs. 'I couldn't,' she said. 'I promised Ruby.'

'And what about me?' His voice was raw with emotion. 'Or don't I matter to you?'

She lifted her gaze to meet his. 'You know you do.'

'I don't know anything any more.'

'Nick, listen–'

'You know, the funny thing is I could almost forgive Ruby for what she did. I know what she's like, I shouldn't expect anything better of her. But you...' He shook his head. 'You were the only one I ever trusted. The only one in this whole stinking, ugly world I felt I could depend on. And you let me down.'

'No! Nick, that's not fair. I wanted to tell you, so many times. You're the last person on earth I'd ever want to betray. Nick, please! You've got to believe me.'

The bleak contempt in his eyes shocked her. 'Believe you? I don't think I'll ever believe another word you say.'

He turned and walked away from her. Dora wanted to follow him but her feet were rooted to the spot.

Chapter Forty-Five

'I want to thank you, Nurse.'

It was Sunday afternoon and visiting time was over for the week. Staff Nurse O'Hara was very punctual about ushering patients out on the dot of three o'clock. She hovered at the doors to the ward, looking at her watch and sighing with frustration when Sister Blake waylaid them for a chat about their loved ones.

But this time it was Helen who was waylaid, by Marcus Forster's mother.

'My son has been telling me how well you've been looking after him,' she said. There was no mistaking the family resemblance; she was as tall and skinny as her son, with an identical shock of tight light brown curls, although hers were concealed under a stylish hat.

'Your son is a remarkable young man, Mrs Forster.'

'Oh, I know. His father and I were always quite at a loss as to how we produced such a child prodigy!' she smiled. 'But I know Marcus can be rather – temperamental,' she went on, 'so I do appreciate your making so much of an effort. Not everyone is prepared to take the time to understand him.'

Helen looked away, embarrassed by the unexpected praise. Mrs Forster went on looking at her, that strange brown gaze as direct as her son's.

'I was a nurse myself, you see, so I know how difficult it can be when you have a patient as demanding as Marcus,' she said. 'My son tells me you're in your third year?' Helen nodded. 'When are you taking your State Finals?'

'In two weeks.'

'I expect you're all prepared for them?'

'Yes.' She often took comfort in sitting up all night with her textbooks, when sleep eluded her.

'That must be very difficult for you, since the death of your husband. I'm sorry, do forgive me,' Mrs Forster added hurriedly, seeing the dismay on Helen's face. 'That's the problem with having a son like mine, I'm afraid. I've become as forthright as he is!'

'No, no, it's quite all right,' Helen muttered. Her eyes darted here and there, looking for a way to escape. 'But if you'll excuse me, I have jobs to do...'

'Oh dear, I've made you uncomfortable, haven't I?' Mrs Forster regarded her sympathetically. 'I'm so sorry, my dear. I was the same when my husband died, so I know what it's like. You're struggling through each day, trying to keep a lid on your emotions and pretend life is normal. The last thing you need is a stranger blundering in and making you feel worse. Isn't that right?'

But I am normal, Helen wanted to shout. Look at me. I get up every morning and I wash and dress myself and report for duty and do everything that's asked of me. What could be more normal than that?

Why did everyone keep insisting that there was something wrong with her, that she was grieving?

She had bidden goodbye to her grief at Charlie's graveside. Now she had to get on with life.

She flinched as Mrs Forster patted her arm. 'Look, I know it's probably of small comfort at the moment, but time is a great healer, my dear.'

'Thank you, Mrs Forster, but I really don't need to be healed,' Helen replied sharply. 'I can assure you there is nothing wrong with me. Now if you'll excuse me—'

She backed away, and collided with Sister Blake who was coming in the other direction.

'Oops, watch out, Nurse Dawson!' Her smile vanished when she looked at Helen's face. 'Are you all right?'

'Yes, Sister.' Helen fought to keep a tremor from her voice. 'I'm sorry, I – I wasn't looking where I was going.'

'And where are you going, Nurse?' Sister Blake enquired patiently.

Helen's face coloured. 'I'm not sure, Sister.'

'In that case, why don't you go and help Nurse Patrick with the dressings?' she suggested kindly. 'She hasn't done them before, and I'm afraid she's about to get herself in rather a muddle without someone to show her.'

Helen hurried off, relieved to have a purpose. Showing the pro how to remove and dispose of a used dressing, clean a wound and apply a new one took up all her concentration so she didn't have the time to ponder Mrs Forster's comments.

At five Sister Blake retired to her sitting room for a cup of tea. Several of the other nurses went into their kitchen to put the kettle on, leaving Helen alone on the ward. She went around each bed, checking pulleys and traction tension, tightening drawsheets, smoothing mackintoshes and turning down sheets to an exact fifteen inches.

'Excuse me, Nurse. Are you busy?' Mr Casey said, as she checked the blocks under the foot of his bed.

Helen fixed a bright smile on her face. 'What can I do for you, Mr Casey?'

'I wondered if you could do me a favour?'

'If I can.'

'Have a look in the paper, will you? The Speedway was on last night, and I want to know the result.'

'The Speedway?' Helen heard herself say faintly.

'Yes, I like a bit of racing. Not that I get to see it much these days,' Mr Casey said ruefully. 'I don't suppose you know much about the Speedway, do you, Nurse?'

'Yes, I do, as a matter of fact. My husband–' Helen took a deep breath and picked up the Sunday newspaper. 'The results are at the back, aren't they?'

'That's right. The sports pages. There might be a match report too.'

It's only a newspaper, Helen told herself as she flicked through the pages. Just because she had avoiding reading one, or even touching one, since that day she'd asked Mr Hopkins for a copy of the *Evening Standard*, didn't mean she could avoid them for ever.

'Is there a report?'

'Yes. Yes, there is.'

'I'd be obliged if you could read it to me. Only my daft missus has gone and taken my specs home with her, and I'm lost without them. Nurse?'

His voice was muffled under the roar of blood in Helen's ears.

Read it, she urged herself. Stop making a fool of yourself and read the wretched newspaper.

She cleared her throat and started to read. But her hands were suddenly shaking so much she couldn't hold the newspaper still.

'Nurse?' She heard Mr Casey's voice. He seemed to be shouting. 'Nurse!'

'It's all right, Mr Casey, you don't have to shout,' she tried to say. Her tongue felt thick in her mouth and she stumbled over the words.

Then she saw a blur of blue uniforms converging on her and realised he wasn't shouting at her. He was calling to the other nurses to help.

She saw Sister Blake's face, distorted as if she was looking at her through the bottom of a very thick glass.

'I'm sorry, Sister, I don't think I'm feeling quite well–' were Helen's last words, before the world started sliding slowly sideways and she slipped to the floor.

Helen had recovered by the time Kathleen Fox reached the sick bay, thanks to a generous whiff of sal volatile. She lay against the pillows, still half asleep.

Sister Blake sat at her bedside. She rose as Matron walked in, but Kathleen waved her back into her seat.

'How is she?'

'Better than she was. She became rather agitated when she came round, so Dr McKay gave her a mild sedative. Not that she really needed it – I don't think she's slept in weeks.'

'Did he say what was wrong with her?'

'She doesn't have a fever, and her pulse is normal. Dr McKay thinks it might be nervous exhaustion. It's not surprising, really. The poor girl has been struggling to cope for such a long time.'

Kathleen looked at Helen. Her skin was so translucent she could see the fine network of blue veins on the closed eyelids. 'I should never have let it go on like this for so long. I should have sent her home straight away.'

'You mustn't blame yourself,' Sister Blake said. 'She wouldn't let anyone help her. She wore herself out trying to prove to everyone that she could cope.'

'She's paying for it now, isn't she?' Kathleen sighed. 'Look at her. How young she looks. You forget these nurses aren't much more than girls.'

As if she knew she was being discussed, Helen's eyes fluttered open.

'Wh-Where am I?' She looked around, dazed and dishevelled, then caught sight of Kathleen. 'Matron!'

She struggled to sit up, but Kathleen moved to her bedside and put a reassuring hand on her shoulder.

'It's all right, Dawson, don't try to get up,' she said. 'You're in the sick bay. You collapsed on the ward.'

'You gave us all quite a scare!' Sister Blake put in.

A faint blush swept over Helen's high cheekbones. 'I'm so sorry, Sister ... Matron. I don't know what came over me.'

'Don't you? I do.' Kathleen sat down beside her so they were eye to eye. 'You are physically and mentally exhausted. You need to rest.'

Helen shook her head. 'I need to go back to work...'

'Not this time. When you are feeling well enough, you may return to your room and pack a bag. I will telephone your mother to come and collect you.'

'No!' A look of panic flashed across Helen's face. 'Please, Matron, don't call my mother. I'm feeling perfectly all right, honestly. I think it must have been the heat.'

'Dawson, you are far from all right!' Kathleen's voice was firm. 'You should never have been allowed on duty in the first place. You need to go home and rest. You can't take care of other people if you don't take care of yourself.'

'But couldn't I just stay here?' Helen pleaded.

'Out of the question,' Kathleen said. 'Your mother would never allow it, and quite rightly too. Your place is with her.'

She caught Helen's beseeching look, and suddenly she understood.

'Give your mother a chance,' she urged. 'You never know, she may surprise you.'

And I hope for everyone's sake she does, Kathleen added silently to herself.

Chapter Forty-Six

'Have you seen what they're doing now?'

Dr Adler tossed a copy of the *Daily Mirror* down on to Esther Gold's bed. It was the middle of the morning, and Dora was in the middle of the locker round.

'Do you mind, Doctor?' She snatched up the newspaper. 'There'll be hell to pay from Sister if that print gets on the sheets.'

It was lucky Sister Everett was supervising a pro's first enema behind the screens at the far end of the ward, otherwise she would have been most displeased by the interruption.

Esther looked up at him blankly. 'What's going on?'

'The Blackshirts are planning a march through the East End. Read it for yourself.' He took the newspaper out of Dora's hands and handed it to Esther.

'The Blackshirts are always marching,' Dora said, wiping down the tiled top of the locker. Barely a Sunday afternoon went by without her seeing them parading down the street in their black uniforms, heading for some street corner rally or other.

'This is different,' Dr Adler said. 'It's supposed to be some kind of anniversary celebration. Every Blackshirt in the land is going to converge on London, and march from the City out through

408

the streets of the East End to a rally in Bethnal Green. Can you imagine it? There'll be thousands of them.'

'It says here Sir Oswald Mosley himself will be addressing them,' Esther said, reading from the newspaper.

'But I don't understand. Why are they coming here, to the East End?' Dora asked. 'Surely they'd be better off having this rally somewhere up west?'

Dr Adler sent her an almost pitying look. 'Because they want to cause as much trouble as possible, I imagine. They're marching through our streets, past our shops and businesses, just to provoke a fight.'

'Do you think they'll come past the factory?' Esther looked up, her dark eyes full of fear.

'I told you, they want to provoke us – what do you think you're doing?' he broke off, as Esther threw aside her bedclothes.

'What does it look like?' She swung her legs out of bed and started searching for her slippers. 'I need to go home.'

'Get back into bed before Sister catches you!' Dora threw Dr Adler a despairing look. 'You can't discharge yourself.'

'I'm not going to stay in this hospital bed while my home is being attacked by those thugs.' She searched around. 'Where are my clothes? I need to get dressed.'

'Esther, please.' Dr Adler stepped in. 'The march isn't happening until the beginning of October. You'll be home by then.'

'But my father–'

'I told you, I'll look after him. I'll look after both of you.' Dora saw their hands brush against each other on the bedcover, and looked away quickly.

'Let's get you back into bed,' she said briskly, to cover her embarrassment.

'You'd best do as Nurse Doyle says,' Dr Adler advised, the moment broken. 'She's a very hard woman if you get on the wrong side of her.'

Esther smiled at her. 'Dora isn't hard. She's strong, like me.'

Just then Sister Everett emerged from behind the screens and spotted Dr Adler.

'Really, Doctor, we are running a hospital, not a social club!' she snapped as she ushered him out of the double doors.

'Will your brother be going on that march, do you think?' Esther asked as she watched Dora scrubbing out her locker.

She stopped, the brush in her hand. 'I hope not.'

'He's still involved with them, then?'

Dora felt herself blushing. She had truly believed that Peter had had a change of heart about the Blackshirts after what they'd done to Esther. But gradually he had allowed himself to be drawn back in. He swore to Dora that he no longer roamed the backstreets at night looking for trouble, but he still went to the meetings and marches, and she had seen him handing out pamphlets in the street.

'I told you, you don't know what they're like,' he insisted. 'I'm scared about what they might do to Mum or the kids.'

'Keep him out of it, *bubele*,' Esther urged her

410

now. 'For his sake, try to get him to stay away.'

'I'll do my best,' Dora promised.

'Stick your moniker on here, will you?'

Nick looked down at the piece of paper Harry Fishman had thrust under his nose. 'What's this?'

'A petition against this march the Blackshirts are planning. We want to send 'em the message that we don't want their kind in the East End.'

He glared across the Porters' Lodge at Peter Doyle as he said it. Peter didn't look up from his newspaper.

'Now, I'm not sure I approve of political activity in this lodge,' Mr Hopkins spoke up as Nick scrawled his signature across the paper. 'It's not good for morale.'

'Better tell him that, then.' Harry glowered at Peter. 'He's been spouting his Blackshirt rubbish in here long enough.'

'Leave it, Harry,' Nick warned wearily.

'Anyway, we're planning to fight back,' Harry said. 'We're going to be out on the streets on that Sunday, protesting against the march. Let Mosley and his lot see if they can get past us!' His broad chest swelled with pride. 'You'll be with us, won't you, Nick? We could always do with a bit more muscle on our side.'

'Count me out,' he said.

Harry stared at him. 'Don't tell me you're siding with the Blackshirts?'

'I ain't siding with nobody, all right? I just don't want to get involved.'

'You live round here, don't you? I reckon that makes you involved whether you like it or not.'

'All the same, I'm staying out of it.'

Harry opened his mouth to argue, but Arthur, one of the other porters, jumped in. 'Best leave it, Harry,' he murmured. 'He's like a bear with a sore head at the minute.' He lowered his voice. 'Between you, me and the gatepost, I reckon he's lovesick.'

'Sick of kipping on my settee since his missus kicked him out, you mean!' Harry put in.

'I ain't surprised.' Arthur leered. 'That missus of his was a bit of all right. I bet he's regretting not having her to cuddle up to at night!'

They weren't wrong, Nick thought as he made his way up from the laundry pushing a trolley laden with freshly washed linen. He was lovesick all right, but not for Ruby.

He missed Dora so much it hurt. Even before, when they were keeping their distance from each other, he was always aware of her. He could watch her tending to a patient on the ward, or hear her laughter coming from the kitchen, and somehow he would feel connected to her.

But now it was as if there was a high brick wall between them.

Part of him bitterly regretted lashing out at her, but he'd been angry and hurt. Even now he'd had time to calm down, he still felt betrayed. He wasn't sure if he could ever forgive her, or trust her again. And that made him feel so lonely.

But never so lonely that he even considered going back to Ruby. She had left him notes at the Porters' Lodge – his love letters, the other blokes teasingly called them – begging him to give her another chance. But Nick had no intention of re-

412

turning to her, or to Victory House. He'd even written to tell her their marriage was over, but he should have realised that Ruby wouldn't give up that easily.

Not like Dora. Since their last meeting in Griffin Street, she had avoided him completely. If they ever came face to face in the corridor, she would quicken her footsteps, avert her face and pretend she hadn't seen him.

He might have known that, too. Unlike Ruby, Dora had her pride. And so did he. That was the problem.

Chapter Forty-Seven

Millie's make-up and perfume were scattered haphazardly on top of the chest of drawers, along with her silver-backed hairbrush, comb and mirror. Helen put them away without thinking. Poor Millie, how would she ever manage to escape Sister Sutton's wrath without a friend to watch over her? Helen wondered as she straightened the brush and mirror into perfectly parallel lines.

She was glad she didn't have to say goodbye to them. Dora was on duty, and Millie was spending the weekend at her family's country estate with Seb. Helen didn't want to have to face anyone, least of all the girls she had come to think of as her friends.

But just as she was wrapping up her washing things to put into her suitcase, she heard a familiar light tread hurrying up the attic steps, and Millie breezed in.

'What are you doing here?' Helen said. 'I thought you were down in Kent.'

'Daddy was called up to London for an important meeting, so we decided to come back with him.' Millie plonked herself down on her bed and pulled off her hat. 'I've only come back to change, and then Seb and I are going to–' She stopped, taking in the suitcase open on Helen's bed. 'What are you doing?'

'Matron's sending me home.'

'Well, that's a relief,' Millie said. 'You need some time off. I know you think you can cope, but we've all been so worried about you. A few days at home and you'll be as right as rain.'

Helen said nothing as she went on folding her clothes and arranging them in her suitcase. Luckily, Millie was in one of her chatty moods and didn't notice.

'Daddy wouldn't say why he had to go to this meeting, but he was in a frightful state,' she said, shrugging off her coat. 'Between you and me, I think it's all to do with the King and that dreadful American woman, as Granny calls her.'

'Oh, yes?' Helen tucked her washing things into a corner of her suitcase.

'The Prime Minister's in an awful flap about it, and so are most of the Privy Council,' Millie went on. 'They know it's been going on for years, but they all thought he'd give her up as soon as he came to the throne. But now she's got her claws into him and he's utterly besotted. Spends all his time locked away in Fort Belvedere with

her and her American cronies. Granny says the
writing was on the wall when he swapped the
state Daimler for a Buick.' She flung open the
wardrobe, then turned to Helen. 'I say, you're
packing rather a lot for a few days, aren't you?
Anyone would think you weren't coming back!'
She laughed, and then her face grew serious.
'You are coming back, aren't you?'

'I—'

'Of course you are, how silly of me,' Millie went
on before Helen had a chance to speak. 'You're
not going to leave a week before your Finals, are
you?'

She pulled out a dress and started to get
changed, chatting away about Seb, her weekend
in Billinghurst, and the latest scandals at court.
Helen finished her packing and locked up her
suitcase.

'All done,' she said. 'Will you say goodbye to
Doyle for me?'

Millie nodded. 'I don't know how she'll put up
with me without you to sort out our squabbles.'

'You'll be all right.' Helen smiled bracingly.
'Try to keep your room tidy, won't you? And
don't break your neck getting in through that
window after lights out.'

Millie laughed. 'Really, I'm sure we'll manage
without you for a few days! You never know, we
might be reformed characters by the time you
come back.'

'I hope not.' Helen put down her suitcase and
hugged Millie impulsively. 'I'll miss you,' she
said, breathing in her Guerlain perfume.

'I'll miss you too.' Millie pulled away from her,

her expression quizzical. 'You are coming back, aren't you?'

Helen took a deep breath. If she told Millie the truth, it would mean so much explanation. And she wasn't sure she could face it.

She was saved from answering by the sharp toot of a car horn outside.

'I have to go,' she said. 'My mother's waiting for me.'

'I'll come down with you and wave you off.'

'No, don't.' Helen smiled at her. 'Let's just say goodbye here, shall we?'

Constance was sitting in the back of the taxi, stony-faced. She turned to face Helen who stiffened, waiting for the usual critical comment. But for once none came.

'Hurry up and put the suitcase in the boot,' her mother said, tight-lipped. 'We'll be late for our train.'

Constance stared out of the window at the passing scenery and struggled to find something to say.

Helen hadn't spoken a word to her since she'd got into the taxi. Constance could feel waves of resentment coming off her, though she didn't understand why.

She supposed it was because Helen hadn't wanted to leave the hospital. Matron had made that very clear when Constance took her to task for not sending her daughter home earlier.

'She was most adamant she didn't want me to contact you,' Miss Fox had said.

'But I'm her mother!'

416

Miss Fox had given her one of those knowing looks that Constance found so irritating. 'I believe she's afraid of letting you down,' she commented.

'Well, I can't think where she's got that idea from.'

As they were leaving, Miss Fox had taken Constance to one side.

'Please take care of her,' she had urged. As if it had ever occurred to her to do otherwise. What did Matron think she was going to do, take Helen home and beat her?

But now they were together, travelling homewards on the train, she struggled to find words of comfort.

She wished she had been more generous and loving to her daughter, and towards Charlie. If only she'd realised how ill he was, of course she would have done things differently. She knew Helen resented the way she had behaved. But she couldn't turn the clock back, as much as she wanted to.

She took a deep breath, and plunged in.

'I'm sorry to hear you've been ill,' she said. 'But a few days' rest should make you feel a lot better.'

She saw the cold look Helen sent her, and realised immediately she had said the wrong thing.

'I'm not ill, Mother,' Helen said in a chilly voice. 'I've lost my husband, I'm not recovering from influenza.'

'No, of course not, I didn't mean it like that.' Constance looked down at her hands, flustered. Helen seemed like a different person – distant, more grown up somehow. 'What I'm trying to say is that you need to start looking forward. Once your State Finals are out of the way...'

'I'm not taking my State Finals.'

Constance stared at her. 'What do you mean, you're not taking them?'

'Just what I said.' Helen faced her, her gaze level.

'And how do you expect to become a nurse if you don't take your exams?'

'I don't. I'm giving up nursing.'

Constance felt dizzy with panic. 'Don't be absurd. You're not thinking straight,' she dismissed.

'And you're not listening.'

'I am listening, Helen, but what I'm hearing is utter nonsense!'

'Why is it nonsense? Just because you don't agree with it.'

Constance glanced around. The other passengers in the carriage were sending them interested looks. 'We'll talk about this later,' she said firmly.

'You can talk about it all you like, but I won't change my mind. I'm sorry if you think I've let you down, Mother, but that's the way I feel.'

'But you haven't–' Constance started to say. Helen had already turned away to stare out of the window again.

Chapter Forty-Eight

'I don't care what you say, Dora. I'm going on that rally.'

Reflected firelight from the incinerator flickered across Peter's obstinate face as he threw more rubbish into the stoke hole and watched it burn.

It had taken Dora three days to get her brother on his own. She had finally tracked him down to the basement on the pretext of needing to go there and burn some dressings.

He had been so worried and contrite after what happened with Esther Gold, Dora would have bet a month's wages on him not going anywhere near the Blackshirt rally. So she was shocked when he told her he was not only going to be there, he was also going to be one of the men guarding the platform at Victoria Park Square where Sir Oswald was going to speak.

'It's expected of me,' he said, eyes fixed on the dancing flames. 'Besides, it's a big honour for Bethnal Green to have someone like him come to speak here.'

'We don't want him here.'

'Speak for yourself. There's plenty who want to hear what he's got to say.'

'Then let them go and listen to him up west. We don't want them in the East End.'

'It's a free country,' Peter protested. 'We're allowed to march where we like. That's what it's

419

all about, ain't it? Defending our rights.'

'And what about the rights of all those Jewish shops and businesses who get turned over by your lot every day?' Dora went up to him, feeling the heat of the stoke hole on her face. 'Have you forgotten what they did to Esther Gold, Peter? They would have killed her if I hadn't come along...'

'They wouldn't,' he mumbled, emptying another sack of rubbish into the gaping, fiery jaws of the furnace. 'Anyway, if she'd turned around and walked away, then no one would have got hurt.'

'So Mosley and his gang have the right to walk where they like, but Esther and her family and friends don't, is that it?' Dora stared at her brother with contempt. 'I can't believe you, Pete, really I can't. You saw her yourself, lying unconscious in that hospital bed. You were so scared for her, remember?'

'Yeah, well, I've had time to think since then.'

'Time to let someone else do your thinking for you, you mean! What did your mates say to you, Pete? Did they tell you she deserved it? That she had it coming to her? Come on, they must have said something. How else can you sleep at night?'

Peter slammed the stoke-hole door shut and drew the heavy bolt into place. 'I told you, I've got to think of our family,' he muttered. 'You don't know what those men are like...'

'Oh, I do. I've nursed Esther, remember? Helped stitch her up where they caved her skull in with their boots.' Dora saw him flinch but went on, relentless. 'I know what they can do all right, Peter.

But do you think that's what Mum would want? Do you really think she'd want your protection, knowing what it cost? No, she wouldn't. She brought you up to do the right thing, Peter Doyle. And I reckon she'd be ashamed of you, just like I am.'

He tried to turn away from her but Dora grabbed his shoulders, swinging him back to face her.

'And let me remind you of one more thing,' she said. 'You would have been locked up by now if Esther had told the police you were there that night. She kept quiet because she's a decent person, and she hoped that you might see sense and do the decent thing. You just think of that when you go out marching with your bully-boy mates!'

Constance Tremayne had never been afraid to speak her mind before, but now she felt as if she was tiptoeing across eggshells.

Helen had been at home for three days, and her mother still didn't know what to say to her. Every word she uttered seemed to inflame the situation further.

Constance wanted to reassure Helen that all was not lost, that she still had a future to look forward to. But Helen turned it around, made it seem as if her mother was forcing her into something against her will.

She even made it sound as if Constance had cajoled her into taking up nursing. Constance couldn't recall doing any such thing. She had only suggested nursing because it seemed a sensible way for a respectable young woman to earn a living. Everything she had ever done, she had done for Helen. So why did her daughter make it sound as if she was the enemy?

And all the time she was conscious that the days were passing, the Finals were getting closer, and Helen's textbooks remained abandoned in the bottom of her suitcase. Constance had to talk some sense into her before it was too late.

She tried again on Thursday evening, while they were having dinner together. It was the only time Helen ever emerged from her room, so Constance had to take the chance.

'Have you thought any more about the exams?' she asked, ignoring her husband's warning look.

Helen sighed wearily, her gaze still fixed on her plate. She had been pushing her food around un-touched for ten minutes. 'I've already told you, I'm not going to take them.'

'And do you think that's what Charlie would have wanted?'

Helen's head went back. Constance saw the flare of anger in her eyes and realised she had thrown petrol on a blazing fire.

'How dare you!' Helen snapped. 'How dare you bring Charlie into this! How do you know what he would have wanted? You didn't know anything about him.'

'Helen, please. She didn't mean–' Timothy tried to step in, but his daughter was too angry to listen.

'I know exactly what she meant, Father. I won't let her talk about Charlie like that. She has no right.' She turned back to her mother, face rigid. 'You despised him when he was alive ... wanted nothing to do with him. You couldn't even bring yourself to come to his funeral! And yet now you think you can tell me what he would have wanted? You're just using a dead man to get me to do what you want. I didn't think even *you* would stoop that low!'

She threw down her knife and fork and blundered to her feet, pushing back her chair with a clatter. She had reached the door before Constance could speak.

'He came to see me,' she said quietly.

Helen stopped, her back still turned. 'When?'

'In the summer. Just before the ball.' She turned to her husband. 'You remember, don't you, Timothy?'

He nodded. 'Charlie wanted to speak to you in private, as I recall.'

It was the last time Constance had ever seen him. A hot wave of shame broke over her as she remembered how ungraciously she had behaved.

Helen hesitated in the doorway, her expression wary. 'Why did he come?'

'He wanted to make peace between us.' Constance smiled, remembering. 'He told me how much our disagreement was hurting you.'

'But you didn't listen to him?'

'No, I didn't.' How she wished she had now. If she had only allowed herself to admit her mistake, to accept how much Charlie and Helen loved each other, perhaps none of them would be in so much pain now. 'But I admired him for coming here and having the courage to face me.'

Helen managed a trembling smile. 'Charlie was always brave.'

'And he loved you. I can see that now.' Constance looked up at her daughter, standing in the doorway, her head bowed. 'I know we didn't always see eye to eye, but we did both want the best for you. That's why I think he'd be so disappointed now, to think you were throwing your studies away–'

'No!' Helen cut her off angrily. 'You just can't stop yourself, can you?' she said, her face full of contempt. 'Just when I think you might understand, you have to go and ruin it by ... by being you!'

'Helen!'

But she'd already gone, slamming the door behind her.

Constance turned to her husband, at a loss. 'I – I don't know what to say,' she said. 'I can't reach her.'

'She'll come round. She just feels very lost at the moment.'

'But I want to help her!'

'Then perhaps the time has come for you to be honest with her?'

Constance stared at him. 'What do you mean? Of course I'm honest. I'm always honest. I thought that was the problem...'

'I mean, be honest about yourself.'

His smile was bland, every inch the expression of a kindly country vicar. But behind his spectacles, there was a look in his eyes she hadn't seen before. A look that told her there was no sense in pretending.

'I don't understand,' she tried.

'I believe you do, my dear. That secret from

your past you've always tried to hide?'

'Secret?' said Constance faintly.

'Please, Constance, we've been married far too many years.' He looked amused. 'I knew the moment I met you that there was something you weren't telling me, something that had happened in your past that you felt you had to hide.'

Panic washed over her. She opened her mouth to deny it, but Timothy held up his hand. 'It's all right, my dear, I don't want to know. I've always taken the view that the past is the past, and that if you wanted to tell me you would in your own good time. But I wonder if now might be the right occasion to share some of your lessons learned with Helen? You never know, perhaps it might help to bridge the gap between you.'

Constance looked into his mild, smiling face. She had always thought her husband such an innocent, unworldly person. But he understood far more than she'd given him credit for.

She smiled sadly. 'You're a very wise man.'

'Of course I am, my dear. I married you, didn't I?' He stood up and kissed the top of her head. 'So will you talk to Helen?'

Constance hesitated. 'I'll try,' she promised finally.

It was Katie's birthday, and as they had both just been assigned night duty on Male Orthopaedics, Dora had treated her to a Saturday afternoon matinee of *My Man Godfrey* at the Palaseum.

'I love William Powell, don't you?' Katie sighed as they came out of the darkened cinema into the foyer afterwards. 'Isn't it strange that he and

425

Carole Lombard can pretend to be in love in the film when they're divorced in real life? I don't think I'd be able to speak to my Tommy again if we ever parted. How about you?'

'I'm about to find out, aren't I?' Dora nodded across the foyer. Penny Willard was coming in through the doors, arm-in-arm with Joe Armstrong.

'Oh, no!' Katie squealed. 'Quick, let's go!'

'Why?'

'You don't want them to see us, do you?' Katie tugged on her sleeve, but Dora stood her ground.

'Too late, they're coming over.' She waited to feel a pang of jealousy, but nothing happened. Even when Joe spotted her and put his arm around Penny's shoulders, she was unmoved.

'All right, Dora?' he greeted her. 'Been to see the film, have you?'

She bit back the sarcastic retort that sprang to her lips. 'Yes. It's good. You'll enjoy it.'

'Not sure how much we'll see, stuck in the back row!' Joe leered.

Dora glanced at Penny. She looked mortified, poor thing. She tried to squirm away from Joe's embrace, but he held her tightly. 'What do you reckon to this march tomorrow?' he said. 'Bet your brother can't wait, can he?'

Dora sent him a level look. 'Neither can I,' she said.

Joe sneered. 'You're not thinking of joining that protest, are you?'

'Why not?' She hadn't been considering it until that moment, but something about Joe's arrogant grin incensed her. 'Someone needs to stop the

Blackshirts. And the police don't seem to be doing anything about it,' she added, pointedly.

Joe's face flushed. 'You can't,' he said. 'It's too dangerous. Besides, there's no point. We've all had our leave cancelled. There'll be thousands of police on the streets, making sure the march gets through.'

'All the more reason why I should be there, then.'

She glared up at him, holding his gaze, fierce and determined. Then Joe laughed.

'Suit yourself,' he said. 'But if you think a few protesters will be any match for the police, you've got another think coming!'

'You weren't really serious, were you?' Katie said as they watched the couple head off towards the ticket office. 'You're not really thinking of joining that protest?'

'I want to do something,' Dora said. 'Dr Adler is going to set up a first-aid post in Cable Street. I thought I might go with him and help.'

'Matron would never agree to it.'

'Matron wouldn't have to know, would she? I'm on nights, so what I choose to do during the day is my business.'

'All the same, I don't think she'd like it,' Katie said. 'And Joe's right. My Tommy reckons it's going to be murder out there on the streets. What if you get hurt?'

'I won't. I told you, I'm going to offer first aid.'

Katie sent her a level look. 'I know you, Doyle. You say you're going to stay on the sidelines but before you know it you'll be in there, getting mixed up in it all. Well, you wouldn't catch me

427

going. Tommy's already told me I'm to stay in the nurses' home and not come out until it's all over.'

'Lucky for your Tommy I'm not his girlfriend then, ain't it?' Dora replied.

Chapter Forty-Nine

'You have a visitor,' Timothy Tremayne said.

It was Sunday morning, and Helen was brushing her hair in front of her bedroom mirror, ready to go to church with her parents. She looked up at the sound of her father's voice on the other side of the door.

'A visitor?'

'She says she's a friend of yours from the hospital. Miss Hollins?'

'Hollins?' Helen went to the door. Her father stood there, looking smart in his cassock and dog collar. 'What does she want?'

'You'd better go and find out, hadn't you? I've put her in the drawing room.'

Helen looked at her watch. 'But what about church?'

'I'm sure the Lord won't mind you missing the morning service just this once. You can always catch up with Him at Evensong, can't you? And if you're worried about your mother, she's already gone down to the church to bully the sexton.' He smiled. 'You go and see your friend. It will do you good to chat to someone your own age. You've been cooped up with us for a week now.'

Amy was perched on the edge of one of the chintz-covered sofas. She jumped to her feet the minute Helen walked in.

'Oh, thank heavens.' She put her hand to her heart. 'I was terrified of meeting Mrs Tremayne.' Her eyes darted around anxiously. 'She's not here, is she?'

'Don't worry, you're quite safe.' Helen ushered her back on to the sofa. 'This is a nice surprise,' she said.

'What you mean is, I'm the last person you expected to see!' Amy's mouth twisted. 'To be honest, I don't even know why I'm here,' she admitted frankly. 'I just knew I had to get out of the house, and you were the only person I could think of to visit. I'm sorry, that sounds awful.' She blushed. 'I wanted to come and make sure you were all right, too. Bevan wrote and told me you'd left.' She regarded Helen sympathetically. 'How are you feeling now?'

'Better than I was, I suppose.' She was feeling less anxious, but a heavy cloud of depression still settled on her. 'Would you like some tea?' she offered.

She rang for the maid and ordered it, then settled down in the armchair. 'So are things very difficult at home?'

'It's awful!' Amy grimaced. 'My parents are disgusted with me, as you can imagine. My mother can hardly bring herself to look at me, let alone speak to me. The only time she utters a word is to tell me how disappointed she is with me.' Amy sighed. 'How about yours?'

Helen considered it. Much as she resented her

mother, she had to admit Constance hadn't criticised her at all. And she certainly hadn't stopped trying to speak to Helen. 'My mother is obsessed with the idea of my taking the exams,' she said.

'Gosh, yes, the State Finals are tomorrow, aren't they? I wish I could sit them.' Amy laughed. 'I never thought I'd hear myself say it, but I miss the hospital. I even miss Sister Parker's lectures!'

'Me too,' Helen said.

Mary knocked softly and brought in their tea. When she'd gone, Amy said, 'It must be nice to be waited on, though. That's something you definitely don't get in the nurses' home!'

'I'm sure Sister Sutton would have brought you a pot of tea if you'd asked her nicely!' Helen smiled, handing her a cup.

Amy was thoughtful as she sipped her tea. 'You haven't asked me about my scandalous affair?' she said. 'That's all any of the other girls are interested in.'

'Do you want to tell me?'

'There isn't much to tell.' Amy shrugged. 'I behaved like an idiot. I fell in love with a married man, and I thought he loved me too.'

'You knew he was married when you met him?'

'Yes, I did.' Amy's chin lifted defiantly. 'But I didn't care, at first. I didn't mean to fall in love with him, you see. It was just a bit of fun. He was just a rich, successful man who could give me everything I wanted. He wined and dined me, and took me to expensive places. He was much more fun than the penniless medical students I'd been out with before.' She smiled at the memory. 'But then I started to fall in love with him, and I

430

wanted more.' Her face grew wistful. 'I thought he loved me, too. He told me he didn't love his wife, that he'd only married her because she was rich. He said that once he'd established himself in his career, he wouldn't need her any more and he was going to leave her. And I believed him, because I wanted it to be true.'

'When did you realise it wasn't?'

'I don't know,' she said. 'I suppose it really struck me on the night of the Founder's Day Ball. I so wanted to go with him, to be seen with him, and he wouldn't allow it. And then when you got married, and I saw the way Charlie stood in front of all those people and told the world he loved you, I suddenly realised that my lover would never have the courage to stand up in front of anyone and say that about me.'

Amy's teacup rattled in the saucer as she put it down. 'You were so lucky to have Charlie,' she said. 'I know it might seem heartbreaking for you now, but one day you'll look back and realise how fortunate you were to have someone in your life who loved you with all their heart.'

Helen swallowed hard. Even now she tried not to think about Charlie. If she opened up that part of her brain she was afraid the pain would just engulf her and leave her paralysed.

She tactfully changed the subject. 'How did his wife find out?'

'I told her.'

Helen jerked, sloshing tea into her saucer. 'You did what?'

'He didn't seem in any hurry to do it, so I thought I'd force the issue. I wrote her a note. I

431

thought she would confront him, throw him out. But she took it straight to Matron instead.' Amy looked pensive. 'Even then, I thought he would step in, come to my rescue and protect me. But he just stood back and let me take the punishment. He didn't say a word.'

As Amy was speaking, a thought suddenly occurred to Helen. 'This lover of yours – it wasn't a doctor, was it?'

Amy paused for a moment. 'I suppose you might as well know ... it was Simon Latimer.'

'Mr Latimer?' Helen nearly choked on her tea.

'I thought you'd guessed,' Amy went on. 'You almost caught us together once.'

Helen vaguely recalled the scent of rose perfume at the top of the staircase that led from the operating theatres. Amy's perfume. 'I had no idea,' she said.

'You see why I thought he'd protect me?' Amy said. 'I should have known better. I haven't heard a word from him since I left the hospital. He's completely abandoned me.'

She looked so devastated, Helen's heart went out to her. 'You poor thing.'

'Poor?' Amy flashed her a bitter look. 'Not stupid, or evil, or a homewrecker?'

'Why would I think that?'

'Because that's what most people think. That's what my mother thinks, anyway.'

They finished their tea and Amy got up to leave. 'What will you do now?' Helen asked.

'Keep writing to hospitals asking if I can finish my training, I suppose. Although I don't hold out much hope, if the responses I've had so far are anything to go by. How about you?'

'I have no idea.' Helen shrugged. 'I haven't even thought about it.'

'At least you have a choice.'

'Hardly! The State Finals are tomorrow morning, remember?'

'I'm sure your mother could pull a few strings, if that's what you wanted.' Amy looked at her consideringly. 'You know, I've always been rather jealous of you.'

'Me, why?'

'Because your mother cared about you.'

Helen snorted. 'Interfered, you mean?'

'Call it what you like,' Amy said. 'But perhaps if my mother had interfered a bit more, I might not be in this mess!'

Constance returned from church an hour later.

'Has your friend gone?' she asked, pulling off her gloves.

'She had to catch her train back to London.' Helen didn't add that Amy was terrified of coming face to face with Mrs Tremayne.

She waited for her mother to make a comment about Helen missing church, but she didn't. 'It was very nice of her to come and visit you on her day off, I must say.'

'It wasn't her day off. She's been dismissed from the Nightingale.'

Constance looked round sharply. 'Oh? For what reason?'

'She had an affair with a married man,' Helen announced. 'A surgeon at the hospital.' Her mother went very still. 'It's a pity she wasn't

433

allowed to take her Finals,' Helen added.

'If that's Matron's decision.'

Helen watched her mother unpinning her hat and smoothing down her scraped-back hair. She might have known her mother would take that attitude.

'I daresay you agree with it,' said Helen. 'I expect you think she deserves everything she gets.'

Constance turned to her. 'Is that what you really think of me, Helen? Do you think me so lacking in compassion?' Helen was taken aback by the hurt in her eyes. 'If you must know, I think it's a harsh punishment to take away a girl's future for the sake of one foolish mistake. Very harsh indeed.'

Helen stared at her in surprise. She had never known her mother show any compassion towards other people's failings.

But then Mary appeared and Constance immediately returned to her usual self, briskly giving the maid orders about when and how to serve lunch. Mary was taking it all in, her face a carefully composed mask of attentiveness. Helen smiled, wondering what the maid was really thinking behind that blank expression. Over the years Mary had been in service with them, she had become more and more inscrutable.

But even then, Constance wasn't satisfied.

'Really, that maid will have to go,' she said. 'I truly don't know whether she is stupid or just difficult. She never seems to take in a word I say. I'm sure she's out there in the kitchen, peeling away half the potatoes...'

'I daresay you're right, Mother,' Helen sighed

in agreement. She headed for the stairs to return to her room, but her mother called her back.

'If you have a moment, I would like to speak to you in the drawing room?'

Helen paused, her hand resting on the polished wood of the newel post. Could she really face another argument with her mother? They had barely spoken after their last short, angry outburst two days earlier. But Helen had the feeling Constance was biding her time, waiting for the chance to point out her shortcomings yet again. It was like a storm brewing, turning the air heavy.

She knew she would have to get it over with sooner or later, but not now.

'Do you mind if we talk later, Mother? I have a letter I would like to finish.'

Her bedroom had been Helen's sanctuary for as long as she could remember, but never more so than now. It reminded her comfortingly of her childhood, decorated in light pinks and greens, with its window overlooking the garden, framed by flower-sprigged curtains, and her bookshelves crammed with all her childhood favourites. Her bed, well stuffed and luxurious compared to her hard, narrow horsehair mattress at the nurses' home, was covered in the patchwork quilt her mother had made for her. The whole room was bright, sunny and smelled of lavender polish, a smell that took her right back to a time when her life was far less complicated.

As she sat down at her dressing table, she noticed a small glass vase filled with violet-blue Michaelmas daisies. The maid must have put them there for her while she was talking to Amy.

Helen sat down, opened the drawer and pulled out the letter she had been writing. She had barely taken up her pen when there was a soft knock on the door and her mother appeared.

'I've brought you a cup of tea,' she said.

'Thank you.' Helen looked curiously at the cup in her mother's hand. Serving tea or any other kind of refreshment in bedrooms was one of the many things of which Constance disapproved, smacking as it did of indulgence and 'pandering'. Even when she was ill as a child, Helen had had to struggle down to the dining room for her meals.

But the tea was just an excuse for her mother to continue their conversation, Helen realised.

Sure enough, after she had placed the cup on the dressing table, Constance perched herself awkwardly on the edge of Helen's bed.

'Who are you writing to?' she asked.

'Charlie's mother.'

'Ah.' Constance was silent for a moment, taking it in. 'That must be a great comfort to her?'

'I hope so.' Although it was hard to know what to write, or whether hearing from Helen helped Mrs Dawson at all. All Helen knew was that it made her feel as if Charlie hadn't left her.

'You're close to his mother, I gather?'

Helen stiffened, sensing criticism. 'She's been very kind to me.'

'Kinder than your own mother, I daresay,' Constance sniffed.

Helen stayed silent. She tried to write her letter, but she could feel the weight of her mother's expectation as she sat gazing around the bedroom. Finally, Helen put her pen down. 'Was there something you wanted?'

Constance didn't reply. When Helen glanced over her shoulder, she was surprised to see an expression of what looked like uncertainty on her mother's face. She had never before known Constance ever have a moment's self-doubt.

Finally, she spoke. 'There's something I need to tell you,' she said, looking down at her hands. 'Something I feel you ought to know, at any rate,' she amended. 'I can't say it's something I wanted anyone to know about, but I thought it might help – explain the way I am.'

Helen twisted around on her chair so that she was facing her. 'Go on,' she said.

Constance kept her gaze fixed on her hands. Her fingers laced and unlaced themselves in her lap as if they had taken on a life of their own. 'When you talked about your friend Amy's ... predicament,' she began, then stopped, gathering her thoughts. 'You expected me to condemn her for what she did, but I couldn't. Because I was in her shoes myself once.'

The world seemed to tilt on its axis.

'I don't understand?'

Constance managed a small smile. 'Really, Helen, you don't have to sit there with your mouth open. Is it so hard to believe I was young and foolish myself once?'

Yes, Helen thought, it is. Although from the way Constance's hands trembled as she smoothed her skirt primly over her knees, perhaps her mother still wasn't as self-assured as she liked to make out.

'What happened?'

Constance paused for a moment, composing herself. 'As I said, I was very young,' she began. 'I had just finished my training, and I was in my first Staff Nurse post on a TB ward.'

'At the Nightingale?'

'No. St Cecilia's, on the south coast. That was where I did my training, before I moved to the Nightingale.' Constance shot her a cross look. 'Really, Helen, it has taken me thirty years to tell this story. If you are going to interrupt me, it may take another thirty.'

'I'm sorry,' she murmured. 'Go on.'

Constance resumed her tale. 'As I said, I was in my first Staff Nurse post. He was a consultant surgeon, very dashing and extraordinarily clever. Even the other consultants were wary of him.'

'A bit like Mr Latimer,' Helen murmured, then caught her mother's warning look and promptly shut up.

'We used to be so in awe of him when he walked into the ward. Of course, I never dreamed he would notice me.' Constance smiled, remembering. 'How very special I felt when he picked me out from the other nurses to pay me attention. I had no idea at the time, of course, that he always went for the younger, less experienced girls because they were easier to dazzle.' Her mouth set in a thin, bitter line.

'And did you know he was married?' Helen asked.

Constance's gaze drifted towards the window. A guilty flush spread up her thin neck. 'I'm ashamed to say, I did,' she said. 'But he convinced me it didn't matter,' she added quickly. 'He told me he

438

didn't love his wife, that he had never loved her, but he couldn't divorce her because of the shame it would bring on his family. He convinced me that if I could only be patient, then one day we would be together. And, of course, I believed him,' she said. 'I believed him because I loved him and it never occurred to me that he might be – taking advantage of me.' She lowered her eyes, and Helen could see the shame washing over her still, even after so many years.

'What happened?' she asked.

'People talked, as they do. And before long, the gossip reached Matron's ears. I was hauled up before her and made to explain myself.' Constance's smile was full of self-mockery. 'When I think about how I stood there in her office, so sure of myself, I hardly know how I dared. I told her that this man and I were in love, and that we were planning to marry one day. I all but demanded that she should summon him to back up my story.'

'But she didn't?'

'How could she? He was a consultant, she couldn't very well summon him as if he were some probationer. Besides, she already knew he would deny everything. Because this wasn't the first time she'd been in this position, you see. I was just the latest in a string of young girls who had fallen prey to his charms.' Constance shook her head. 'I could tell she pitied me, in a way. She understood the situation far better than I did, naive as I was. But even so, she had no choice but to dismiss me from the hospital.'

'Did you ever see him again?' Helen found herself perched on the edge of the stool, leaning forward eagerly.

'I tried, but he wouldn't have anything to do with me. He cut me off just like that.' Constance made a sweeping movement with her hand. 'But even then I refused to believe that he could abandon me. I convinced myself that it must be his wife's doing, that she had some hold over him and was forcing him to turn against me. I wrote him letters, sent them to his home, the hospital, his club – anywhere I could think of. I was desperate, you see. But none of them were ever answered.' Her face was desolate. 'I don't think I have ever felt so alone and betrayed in my whole life. I'd lost everything, and I didn't think I would ever live down the shame.'

'But you did,' Helen said.

'Eventually.' Constance allowed herself a smile. 'After a while, I found a new place at the Nightingale, and I met your father, and slowly I began to piece my life back together again. But I've never forgotten the terrible mistake I made. How I lost everything, just because I fell in love with the wrong man. That's why I've always protected you, watched over you so closely. I didn't want you to go through the same pain as I did.'

As Helen watched her mother, slowly the truth began to dawn. 'And you thought Charlie was the wrong man, too?' she said.

'I was afraid for you. I saw how your love for him consumed you. Perhaps I was wrong,' Constance conceded. 'That day when he came here, I realised how much he loved you. How he was prepared to fight for you... But even then I still thought that he would drag you down, stop you being the bright, successful young woman I'd always hoped you would be.'

'Charlie would never have stopped me from doing anything,' Helen said. 'He loved me too much for that.'

Constance sent her a wistful smile. 'And yet here you are, without a future, because of him.'

Helen remained silent. 'I'm sorry,' her mother sighed. 'I shouldn't have said that. I promised myself I wouldn't nag you about your exams any longer.' She smiled. 'You have to make your own decisions. If nothing else, the past few weeks have taught me that.'

She rose from her seat. 'Now, I'll have to go and see what that silly girl has done to the potatoes. They were as hard as bullets last time.'

'I'll do it,' Helen blurted out.

Constance frowned. 'I beg your pardon?'

'I'll take my Finals,' she said. 'If it's not too late?'

Her mother smiled and Helen was relieved to see her supreme confidence back in place. 'Of course it won't be too late,' she said. 'I'll see to that.'

Chapter Fifty

They shall not pass.

Everywhere she looked Dora saw those four words. Scrawled in white paint across brick walls; pasted across shop windows; on bed sheets fluttering from lamp posts and banners held aloft by

441

the noisy, seething mass of people that crowded into Cable Street on that Sunday afternoon.

Everywhere she looked there was a bobbing sea of heads, arms and waving flags. 'Bar the road to Fascism!' came the booming message from a loudspeaker van as it nosed its way through the crowd. As if anyone needed telling. Shopkeepers were busy putting up shutters, while above them women and children hung out of the upper windows, passing down furniture to the street so the people below could create barricades out of old bedsteads, tables and chairs. A few were even tearing up paving slabs to build a makeshift wall.

They had been told that the march would be coming down three routes through the East End. But one had been abandoned before the march even started, and now thousands of protesters were crowding into the other two routes to cut them off too.

'Have you heard what happened at Gardner's Corner?' someone shouted. 'A tram driver just got out of his van and left it there, right on the corner. It's causing chaos to the marchers, they can't get past it!'

A roar went up from the crowd. 'Let's see if we can't do the same down here,' someone else yelled.

It took Dora a while to find Dr Adler in the middle of all the chaos. He had set up a temporary consulting room in the back of a bagel bakery. Dora found him in his shirtsleeves, unpacking dressings from a bag.

'Need any help?' she asked.

He swung round. 'Nurse Doyle! What are you doing here?'

'Same as you.' She took off her coat and rolled up her sleeves. 'Right, what have we got?' She nudged him aside and delved into the medical bag. 'Did you remember to bring any elastic bandages? Oh, well, never mind, I suppose we can make do with what we've got. How about medicated lint?'

He ignored her. 'You've got to go back, it's too dangerous. You can hear them out there. I can't be responsible for your safety.'

'Then I'll just have to look after myself, won't I? Now, have you brought any carbolic? We're going to need that, whatever happens. Never mind, I'll go and get some. I'm sure I passed a hardware shop further up the road...'

Just at that moment the door burst open and a boy charged in, his face alight with excitement. 'We've just got word, the marchers have been turned away from Gardner's Corner!' he cried.

Dora looked at Dr Adler. 'Does that mean they'll be turning back?' she asked.

'Either that or they'll all be coming down here,' he said grimly.

Dora grabbed her coat. 'Better get that carbolic then, before the rush starts.'

It was a quiet Sunday afternoon in Casualty. Nick had been summoned to replace a lightbulb in the waiting room. 'The calm before the storm,' he heard Sister Percival saying to Nurse Willard as he balanced on top of the stepladder, unscrewing the bulb. 'You mark my words, we'll be turning them away before the end of the day.' She tutted. 'We could have done without Dr Adler swanning off, today of all days. How Dr McKay is going to manage on his own when the casualties start to arrive, I've no idea.'

'You heard Dr Adler,' Nurse Willard said. 'He was determined to go and do his bit.'

'Irresponsible, I call it,' Sister Percival huffed.

'He's not the only one,' Willard said, idly examining her fingernails. 'Doyle's gone off too.'

The lightbulb crashed to the ground, splintering into fragments.

'Really!' Sister Percival looked up, irritated. 'I hope that wasn't the new bulb you've just broken. It will be coming out of your wage packet if it is!'

Nick ignored her, coming down off the ladder to pick up the pieces. He moved slowly, listening to their conversation.

'Are you certain Doyle's gone?' Sister Percival was saying. 'I'm sure Matron would never allow it.'

'Allow it or not, she's gone. She told me herself. Joe warned her it would get nasty out there, but you know how headstrong she is.'

'Serves her right if she ends up in here injured herself – where do you think you're going?' Sister Percival turned round to Nick, who was stripping off his overall. 'Come back here, you haven't finished the job–'

But he was already gone, the double doors crashing shut behind him.

Outside the bagel shop the crowd were getting restive, jostling each other. People were shouting and singing. Kids hung off lamp posts, acting as lookouts. Women in aprons and old men in silk coats with shawls around them stood shoulder to shoulder with big Irish dockers and young communists with their red banners flying high above them. It felt as if the whole world had converged on Cable Street.

A crash shook the pavement under her feet, briefly silencing the crowd. Dora cowered, terrified a bomb had been dropped. But then one of the children called down from his lamp-post look out, 'They just pulled a lorry over on its side!'

But no sooner had a cheer gone up than someone else called out, 'Watch it! The police are coming.' Dora looked over her shoulder, just in time to see a dark tide swarming towards them over the barricades, policemen on foot and on horseback, pushing their way into the crowd. She saw bricks, bottles, lumps of wood and concrete flying through the air, truncheons raised, horses' hooves pawing the air, coming down on the crowd, followed by screams and roars of outrage.

'Bloody coppers! Let 'em have it!'

The next moment hell rained from the skies. The women were hanging out of the upper windows, throwing jars, bottles, tin cans and anything they could find down on the policemen. The air was suddenly filled with the stench of vinegar, pickles and a lot worse.

Dora dodged into a doorway, just in time to avoid a chamberpot smashing at her feet.

'Watch it!' someone laughed. 'Don't hit us, we're on your side!'

She inched her way along the street, dodging the scuffling crowd that surged around her. She got to the hardware shop just as the owner was boarding

445

up his windows. He gave her the carbolic and refused payment.

'It's good of you and the doctor to help us,' he said, pressing the brown paper package into her hands.

She was on her way back up Cable Street when she saw a man, slumped down an alleyway just off the main street. Blood poured from a gash in his head. A little girl in a green coat stood beside him, whimpering.

'It's all right, love, I'll see to him.' Dora crouched down beside the man. 'Hello?' she said. 'Can you hear me?' He groaned a response. 'I'm going to get you somewhere safe. Put your arm around me ... do you think you can walk?' She turned to the little girl. 'You come with me too, ducks. It's not safe for you round here.'

The man was a dead weight. No matter how hard she tried, Dora couldn't shift him. She was still struggling to get him upright when a voice behind her said, 'Here, let me.'

She looked around. There was her brother, a coat slung over his black shirt.

'Pete! What are you doing here?'

'I could ask you the same question.' His face was grim.

'You never know when to stay out of trouble, do you?'

Dora looked him up and down. 'But why are you—'

'Let's just say I thought better of it. Come on, let's get this bloke moved before the police really move in.' He slung the man's limp arm around his own shoulders, lifting him easily. 'Which way?'

'Down here. On the next corner.' Dora directed him through the crowd to the bakery where Dr Adler had set up his surgery. A small crowd had already gathered there, waiting for attention. Dr Adler was cleaning a cut on a woman's arm, his white coat smeared with blood.

'Thank God you're here, I was beginning to–' He glanced over his shoulder and saw Peter, helping the man into a chair. 'What's he doing here?'

'I think he's come to help,' Dora said.

'We don't need help from the likes of him.' He shouted over to Peter, 'You're in the wrong place. Shouldn't you be up at Victoria Park, polishing Mosley's boots?'

Peter didn't reply. 'Surely we can put him to some use?' Dora pleaded. 'He's a porter, so he's used to lifting patients.'

'Dora?' Peter called to her. 'This bloke we've just brought in... I think he's lost someone. He keeps calling out for Anna.'

Dora went over to him. 'Who's Anna, mate? Your missus?'

'*Tochter*...'

'He's asking for his daughter,' Dr Adler translated.

Dora and Peter looked at each other. 'There was a little girl with him,' Dora said. 'I told her to come with us...'

'I didn't see her.' Peter frowned. 'She must have run away.'

'Probably saw that black shirt of yours,' Dr Adler muttered.

The man started to get agitated. 'Anna,' he pleaded, looking from one to the other of them

447

desperately. 'My Anna...'

'I'll fetch her, love, don't you worry.'

Dora headed for the door, but Peter barred her way. 'You're not going out there again.'

'I've got to find that kid. She's out there by herself, I can't leave her.'

'Let me go, then.'

'You don't know what she looks like.' Dora glanced back at Dr Adler. 'You stay here and help the doctor.'

Dr Adler and Peter glared at each other. 'Do you know anything about putting on a bandage?' the doctor asked.

Peter's chin lifted. 'A bit. Our Dora's practised on me a few times.'

'Then make yourself useful.' Dr Adler tossed him a dressing. 'That's if you don't mind putting your hands on a dirty Jew?' he added.

Chapter Fifty-One

The police had broken through the barricades and were tearing through the crowds, charging them with truncheons raised. Horses thundered past, so close Dora could feel the heat coming off their flanks. Everywhere she looked there were running battles, people fighting hand to hand with the police, blood running down faces.

A young policeman lay injured in a doorway, nursing his leg. As Dora watched, a man dashed out of the crowd towards him, a blood-stained lump of brick in his hand.

'No!' She flung herself on him, pushing him away. 'For God's sake, what do you think you're doing? Leave him be, or you'll be no better than those bloody Blackshirts!'

She helped the policeman to his feet. 'Can you walk?'

'A bit.' He put his weight on his leg and cursed in pain.

'Let me help you. Put your arm around me.'

Together they struggled the length of the street almost to the door of the bakery. 'Go in there,' Dora said. 'The doctor will sort you out.'

She left him and turned back into the mêlée. The police were closing around her on all sides now, charging and thumping and kicking and punching out at anyone who came near them. The protesters were giving as good as they got, while rubbish still rained down on all of them from above.

She plunged into the crowd, head down, looking for the little girl.

'Anna!' she called out, but her voice was lost in the roar of the crowd.

And then, by some miracle, she caught a flash of green out of the corner of her eye. She swung round. The little girl was cowering in a shop doorway near where Dora had found her father.

'Anna?' Dora started across the road towards her, pushing her way through the crowd. But just as she reached her, a lump of wood came down from an upstairs window, hitting Dora on the shoulder and sending her sprawling across the road. Next moment, a huge grey police horse plunged out of the crowd towards her, its eyes wild, nostrils flaring.

'No!' She heard a roar as the massive beast reared up, casting its shadow over her. She saw its iron-shod hooves pawing the air, and instinctively curled up to protect herself, moments before they came crashing down.

Suddenly she felt strong arms around her, pulling her up, snatching her out of the way as the horses' hooves descended.

'Jesus, Dora!'

She breathed in the familiar scent of him before she dared to open her eyes and found herself crushed against Nick Riley's rapidly pounding chest.

'Thank God,' he whispered, over and over again. 'When I saw you lying there... I thought I'd lost you.'

Dora clung to him, not wanting to let him go, even as the crowds surged around them, pushing them this way and that.

Finally he released her, his hands moving up to cup her face. His was only inches away, closer than he had dared to be in so long, and for the first time in months Dora didn't try to fight it.

'You could never lose me,' she whispered.

The riot around them ceased to exist for a moment as she drank in every detail of his face: the tears glistening on his thick black lashes, the flecks of navy in his blue eyes, the beautiful long curve of his upper lip ... moments before his mouth came down to claim hers.

Joe Armstrong clambered over the barricade, raised his stick above his head and lashed out left, right and centre, blindly striking down anyone in his path. On either side of him a wall of uniforms was advancing, pushing forward into the crowd. Ahead of them was an unruly mass of people, waving flags and jeering. He could see their mouths moving, but their angry taunts were lost in a deafening chorus of police whistles, ambulance bells, horses' hooves and chanting.

'Oi, copper! Over here!' He turned around just as a woman took aim and pelted him with a rotten apple. It exploded as it hit the side of his face, rotten mushy flesh dripping down his cheek.

A young man laughed. Joe spun round, blinded by rage.

'You think that's funny, do you?' He picked up the boy with both hands and hurled him through an ironmonger's window, splintering the glass.

'Careful, mate.' Tommy sent him an uneasy sidelong look.

'We've got our orders, ain't we? Hold the line and get rid of anyone who stands in our way. That's what the sergeant said.'

'Yeah, but you don't have to be violent, do you?'

'Have you seen what they're doing to us?' Joe dodged a brick as it flew through the air. 'We're allowed to defend ourselves, ain't we?'

'You weren't defending yourself when you threw that kid through the window. You looked like – well, like you were enjoying it.'

Joe shot him a dirty look. 'You get on with your job, mate, and I'll get on with mine.'

Truth be told, he *was* enjoying it. All the shouting and the fighting had got his blood raging. He

451

didn't really care who he lashed out at. Just like being in the ring, he'd taken a few blows but he'd delivered a damn sight more. And so what if they hadn't all been in self-defence? Those bastards shouldn't have been on the streets if they didn't want trouble.

And then he saw them.

For a moment he thought he must be dreaming. But when he looked again, there they were, Dora and Nick, standing on the side of the road, kissing.

Blood roared in his ears, deafening him. A missile came out of nowhere, knocking his helmet sideways, but he barely noticed as he stood stock still, staring at them.

'Hold the line!' their sergeant urged them on. Joe saw them, still locked in an embrace as the police surged past, pushing back the crowd, a relentless wall of blue uniforms. Still he couldn't take his eyes off them, looking back, picking out Dora's red curls in the crowd.

And then, suddenly, he couldn't stand it any longer. 'Joe!' he heard Tom calling to him. 'Come back! We've got to keep going.'

But Joe had already disappeared, clambering over the broken furniture strewn in his path, smashing his way through the crowd, oblivious to the missiles that whizzed past his ears.

'Anna!' Dora broke away from Nick, suddenly remembering why she'd come. She turned round, and heaved a sigh of relief. The little girl was still there, hiding in the doorway.

'Thank God.' She reached for the child's hand.

452

'I've got to take her back to her dad,' she explained to Nick. 'He's worried sick about her.'

'I'll come with you.'

'No, you should go.'

'And leave you?' He shook his head. 'If you think I'm letting you out of my sight for a second, you're wrong.'

He bent down and picked up a broken piece of chair leg.

'What's that for?' Dora asked.

His mouth lifted at one corner. 'Well, I ain't going to sit on it, am I?' he said, testing the weight of it in his hands.

'I don't want any rough stuff, Nick.'

He glanced around him. 'Bit late for that, ain't it?'

'You know what I mean.'

'It's only for protection.' He saw her expression and dropped the stick with a clatter. 'All right, have it your way. I'll just have to fight them off with my bare hands, won't I?'

'No one's going to be fighting anyone,' Dora said firmly. 'We're taking this little one back to her dad, and then we're going to...' Suddenly she caught a flash of dark blue and silver, running out of the crowd towards them. She saw Joe's face, contorted with fury, arm raised above his head. 'No!'

Nick turned round, and in that split second Joe struck. His arm came down with massive force, striking Nick a single blow between his shoulder-blades.

'Run, Dora!' she heard Nick cry as Joe launched himself, raining down blow after blow.

'Joe!' she screamed out, but he was like a

453

madman, demented by rage, bringing his fists down again and again.

'Go Anna. Run to the baker's shop.'

Dora released the little girl's hand and ran back to Nick. 'Leave him!' She tried to drag Joe off, but he was too strong for her, and batted her off with a jerk of his arm.

She spotted the chair leg Nick had thrown down, and made a grab for it. Without stopping to think, she swung it with all her might at Joe. It caught him on the shoulder and sent him flying sideways where he lay, clutching his arm and howling in pain.

'Nick!' Dora dropped to Nick's side. He lay silent on the pavement.

'They're turning back! The marchers are turning back!' someone shouted. Within seconds the cry had been taken up all along Cable Street.

'They shall not pass! We've done it! Down with Mosley and his fascist mob!' People cheered, hugging each other and slapping each other's backs.

But none of it meant anything to the girl who sat crying in the middle of the street, cradling a young man's broken body in her arms.

Chapter Fifty-Two

Dora could hardly bring herself to look at Nick as she busied herself arranging towels and blankets around him in the back of the ambulance.

'Do I look that bad?' he whispered hoarsely.

'I've seen worse.' She forced herself to smile. She had seen a lot worse – his face was almost untouched, just a graze across his cheekbone. But it was what was going on under his blood-stained shirt that worried her. 'Your movie career might be finished, though.'

'And my ballet career, I reckon.' He tried to shift his weight, cursing at the pain.

'Don't try to move,' Dora said.

'I couldn't if I tried.' He shifted again, gritting his teeth against the pain. 'I can hardly feel my legs...'

Dora glanced at her brother Peter, sitting beside her in the ambulance. His expression was grave.

'Just keep still until we get you to hospital,' she begged, reaching up to stroke a dark curl off Nick's face. His skin felt clammy and cold.

She moved her hand down to his neck, searching for his pulse. It skipped lightly under her fingers, missed a few beats, then skipped again.

Nick's eyes followed her every move. 'I'm not dead, then?'

'Not yet.' She pulled the blankets up to his chin, tucking them around him.

'That's the last time I take on one of your jealous boyfriends. If he hadn't jumped me from behind...'

'Don't.' Dora shuddered. 'Don't talk about it.' She couldn't get the picture out of her head: Joe, his face contorted with rage, raining blows on Nick's helpless body.

'I wouldn't worry about it, mate. Our Dora gave him what for!' Peter grinned. 'Set about him with an old chair leg, she did. He's in one of the other ambulances now, nursing a broken shoulder!'

'An old chair leg, eh?' Nick turned his gaze towards her, his blue eyes glinting with amusement. 'What happened to no rough stuff?'

'I didn't know what else to do. I thought he was going to kill you.'

Dora gulped in a breath to steady herself. But she couldn't stop a single tear from escaping.

'There now.' Nick put his hand up, brushing it off her freckled cheek with his thumb. 'You should know by now, you don't get rid of me that easily,' he whispered.

At the hospital, he was rushed straight into Casualty. Dora wanted to follow him, but Sister Percival blocked her way.

'You can't go through there, you should know that,' she warned.

Dora craned her neck, watching as the door to the consulting room swung shut behind him. 'I want to stay with him,' she pleaded. 'He needs me...'

'Are you his next-of-kin?'

'No, but–'

'Then you need to give us their name and address.' Sister Percival sent Dora a disapproving glance as she handed her a piece of paper. 'And then, if I were you, I'd go and clean yourself up,' she added, looking askance at the girl's crumpled, blood-spattered dress. 'And stay well away from him, if you know what's good for you,' she whispered.

But Dora didn't know what was good for her. As

soon as she had changed, she hurried back to the Casualty department. The rows of benches were filled with walking wounded from the protest; every time the double doors opened, more people came stumbling in, nursing bleeding faces and broken limbs.

Behind the counter, Penny Willard was taking names as quickly as patients arrived. Dora wondered where Joe might be. She hoped for everyone's sake he had been taken to another hospital. She wasn't sure what she would do if she came face to face with him again.

The double doors swung open and Ruby came in, followed by Lettie. Dora sat still as she strutted up to the counter, heels tapping. She saw Ruby talking to Penny Willard, then Penny pointed her pen in Dora's direction.

Lettie turned around, her scowl deepening. She stamped over, Ruby following her.

'What are you doing here?' Lettie demanded.

'Never mind that now!' Ruby cut her off. 'What happened?' she asked Dora. 'Why is Nick here?'

Dora licked her dry lips. 'He was injured ... a policeman set about him.'

Ruby stared at her, blank-faced. 'What policeman? Where?'

'On the protest.'

'The protest?' Ruby stopped for a moment, uncomprehending. 'What was Nick doing on the protest?'

Dora lowered her gaze to the floor. 'He came looking for me.'

'So this is all your fault, then?' The other girl's voice was cold.

Dora nodded, her heart heavy with guilt. Ruby was right, there was nothing more she could say about it. If it hadn't been for her, Nick would never have been in Cable Street, and none of this would have happened.

'I knew it!' Lettie spat. 'You shouldn't even be here. You've got no right. My Ruby's his legal wife, you're nothing to him!'

'Leave it, Mum,' Ruby said wearily, but Lettie was in full flow and there was no stopping her.

'You should be ashamed of yourself, running after a married man! See what you've done? See what trouble you've caused?'

'I said, leave it. I ain't exactly been whiter than white myself, have I?' Ruby snapped. She turned back to Dora. 'How bad is he?'

'I don't know. They won't tell me anything because I'm not family.' She ignored Lettie's grunt of disapproval. 'But it's not good. His back is damaged, and there's a risk of internal bleeding, too. He was talking all right in the ambulance, but his pulse was weak so there's a risk he might go into shock–'

Ruby took a deep breath. 'So he might die, is that what you're saying?'

'I don't know, Ruby. I wish I did.'

Neither of them spoke for a moment, then Lettie started up again, filling the silence. 'None of this would have happened if you'd left him alone,' she squawked. 'He was happy with my Ruby–'

'Go home, Mum,' Ruby said, eyes still fixed on Dora.

'What?' Lettie's eyes bulged in outrage. 'Oh, no, I'm not going anywhere! If anyone's leaving, it should be her!' She jabbed an accusing finger at Dora.

'Please, Mum. This ain't helping anyone, is it?' Ruby turned to her. 'I'd rather wait by myself, if you don't mind?'

Lettie pursed her lips. 'All right then, I'll go,' she huffed. 'But I won't forget this,' she added, shooting them both a warning look. 'Of all the ungrateful ... and after I gave up my Sunday afternoon to traipse all the way over here!' They heard her grumbling all the way across the waiting room, until the doors finally closed behind her.

Ruby's mouth twisted. 'Anyone would think she'd come from the North Pole!'

'She's right, though. I should go.' Dora got to her feet, but Ruby stopped her.

'Don't think you're leaving me here by myself,' she said. 'We're sitting this out together, you and me.'

Dora read the unspoken message in her blue eyes. 'Thank you,' she whispered.

'It ain't a question of thanking me,' Ruby said, sitting down next to her. 'Truth is, I've never liked hospitals.' She shuddered. 'And besides, you know your way round this place better than I do. And you know what to say to doctors. You've always been the clever one,' she said, sending Dora a sidelong look.

'And you've always been the pretty one!' Dora smiled, remembering what they always used to say to each other when they were at school.

'Much good it's done me,' Ruby sighed, looking down at the chipped scarlet polish on her fingernails. 'Maybe if I'd been as clever as you I wouldn't have got myself into this mess.'

Dora put her hand out. Ruby looked at it, then at Dora. Then, after a moment's hesitation, she reached for it. 'I'm sorry,' she whispered.

'Me too,' Dora said.

'Still mates?' Ruby gave her a shaky smile.

'Always.'

They were both silent for a moment. Then Ruby said, 'He'll be all right, won't he?'

Dora dragged in a deep breath. 'I hope so.'

'So what do we do now?' Ruby asked.

Dora stared into her friend's helpless face. There were so many times she had hated Ruby, but looking at her now she couldn't feel anything but pity. All Ruby had done was try to fight for the man she loved, and Dora couldn't blame her for that.

She squeezed her friend's hand. 'We wait,' she said. 'And hope. It's all we can do, Rube.'

It was as if Fate didn't want Helen to sit her State Finals.

First their train was delayed by a fallen tree on the line. Then, when they finally reached London, there was no taxi to be found anywhere.

'We might as well give up, we're never going to get all the way to Hampstead in time,' Helen said as they stood on the pavement, scanning up and down the street.

'We'll get there,' her mother said grimly. 'I told you I'd see to it that you sat this examination, and I meant it. Even if we have to travel there on the back of a coal wagon.'

A mental picture of her mother perched on top

of some sacks of coal, handbag clutched tightly on her lap, made Helen smile in spite of her nerves.

Finally they found a cab to take them to St Jude's.

'The patron saint of lost causes,' Helen murmured, as her mother paid the driver. 'How appropriate.'

'Do be quiet, Helen,' Constance snapped. 'Go and get changed into your uniform while I get you registered.'

The clock was striking a quarter to eleven and sets of nurses, all in the uniforms of their various hospitals, were already filing into the examination room. Helen changed hurriedly in the nurses' cloakroom, her hands shaking so much she could barely manage to fasten her collar stud.

Help me, Charlie, please, she prayed silently to her reflection in the mirror.

'Dawson?' She turned around. Brenda Bevan stood before her looking neat in her blue striped uniform. Helen's knees buckled in relief at the sight of a friendly face. 'Here, let me.'

'Thank you.' Helen lifted her chin for Brenda to fasten her collar stud.

'Terrifying, isn't it?' Brenda said. 'I didn't sleep a wink last night.'

'Me neither.'

'Oh, well, it's too late to turn back now, isn't it?' Brenda finished fastening her stud and stepped back. 'I'm glad you decided to come,' she said.

'So am I,' Helen replied.

As she walked up the wide green-painted passageway towards the examination room, Helen

461

could already hear her mother's voice raised in indignation at the far end.

'What do you mean, she's not registered?' Constance stood at a table outside the doors to the room, berating the man who sat behind it. 'Of course her name is on the list. Check it again.'

'Is something wrong?' Helen asked, coming up to join them.

The clerk looked up at her. 'I've just been explaining to your mother, you can't register for the examination because your name is not on my list of candidates.'

'Then your list is wrong, isn't it?' Constance said, tight-lipped.

'Perhaps the hospital didn't put my name forward because they didn't think I wanted to sit the exam?' Helen suggested to her mother.

'No, but I did. I telephoned the examination office last Thursday. Oh, don't gawp at me like that, Helen,' Constance dismissed her impatiently. 'I knew you would see sense eventually.'

'Oh, Mother!' Helen laughed, too amused to be angry. What was the point? Constance Tremayne would never change.

Her mother turned back to the clerk. 'There has obviously been some mistake,' she said, in the voice she always used when she believed she was talking to a simpleton. 'Let me speak to someone in authority.'

The man drew himself up in his seat. 'The Chief Examiner is busy,' he sniffed.

'Not too busy to speak to me, I'm sure,' she said. 'Please inform the Chief Examiner that Constance Tremayne, Trustee of the Florence Nightingale

462

Hospital, is here and would like to speak to him.'

The man looked unimpressed. 'I told you, the Chief Examiner is busy.'

Helen saw her mother quivering with suppressed fury, and wondered if the man knew how close he was to being throttled. 'Do you know who I am?' hissed Constance.

'No, but I know who *she* is.'

They looked up. A woman stood in the doorway to the examination room, tall, thin and ramrod-straight. Helen didn't recognise her at first in her dark grey uniform, her tight light brown curls concealed under a starched bonnet.

'Mrs Forster?' She blinked in surprise.

'Hello, Helen. I told you I used to be a nurse, didn't I?' Mrs Forster smiled, her dark brown eyes twinkling. 'But I wasn't sure if it would be fair to tell you I'm Chief Examiner now.'

'I was just explaining to this person – Mrs Forster, that it isn't possible for her daughter to sit the State Final Examination because her name isn't on the list,' the clerk explained.

'Oh, I'm sure we could make an exception for Nurse Dawson.' Mrs Forster sent her a smile of understanding. 'Come along, my dear, the written paper is just about to start. I will sort out all the paperwork for you before the practical examination.'

As she followed Mrs Forster into the examination room, Helen heard her mother berating the hapless clerk.

'You see,' she was saying, 'if you'd only done as I told you earlier, we could have all saved ourselves a great deal of time.'

The examination room was a cavernous space, like a cathedral, with a pitched ceiling that seemed to go upwards for ever. Sunshine streamed in through the high windows, illuminating dancing dust particles.

Nurses were already sitting at small desks, set out in neat regimented lines that reached as far as Helen's eyes could see. At the back of the room, she could make out the blue striped uniforms of the rest of the Nightingale set, Brenda Bevan amongst them.

Mrs Forster directed her to an empty desk near the door and placed an examination paper face down in front of her. Helen stared at it, feeling sick.

This was a mistake, she should never have come. How could she ever have imagined she was ready to take an exam? Her brain was suddenly a fog of jumbled facts, none of them making any sense.

The clock struck eleven. 'You may turn over your papers, Nurses,' Mrs Forster instructed, her voice echoing around the room.

There was a rustling sound. Helen picked up one corner of her exam paper as if it were a venomous snake, flipped it over and read the first question.

Which drugs or agents could be locally applied to check haemorrhage?

Suddenly she was transported back to the summer. Perching on Nellie Dawson's moquette settee, preparing a cold compress while Charlie helped her revise.

She smiled, feeling her confidence trickling

back. Perhaps she could do this after all.

Thank you, Charlie, she thought, picking up her pen.

Chapter Fifty-Three

Nick opened his eyes to a blinding white light and a smell of carbolic and polish. It took him a full moment to work out that he was lying in a hospital bed, surrounded by screens.

He tried to move, and instantly everything hurt. From his thudding temples to his painful ribs, there wasn't an inch of him that wasn't in agony. Except for his legs. He couldn't move them.

Panic surged through him until he looked down and saw that he was heavily bandaged from the waist down, and held fast in some kind of complicated sling contraption, which in turn was attached to an overhead frame. He didn't know whether that was more or less alarming than being paralysed.

He closed his eyes against the blinding pain in his head. When he opened them again, Sister Blake's smiling face swam into focus above him.

'You're awake at last. How are you feeling?'

'Like I've just gone ten rounds with Max Baer.'

'I'm not really surprised. You took quite a beating. The doctor had to put you under general anaesthetic while he set your fractured pelvis.'

Nick's eyes widened. 'I fractured my pelvis?'

'I told you you took a beating, didn't I?'

He tried to breathe in, but it felt as if he had several daggers buried in his breastbone. 'Will I live?'

Sister Blake pretended to consider this. 'Luckily it was a simple fracture, and there was no damage to the visceral organs,' she said. 'I'm afraid you won't be up and about for a few weeks, but yes, I reckon you'll live.' She checked his pulse. 'Do you feel sick at all?' He shook his head, then wished he hadn't as the room rolled like a ship around him. 'Your pulse is very strong now, so that's a good sign.'

She set his hand down on the bed. 'Do you think you're well enough to receive a visitor? Only there's someone who's very anxious to see you.'

He turned his head, his gaze following Sister Blake as she slipped out between the screens. 'Dora?' No sooner had the name left his lips than the curtains parted and Ruby appeared.

'Hello, Nick,' she said.

'Ruby.' He thought he'd hidden his disappointment well, but her expression was wry as she looked down at him.

'Sorry, were you expecting someone else?' she asked, mock innocent.

Nick didn't reply. Ruby looked him up and down. 'Blimey, I wouldn't like to see the other bloke!' she commented.

Nick grimaced. 'For once I reckon I came off worst.'

'At least you're alive, that's the main thing.' She sat down on the chair beside his bed. 'We were all so worried about you.'

He managed a smile. 'It was nice of you to come.'

'Well, don't get too excited, I haven't come to mop your brow or anything.' Her tone changed, becoming brittle and businesslike. 'I just wanted to let you know I'm leaving the flat, going back to live with Mum.' She pulled a set of keys out of her bag and put them down on the locker. 'The place is all yours if you want it.'

'I don't,' Nick said. 'That flat was always your dream, not mine.'

'A bit like our marriage then!' she said, with a trace of bitterness.

'Ruby–'

'It's all right, I haven't come here to get all miserable. I finished crying over spilled milk a long time ago.' She gave him a tense smile. 'But if you wouldn't mind, I'd rather you didn't move back to Griffin Street. I don't know if I could stand bumping into you in the back yard every day!'

He shook his head. 'You don't have to worry about that. I'll find lodgings somewhere, once I'm back on my feet.'

'That's all right then.' Ruby's mouth twisted. 'I mean, it could get awkward, couldn't it, if you're chasing up the stairs all the time, begging me to take you back!'

Nick smiled. Even after everything they'd been through, she could still make him laugh.

But Ruby wasn't laughing as she looked down at him. Her large blue eyes were swimming with tears. 'I'm sorry,' she blurted out. 'I never meant to hurt you, you have to understand that. It was

467

the last thing I wanted.'

'I know.'

'Look at me, blubbing like a baby. I'll ruin my make-up if I'm not careful.'

He watched her mopping her eyes with her handkerchief, being so careful not to smudge her make-up. She wasn't perfect, but she was a lovely girl and she deserved to be happy.

'Will you be all right?' he asked.

'What do you care?'

'Of course I care.'

He reached out for her, but she pulled away. 'Don't you dare go soft on me, Nick Riley!' she warned.

She slid off her wedding ring and put it down on the locker beside the keys.

'Keep it,' he said.

'I'd rather not, if you don't mind.' She looked at it for a moment, her face wistful. 'Besides, I expect Dad or the boys would only take it down to the pop shop and pawn it!'

She stood up to leave. 'Well, I'd best be off. Don't want to wear out my welcome, do I?' She looked down at him. 'But there was one more thing before I go. It's about Dora.'

He eyed her warily. 'What about her?'

'I just wanted you to know, she never wanted to keep that secret. She wanted to tell you the minute she found out, but I begged her not to. You were right, Nick, she's a good friend. Probably better than I deserve.' Ruby smiled bravely. 'I just thought you'd want to know that,' she said softly.

'Thank you.' Nick watched her gathering up her belongings. 'Be happy, Rube,' he said.

She gave him a sad smile. 'I'll try,' she promised.

She slipped out through the screens, and he heard her voice saying, 'He's all yours.' Then Dora appeared, dressed in her uniform. Her freckled skin was as pale as her starched white cap, her green eyes anxious.

She looked so straight-laced and formal, Nick's heart started to pound. She'd changed her mind, he thought. That moment out on Cable Street where she'd kissed him had been a wild, heat-of-the-moment thing. Now she was wondering how to break it to him...

He swallowed hard, determined not to make a fool of himself a second time.

'Don't ask me how I'm feeling,' he warned. 'I've only been awake ten minutes, and I'm already sick of it.'

'It's my job,' she said briskly, reaching for the chart at the end of his bed.

'And is that the only reason you're interested?' he asked.

He saw the smile kindling in her eyes and suddenly realised she was as unsure as he was. 'I wouldn't say that.'

Relief flooded through him. 'So I didn't dream it, then? Only I thought I might be imagining what happened – because of the pain, or something.'

'No, you didn't dream it.'

He watched as she bustled around, straightening the bedclothes around the frame. 'So you're working on this ward, then?'

'That's right. I'm on nights.'

He grinned. 'Looks like we'll be seeing a lot of each other, then? Reckon you can put up with me?'

He caught the mischievous glint in her eyes. 'We'll see, won't we?'

Constance Tremayne didn't need anyone to point out Simon Latimer. She spotted him immediately, heading towards his Bentley. He looked every inch as arrogant as she'd thought he would, with his affected bow tie and girlish mane of wavy hair. God's gift to young nurses, in his own mind.

'Mr Latimer?'

He turned around, frowning. 'I'm sorry? Have we met?'

'My name is Constance Tremayne. I am on the Board of Trustees at this hospital.'

'Mrs Tremayne, of course! Please forgive me.' Mr Latimer was instantly all smooth charm. He held out his hand, but Constance ignored it. 'What can I do for you?'

'Nothing, Mr Latimer. I just wanted to get a good look at you, so I know what a lothario looks like.'

'I beg your pardon?'

'A lothario, Mr Latimer. A libertine. A dissolute or licentious man.'

'Yes, yes, I know what it means! But I'm sure I have no idea what you're talking about.'

'Is that what you said to your wife, when she asked you about Amy Hollins?'

Mr Latimer's face suffused with colour. 'That was all a mistake. A misunderstanding,' he blustered. 'She was a silly young girl who got the

470

wrong end of the stick–'

'I don't disagree she was silly, but I have no doubt you encouraged her in her delusion,' Constance snapped. 'And then, when it all came to light, you abandoned her. Now poor Miss Hollins has lost everything while you have got off scot-free. But that's the way it works, isn't it? The man always walks away, while the innocent young girl pays the price.'

Mr Latimer's gaze darted around, making sure no one was listening. 'Look,' he said in a low voice. 'I have no idea why you've decided to ambush me like this, but I can assure you it will serve no useful purpose to drag up this sordid business. I am a respected surgeon in the hospital–'

'For now,' Constance put in. 'But that situation can easily change, can't it?'

He stared at her, his mouth opening and closing but no sound coming out. 'Are you threatening me, Mrs Tremayne?' he managed finally.

'No, Mr Latimer. But I am giving you fair warning that I will be keeping my eye on you. And if I think you have so much as looked at another young nurse, you can be sure I will bring the might of the Board of Trustees to bear on you. And I can assure you, we will not be nearly so forgiving as your wife!'

471

Chapter Fifty-Four

'Pay attention, Nurses. I know this is a very proud moment for you all, but that is no reason to start squawking like parrots. May I remind you, this is still a classroom!'

Sister Parker clapped her hands for silence and surveyed the third-year set for the last time. It seemed like only a few months ago they were fresh-faced eighteen year olds and she was teaching them how to wash their hands properly. Now on their starched collars they all wore the tiny enamel badge of a State Registered Nurse from the Florence Nightingale Hospital.

Her gaze fell on Helen Tremayne – or Dawson, as she was now called – sitting in the front row, her hands folded demurely in front of her. As Sister Parker had predicted, she also had the Nightingale Medal pinned to the bib of her apron.

And never had it been more thoroughly de-served, in Sister Parker's opinion. The poor girl had been through so much, there was a time when everyone at the hospital had wondered if she would survive. But fortunately she had proved them all wrong. She had returned to the Nightingale filled with new confidence, although her dark brown eyes still had a haunted sadness that Sister Tutor knew would take a long time to heal.

'Now, Matron will be calling you all into her

office in due course, to discuss your future at the Nightingale. For some of you, this may be good news. For others...' She eyed Brenda Bevan, gossiping on the back row as usual.

'Well, I daresay you have your own plans for the future. But whatever path you take, I hope the training you have received here will stand you in excellent stead. Remember, girls, you are Nightingale Nurses, and that will always mean a great deal, both in the nursing profession and in life.'

She stepped back and allowed her gaze to travel along the rows of faces, memorising every one. Even after more than twenty years as Sister Tutor, she could still remember all the nurses she had trained. Some of them were kind enough to remember her too. They often wrote to her, or came back to the hospital to visit. Many of them had stayed at the Nightingale as ward sisters and staff nurses.

She wondered how many of the set before her would do the same.

Helen was barely surprised to see her mother waiting for her as she came out of Matron's office and stepped into the courtyard on that brisk November afternoon.

'What are you doing here?' she asked, although she already knew the answer. This was the day she found out what her future held, and there was no chance that Constance Tremayne would want to miss that. 'I've already had my interview with Matron, if that's what you've come for?'

'Don't be absurd, why would I want to interfere?' At least her mother had the grace to look away when she said it. 'I had to come here to meet the Head of the Trustees,' she went on. 'But since I am here – how did you get on? What did Matron say?'

Helen took a deep breath. 'She has formally invited me to take up a post at the hospital,' she said, unable to keep the pride out of her voice.

'Well, of course she has!' Constance dismissed this impatiently. 'For heaven's sake, you came top in your State Finals and you won the Nightingale Medal. She's hardly going to turn you away, is she? But what has she offered you? I hope it was Theatre,' she said, without waiting for an answer. 'It's the very least you deserve, after all your hard work. She would be foolish not to offer it to you...'

'She did offer it to me,' Helen said. 'But I turned it down.'

Constance shot her a disbelieving look. She couldn't have looked more crestfallen if Helen had told her she was going to give up nursing and go on the stage instead. 'But why? You didn't! Oh, Helen, what on earth possessed you?' She seized her daughter's arm. 'We must go back to see Matron immediately, tell her you've changed your mind...'

She caught Helen's half smile and stopped. 'Is this a joke?' she asked suspiciously.

Helen grinned. 'Yes, Mother, it is. You'll be pleased to hear I have accepted a post in Theatre. But only because it's my decision,' she reminded her.

'Of course.' She could see her mother fighting to keep the self-satisfied look off her face. 'Now, why don't we have some lunch to celebrate your new

474

position? Perhaps we could go to Fortnum's?'

Helen glanced at her watch. 'I'm sorry, Mother; but I have to catch my train in less than an hour.'

'Oh? Where are you going?'

'Southend. I'm going to visit Hollins.'

Her mother nodded understandingly. 'How is she settling in at her new hospital?'

'Very well, I think.' Helen paused. 'She's very grateful to you for arranging for her to finish her training at the Victoria,' she said. 'If you hadn't talked to the Matron there, she might never have been accepted.'

Constance waved aside her words. 'Everyone deserves a second chance,' she said quietly.

Including you, Helen thought. Her relationship with her mother might not be perfect, but at least they understood each other a little better. And she could see Constance was trying hard to be less overbearing, although there were times when she still couldn't help herself.

'And what about you?' Constance asked. 'Are you sure you're doing the right thing, staying on at the Nightingale?'

Helen turned to her, surprised by the question. 'Why do you ask that?'

'I just wondered if, under the circumstances, you might prefer a change of scene? This place holds a lot of memories for you.'

Helen looked around at the courtyard, surrounded on all sides by a higgledy-piggledy sprawl of ward blocks, outbuildings and extensions.

Her mother was right, it hadn't been easy coming back. Sometimes just walking across the courtyard she would remember the day Charlie died and the pain would make her stop and catch her breath. And she had managed to avoid Judd ward completely since her return. She wasn't sure she would ever be able to set foot in that corridor again, or see those double doors without remembering that awful day.

But the Nightingale Hospital wasn't just full of bad memories. There were good ones, too. Like the day she'd met Charlie, so full of life and laughter, on Blake ward. And their wedding day, poignant though it was, was one of the happiest of her life. Because she knew she was surrounded by loyal friends who had rallied round and stood by her. Friends she would have for the rest of her life.

It was those friends who helped her face each day. When she opened her eyes every morning and had to endure that awful moment of realisation that her dreams of Charlie hadn't been real and that he was really gone for ever, they were there to distract her. And when she saw or heard something funny and stored it in her mind to tell Charlie, only to remember once again that he would never be there to share her funny or sad moments, at least she knew she wasn't completely alone.

She would be in pain wherever she went. But at least at the Nightingale she knew she was among friends.

'I think I'm in the right place,' she told her mother.

After all, if you wanted to heal, where better to go than a hospital?

The publishers hope that this book has given you enjoyable reading. Large Print Books are especially designed to be as easy to see and hold as possible. If you wish a complete list of our books please ask at your local library or write directly to:

Magna Large Print Books
Magna House, Long Preston,
Skipton, North Yorkshire.
BD23 4ND

This Large Print Book for the partially sighted, who cannot read normal print, is published under the auspices of

THE ULVERSCROFT FOUNDATION